I0810713

Advance praise for *The Girl Upstairs*

"Jessica R. Patch is the new Alfred Hitchcock, brilliant at plotting and at scaring readers!"

—*New York Times* bestselling author Lisa Childs

"*The Girl Upstairs* is a chilling thriller that you can't put down."

—Rick Mofina, *USA TODAY* bestselling author

"Jessica R. Patch is the best suspense writer out there today. Suspenseful and compelling with lots of twists and turns that are impossible to guess. Highly recommended!"

—Colleen Coble, *Publishers Weekly* and *USA TODAY* bestselling author

"Riveting and utterly unputdownable, *The Girl Upstairs* is a chilling thriller that had me turning pages with one eye open and my heart racing. Fans of Lucy Foley, Lisa Jewell and Freida McFadden will devour this story, but what sets Jessica R. Patch apart is the way she threads hope through the darkest corners. *The Girl Upstairs* isn't just a must-read—it's a must-experience."

—Natalie Walters, bestselling and award-winning author of the Harbored Secrets and SNAP Agency series

"This psychological thriller kept me flipping pages until the wee hours of the morning. Jessica R. Patch has outdone herself!"

—Patricia Bradley, ECPA, Parable and *USA TODAY* bestselling author

"*The Girl Upstairs* entertains and enlightens, all while probing the meaning of justice, of motherhood and of faith. Jessica R. Patch delivers!"

—Lis Wiehl, *New York Times* bestselling author

Also by Jessica R. Patch

Love Inspired Trade

Her Darkest Secret
A Cry in the Dark
The Garden Girls
The Other Sister

Love Inspired Suspense

Elite Protectors

Attempted Mountain Abduction
A Killer in Texas

Texas Crime Scene Cleaners

Crime Scene Conspiracy
Cold Case Target
Deadly Christmas Inheritance

Quantico Profilers

Texas Cold Case Threat
Cold Case Killer Profile
Texas Smoke Screen

For additional books by Jessica R. Patch,
visit her website, www.jessicarpatch.com.

THE GIRL UPSTAIRS

JESSICA R. PATCH

LOVE INSPIRED

Stories to uplift and inspire

LOVE INSPIRED®
Stories to uplift and inspire

Recycling programs for this product may not exist in your area

ISBN-13: 978-1-335-00136-8

The Girl Upstairs

Love Inspired
22 Adelaide St. West, 41st Floor
Toronto, Ontario M5H 4E3, Canada
www.LoveInspired.com

HarperCollins Publishers
Macken House, 39/40 Mayor Street Upper,
Dublin 1, D01 C9W8, Ireland
www.HarperCollins.com

Printed in U.S.A.

1 2 3 4 5 6 7 8 9 10 HDC 28 27 26 25

For every "girl upstairs." Your life has value and meaning. The trauma and pain you've endured becomes a part of you—you can't erase it. But it doesn't *define* you.

Part I

Secrets

"There are some secrets which do not permit themselves to be told."

—Edgar Allan Poe

Chapter One

She can breathe easy since she feels no consequences.

I, on the other hand, feel suffocated every day.

"What are you thinking?" Steven slips his hand in mine as the U-Haul trailer bounces behind us. He rubs my wedding ring with his thumb. We've been married almost eleven years. I was thirty and thought we would have forever, grow old together. Now I'm not so sure that's going to happen.

I cast a glance at him; the crinkles around his eyes have deepened in the past year, but his hair is still full, dark and wavy with only a few traces of silver. The right lens of his glasses is smudged, but I don't comment; however, it's going to bug me now. Steven rattles my hand in his. "Deep thoughts, huh?"

Yes. But if I tell him *she's* on my mind, the atmosphere in the SUV will plummet by twenty degrees, and the rest of our night will go to pot. He's made it clear I am no longer to discuss *her*, mention *her* or look *her* up online. It's over. We're moving, and that means forward living and thinking, which doesn't include *her*. She's in the rearview mirror—back in Baltimore.

Cold Harbor, Maine, is the place where we'll settle and plant new roots. Kick off the Labor Day weekend by laboring to move in. I squeeze his hand and smile. "I'm thinking I'm ready for this new chapter in our lives, and we should hurry inside the house, make it our own. Settle in."

We bought the most perfect home on the cliffs overlooking Cold Harbor. I knew we had to snap it up, and it was a steal. We put down an offer sight unseen—minus the photos—and then Steven flew out a few days later to do the walk-through while I stayed home and packed and finalized the sale of our Baltimore home. It sold for a mint and fast.

Gotta love the seller's market.

Moving here and fixing up this house will be the perfect way to start over, keep my mind off *her* and begin a new chapter. Find myself—as Steven puts it.

Find myself? As if I'm lost.

The past few weeks have been a whir of busyness. But he's acted excited, and I do mean acted. Steven says leaving his prestigious career at Johns Hopkins could be for the best, and he looks forward to working in a small-town clinic. But I don't buy it. Probably because he's not selling it well.

I'm not happy about why we're leaving, and I'm not selling it either.

As the green sign signals we're approaching Cold Harbor, my heart beats faster, and my stomach twists and turns like a rickety wooden roller coaster.

He brings my hand to his lips and kisses my knuckles. "I'm happy to see you happy."

Okay, maybe I'm selling it better than I thought.

"This will be good for you, Gwen. A chance to throw yourself into something productive." A slight scowl creases his brow. "Something healthy."

Bristling, I let his passive-aggressive remark go unanswered. I'm sick of my emotional and mental health being tossed in my face like a cold wet rag. Steven is a primary care physician. An excellent doctor. Recognized for his clinical work as a 2020 inductee into the Johns Hopkins Community Physicians Academy of Clinical Excellence. Which makes him a terrible patient himself and a know-it-all concerning my mental health, which is not his specialty. Internal medicine is what he's good at.

"Yeah," I murmur. "It really is gorgeous here. Much prettier than the photos or what I remember as a child."

"I told you," he says.

We're surrounded by forest, and the leaves haven't quite changed color. That will come later this month and peak mid-October. Fall is my favorite. I love the blending colors of terracotta, crimson, gold and chocolate. Love the colder nights and crisp mornings.

"Yep, you did, and you're right." Steven is always right, even when he's wrong.

"I thought we might have a picnic dinner tonight out by the cliffs, overlooking the water. Might even kindle that firepit that's out there. Just the two of us." He kisses my hand again. I shift and look at the car seat.

"And Baby Tara, of course." She's in her seat, eyes closed and a pacifier in her mouth. She's precious with soft caps of brunette hair, like Steven, and deep blue eyes, almost brown. Steven and I both have brown eyes.

Now it's Steven's turn to stiffen. "Of course." He clears his throat. "Can you call Teresa and let her know we're five minutes out? She's going to bring the keys by." Cold Harbor is *Gilmore Girls*–ish, which means no one lives that far away. Steven says *Teresa* as if he's known her his entire life. She's twenty-four and single with everything in the upright position and gorgeous walnut hair. Total opposite of me.

"Sure." I dial, and her perky voice pierces my ear.

"Oh, awesome! I'm already here, actually, excited to hand over the keys to you. This is my second house I've sold since becoming a real estate agent. I think I already told you that, though."

Four times, but who's counting? "You did. Congrats. See you in a few."

After ending the call, I take in the blue skies and gorgeous scenery as the road winds upward. Our house is nestled in a cluster of woods and overlooks the harbor. We're secluded, and to be honest, after city living, I'm here for it. As a former homicide detective with the Baltimore PD, I'm peopled out. Criminals and good humans, though I've rarely found a human good. We all harbor secrets, cover up sins with lies and learn how to deceive others and ourselves. I'm cynical, but that's par for the course when you see what I do—did—every day.

The narrow road winds through a tunnel of trees, their branches arching overhead like a canopy, filtering the afternoon light into dappled gold. Our driveway veers off halfway down, a gravel path that crunches beneath the tires and leads to our new house—secluded, quiet and wrapped in green. Before this, we lived in a cramped row house in Baltimore, hemmed in on both sides by nosy neighbors. Their dogs barked like alarms at all hours, and their kids shrieked in the street until dusk. I hated both—but for different reasons. The dogs were relentless, the kids unpredictable. Noise without pause, chaos without end.

We approach the large, ancient home, and my belly hitches. I rub it and frown at the unsettling feeling. As a child, I loved our vacations in Acadia National Park. Me, Mom, Dad all camping, hiking, playing in the water and roasting hot dogs. Maybe that's why I chose here to live. I want that again. Good times. Making fond memories. Losing Dad six years ago to cancer was hard, and Mom passing from an aneurism a year ago even tougher. She would have loved visiting here, moving in with us even. We now have the room. Many rooms, and I hope to fill them all.

We park but don't exit. Instead we take it all in silently.

The house looms over the harbor, its whitewashed exterior faded. It perches on the bluff like something forgotten, left to rot against the salt and wind. The porch wraps around the front, its boards warped and buckling. I can tell they'll protest beneath my feet when I approach. Two barrels of dead flowers flank the doors.

The windows are the worst—too many, too large. They stare blankly, smeared with age and dust, clouded, like the house has been watching for so long it's gone blind.

According to Teresa, the house caught fire in 1980, but it was contained to the main floor's primary room and the bathroom beside it. Tragic accident around Christmastime.

The roof curls at the edges, blackened with damp, and the chimney stands like a broken spine, bricks crumbling away one by one.

Behind it, the forest presses in. The trees of Acadia stand silent, the pines too still, the birches stripped bare like reaching bones.

Something about the house is jarring. Not just old or neglected. Plenty of houses wear their history in their walls, in their beams, in the way the air inside feels heavy with time, but this one feels like the years left behind something that never quite settled.

We finally step out of the vehicle. I stand a few feet from the porch steps. The wind shifts, cold and sudden, and I swear the house exhales. Like it's been holding its breath.

Like it's been expecting me.

Teresa leans on her black Volkswagen Tiguan and chats away, but the icy pull of the house has made me miss whatever she said. The pictures couldn't have been photoshopped, could they? Are homes like people? Some photogenic, others not so much.

Teresa's grinning now, but I can't focus. My lungs seize as my insides flush like I have the flu. I might be sick.

Sweat breaks out like an underground fountain springing up

across my body, and I rest my hand on the SUV to steady myself. Panic attack. Why now? Why in front of Steven and Teresa?

Steven strides to her, ignoring me, thankfully.

His hand is already outstretched in greeting, greedy to claim hers. Slow down, tiger. She isn't going anywhere. I might not be either. My legs are frozen in place.

Teresa continues discussing the house's potential with him, but her words are garbled due to the blood whooshing in my ears.

Finally, he turns back to me. "Gwen, you okay, hon?"

"Yeah."

Teresa clutches her chest. "I hope it's not the history of the house making you uncomfortable. I told your husband it was a long time ago, but no one likes to hear a child was murdered in the home they're buying."

What? I whip my gaze to Steven, who has clearly held out on me. Not that a murder house would deter me. I've seen crime scenes before. But I know exactly why he happened to forget this tidbit of information. Did the fire in 1980 take the child's life? "Refresh me again, will you?"

"Wouldn't you rather go inside?" Steven asks.

"No. I wouldn't."

He knows I'm a dog with a bone and backs down.

Teresa's cheeks redden, and she's realized her faux pas. "Well, okay. In '74, Thomas Barkley murdered his wife, Gina, and their daughter, little Lizzie. They'd been in the house… I guess ten years by then. On Halloween night too. He chased them into the attic and shot them both. Story goes he made Gina watch as he shot Lizzie. Then he came downstairs and to the dock and killed himself."

"The story goes or the story is true?"

"Well, we don't know if he made Gina watch, but they were both found dead in the attic. Every generation the story changes. Campfire stories, you know. Teenagers will be out here looking to see Lizzie's ghost, but it's all in good fun. Nothing to be concerned about."

My ire rises. Is that what is bothering me? Am I feeling a murdery vibe?

I'm waiting on Teresa to holler, *No takebacks!*

Steven eyes me warily, waiting for me to have a meltdown over the story—over Lizzie Barkley in particular.

"I'm just carsick. It's not the house."

Teresa's shoulders relax. "Oh, good. Come on in and splash some water on your face. Maybe you'll feel better." She talks as if this is her murder house and I'm the guest, which is better than victim. But I nod and follow her, my chest twisting tighter with each step toward the long front porch. I don't want to go inside the house. The wooden double doors squeak open, like a yawning mouth ready to suck me in whole and never let me leave.

My mouth turns dry, and my legs are shaky.

What is going on with me? "Steven, can you bring Tara inside, please?" I can barely manage myself.

"Sure," he says dryly. The back door of the SUV opens, then slams, and I flinch.

I step into the empty parlor, and an uneasy warmth scrapes over me. The home, built in 1896, stands barren—no rugs, no furniture—just the echo of a long-forgotten life. A grand stone fireplace roars with a lively fire, its dancing glow illuminating the bare, timeworn walls and exposed wooden beams overhead. The space should feel inviting, yet the heat feels like a dissonant reminder of secrets buried within.

I catch a whiff of sugary marshmallows and hot dogs roasting. Wiping the sweat from my brow, I catch a movement out of the corner of my eye and turn.

Perched between the newel post and the wooden stair rail sits a little girl in a sundress—too thin for the nip in the air. Her curly blond hair is tied into pigtails, and she clutches a jump rope in one hand, the frayed ends brushing the floor. Her bare feet dangle over the edge, swinging idly, like she's waiting for someone to play. She looks eight, maybe nine—though something about her feels older, like she's been sitting there longer than she should have.

Our real estate agent must have a daughter from her teenage years. "Teresa, I didn't realize—" My words die on my lips.

Teresa sits on the inglenook by the fireplace, her legs crossed, but there's no longer a fire. I rush toward it and touch the brick, hold my hands out to feel that lingering heat.

Nothing. It's cold.

"The stone is original to the house, hewn from the cliffs and sanded smooth. Cool, huh?" Teresa says. She eyes Steven as I continue to touch the hearth, my mind fuzzy.

Not only is the stone frigid, but the house is now drafty. Glancing toward the stairs, I see the girl is gone too, vanished as if she was never there. Gooseflesh breaks out along my arms as Steven sidles up next to me, Tara in her carrier, quiet. Teresa blinks and stares at her as if she has seven heads and horns. Steven's mouth is grim.

"Home sweet home," he says tightly.

I pinch the bridge of my nose. I did just see a little girl. A pool of dread forms in my gut.

Teresa frowns. "How about that water? You look like you've seen a ghost. Too soon?" She snickers as she guides me into the kitchen, but my mind is on the little girl on the stairs and the fireplace that no longer burns. The scent of campfire snacks is gone.

"Did you have the fireplace on earlier?"

Teresa turns on the faucet, signaling for me to cool my cheeks. "No. I haven't been inside today. But we can start one from the big woodpile out back. Left from Brad—the homeowner before you. Transferred to Japan. Happened so quick."

She already told me this when I inquired about the house

once it went on the market. "Okay, thanks." I splash the water on my cheeks and use my sweater sleeves to pat them dry. "Do you have children?"

Steven heaves a sigh, and I cut him a glare. I can ask about children. It's not an intrusive question…except for when it is.

"Me? Hardly. I'd need a man for that." She laughs, and her gaze lands on Steven. He chuckles. My hands curl into fists.

If Teresa doesn't have a child, then who was on the stairs? Because I know I'm not seeing Lizzie Barkley—that's preposterous, and if I dare mention it, I'll be sent to some ward for mental health recovery.

But I did see a girl and a blazing fire. Now I simply smell hints of time gone by, a faint lingering scent of Pine-Sol and Murphy Oil Soap mixed with Teresa's cloying perfume.

"Well, what do you think so far?" Teresa asks and steals another peek at Baby Tara.

I think… I think something is very wrong.

Chapter Two

Steven has lit the firepit, and blazing heat attempts to penetrate the chilly atmosphere as I sit on one of four Adirondack chairs that are arranged in a semi-circle. The sun has almost made its descent and has now cast eerie shadows that loom over the harbor. Waves crash like warning bells against the rocks below. A murder of crows hovers on branches, and an owl hoots in the distance.

After Teresa left, my panic attack subsided, but I've been skittish all evening. Seeing her must have set it off—set off insecurities. Steven's been casting extra-wary glances my way but hasn't broached the subject, and I'm grateful. I love my husband, but I'm not always honest with him, and discussing my feelings isn't something I do. I used to think he appreciated that about me. Now I'm always wondering if I have a clue who he is. Who I am.

Tara is nestled against me, wrapped in a heavy quilt, and I cuddle her close, feeling her chest rise and fall against mine. She's been a solace to me, as I suspect most infants are to their moms. Earlier, while we carried in boxes and the movers arrived with the big furniture, she lay in her cradle near the fireplace.

A fireplace that wasn't ever burning.

My mind is playing tricks on me. I may be on anxiety medications, but they don't have hallucinatory side effects. I've been on them for six months. Never have I seen something that wasn't there.

Well…that's not entirely true.

But this is a completely different circumstance. And the little girl? I turn back and peer up at the house from this viewpoint. As I stare, the faint light from the porch casts trembling shadows that shift and merge on the eaves. My heart pounds with a mixture of dread and anticipation. Out of the corner of my eye, I catch a glimpse—a pale, fleeting outline at the edge of the attic window.

Was that her?

It's too brief, yet too vivid, to dismiss as mere trickery of light. A shudder vibrates down my spine, and I grip the armrest, unable to shake the feeling that the house is watching me, waiting for something to happen. Thoughts of her raise gooseflesh along my arms again. She was real, but clearly not.

"Why didn't you mention a family died in this house, Steven?" Though I already know. I want to hear it from him.

"I didn't want you to dwell on the fact a child…died. You've been doing so well. I thought it might trigger you. That's all. Really. I'm sorry. Was I wrong?" He hands me a steaming cup of hot chocolate, cradles his own and collapses in the chair next to me, shivering. "Found some Swiss Miss in the kitchen pantry tote."

"Thank you." I sip the sweet concoction, but nothing out here feels sweet. "No, you weren't wrong per se. I just think a family blown to bits in my house on Halloween might be something worth mentioning."

"Would it have swayed your decision?" He slurps, and it annoys me.

"No."

"I didn't think so either. I've always done what was best for you." His gaze lands on me, but I don't look at him or respond. Instead I quietly sip my hot chocolate since it's quickly becoming cold.

"Bed's set up," Steven says after a few beats. "We can start the nitty-gritty tomorrow. Still not sure where a good office would be. I'd love a room overlooking the water, but not too close to the kitchen where it gets noisy. The two bedrooms at the back of the house feel too closed in. I need space to spread out—and enough room to fit my exercise bike."

I continue to sip my drink and try not to shudder as the sun slips away, leaving us drenched in darkness. Pewter clouds perch on the night like the crows in the trees, blocking light and bringing a sharper nip to the air.

"Not the basement. Dreary and damp. Maybe the attic? It's actually pretty spacious. We could add a few more windows?" He sighs.

"Maybe. I'll look at it later." My dad was a contractor, and I know renovations better than Steven. "Diagnose it."

He smirks at my teasing. We teased a lot in the early years. When the world was our oyster, whatever that means.

"I don't have to be in the office until Tuesday—though I may go in Monday and get a head start—so that gives us all weekend to unpack the main things. I also saw a Labor Day sale. I might go car shopping." He wants something less ostentatious in this new town. Nothing to draw too much attention. He sold his Porsche before we left Baltimore. He holds up his steaming mug. "Here's to hot drinks on cold nights and fires to keep us extra warm."

Water laps at the rocks at the edge of the cliff, and smoke plumes from a house across the harbor. A single light shines from the attic window. I focus on it and forget about our drinks.

Steven brings me back to reality. "Gwen, are you happy? Was

this move too fast? You had a panic attack earlier, and you're not yourself tonight. Do I need to up your anxiety med doses?"

My breath is shaky. "I'm fine. The meds are fine. The house has great bones. What's not to love? Needs some TLC, but we'll fix that. I'll run to the hardware store on Monday if they're open on the holiday." I've always been skilled with my hands. I'm no Joanna Gaines, but I'm not bad with DIY projects. As a former detective, I didn't have a lot of time to start home renos. Now I have all the time in the world.

And I hate it.

"Sounds good. It's quiet," he comments as he lays his head back against the chair. His eyes close, and a peaceful expression fills his face.

I expected to mimic these features, but I'm a bundle of nerves, and my neck muscles are tighter than a wind-up toy. Guess it's the move. A new place. New people. Everything that was me is back in Baltimore. Old friends. Old job. Old life. Old house. That's enough to rattle anyone's cage.

"Too quiet, almost, don't you think?" Is he not picking up on the ghoulish vibes? Is it just me?

He sets his cup on the right side of his armrest, leans over, and takes my hand. "I can get used to it. The slower pace will be good for us." He means me, but I appreciate him considering us as a unit, or maybe he wants to avoid a discussion. He never fights. We discuss.

He yawns, which ends dramatically, and leans back in his chair again. "I thought we might go into town tomorrow, have brunch and look around. Familiarize ourselves with the businesses and people. And Dr. Mansfield has invited us to a dinner at his home across the harbor. Be a nice way to meet colleagues and their spouses. A Labor Day celebration for our arrival."

"I don't have a babysitter." He acts like we can just jet-set like we used to.

He heaves a sigh. "Right."

Tara seems to be more of an inconvenience to Steven than anything else, but I let it pass for good reason.

"What about Teresa?" he suddenly asks, and perks up as if he's not quite as sleepy as he was three seconds ago.

"What *about* Teresa?"

He leans forward in the chair. "Maybe she'd be willing to babysit?"

"Why would you pick her?" I hear the accusation in my tone, but it's too late. Can't take it back now.

"She's the only one we know so far, and she's young." He remains calm as if my passive-aggressive behavior has flown over his head, but Steven is the most intelligent and observant man I've ever met.

Yeah, she is. Young and gorgeous without laugh lines and crow's-feet and a gooey middle.

"She's home most nights—not much to do in town."

I rise up and slowly turn to face him. "How would you know that?"

"She told me," he says innocently. "When I came and did the walk-through. I did spend a whole weekend here."

I eye him to catch a tell, but it's dark. He's nothing but shadow.

He points to the baby. "She's already accustomed to Tara. And she's our only choice at the moment. I'd really like you to be there. I can call her—or you can." He adds those last few words in quickly. Too quickly.

I don't want to go, but he's trying, and that means a lot to me. "Okay. I'll call her in the morning, but it's short notice." Not to mention we don't actually know this woman. Do I want a stranger roaming freely through my home?

"Good. That's good, Gwennie."

"I hate it when you call me that."

"I know. But sometimes I like putting a bee in your bonnet."

I snort. "You sound like an old Southern woman."

"When have you been down South?" He laughs.

"When I watched *Steel Magnolias* and *Driving Miss Daisy*."

He shakes his head and stands, then leans down and kisses me. It's soft and full of intention, but I'm exhausted and still unsettled over what I thought I saw when we arrived. Maybe Teresa's little history lesson played on my mind too hard. I do have a big imagination. I've been told that before—in a myriad of ways.

"You coming to bed?" he asks. It's more of an invitation than a question. "I put the sheets on earlier. We're all set."

"Yeah. I'll be right in. Thanks for the hot chocolate. It was sweet."

He kisses me again and heads up the stone steps to the back porch. A portion is screened in—one of my favorite things about the place—and that connects to a sunroom that looks out over the water. Wind rustles the trees, and the water laps at the rocks below. I close my eyes and breathe in fresh air not tainted with smog and car exhaust or the rubbery scent of hot asphalt.

I want this new home and new chapter to work out. I really do, but I'm already off to a rocky start. I'm tired. That's all. I've been exhausted for four years. Spinning my wheels. Going through motions. My eyes grow heavy, and finally my neck muscles relax.

A piercing cry shatters the silent moment, and I jerk from the chair, knocking over the now cold hot chocolate, my heart pounding. I jump to attention. Tara lies quietly against me, but I already knew it wasn't her.

But I did hear a baby.

The fire is nothing but embers and ash, and I shiver and check my Apple Watch. It's after midnight. I've been out here for over two hours sleeping after telling Steven I'd be up to christen the house. He's mad. Otherwise he'd have come out and woken me.

Another promise I haven't made good on in his eyes.

After snatching the mug, I head up the stone steps as hairs prickle along my neck, giving me pause. Scanning the night, I see nothing, but it's Bible plague kind of blackness out here, and there's no amount of eye adjusting to see past it, through it or beyond it.

Nighttime terrified me as a child. Dad would sit by my bed and sing me lullabies until I fell back asleep. It's one of my few but vivid memories. I wish I could remember the early years with clarity, but it seems with every passing year, I forget more than I remember. I have some old home movies packed away and every so often watch them.

At the moment, all I want is to get inside and into the safety of my new home, except it doesn't feel safe. As I enter the back door, I tell myself that I'm not used to living in the country. I'm a city girl. But it's not the environment that has my teeth on edge.

The microwave's surface light is on, giving me a sliver of peace. I slip off my shoes, and the cold of the hardwood seeps through my socks and sends a new shiver through my bones. The house is chilly, but I'm okay with that at night. I like it cooler when I sleep, and so does Steven. As I tiptoe through the living room and parlor to the stairs, joists creak and groan. I need to become accustomed to the house is all, until it's my own with our own scents. I pause at the staircase, remembering the little girl sitting here earlier with her jump rope.

As I pass where she stood, a new icy stream runs through me, and I take the stairs two at a time, my heart leaping into my throat as if someone is behind me, following me. Coming for me. The joists cry out and screech beneath my feet, and I can't move fast enough. At the top of the stairs, I glance back down, and a murky silhouette flashes by the front door.

But it's gone as fast as it came. Like a ribbon of smoke.

I stand there a moment longer, waiting for further movement, but it's quiet. Was it inside or outside? It can't be anything but the house settling and the weak heat blowing through vents. On the second floor, the hallway unfolds in a U shape, wrapping around the stairwell. Doors line both sides, their chipped frames standing like sentinels. The ceiling is lower up here, the walls closer, giving the space a claustrophobic feel, as if the house is pressing inward, listening.

A draft moves past me—soft, but deliberate. I stop, my breath caught in my throat. There's nothing ahead but closed doors and silence, but I can't shake the feeling that something else is here, just out of sight, waiting in the bend of the hallway where the light doesn't reach.

Inside our bedroom, Steven lightly snores on his side of the bed—the left side. He's kept a night-light on in the bathroom for me. He's thoughtful in this way.

After I lay Tara in the bassinet by my side, I go into the bathroom and wash my face, brush my teeth and change into a nightshirt, then slither into bed, reaching over and carefully opening the bedside table drawer. Slowly I remove my Glock 22 and slip it under my pillow.

I haven't been on the force in three long months, and this is the first time I've felt the need to have my gun near me. As if danger lurks and prowls this house, though I'm not sure bullets would be able to stop it. It's an unseen enemy.

And if it's unseen, then I'm not sure how to fight or protect my family from that kind of deadly threat.

Chapter Three

Birds chirping outside wake me, and I blink a few times, disoriented by the smells and surroundings, then remember it was our first night in our new home in Cold Harbor.

Three little brown, white and black birds sit on the window sill, the middle one pecking the glass. He's cute. A robin of some kind maybe. His little head swivels and he looks right at me, and it's calming. Friendly. Familiar even. As if he's saying joy comes in the morning. The night is gone.

Steven's side of the bed is cold, and the nightlight has been turned off in the bathroom. My gun is still under my pillow, and I place it inside the night table drawer before slipping out of bed and heading to the bathroom. I stare into the mirror, wondering where the young me went to. My short, chin-length blond bob is a disaster, but it's thick and easy to brush. A few pops of gray are coming in at the roots. Finding a good hair stylist is on top of my priority list. My skin isn't dewy and fresh like in my thirties. It's pasty and wan. Blech. I pinch my cheeks, brush my teeth and pad over to the bassinet, where Tara lies quietly.

"Come on, baby. Time for a diaper change." When I finish changing her diaper, we trot downstairs, and I pause at the front door, where it no longer feels sinister.

Steven is at the kitchen table with his iPad and a cup of coffee, which smells like glory and sunshine. "Morning," he says, but it's cool. He's still upset that I didn't come upstairs earlier last night.

"I'm sorry. I fell asleep outside. Didn't mean to."

"It's okay," he murmurs, engrossed in his online news. Steven's life is like clockwork, and he rarely if ever deviates from his routine. If it was a normal weekend, he'd go for an eight-mile run, then shower. By nine, he'd want egg whites on whole grain toast with no butter, a slice of avocado and orange juice.

"Hey, did you notice any weird noises last night? Like a… cry or something?" I don't mention baby cries. His mind will go where I don't want it to.

He peers at me over his mug, and a plume of steam rises. "No. I did notice the house settling, which is a tad unnerving. We'll acclimate soon enough, hon. Also, we live in the country now, and I suspect we'll hear all sorts of nocturnal animals that cry and screech. You might have heard an owl or a rabbit squeal if a coyote caught it—or a fox."

The image is disturbing. Rabbits screaming in the mouth of a predator. I've seen domestic violence, homicide, you name it. But helpless rabbits give me the willies. I pour a cup of coffee and bring it to the table.

"I put the baby's swing together. I know how you like to put her in it while you drink your coffee. It's by the inglenook."

Reaching across the table, I squeeze his hand. "I appreciate that, Steven." It's progress.

"Mmm-hmm."

After placing the baby in the swing, I return to the kitchen and stare outside through floor-to-ceiling windows that reveal the entire expanse of the backyard and a breathtaking view of our deck, the cliffs and harbor, and autumn soon approaching. I'm in some kind of painting and it's incredible, a stark contrast from last night's veiled landscape. "I'm going to call Teresa, and I'll be ready to go with you into town when you return from your run. Sound good?" I sip the rich brew, and he nods.

I thought he'd be more enthusiastic over my decision to attend the dinner tonight at the senior doctor's home. "What's the attire?"

His nose scrunches. "I'll have to ask. Casual, I'd assume."

Silence fills the kitchen, and I drink my coffee and scroll through my phone. Kent Masters, my old partner in the homicide unit, won his division in a 5K this morning. Good for him. He was always fast on his feet and looking out for me, until he wasn't. Doesn't matter if he insisted he was—or maybe he was. I don't want to think about him. The past.

What happened.

And of course, seeing his post reminds me of everything I've lost.

Of *her.* My coffee sours in my gut, and I try to focus on the relaxing scenery. "I'm going to walk down to the water."

"Nippy out. Wear a jacket."

"I will." I snag his since it's hanging on the chair and walk out on the deck, the gales off the water slapping me, brisk and biting. My coffee isn't going to stay hot long, though. I pad down the stone stairs that lead to the edge of the water, where a canoe and oars are tied to our own private dock. Fenders that look like red bouncy balls cushion the hull from bumping the dock.

Steven mentioned a couple of kayaks, a canoe and a paddleboard. Not sure which previous owner left them behind. Maybe I'll take up a hobby. I don't have one now, unless occasionally reading counts. I like murder mysteries. But as a cop, I already know what's going to happen in most of them, and when the procedurals aren't done according to real protocol, it only serves to tick me off. Not to mention it means sitting still for longer periods of time than I can stomach. Yet I still buy them.

I have pent-up energy. Steven says it's probably ADHD, and I should be tested. Some people simply need to move more than others. Why does every little tic or action require a label and a medication?

The dock sways as I lean against a post, looking out across the water at the one house I can clearly see from here. It's a Tudor style and stark white with a big porch and a dock, a canoe or kayak tethered to it. I wonder who lives there. Maybe a woman who needs a hobby like me. A fish plops in the water, and ripples span out. I inhale the brine and brew. That should be a café name around here—Brine & Brew. Maybe I'll take up a coffee bean hobby and learn to roast them, open a café . More likely, it's just a clever name.

"Yoo-hoo! Helloo!" A cheery voice draws my attention, and a woman carrying a basket approaches. She's early sixties if I had to guess, in a blueberry-colored tracksuit and as plump as one too. Her hair is bottle-black and coiffed, and I fear she's going to roll down the hill and land in the water. "I'm Deena Richardson, the Welcome Wagon."

They still have those?

"Oh, I know it's a thing of the past, and they send gifts to your mailbox, but it's not proper or welcoming."

Neither is showing up at my house unannounced and entirely too bright for a Saturday morning. I'd prefer the junk mail that says *welcome* quietly. She still hasn't made it to the dock, so I meet her in the middle or we might be here all day. She thrusts the basket of goodies toward me. It includes homemade jams, coffees and tea biscuits as well as a map of the town. The town is walkable, so a map seems unnecessary, but I thank her anyway. "I'm Gwen McDaniel."

"Oh yes, I know. Your husband is the new doctor. We're so thrilled to have one—a younger one, that is." Her chipmunk cheeks blush, and her powdery scent wafts in my direction. "How was your first night here?"

Creepy as all get-out. I slept with my gun. "Pleasant. It's so quiet."

"Oh, indeed, indeed. What do you do?"

"Nothing." I literally have no identity. I do nothing. "I mean, I was a homicide detective in Baltimore for eight years, and before that a patrol officer for six."

Her eyes briefly widen as she sizes me up. I'm a little fluffier since leaving the force, but I can hold my own. "I see. I suppose being a homicide detective makes you less squeamish about the house's history." She covers her mouth. "Not very Welcome Wagon kind of talk."

"I know about the Barkley family, yes. I'm fine. It was decades ago."

She eyes me as if she wants to spill more tea. Instead she waves her hand to dismiss the ghoulish talk. "Well, we don't have much more crime than a drunk and disorderly over at Hal's Tavern. We pride ourselves on being one of the safest little towns in the United States. Our motto is Calm Waters, Safe Shores, Strong Community. Did you see that on the sign when you entered Cold Harbor?"

"No, afraid not."

"It's true. We've even been in magazines, real and online." Online magazines are real, but I refrain from pointing that out, or the fact that crime can happen anywhere and does. Even in safe neighborhoods. I've been on the scene at several.

I look at the white house across the harbor again. "Who lives over there?" Might as well let her scratch my itch.

"Oh, Dr. Adrian Rivera, but he no longer practices. Alzheimer's. Kristin White is his live-in nurse. Real pretty redhead. That house was built in '69."

"The summer of?" I joke, but she squints as if Bryan Adams has gone over her helmet hair. "Sorry. It's a song." One I'll now be singing or humming the rest of the day, but it's a good one, so I don't mind.

"You have plans for the house?" she asks. "I'd hate to see it become some modernized farmhouse. This place has character. Don't you think?"

When she pays the bills for it, she can do whatever she wants. "It definitely has something. You like architecture, do you?"

Again her cheeks redden. "I'm being off-putting. My apologies."

"No, it's fine. I'm just not an early bird. I'm completely fine forgoing the worm."

She laughs, but I'm still not convinced she understood the joke. I should invite her in to meet Steven and have coffee, but our day is crazy busy, and I wasn't expecting visitors or polite conversation. I hope this isn't a prelude to my new life. "Deena, you'll be happy to know I'm not doing anything to the outside other than having it painted and roofed and the windows cleaned, but I am going to work on the inside. It's not been updated in some time and needs a little TLC. Steven wants to remodel the attic into his office like a modernized bonus room, but that's just one room."

"Oh," she says as if she's shocked.

"I don't love the mahogany beadboard inside. It needs freshening up, but I'm keeping the texture it provides."

"Well, that sounds like a big job. My dear friend Marcia Tremell's husband, Curt, owns a construction company. They could do all the work for you. I'm happy to call them or give you his number. Good people."

"Thank you, but I'm a DIY girl, and I'll be taking on the project myself. If I need a subcontractor, I'll call him for a reference, though. I appreciate that."

Deena's toothy grin has now turned close-lipped. She's not happy I've turned down her BFF for the job. Maybe she's out a kickback, but I honestly don't care. "Well, that would be sweet. Fall comes as soon as the ber months hit here." She points to a few gourds and pumpkins in my welcome basket as if to clue me in that my house should already be decked out like a Hallmark movie.

"Oh, nice." I do love fall. I don't love being told when or how to decorate for it.

"And, so you know, we go all out around here come October too. I noticed your flowers are dead on the porch. We have several garden shops where you can freshen those up. Spruce them up for all those little trick-or-treaters."

I frown. Our driveway is long, and we're out away from subdivisions and town. "I don't foresee little goblins coming for treats, Deena."

Her eyes widen. "You don't know, do you?" She puts a hand over her ample chest. "Your house gets more trick-or-treaters than anyone. You know…with it being haunted and all."

I cock my head. "Haunted?"

"Be back…" Steven's words die on his lips when he sees we have a guest. He beams and gracefully jogs down the steps and to us. I've always loved Steven's easy manner and gait. Confident. "Hello," he says with pep because, unlike me, he is an early bird and more extroverted. "I'm Dr. McDaniel, but please call me Steven."

"Steven, so glad to meet you." Deena goes through the entire spiel with him, and I hold up the basket like Vanna White showcasing a vowel.

"I'm about to go out for a run," he says. "Keep that heart healthy and tick, tick, ticking."

She finds this humorous, but not my Bryan Adams joke?

"Well, we're so happy to have you here. If you need anything, you only have to holler."

Literally. This town is tiny.

"I won't keep you," she says.

Too late. And it's too late to press her for more about the house. Haunted? That's just silly talk.

"I'll walk you out." Steven holds out his arm for her to cling to so she doesn't tumble down the steep yard. I toss my cold coffee, glance back at the old doctor's home and then sprint up the stairs into the house. Tara is swinging peacefully, pacifier in her mouth and eyes closed, her little lashes fanning across her velvety skin. My heart aches at the sight. "Sweet baby," I whisper and head upstairs to change clothes, wash my face and apply a little mascara and blush. Look human when I meet the townsfolk.

I'm halfway up the stairs when a rattling noise startles me. I pause and listen, turning my head side to side to gauge from where I'm hearing it. One more step, the joist squawks, and there are rattling sounds again, reminding me of Jacob Marley's chains in *A Christmas Carol.* They're coming from underneath the stairs.

What in the world?

I return to the living room and stare at the wall and the closet door under the stairs. Will I find Harry Potter? My insides flush fever-hot as I approach the door, but my hands are ice-cold. I touch the knob and twist, then yank open the door.

Nothing.

But this is exactly where the rattling of…chains banging on hardwood?…came from. Or something. I'm not sure what it was, to be exact. I only know that I heard it plain as day. Steven's not here to corroborate it. That's convenient.

The back door slams, and I jump and grab a fire poker, then bolt into the kitchen.

No one is there. No one is outside.

Maybe I left the door cracked and the wind caught it. I peer outside and see a blurry figure on the dock.

I blink and it's gone.

No, *he's* gone.

What is going on with this house?

Or what is going on with me?

Chapter Four

Our bedroom is stacked with boxes that need unpacking, including my clothing. I've never been a big shopper. I can't tell you trends or fashion brands. These things are not my cup of tea, but I do have a few upscale items for when Steven and I attended important events—like his honors and awards. Those pieces might be too upscale for the gathering at the senior doctor's home tonight. I want to look presentable and put together even if I feel neither of those things.

Steven could wear a bathrobe and appear sophisticated and confident. My main clothing used to consist of businesswear as a detective. Pantsuits and button-up shirts. Sensible shoes. Another reason I never watch cop shows. Female detectives in spiky boots or heels are nothing but Hollywood's version of a cop. In the real world, you can't chase a criminal in heels, and you're on your feet often.

Back from his run, Steven enters the bedroom, freshly showered and in a pair of jeans and a long-sleeved T-shirt that brings out the tiny amber flecks in his espresso eyes. His hair is wet and curls around his ears. He's always been attractive, and he goes nowhere without at least a handful of women noticing and appreciating him.

"I called Teresa while you were gone, and she hesitated at first but agreed to babysit Tara while we attend the dinner tonight." I rip open a box labeled Dressy-Casual and haul out a few items. I have fifteen extra pounds loading down my body, and I'm not sure any of these items will fit me well. Or maybe it's me. I don't like the way I look. I should remedy that and tell myself I'll start tomorrow. I've been starting tomorrow for a while now.

Steven grunts and slips his wedding band onto his ring finger. Nice to see him wearing it again.

"Did you find out the dress code for tonight? I don't want to be over- or underdressed."

"Cocktail attire. Dr. Mansfield said it's a catered event with a string quartet. I'm going to wear a suit with no tie."

Then I need a cocktail dress but not a shimmery one. A little black dress. I keep one on hand as it serves many purposes. "Good to know." I empty out one box onto the bed, but no black dress. I have one more that's labeled Dressy. Surely it didn't end up in my loungewear box. After twenty minutes of digging, our bedroom looks like a closet puked, and I have no little black dress for tonight. But even if I did, I'd look like a can of busted biscuits in it.

Frustration leaches into my muscles, tightening them, and tears burn the backs of my eyes. I'm not a crier. Never have been that I can remember, but the past few months have taken a toll on me, and now I cry at the drop of a hat. Moodiness is my best friend, along with queso and chips and tacos. I should turn them down more often. But I know that will never happen. "I'm going to see if I can find something when we head downtown. What time are we leaving?"

"I'm ready if you are." He grabs his keys and wallet from the bowl on his chest of drawers, and I lift Tara from her bassinet.

Steven eyes her like a nuisance cutting into our day, but it's not like she'll scream and cry or interrupt his shopping plans. I say nothing, and he says nothing in return. That's how marriages go. Two people making eyes and pulling faces but never discussing the root cause. It's also how marriages end, and I can't deny that ours is walking a fine line, a loose and flimsy line that stretches across a chasm that's graveyard-dark. A place all dead marriages go to die.

I buckle Tara into her car seat and check to make sure the stroller is in the hatch of the SUV. Tension builds around us, and Steven cranks up the radio as if noise will drown it out. The '80s rock is simply the death knell, the "ba-dum" before Jaws takes a bite and we bleed out.

Downtown is less than ten minutes from our house. Barrels of mums sit by every wooden bench, reminding me to buy some myself to replace the dead ones in those large wooden barrels on my front porch.

Pumpkins already dot the cobblestone sidewalks. Deena wasn't kidding around about fall coming to town when the ber months hit.

The sky is overcast, ripe with rain, and the wind pushes the scent of salt and fish through the air. Patrons weave in and out of shops, cafés and boutiques, pausing to chitchat on a dreary Saturday afternoon. They pay no attention to the gloomy clouds rolling in or the weeds springing from between the cobblestones. All a weed needs is a sliver of space to grow until the area is riddled with them.

Steven draws the cover over the stroller, and I bristle but keep silent. Cold Harbor residents nod as we pass, noticing we're strangers, unsure if we're tourists or new residents. My cheeks hurt from all the smiling. I haven't smiled this much in a solid year, but I'm the doctor's wife, and it requires playing a part I've never been fully comfortable with. But I can pull it off. I have a closet full of metaphorical Oscars. Most of my interactions with people have consisted of filtering out lies, watching for deception and comforting grieving families due to crime. I have frowning down to an art, a penetrating gaze perfected.

Smiling? Smiling is not my gig.

"That's my office," Steven says, and points to a brick building with a bay window displaying more purple and gold mums and an assortment of gourds and pumpkins.

Those pumpkins are going to rot before October, but who am I to interrupt the town's tradition? Yet it's almost like the insistence on rushing fall is shellacking something darker.

The thought of rot and death brings to mind the death of the Barkley family on a Halloween night. Old houses are rife with history as families cycle in and out over time, making it their own space. The walls stand and hold secrets from one generation to another. I wonder what secrets my home holds that I don't know?

"What do you think?" he asks, and a pinch of excitement fills his voice.

His building is at the end of the strip near the water. Beside that is a small wooded park where children are playing, laughing and shrieking in good fun.

My insides stir and twist as a strong sensation of doom strikes against my pulse, quickening it. Parents converse, ignoring their children as they race around the swing set poles and zip down yellow plastic slides.

"One of those children could be snatched. I have half a mind to go over there and tell them what happens to the children of parents who don't pay attention." Anger breaks loose in my veins. I've seen it happen. Found lifeless bodies of small children whose parents only turned around for a second. A second is all it takes. But this park, this town, exudes a false sense of security.

"Gwen, we're not in Baltimore anymore. They're paying attention. Let's not have this conversation again, okay? Please. It's a nice day. We should enjoy it. Can we? You didn't even answer my question about my office." Steven's tone is firm, but his desperation rides the undercurrent.

I shake off the dread and force a smile. "Of course. Sorry. It's a great building with views. Can't wait to see inside." I toss him an apologetic grin. "I guess you can take the girl from the force, but you can't take the force from the girl."

But then, from the obscurity of the trees, a man emerges. He's wearing gray jeans and a black jacket that matches his hair. He leans on the tree and watches the children, one little girl in particular. I pause and pretend to tie my shoe, but I'm watching him. Mothers continue to squawk over coffees and completely ignore the danger lurking. Like a human crow perched on a branch, watching, studying, learning.

Every nerve in my body hums as the little girl wanders farther away from the other children and toward him and the dense woods surrounding the play park. He squats and holds something in his hands. Is that a puppy? A puppy! I believe it is.

Steven is still walking toward his office, oblivious to my abrupt stop and what is transpiring before my very eyes. The girl is eyeing the fluffy little pooch and continuing her walk to the stranger. He says nothing. He's still, like a person coaxing a timid stray dog to approach.

My warning bells blare. I finally stand and begin my way into the park and toward them. He is not taking a child on my watch.

And then she giggles and cries, "Daddy, you found him! You found Chucky."

"Yeah, baby. He was down by the dock. You have to take better care of him if you want a real puppy." She grabs her stuffed puppy and hugs him.

Her father.

Steven has now paused and turned, walking back to me with a grim expression on his face. When he closes the distance between us, he studies the man with the child and then looks at me again. "This right here..." He motions from me to the father and daughter. "This is why I worry about you. Jumping to conclusions and about to take down an innocent man for what? Giving his child back her stuffed puppy. Don't ruin this for us. We have a lot to lose, Gwen. You know it more than I do."

"Better safe than a child dead." It's all I can muster. Because he's right. We have so very much to lose if we don't tread lightly in this town. I glance at Tara. *I* have so very much to lose.

"Come see the office." Steven grabs my hand and brings me inside Cold Harbor Medical Clinic. The waiting area, drenched with the scents of cinnamon and maple, is empty. No crime in this town, and no sickness either, from the looks of it. A pretty brunette sits behind a big counter wearing cheery scrubs. She beams, and recognition dawns as she sets her gaze on Steven.

"Dr. McDaniel. It's so great to see you. Are you working today?" she asks.

"No, Lynn. Not today. I'm showing my wife my new digs. This is Gwen."

She laughs as if his word choices are hysterical. They aren't. I shake her hand. She stands, noticing the stroller, and Tara, who is concealed under the shade cover. "How precious. I didn't realize you had a baby. You look amazing."

Steven bristles. "Can we come on back?"

"Of course, Dr. McDaniel. You can do whatever you'd like." I catch her innuendo and shoot her my interrogative expression, feeling the satisfaction as she flinches slightly. We enter the hall and walk past a total of ten examination rooms and a small nurses' station where two nurses are present. Steven introduces them, and they titter about the event tonight. We visit his cozy office, and he tells me his plans for decorating, which is really explaining on which walls he'll hang his license and accolades.

After, we enter the fray outside. People are moving a bit quicker as the clouds thicken, and the waves are rolling in faster, harder.

"Well, what did you think?" he asks.

Honestly, it's pitiful. Beneath his pedigree and capability, but he can't go back. *We* can't go back. Guilt nips at my heart, and shame fills my drowning soul. "It's going to be perfect. You'll be loved and adored by all." And he might be paid in pies. I refrain from that smart remark. I picked this town. This house. This place. He compromised, and for that I'm grateful.

"Yeah. I can make it work." He flashes me a smile, but I catch a flicker of disappointment in his eyes.

I wish he didn't have to *make it work*, but when life hands you lemons and all that. "I'm going to head into that boutique." I point to an adorable shop with painted white brick and a wooden sign in the shape of a smooth pine cone. "The White Pine Cone. See if I can come up with something dazzling for tonight. Do you have a preference?"

"Gwen, you'll be gorgeous in anything. I'll meet you in thirty minutes for brunch. You want to try that little place on the water? The Lighthouse Café with the signature bisque?"

Lobster bisque sounds like a dream. "Perfect."

He kisses my cheek and jogs across the street to a little bookshop. Steven can't seem to read enough spy fiction. I breeze inside the boutique and instantly know I'll find the perfect little dress. It's upscale, and the girls working the counter are barely out of high school if at all. They'll insert the word "like" between every other word. It's a pet peeve of mine.

"Can I help you?" a blonde with a perfectly contoured face asks.

"No, just browsing."

"Okay. Well if you change your mind, let me know." She grins and resumes her conversation with the other girl.

"My mom was like freaked out this morning," the blonde says in a hushed tone.

She *was* freaked out or she was *like* freaked out? I roll my eyes and move to the clearance rack first, pushing the stroller through the tight shopping racks.

"Well, when I was grabbing an iced latte this morning, I heard John Markum say it wasn't an animal bone because Wilt would have known that. He's like a major hunter, you know? Also, John is so hot. He can live rent-free in my head for as long as he wants."

Now I don't much care if they insert the word *like* into their conversation. New interest is piqued.

If a bone was found by an avid hunter and it wasn't an animal bone…

Then it must be human.

Chapter Five

I don't receive all the answers I'd hoped from the two teenagers discussing a possible human bone that was found earlier this morning, but what I do overhear is the location. It's the east side of my property in the woods behind the house. I lay my dress and a pair of earrings on the counter, and the girls stop talking.

"I hear a bone was found this morning near the house we just moved into." I lean in as if I enjoy a little gossip myself.

"Ack!" the blonde says. "We heard a new doctor was moving to town with his family."

"I bet he'd be able to tell if it was animal or human," the brunette returns.

I have them. Not that it took much. Girls do love to dish. "He would. Do you know anything else?" What kind of bone? Are there more bones? I have a million questions, but these girls are all about spilling the tea and not necessarily the truth. Next door is a coffee shop, and in small towns, the cafés are the place to be—and post offices. The truth might be steeping over there.

The blonde shakes her head. "No. Just that Wilt Dinner's dog found it and he took it into the chief's office. But it's kind of a big deal. Nothing ever happens here, and if it's a legit human bone, Cady's podcast might really take off. If she starts it. Our town will be famous." She rings me up and glances at the stroller. "She's cute."

She's hard to see with the cover pulled over her, but the gesture is kind. "Thank you."

I leave and scan the sidewalks. I've only been in the boutique twenty minutes. I have time before lunch and slip inside the busy coffee shop, Black Capped Coffee, whose sign has a little black, white and beige bird sitting on a pluming cup of coffee—the same as the sweet little birds on my window sill this morning. Coffee drinkers are sitting at booths and tables, indulging in conversation, and I strain to hear if any of it is centered around a possible human bone on my property.

The foreboding ripples in my gut as I approach the wood-and-tin counter and scan the menu. A woman in front of me orders and scoots to the side, and then it's my turn. The woman behind the counter is young and fresh-faced with shiny blond hair that hangs like a long silk curtain around her apple cheeks. Her blue eyes could only be described as sparkling. She offers a bright greeting and patiently waits for me to order a coffee.

"You passing through?" she asks while I peruse the chalkboard menus on the wall, each coffee cleverly named. Pumpkin drinks and muffins are on the menu too.

"No, we moved here yesterday. My husband—"

"The new doctor," she exclaims. "My mom told me." She extends her hand. "I'm Cady Tremell. I own this lovely establishment."

Cady the podcaster? And Tremell as in the construction guy friend of the Welcome Wagon blueberry lady? In this small town, it would have to be.

"Gwen McDaniel," I say as I shake her hand. "I'll have an Americano with honey and heavy cream."

"Excellent choice."

I reach inside my purse, but she holds out her hand to halt me. "On the house. A little gift. Welcome to Cold Harbor."

She's kind. I can spot genuineness a mile away, and Cady Tremell is loaded with kindness. It's refreshing. "Thank you."

Cady spots the stroller, the cover down. "I don't know how your baby is sleeping through all this ruckus."

I only smile. Bones are on my brain. "I heard about the bone found this morning near our property line."

She pauses. "Oh…uh. Yeah. That's been the buzz." She hurries behind the counter and works on making my coffee. Her shoulders are tight, and it's clear she doesn't want to talk. While it doesn't help me, I appreciate she's not a tea-spiller like the girls next door. Which means what she does say will hold some weight.

"And where might the truth land? I mean, it is our property."

She looks at me and bites her bottom lip. "Chief was in here earlier—Chief Ellersby, that is, our police chief. He came in for his usual house brew, and he was swarmed with customers asking, especially since it happened at your house." She almost winces.

"I know about the Barkley family," I reassure her in case the history is her reason for hesitation. "And the fire that killed a family." Though I don't know the details.

"Right. Wilt Dinner says it was too big to be an animal. Even a wolf or coyote. Definitely human. Chief says it's not. But I'll be honest… Wilt knows what he's talking about, and I believe him."

"Why do you believe him?" I ask as she hands me my coffee. "Because he knows bones or because the house creeps you out? You can be honest. The house creeps me out too—at least at night." I refrain from sharing my reasons.

"The house is a little creepy," she says apologetically, and her cheeks flush pink. She's withholding, and two women now stand behind me. Cady points to my cup. "Again, on the house."

"Thanks." I sip it. It's perfectly sweetened and has the right amount of cream. "Delicious. I'm sold. You have a new regular." Not to mention, I want more information on this bone, Wilt Dinner and the house I nabbed at a steal. I turn to leave and pause. "Hey, are you the Cady that has a podcast?"

Her eyes light up. "I am. Well, I'm in the fledgling stages. True crime."

"I'm a former homicide detective with the Baltimore PD. I'd be happy to help you. If that bone isn't an animal's, we might have ourselves a podcast. Also, the girls next door want in." I wink, and she laughs.

"I bet they do. I would actually love to pick your brain. We aren't open on Sundays—it's not just Chick-fil-A. But next time you're free, come by any day around ten—that's my slow hour—and we'll talk." We exchange phone numbers, and I'm actually excited to make a friend. Have another woman to gab with.

"Great. I'm sure I'll be in town for supplies off and on. I'm remodeling the house. Maybe it won't stay so creepy."

She laughs again. "I like you, Gwen. See you soon."

By the time I arrive at the Lighthouse Café by the edge of the water, Steven is sitting on the deck with a glass of iced tea, and a club soda is waiting for me. "You been here long?"

"Fifteen minutes. Locals say we have time before the storm hits. How was dress shopping?" He spots the bag from the White Pine Cone and the coffee in the cupholder on the stroller, and he raises an eyebrow.

"Oh, I thought I'd pop into the hubbub of the town and feel it out."

"And?"

"Excellent coffee, and I may have made a friend." I tell him about Cady, leaving out the true crime podcast and the bone found on our property, but if it's all the buzz, then he might have caught wind in the bookstore or while being seated.

Steven nods, satisfied I'm doing normal stuff. Making normal friends—as far as he knows. Drinking coffee and mingling around town. The server sidles up. Steven orders a lobster brunch roll, and I order the bisque and eggs Florentine. "You buy a new book?"

"Two. A Dugoni, and I thought I'd try a new genre. Bought a psychological thriller with some serious Hitchcock vibes."

As if on cue, I notice several crows circling as if they've been following me from the house, watching. An omen. I shiver. "Nice." I can hear the distraction in my own voice, and Steven's eyebrows bump upward, but he doesn't call me on it.

Instead we talk about the weather and the town. He seems genuinely interested and on board with acclimating to it all. He can fit in anywhere, though. The server brings out food, and I immediately dive into the thick, creamy bisque loaded with hunks of fresh lobster. "Well, this confirms it. I picked the right place to live and eat." I'm going to weigh ten tons if I eat this rich food all the time.

Steven chuckles and offers me a bite of his meal, and I return the favor. I can't remember the last time we shared food. Our life has been fractured and lately broken. I want to try because I love my husband, faults and all. I'm certainly not perfect—flawed to the core, in fact—and here he is doing this new thing for me, for us. I put my racing thoughts on hold and ask him questions about the new practice and his hopes for what he can do here, and I mean every word. I've always been impressed by Steven's keen mind and high aspirations.

About halfway through the meal, when our conversation eases into comfortable silence, I recall what I learned earlier, and I decide to test the waters. After all, if that bone is human, then forensic teams, dogs and officers will be milling around our land, hunting for further remains.

"I heard something in the boutique. About a discovery this morning on our property line."

He polishes off his lobster roll and waits for me to continue.

"They found a bone. Possibly human," I whisper. "That's crazy town, right?" I brace myself for his reaction in case it's what I'm expecting.

Steven inhales sharply. "Or it could be anything, Gwen."

And I'm right.

"I'm just saying that it might not be nothing."

"And our privacy could be invaded if a search happens. We don't need that. I feel like I have to remind you of this more than I should." Steven has never been one to enjoy gossip or rumor mills, and neither have I, but this is fact. A bone of some kind has been found.

I rock the stroller with my foot, which is more about my own need to self-soothe. It could be anything, but with what I've already experienced in the house, my gut screams evil things have happened in this town that prides itself on safety and small-town hospitality. Something transpired yards from our house—as well as inside decades ago. But what if that's not all?

Why did the last owner move so quickly? Was it really a transfer, or did he have a more sinister reason to skip town?

Steven lays his napkin onto the empty tray and reaches across the table, taking my hand. "Gwen, you're not a cop anymore. I know it's hard to swallow. The circumstances are still tender, but this doesn't concern us, and it's probably nothing. I think it would be best for you to focus on making friends and making our new house a home. You haven't done a home project in a long time."

"My gut—"

"Your gut isn't always right. I'd think by now you'd know that and not act on every single impulse. We have a clean slate here." His words, while spoken softly, lance wounds that have been healing. No one's gut is always right. That's true, and I had mitigating circumstances that surrounded a lapse in judgment. Now? Nothing is hindering an unbiased view. I have no skin in this game, and my gut screams something volatile happened in that house besides the Barkleys' tragedy, and that bone is anything but an animal's.

And come Monday morning, after I visit the hardware store, I'm going into Cady's with every intention of finding out what is going on in this town that boasts utter safety and good neighbors.

I can reno a house while digging into the town, the past and the secrets Cold Harbor hides. Because I know for certain, deep in *my* bones, at least one secret has been unearthed.

How many more will those eerie woods and this veneered town give up?

Chapter Six

Lily Ann

She sat by the lake, picking dandelion puffballs and blowing the seeds into the air. It'd been an almost perfect day. The clouds blobbed the blue sky like the tops of Disney's DOLE Whips—her favorite when Mom and Dad took her last year for her birthday.

It had been epic.

She glanced back toward the campsite, inhaling the scents of charcoal and beef. Mom was grilling burgers and dogs for dinner. Dad took her fishing earlier, but they didn't catch anything worth keeping. So much for a fish fry.

She liked to come down to the lake to watch people canoe and kayak. They looked like specks of color on the water. She couldn't find anything to catch her attention. Mom said she had ants in her pants all the time, but not real ants. She didn't need to add that last part. No ants had ever been in her pants. But once they found their way into her socks and bit her ankles, burning like fire. Dad had sprayed her with the hose to rinse them away, and Mom had put anti-itch cream on them, but it hadn't helped.

"Hi." A deep, raspy voice caught her attention, and she glanced up, shielding her eyes from the sun. A big man in a uniform stood over her. A park ranger.

"You been fishing?"

She pointed to her fishing pole. "Yessir, but we didn't catch anything, and I didn't catch nothing by myself either."

"What part of the lake did you fish?" he asked. He squatted beside her, his knee cracking, and the smell of cinnamon toast filled her nose. She loved cinnamon toast. The ranger reminded her of Dad. Thick hair and some wrinkles around his eyes, mouth and neck. But his smile stood out most. Bright. Straight teeth, just a little yellow. Like Gramps. He said it was from drinking too much coffee his whole life.

Her heart hurt because she missed Gramps. He died two months ago. Cancer. Dad had been pretty blue—Mom's words to her, but when she was on the phone with Aunt Sally, she used other words like "depression" and "distant" as well as phrases like "not coming out of it." Dad and Gramps had fished all the time and taken her too. They'd even been in tournaments.

"I think that side." She pointed to where she'd been fishing and dropped her dandelion stem.

"You make a wish?" he asked.

She squinted at him. "Wish?"

"Yeah. You close your eyes—" he closed his "—and make a wish." The ranger waited a second.

She wondered what his wish was. Was it like blowing out birthday candles? If you told your birthday wish, it wouldn't come true.

"Then you blow the pappus—the white fuzz—and your wishes come true."

She cocked her head. Could blowing dandelion fuzz really make a wish come true? She wished for an American Girl doll last year and had gotten the very one at Christmas. "Are you sure?"

His smile stretched wide. "I would never lie to you, especially about wishes. Wishes are delicate matters of the heart, and no one should lie about that." He crossed his heart with his index finger.

Her chest lightened, and she nodded once. What did she wish for? What were delicate matters?

His dandelion fuzz continued to sail into the wind, up into the sky, until it disappeared—maybe to heaven where Gramps now lived.

He handed her the dandelion. "I wished for cooler weather." He wiped the sweat from his forehead with the back of his hand.

Her mouth fell open. "You told your wish!"

He laughed. "It's not like a birthday wish. You can tell it—if you want. But you don't have to."

She held the dandelion in her hands, then closed her eyes. When she opened them, she blew the little white puffs away. "I wished my dad would catch fish. It would make him happy and not blue."

The ranger's smile covered his whole face. "Well, that's a wish that will come true. I know the perfect spot to fish. Tomorrow you can show him as a surprise. Sound good?"

"Yes!" How awesome would it be to help Dad out of that depression Mom talked about?

He stood and held out his big callused hand. "It's on the south side in a cove, covered with trees. Hard to see but easy to find if you know the way."

She stood too, but hesitated, glancing back toward the campsite. "Will it take long? Dinner will be ready soon, and I'm not really supposed to go away with strangers."

He nodded. "You have good parents. They'll never know, and they wouldn't mind you leaving with a park ranger. We help people, and I'm helping you surprise your dad and make your wish come true."

That was true. Park rangers did help people, and if Mom and Dad didn't know, it would be a way bigger surprise tomorrow. "Okay." She placed her hand in his.

But she'd never know if her father stayed blue or not.

All she knew was she'd never be happy again.

Chapter Seven

I don't hate my black dress. I do detest the form shaper I'm wearing beneath to hold in my busted can of biscuits, and I consider taking up running again. Steven already has plans to turn half of the basement into a home gym. The equipment is already down in the dank, musty room, but it's my job to make it look—and I guess smell—better too. Not that I'm not ready for a project, but Steven's list feels condescending and controlling, and even claustrophobic.

And I did not like going down those concrete steps into concrete walls and flickering fluorescent lights. I've never been a fan of basements, but ours is especially cold and unsettling. Or maybe I'm just unsettled. Yes, I definitely am, but with good reason.

Running my hands through my hair, I pull out a few curls I've added to loosen them and give it more of a fun beach wave style. Steven says sometimes I carry stiff shoulders and a mean face. It's just my face, and he knows that. Criminals don't take a bubbly detective seriously. To be honest, I'm too tired to fake it until I make it tonight.

Chronic fatigue has plagued me the last several months. Finding criminals and bringing them to justice energized me and gave me a sense of purpose. A focus. But since leaving the force, I've been whirling in a vacuum. Maybe Steven is right and the renovations will give me a sense of purpose too. And of course I have Tara. She's been such a sweet comfort to me the past two months, pulling me from a depression I didn't think I'd sludge my way out of. To some degree, I'm still underwater, kicking my way to the surface, and it's utterly exhausting.

I open my jewelry box as Steven enters the room. "Teresa will be here in twenty minutes." He lightly touches my hair. "You look amazing."

"I'm contoured, stuffed in a sausage casing and feeling shaky. It's been a while." My nerves buzz, and sweat already trickles along my lower back from the shaper cutting off air to my skin. Yep, tomorrow I'm going back to running.

He grins and kisses my neck. "You're going to do fine. You know how to chitchat and make nice. You're utterly charming when you want to be. You charmed me."

Past tense, I notice. He gently takes the necklace from my hand and puts it around my neck, then clasps it. My skin used to respond to his touch, humming. Now I simply feel his cool skin and that's all. It's the anxiety. Plagued me since childhood.

Steven rubs my shoulders and squeezes. Tara lies quietly in the bassinet. Steven called Teresa earlier—after I had already called her to babysit. He left the room and went outside to talk to her, and I homed in on him like a bald eagle circling for a fish to snatch from the water. He'd paced, laughed and then used hand gestures a lot. Thirty minutes later—which is entirely too long to confirm a babysitting gig—he returned with a flushed neck and tight smile.

Did I ask him what he said? What she said? No. Because the truth is, I don't want to know. Apparently, I look for problems where none exist.

"Tell me whose house we're going to again." I grab the diamond drops, but the post doesn't want to go through the piercing. Has it been that long since I wore earrings? I switch it to the back of the piercing, and it punctures with a pinch. Then I slide it through the front and repeat the procedure with the left ear when the doorbell rings. "She's early."

He waves off my annoyance. "Take your time. I'll let her in and show her around."

"She knows her way her around." Like the post on my earrings, I've pinched a sealed-up spot that Steven calls insecurity. "I'll go. Give her instructions on Tara."

His jaw ticks, and he gives a slight eye roll. Already I'm ruining his evening.

"Fine," he says, releasing a heavy breath.

I hustle down the stairs, my bare feet creaking old joists, and rush to the front door. I open it, and Teresa stands on the porch, a Hobo bag hanging over one shoulder and a bottle of Smartwater in her hand. She smiles and shifts her weight to one side. "Hi again, Mrs. McDaniel. I'm here to..."

"Keep an eye on Tara," I finish for her. That's all she's here to do. "We don't have much in the fridge. I haven't had time to buy groceries." I motion for her to enter the house, and she eases inside, but she's uncomfortable. Cady said the house creeped her out. Does Teresa feel this way too? She's scanning the room. Boxes line the walls, and the room is mostly empty, but it's only been a day. "I'm assuming Steven gave you all the details regarding Tara?"

She runs her top teeth along her bottom lip as her eyes shift anywhere but to my face. "He, uh, did. Yes."

"Good." Steven is still upstairs, and from what I've gathered, Teresa is a local. Locals know things, and it's obvious she's uncomfortable, which works to my advantage. Discomfort is a wonderful motivator to make people talk. I glance upward, making sure Steven isn't on the stairs. "Guess you heard about the bone they found near or on our property." I'm baiting her. It's what I do—did—as a cop.

"Actually, it is your property, right on the edge of the line."

Well then. Now that the real estate agent has stated it, it gives me a right to know what is going on. A man had been hunting on my land, which butts against Acadia National Park. I find it hard to believe he didn't know the house had been purchased. Probably thought he had one more hunt in him before we settled in.

Maybe that was the shadow at the door last night. No, he wouldn't have been hunting at night for a second time. I just need something logical to explain the bizarre things and noises.

Why hasn't anyone knocked on our door to let us know they'll be searching? If they assume it's an animal, then no point, and if they've sent it off to a local medical examiner to determine if it's human or animal, no point searching until they know. However, if remains are left exposed, scavengers could pilfer them, leaving no crime scene if the bones are taken before an examiner can conclude the origin.

"What do you think? Animal or human remains?" I study her body language, her eyes.

Teresa lays a hand over the hollow of her throat. "I hope animal. Don't you?"

"Of course. But there's talk in town that Walt Dinner says it's human, and he should know. He's an avid hunter, and the bone must be clearly identifiable for him to be so adamant. Right?"

"Wilt Dinner." Teresa corrects my purposeful mistake. "And I couldn't say. No one has gone missing recently, and it's a small town."

Recently. Why include *recently*? Who went missing in the past?

"That news would travel at light speed," she says. "I wouldn't worry, Mrs. McDaniel. I think you made the right choice with this house and shouldn't be afraid."

Ah, she's worried I'll come at her for selling me a house with mass graves on the property or something. No wonder she's fidgety. "I'm not afraid, Teresa. I worked homicide in Baltimore. I've seen it all. I'm curious." Steven's footsteps sound on the creaking stairs. "Never mind. Let's keep our chat to ourselves, yes?"

Teresa grins as Steven descends. He's handsome and fit, and his age works in his favor. "Teresa, thank you again for coming."

"No problem, Dr. McDaniel."

"Steven. I'm Steven," he says as he enters the parlor.

I plaster a smile on my face and slip my arm through his. "Ready?"

"Yes. I don't want to get lost on back roads." He gives me a mock expression of fear, and I can't help but laugh. He really is charming.

"You two have a lovely night." Teresa steps onto the porch as we make our way to the car. "See you later."

"Thanks again," I say and slide into the seat. It's cold tonight. My legs are freezing, but we women suffer for beauty. Men never seem to have to, though.

"You nervous?"

Steven nods. "A little. But I can fake it until I make it."

I wish the same were true of me. I can fake it until I tank it. Or the subtitles play on my face, revealing the truth. "You'll kill them. Charm is your middle name." It's actually Robert.

He's pleased with my comment, but it's true. He could wrap a viper around his finger and it wouldn't even bite.

The curves along the ocean bring in a briny scent, but the stars covering the night sky are like tiny pebbles ready to rain down on our parade and bring light to everything we want to stay hidden. Funny. That's exactly what I want to do to this town.

Expose what's being hidden.

GPS lets us know our destination is only five hundred feet ahead, and the trees open up to a gorgeous Shaker house overlooking the water. A much newer house than ours and more ostentatious.

It's showtime.

My nerves hum as we exit the SUV. Steven's hand at the small of my back brings some comfort, but not enough to keep the sweat from dotting my forehead.

"This will be good, Gwen. Relax."

Easier said than done. New places and people in a social setting have never been my jam. "Of course." I paste on yet another plastic expression of joy and we enter the Mansfields' home. The first thing I notice are the ceilings that were built to reach the heavens and the mixed scents of perfumes, aftershaves and lemon polish. It's a sea of black dresses and white starched shirts and flutes of champagne.

All in honor of my husband—and Labor Day.

A portly man with a bulbous nose that gives me Walter Matthau vibes approaches with a broad smile. "Steven. So glad you're here."

Steven shakes his hand and turns to me. "Gwen, meet Dr. Reggie Mansfield. He's the senior doctor at the clinic."

"You are as lovely as Steven said." Dr. Mansfield takes my hand in both of his and shakes, holding on a little longer than I like, and my insides flush hot. I'm not a touchy-feely person—at least not with strangers. This is why I could never live in the South if the sayings are true that they all chat and hug and have no personal space. I would die.

"That was so kind of him." Probably not true, but I'll let it pass, because maybe it's just me feeling less than lovely. Piano music filters through the atmosphere, riding the undercurrent of conversation and polite laughter.

"It's true." Steven wraps his strong arm around me, pulling me close. He's warm, and my heart aches. I've missed the closeness, but this is a show, so I ignore the pangs of longing.

It's been so long, my body bristles without my instruction. Steven quickly lets me go and puts distance between us. I feel it to the marrow of my bones.

Bones. Would that be a topic of conversation tonight? How sad that talking dead bodies and buried bones will get me through the night with comfort. "Well," I say, "it's sweet of you both. Dr. Mansfield, your home is beautiful."

"Please call me Reggie. Both of you. I can't take any credit for the house. My wife, Amanda, has an eye—or that's what she and her friends tell me." He laughs, and we laugh with him, but it's not actually all that funny.

"I would love to meet her." I mean that. She might have some suggestions on stores and contractors—other than Curt Tremell. Not that I don't want to use him, but negotiating bids is the name of the game. While we are financially stable and Steven's salary here is nice, I prefer frugality over opulence. "I'll be doing some renovations on our home. It's quite a fixer-upper, but the bones are good." Back to bones. Would he bite?

"Oh, I imagine so. We didn't even realize the house went on the market. You must have scooped it up the moment it went up for sale."

That's exactly what happened.

He leans in and whispers, his breath tinged with bourbon. "A lot of people would kill for that house. Not a better view in town."

Is that so? I hope he's not serious, but what if he is? Once it's remodeled, it will be even more beautiful than Reggie's. We bought it under market value. Probably for all the repair work that needs done, but maybe not. Why hadn't anything major been done to the house? Nothing seems updated since the early '80s, and even that was minimal.

Steven must have read my face, because he clears his throat

and addresses Mansfield. "You'd be right. We snapped it up as soon as we saw it. Gwen spent some time in Acadia National Park as a child. She happened to be looking around here when the house went on the market. She called right then, and we put an offer on it sight unseen. I flew out for all the details, and the rest is history—or will be." He gives me a smile and shakes his head. "We aren't usually so spontaneous. But she had to have it."

Steven isn't so spontaneous. I'm another story. And I did want the house. I saw a house full of children and a gorgeous view. I saw bonfires and kayaking. Laughter. Maybe I should have done the walk-through, but Steven insisted I stay home. Rest. I might have changed my mind had I visited first. My dreams about living here faded the second I saw it in person. And I can't say a word to him about it.

"Well, it will be wonderful to grow a family in."

I detest these kinds of insensitive comments. Reggie doesn't mean to be, but he doesn't know my history. Or I don't think he does. If so, he's purposely kicking a wound. I had four miscarriages before Tara entered our lives. With each loss, my hope for a house full of pitter-patters slipped away with a piece of me. A piece I'd never reclaim. With each loss, a gap widened between Steven and me. And when gaps aren't sealed fast enough, they create a chasm. Chasms are much harder to close. I wanted to mend our chasm.

Then…life took a desperate turn and spiraled, and the chasm became an abyss.

"Oh! There's Amanda." Reggie waved, and a woman beamed, then glided toward us. Talk about gaps. Age gaps. Amanda must be twenty years younger than Reggie or more. Her ring fingers are full of bling. Her earlobes and necklace match. She's one decked out lady. "Amanda, darling, I was just telling Gwen how you can really make a house a home. She's about to remodel theirs."

Amanda puts a hand over her spray-tanned heart. “I’m so glad someone is going to put some money into that…house.” I catch a twitch at the corner of her eye. “If it’s all freshened up, teenagers might stop skulking around for—”

“Shrimp cocktail?” A young man in a black-and-white uniform sidles up and presents us with a tray. Reggie and Steven help themselves. Amanda passes. Is she, too, wearing Spanx so tight a single shrimp might pop it? Doubt it. And now the moment is gone. What are teenagers skulking around doing?

“I have a list of contractors and home renovation stores that will fit the bill,” she says as the server leaves us. Her gaze travels to Steven, and there’s no hiding her thoughts. Steven is eye candy. “It’s going to be spectacular having another doctor at the clinic. It’s such a reputable place that people from other neighboring towns drive here just to see Reggie and Mark. Now they’ll see you too.”

“That’s so kind of you to say. I certainly hope it’s true.” Steven extends his hand, and she takes it with long manicured nails and grace. Nah, she’s not wearing a body shaper. “You have a beautiful home.”

“You’re too sweet.” She doesn’t draw back her hand, and I can’t help but wonder if Amanda Mansfield has a sweet tooth.

“Let me introduce you to some people,” Amanda finally says to me. “The Tremells are here, and Curt runs a top-notch construction company. He gives good deals to locals.” She winks, and I follow her through the large, open living space to the kitchen. Floor-to-ceiling windows cover the entire back half of the home—more than ours—and the view is gorgeous. The white-capped waves splash along the rocks, and the night sky is glorious. How can our homes—not that far apart and sharing the same backdrop—feel like polar opposites?

“How are you liking Cold Harbor so far?”

“Well, I’ve barely been here twenty-four hours, but the coffee at Black Capped Coffee is scrumptious, and the proprietor was quite hospitable."

"Oh, Cady? Yes, she's a gem. Curt and Marcia are her parents. Curt purchased, remodeled and expanded the shop for her. A gift."

"That's a great gift."

Townies introduce themselves in droves, and thankfully, I'm good at putting names with faces. Part of my job. Was part of my job. I'm invited to bridge club, the garden club, a cooking class, several fall fests—the pumpkins galore make more sense to me now—and the Halloween Monster Mash that takes place downtown in some weeklong event the last week of October.

We enter the dining area. The table is loaded down with fancy desserts on trays and three-tiered holders. I nab a pecan tart, mostly to give my hands something to do as I meet and greet. It's exhausting.

"Chief. Have you met Gwen McDaniel? Steven's wife." Amanda points to me, and I glance up from my pastry to see an attractive man in his late fifties, if I had to guess. Hair as inky as the sky and eyes the same color. The man who says the bone is an animal's.

"This is Chief Ellersby. Grant. We just call him Chief."

The slender man next to him grins. "Pat Dunham. Attorney-at-law. If you ever need one."

"What kind of law do you practice?"

"Family law, mostly." His eye trails across the room. "Excuse me. Nice meeting you." He pats the man on the back. "See you tomorrow. I only have time for nine holes though." He exits, and I return my gaze to Grant Ellersby.

Amanda points to me. "As I was saying, have you met Gwen yet?"

"I haven't," he says in a deep voice. "Welcome to Cold Harbor, Mrs. McDaniel. We're glad to have you." His tone is light and friendly, his handshake warm but firm.

"Thank you. It's good to be here, Chief."

He likes that I've recognized him as being in charge of the town. "I can assure you our hobnobbing isn't always so fancy." He grins under a thick Billy Burke mustache, and I can tell he's not happy about being in a suit and tie.

"Good to know. I'm not a fancy person myself. Jeans are my go-to." I laugh and hold his gaze, softening him.

"If I'm not in my uniform, I'm in jeans myself. And not eating froufrou foods."

"Same, although these little tarts are delicious. I should pace myself." I pat my stomach. He chuckles, his eyes appraising me pleasantly.

"I think you can afford a few desserts, Mrs. McDaniel."

"Gwen. And thank you."

A voice calls Amanda away, leaving me here with the chief. "So, can I expect a forensic team anytime soon? Rumor has it a human bone was found by a hunter on my property."

His warm expression falters for a second. I've caught him off guard, but I can't believe that no one in this town is talking about the big find today. Or maybe they're just not talking to us newbies about it. A new doctor in town is a big deal. They might not want to scare us away. Little do they know it's pulling me, not pushing.

"Rumors." He shakes his head and rolls his eyes. "The bone was animal. Femur and too small to be a human's. I can assure you."

Small…could have been a child. Adolescent. Very petite woman. I'm not buying his story, but I keep my debate to myself. At least I know it's a femur—a leg bone.

He's doing a lot of assuring tonight. No fancy parties. No human parts.

"It's just Walt Dinner didn't seem to think so—"

"It's Wilt."

I've found when you are forgetful with little things, people tend to believe you might be forgetful about big things. Forgetfulness means one might not be too sharp. And I don't want anyone to know just how observant and discerning I can be. It worked for Andy Griffith and Colombo for good reasons.

"Wilt." I face-palm myself. "Of course. Names."

He cocks his head as if he's not buying my blunder. "Wilt was wrong. Stirring up talk to stir up talk. When there's nothing of importance to converse about, folks like to drum up things. But to put everyone—like yourself—at ease, I've sent it off to the medical examiner to determine for sure."

"And how long will that take?"

"I'll likely hear next week, maybe later."

"And if it's human, that's a week of wild animals potentially taking off with the other bones. You don't find that a problem?" I grab a red seedless grape and pop it in my mouth.

His jaw twitches. "I've been out there already with two of my men. Nothing to be found, Detective."

Now it's my turn to be surprised. He's done his homework on us. How in-depth? What does he know about us?

About me?

Chapter Eight

Since we left the Mansfields', Steven has been uptight. We've been married long enough I can sense the energy and tension without having to ask the problem. I know exactly what he's stewing over. I might have cornered not only Chief Ellersby about the bone on our property. I asked a few others, and by a few, I mean pretty much everyone I met after talking to Ellersby.

The Tremells. Pat Dunham the attorney. Wonder if he does divorces. The Arlingtons and Smiths. The Whites and even Reverend Paulson. They all seem to believe the chief. Why don't I? I have no reason not to. Am I looking for a cold case for something to do? To connect me to who I was and will never be again? Maybe Steven's right and I've made paranoia my best buddy. After all, it was teenage talk this morning. None of the adults seem to think it's anything more than what Ellersby says it is, except Cady.

"No one thought I was out of line asking about that bone, Steven. It is our property, and we're new to town. Normal people would be concerned, and they said that. So what is with the cold shoulder?" Steven turns his brights on. The road that leads to Darkwater Road, which is essentially our driveway, is pitch-black.

"It's not the questions or the concern. I agree that asking is normal. It's just…this kind of thing is a pattern with you, Gwen. And before you deny it, don't make me tick off all the things you obsess over, seeing what's not there." He keeps his gaze on the road, but his jaw is illuminated by the thin swath of light fighting to escape the somber clouds. Rain begins to splat on the windshield.

"Thought we weren't talking about *her* anymore." I was not obsessing, and I had every right to even if I was.

His grip on the wheel tightens even more. I've struck a nerve. Good. He's struck one too. When we married, we said we'd never throw our past transgressions up in new arguments, but he's done it every single time to justify the new fight, and that only serves to make me angrier. *Angrier* means I say things I often regret—or more truthfully, things Steven regrets—later.

Some days I wish I had my mom to talk to. She and Dad hardly ever fought. There were times tension flowed through the house, but I don't recall them dishing out nasty blows with fists full of words. Those punches hurt far more than a physical punch—not that Steven has ever laid a single hand on me.

Steven pulls next to Teresa's car. "I'm talking about the pattern. *She* just happens to be the latest, and not moving forward caused more problems upon old problems. Lay off this, Gwen. We need these people to like us. We need to fit in and make a life here. There's no going back." His voice is calm and rational, and it irritates me. He swings open his car door and exits with gentleness. Me? I slam the door and stomp my way up the saggy porch, just hoping it will break open and swallow me up.

I walk inside, defeated, my feet screaming. They've been pinched all night in these stupid heels. I slip them off and nearly groan in relief. Teresa is on the couch, a fire blazing—at least,

I think one is blazing. A blanket drapes her legs, and the baby is in her swing, peaceful.

"I didn't expect you two home for another hour," Teresa says to Steven.

"We're still tired from the move," he says. "And we're no spring chickens."

No, he was sick of me asking normal questions and expedited our night.

"How was the party? The Mansfield home is amazing. The reno Amanda did was perfection." Teresa smiles and folds the fleece blanket over the couch where she found it.

"It was lovely," I say and check on Tara, touching her velvety cheek and watching her chest rise and fall in a soothing rhythm. I'm always in fight-or-flight mode. "Thank you for staying tonight."

"No problem."

"What do we owe you?" I ask.

"Oh. Nothing. I can't take your money." She shifts uncomfortably and cracks a sheepish grin.

"I insist."

"It's a housewarming gift," Teresa counters and glances at Steven, who holds his wallet in hand.

"That's kind of you, but we did take your time up for the evening. Please—"

"No. Housewarming gift." She collects her purse and smiles tightly. "You have a nice night. Get some good rest."

"We will," I say as Steven walks her to the door, grabs an umbrella beside it and escorts her to her car. I pick up Tara. "I missed you tonight, baby girl." Her hair is downy, and she smells of lavender and powder. I carry her upstairs and into her nursery. It's the bare minimum for now. But her changing table is up, and the rocking chair is by the window that overlooks the water out back. I change her diaper and then slip her into sage footie pajamas with little yellow stars. The color is perfect against her creamy skin. Once she's swaddled, I put her in the bassinet in our room. I like having her close to me; it brings me comfort. About all the solace I can muster these days.

I'm already in bed, face washed and my own pajamas on, when he treks into the room, his suit coat hanging over his arm. "What's the plan for tomorrow?"

He's asking without asking if I want to find a church. I don't. I gave up church on the second miscarriage. I know the hard times are when a person of faith should trust the most in a good God. But three of my babies were ripped from my body; another I had to deliver stillborn. Didn't feel so good.

"I thought I'd unpack. Get the kitchen in working order and decide where I want to start renovating first. Everything needs an update. Maybe make pit beef."

"That sounds perfect," he says from the bathroom while brushing his teeth. He slides into bed next to me, and I smell a hint of cologne. "Homemade fries and gravy?"

"Yep. I'll hit the market in the morning."

He stares at me. "You still mad?"

I roll over to my side and face him. "I was never mad. I was curious, but I'm letting it go. It's girl gossip. You were mad."

"Concerned, not mad." He tucks a chin-length bang behind my ear. "Now I'm not either one."

His eyes tell me he wants to pick up where we failed to last night. He kisses me softly. "We'll make this work, Gwen." His kisses trail down my neck. He keeps saying that. To convince me or himself?

Either way, I hope he's right. It hinges on me, and that's what he's implying. I close my eyes and let him take me away a while where I don't have to think about the past or her or the emptiness I still feel or the simmering rage that fights to erupt. And when Steven is sound asleep, I tiptoe from the bed and downstairs for a hot cup of peppermint tea. I'm exhausted but can't sleep. This is becoming the norm.

I make the tea and inhale the peppermint scent. After adding a generous amount of honey, I sip and look out over the harbor to Dr. Rivera's house. A light glows in the second story window. Guess he's a night owl too, but then another light catches my eye.

A moving light. No. Several.

Flashlights flicker in the woods behind my house. My woods. Who would be out here this time of night—or at all? I'm barefoot and in thin Vera Wang pajamas, but I don't care. After leaving the tea on the counter, I rush up the stairs, hoping the creaking doesn't wake Steven. We aren't used to the new house's noises. But in the room, he's sound asleep.

I snatch Steven's hoodie that's still hanging over the back of the chair in the corner, then pull on wool socks and grab my tennis shoes from the closet, not waking him. Once I return downstairs, I quickly slide on my shoes and collect my cell phone to use as a light—if I need it.

My heart races as I slip out the back door, rushing toward the woods, but as I make it to the edge of the tree line, the lights disappear.

Gone or turned off due to my presence?

The night air is cold enough that plumes of my breath waft in front of me as I slink into the dense forest, the soft crunch of dead leaves and pine needles underfoot. I pause, listening.

A hoot owl makes itself known in the branches above.

Swollen clouds cover the oily sky, which is still heavy with rain, the air dank and drizzly. The evergreens, maples and birch trees blanket the stabs of moonlight, and now that I'm deep inside, the night shifts and bends around me, forcing goose bumps to rise along my arms and the hair at the back of my neck to prickle.

I'm definitely not alone out here, and in the rush, I've left my gun in the nightstand.

Cocking my head, I listen. Twigs and branches snap nearby,

and I follow the sound; my foot sinks into something thick and squishy. Not mud. A decaying animal? I'm not sure, but I inhale the rotting earth, musk and the unmistaken scent of death.

At least three separate lights were out here. No doubt I saw them. If it was a forensic team, a perimeter would have been set up along with tape to cordon off the crime scene. Whoever is out here doesn't want to be seen. Which implies that more than myself believe the femur found in these woods did not belong to an animal at all. They're out here to collect the rest of the remains...or hide what's left to find.

Chapter Nine

A baby's cries startle me awake. This has happened every night for the past week plus that we've been in this house.

I gasp and open my eyes, listening. I was having a nightmare, but now that I'm awake, I can't remember the details. I only know I was paralyzed with fear and still am. Sweat has pooled in the hollow of my throat and soaked my pajamas; my hair sticks to my cheeks. I'm not new to nightmares. They began when I became a homicide detective. Steven says it's my brain's way of filtering through the trauma I've seen, which makes sense.

I've been keeping busy in order to force my body into exhaustion with hopes for no cries or nightmares, no fitful sleep. I've bought supplies and hired Tad Michaud from Michaud's Hardware to tear out two walls and turn the living room, formal dining room and parlor into one large living space, which will make a great room for entertaining guests as it will also open up the dining area too. And maybe it won't feel like the walls are closing in on me if they aren't there anymore.

I didn't go with the Tremells. Nothing wrong with Curt,

but the rebel in me at Deena's suggestion turned it into a hard pass. It's my toxic trait.

Tad was eager to start, and after mocking up a few blueprints, he's now ready to come out today and begin. I haven't had time to pop in with Cady with all the hustle and bustle. We have texted a few times with no word on the bone, which I'm champing at the bit to hear about. But likely it's an animal's or the town would be buzzing. Though deep down I don't believe that. Chief said he'd been out himself and found nothing. So who was out there and why?

I'm going by the coffee shop today around ten. Maybe Cady will have heard something, anything. Steven made it clear I was not to call the chief and ask. We are flying under the radar here. Fitting in. Blending in.

I agreed, but it hasn't been easy. To keep my mind off it, I've worked from the early dawn hours to late into the night stripping old wallpaper, then filling cracks with joint compound. Steven helped me tape the entirety of the space we won't be knocking out, and I've rolled two walls in a pretty beige that brightens the house.

The wood trim is mahogany and original. Whoever built it likely was wealthy and had it imported. But it's too depressing. Yet I don't want to paint it white like the trend at the moment.

The faint wail of an infant crying startles me again and signals my protective instincts; she's in danger somewhere. It's not Tara, but I already knew that. Steven slumbers like a rock. How can he not hear that? How does he not feel the same sickening presence that hovers over the house mostly at night?

I grab my gun, check my phone—2:04 a.m.—and slip on my robe and house shoes. I expect a house this big and old to be drafty, but it's terribly cold. Too cold. I walk into the hall. The doors to the rooms that make the U shape are closed. I tiptoe to the stairs and realize the cries aren't coming from below.

Icy fingers of dread crawl slowly down my spine as I shift my gaze upward.

It's coming from the attic. The space Steven wants as his office. Attics are creepy to begin with, full of rodents and bugs. I haven't even been up there yet; it's not on my priority list.

A slim door is flanked by a bathroom and empty bedroom next to Tara's nursery. I inch toward it and glance back at the bedroom before twisting the smooth glass knob. The door squawks open, and I flinch and wait a beat. Then I bat cobwebs from in front of me and flip on the switch, but no light appears.

Spiders. Horrible creatures. You can swipe away their sticky webs and think you've cleared them out, only for them to make a mockery of you and spin more of their silky traps. I'll need to hire an exterminator to keep on top of them.

The cries have softened to almost nonexistent. Did I hear them at all? Were they phantom cries that often come to women who have miscarried babies? Am I having a mental breakdown? I don't know.

I swallow and listen, then proceed, keeping hold of the icy wooden panels to guide me upward into the dark.

I stand silently and hear no cries. Nothing, not even a hum. Just the wind howling through the trees and water pounding the rocks and boulders below.

I rub my left temple, a headache beginning. I know what I heard just now and what I saw when we entered the house that first day. The little girl. The fire blazing in the fireplace. But those things didn't actually exist. I did not see Lizzie Barkley or anyone else on those stairs.

Finally my eyes begin to adjust, and I'm convinced this was an office. A writing desk and chair reside in the corner facing the window, and a Tiffany lamp perches in the middle. Bookshelves line an entire wall. An old record player is covered in dust in the corner, but I don't see any records. I return to the

Tiffany lamp and switch it on. Lo and behold, it lights up the room in dim lighting. Then I notice another light pops on.

Across the harbor, in the top window—the attic, I presume—of Dr. Rivera's home. From here I make out a silhouette that could be him or someone else, but it hovers in the window as if the lamplight here has summoned it. Another wave of chills dots my arms and sends a shiver through my bones.

I switch off the lamp.

Dr. Rivera's light disappears.

Standing at the edge of the window, I peep out and see nothing. If the figure remains, he's hidden in the shadows now, the same shadows that swathe me. Coincidence? With trembling fingers, I reach out and pull the lamp switch again.

My mouth drops open as the light across the harbor mimics my actions and the figure reappears in the window, the curtains shifting. Is he—or someone—spying on me? If so, they aren't being discreet about it. I try again.

Off. On.

The light across the water goes off and on too.

Deena Richardson, the Welcome Wagon lady, mentioned he had Alzheimer's. The horrible disease changes a person. Could he be up in his attic, confused? Either way, there's no baby up here, and I didn't expect to find one. I'm not sure what I expected to find. I leave the room drenched in night, return down the staircase and quietly push open the attic door, bumping into something solid.

I gasp but realize it's only Steven standing at the door.

How long has he been there? Why didn't he call out to me? Or come up?

"What are you doing?" He takes in my disheveled appearance and then the gun. "Why do you have that?"

"I heard something." I don't tell him it was baby cries.

"In the attic?"

No, in the gardening shed out back. "Yes. Why else would I be up here?"

He sighs and grins, picking a cobweb strand from my hair. "Attics are full of mice and maybe even squirrels. You find anything?"

"No."

"Hmm... Could be anything, Gwen. Kids—not like they much care about private property, and Teresa mentioned in the walk-through that kids like to party in the woods near our house. Maybe it just sounded like it was in the attic but it was outside. Our property line and Acadia National Park blur a little."

Maybe. Probably not. I tell him about the light in the attic and the light in the house across the water. "What is that about?"

"You said yourself he has Alzheimer's. People suffering from that disease do all kinds of strange things. Gwen, you're making a mountain out of a molehill. Come back to bed and close that door. It's cold up there."

I close the door as he instructs. He's not wrong. A million different simple explanations could account for the game of lamp tag. But I'm not buying it. And it doesn't explain the baby cries. They were as real to me as anything.

"You haven't heard baby cries, have you?" I can't help it. I have to know even if it's against my better judgment to ask. Steven pauses in front of me before we reach the bedroom. He turns, and his eyes are filled with pity and a hint of frustration.

"Gwen, you know this is normal after miscarriages. Phantom baby cries waking you in the night or echoing during daylight hours. You've had them before." He wraps me in his arms and holds me against his chest. Once upon a time it would bring me comfort, but I feel nothing but trapped at the moment. What unsettles me most is not knowing if it's coming from Steven, from me...or from the house itself.

Steven left an hour ago in his new Mercedes—less ostentatious but not inconspicuous. He got it during the Labor Day sale and says he's enjoying it so far and he's enjoying work at the clinic.

I spent a good thirty minutes sitting on the dock staring at the house across the harbor, then planting new flowers in the barrels on the porch. Pinterest gave me a few ideas on porch decor. I was going to do this before Deena's suggestion.

We've made a dent in unpacking boxes, and I ordered three new rugs for the living room, dining room and entryway, all online. They should arrive within the week.

I also hired a cleaning agency to do a good scrub on the inside and outside windows, and they'll be by this weekend at some point. It's too much for me to do, and I'm taking bids on repainting the outside.

I'm in the living room packing Tara's diaper bag and doing a mental rundown of what I need to bring with me shopping and to visit Cady—lists, my purse…

A giggle sounds from the back of the house. Are kids outside like Steven mentioned? The laughter comes again.

A single string of a child's laughter.

Too young to be a teenager.

High-pitched. Giddy. Unnerving.

Hairs rise on my arms, and I swallow hard as a deep cold sweeps over and around me. I hesitate to turn and look, but I have to. I see nothing. Only hear the laughter and then a slap, slap, slap. I inch my way closer to the kitchen, my breath caught in my lungs and my nerves on high alert.

Slap.

Slap.

Slap.

A small figure is jumping rope in my kitchen. My eyes widen, and my mouth opens, but nothing comes out.

Slowly, she turns and looks right at me—no, through me—and that's when I scream. But she's already fading, vanishing into the kitchen island as if she were made of smoke. Still, the soft slap-slap of her jump rope echoes against the linoleum long after she's gone.

I back myself into a corner and bend at the knees to catch my breath. I have to get out of this house. Something isn't right here. I rush into the living room and hurry to put Tara in the car seat, my hands fumbling. I've seen gruesome sights as a detective. Blood. Gore. Guts. I've been to crime scenes after the most depraved human beings have had their sinister way with a victim. I've even sat across from diabolical psychopaths and listened to their detailed stories of what they did to women and children. It's abhorrent.

And yet nothing has scared me more than the nights in this house. It's like it breathes on its own, watches and calculates so that when I'm alone, it can rear up and seize my heart, mess with my mind. Sneak attacks that keep me in knots and won't let go. Even when it's quiet, its presence hovers like a thick rotting curtain as it waits for yet another opportune time to swallow me alive. I can't shake the feeling it has eyes within the walls that follow my movements.

"Come on, baby girl. Let's get out of here." Homes are not human. Which means something is very wrong with me. Is it the anxiety meds? Just because they aren't meant to cause hallucinations doesn't mean I can't be the one percent that is experiencing them, but why now? Has Steven changed the pills and not told me? He keeps them locked up and allots them when I need them.

I hoist the carrier in one hand, the diaper bag in the other, just as music drifts down the stairs—soft at first, then unmistakable. Not crisp, but warbling, ghostly—etched with the decay of time. The singer's voice is faded, fragile, like it's coming from the bottom of a well.

Beautiful dreamer...wake unto me...

The parlor ballad curls into the air, slow and mournful, drenched in longing, accompanied by the crackle of a needle skipping across scratched vinyl.

Starlight and dewdrops are waiting for thee...

The hairs on the back of my neck rise.

Chapter Ten

I rest the carrier and diaper bag by the front door. "I'll be right back, baby." If someone is up there—someone flesh and blood—I can put a bullet through them. But I'm terrified I'm not up against flesh and blood. Knots form afresh in my gut as a cold sweat breaks out over my body. My breath is ragged.

No one is in this house. A record player doesn't start on its own. There wasn't a single record in the attic that I saw the other day.

But somebody has to put the needle to the vinyl to make it play. With every step up the stairs, the temperature seems to plummet. Finally, I reach the landing, the music now louder. After grabbing my gun, I make it to the attic door and twist the glass knob. As the door opens, the music blares.

Beautiful dreamer, queen of my song, List while I woo thee with soft melody…

I blink rapidly and lick my chapped lips, moving up the dusty stairs that have my footprints in them. A few beats skip on the song, revealing a scratch on the record, and then it sticks.

Beautiful dreamer, awake unto me! Beautiful dreamer, awake unto me!

My legs might as well be lead as I climb the steep staircase.

Beautiful dreamer, awake unto me! Beautiful dreamer, awake unto me!

The refrain scrapes against my nerves like nails down a chalkboard—except it's my spine that's the board, raw and vibrating. My head is just shy of the railing's view, and I stay crouched, careful, counting out the next six stairs in silence. Each one creaks like it knows I'm coming. When I reach the attic, I lift my weapon—not to strike, but to guide my eyes, trembling slightly as I sweep it across the yawning A-frame.

No one's here.

I inspect the small alcove filled with junky furniture, old broken toys and lamps, and a doll with one lone black glass eye, staring right into me. I knock it from the dusty end table and it falls to the floor, where I don't have to see her plastic face or ruby-red smile.

My breath is still ragged, and I want to race to the record player to end the infernal skipping. I finish clearing the room, which doesn't take long. Then I lift the needle and place it back on its holder. The music dies. In its wake is a sinister silence that urges me to dart down the stairs and out of this house forever.

But I can't. I picked this house, for crying out loud.

I should tell Steven, but he's logical. He has an explanation for everything, and it will end with him believing I must be certifiable, which in turn will bring us back to seeing a therapist. I've been to therapists before. Sometimes I made it inside the building and even the waiting area. Other times, I tucked tail and ran before I entered the parking lot. Honestly, they can't help me, and just the thought of them freaks me out.

I scramble down the attic stairs, my foot slipping, and I grab onto the rail to hold me up so I don't tumble headlong to the floor. When I reach the bottom, I slam the door shut. That's when I see it, up close. It's painted brown to match the wood of the door but I'm not imagining it.

A brass sliding lock a foot above my head. A heavy-duty one too.

Why would a person need a lock on the attic door? And why so far above the doorknob?

Standing up on tiptoe, I slide the lock in place. I have no plans to go up there again. I'll have to come up with a few good reasons why Steven should choose another room in the house for his office.

The new question raised is, is someone or some*thing* in my house?

My cell phone rings, startling me. It's Cady.

"Hi, Cady, what's up?" I try to sound calm.

"Hey. I was wondering if you still planned to come by around ten like you texted, or if you'll have to cancel."

Why would I cancel? "No, I'm still coming by. Do we need to reschedule or something?"

"No. Not at all. I just wanted to check since it's ten now."

Ten now? No way. It was just 9:15, according to the wall clock I hung in the foyer yesterday. I glance at my phone. Cady's right. It's ten. I must have bumped the hands when I hung it. "I am so sorry. I clearly have lost track of time. I'm on my way now."

"No worries. Not like I'm going anywhere, but I need to clean out the espresso machine, and that's a chore. I didn't want to be elbows deep when you arrived." She doesn't sound perturbed, and that suits me. I feel terrible, but time just… I really have no idea what happened. "See you soon."

"Thanks." I end the call, then hurry downstairs, glancing at the clock that's an hour behind. I pinch the bridge of my nose. I know I set that right last night. I used my cell phone time to do it. Down to the second. Didn't I?

Growling, I turn around to collect Tara and my things.

But Tara is missing.

Chapter Eleven

My heart skitters into my throat, and I freeze. Panic overtakes me, but I shove it down and force myself into detective mode.

But it doesn't work.

This is my baby!

I fly through the living room, sitting room and dining area and into the kitchen, but she's nowhere in sight. My lungs constrict. I can't breathe. I pull out my cell phone to call Steven and the police—we *have* had an intruder.

And I see a flash of pink and gray.

A strangled sob escapes me as I bolt through the sunroom and the screened-in porch and down the stones to the rocky cliffs, where the car seat teeters on the edge of the dock. Tara is still buckled in, but if one strong gust hits before I make it to her, she'll be lost to the current, the drowning, merciless waters.

"Tara!" I call out, but the name breaks in my throat, more breath than voice. I sprint down the dock as a gale tears across the water, flinging foam into the air. Salt stings my tongue, my mouth hanging open in shock. The car seat wobbles—then tips. It's already falling. I dive, full-stretch, like a ballplayer sliding for home plate, fingers brushing plastic as it slips over the edge. I catch it. Just before the black water swallows it whole.

Her eyes snap open. I let out a choked wail and fumble with the buckle, hands shaking as I free her from the seat. Ocean spray clings to her cheeks like dew. "My sweet girl. My sweet, sweet girl." The sobs come hard, unstoppable—bursting from my chest like water breaking through a dam, wild and wrenching. I hold her against me, rocking, as I inhale her sweet powder-scented neck and then continue my cries for all my babies I've lost. All the babies that tipped into blackness, never to resurface again.

"I won't lose you, precious." I have never needed a child more. My throat burns from the guttural wails unleashed within me, followed by utter fear. I don't know what is in that house. A person? Something ethereal? I don't believe in hauntings and ghosts.

I do believe in things that go bump in the night. And they are usually made of flesh and blood. They lurk and prowl and blend in with night. They don't dissipate or fly out of reach. They can be caught. They can be killed.

Fear takes a back seat to fury.

When I find who did this to Tara—to me—they will rue the day.

I return her to the carrier and ease the fallen pacifier back into her mouth. No one is on my property, but across the harbor, the figure in the window from last night is now on the dock. How long have they been out there? Did they see who did this to Tara? Would he even remember—if it's the doctor?

As I return to the front yard, Tad is walking up. How long has he been here? "Hey, Mrs. McDaniel." He pauses and studies me. Clearly he can see I'm shaken. "You okay? Look like you've seen a ghost."

That's exactly what Teresa said when I arrived.

"Did you see anyone running through the woods or driving away?"

Tad scrunches his thick eyebrows that match his equally thick wavy hair and shakes his head. "No. But you might be getting teenagers on your land. It's early, but..." He shrugs and points to the house.

Great. The bones buzz is now sending teens to scope out the place. Maybe they were in the woods the other night, hunting for remains for a thrill, or could they be playing pranks on me as a new homeowner? Surely they wouldn't have messed with Tara. That is crossing a major line. But if it's teenagers or an adult...that doesn't explain me seeing things that aren't reality, at least not logically.

"Let yourself in. I have to go into town. And I have some Pinterest ideas. Your sister said I could give them to her. She in?"

"She is. You sure you're okay? You look a little frazzled. If it's the walls being knocked out, then don't worry. We know what we're doing."

I wish all that was ailing me was worrying about walls being knocked out. I'm half tempted to tell him to bulldoze the whole enchilada and start from scratch. A clean slate. No dirty history mucking up things. A truly fresh start. Washed clean. Unfortunately, that isn't going to happen.

Once I'm inside my Lexus SUV, I decide to call Steven. He needs to at least know about the baby. I debate calling the chief, but Steven's words echo in my ear. We don't need people prying, and the chief already knows I'm a detective. I can't have him looking into us more than skin-deep. Too much is on the line.

But one or more people have trespassed. Would he take me seriously anyway? I'm not sure. For now, I just want Steven to know.

"Cold Harbor Medical Clinic. This is Lynn speaking."

"Hi, Lynn. It's Dr. McDaniel's wife. Can I speak with him?" I keep my voice tempered as I do a turnaround and start down our drive.

"He's just leaving a patient's room. I'll get him. Hold, please."

By the time Steven makes it to the phone, I'm already halfway down our long stretch of drive heading for the main road.

"Gwen, what's going on?" Steven asks as concern rises in his voice.

"Someone broke into the house. I went to the attic to investigate, and when I returned downstairs, Tara was missing." My voice catches as I relive the fear again. "I found her teetering in her car seat on the dock."

Steven lets out a calming breath. "Did you see them go into the attic?"

"No, but music came from there. When I went up, an old record player was stuck on a repeated verse. An old parlor ballad or something. Stephen Foster."

"So you caught them when you went up?"

"No. No one was in the attic. That's bizarre, to say the least."

"It is bizarre, yes." Steven's tone is cautious, and I know him well enough to know he's working out what the logical explanation could be.

"When I returned downstairs, Tara was gone. Whoever played the record also carried her to the dock and left her there to fall into the water."

I only know of one person who would do something so vindictive and cruel, but she has no idea where we live, and we're a long way from Baltimore, almost eleven hours.

Steven remains quiet a few more moments. "Gwen, if you were downstairs by the front door and music began playing, then you would have seen whoever played the record come out of the attic—if you went straight up the stairs, right?"

"Well...yeah, but—"

"And how did they disappear from the attic to the living room without you seeing that or hearing them on the stairs?"

My cheeks flush hot. I can't explain it to him. I have no idea, but it did happen. "The music was loud. I wouldn't have heard them on the stairs. Maybe…maybe there's a secret passageway?" I'm stretching here, but it's not out of the realm of possibility, and I like this option more than the alternative. Irritation pricks my heart. Shouldn't the fact someone moved Tara to the dock be more important than the record player?

"I won't say it's not plausible, but it's unlikely." He waits a beat, and I can already tell I'm not going to like his next statement. "You were out on the dock with her when I left. Is it possible that in your deep thought, you left her there accidentally yourself? Before you say no, remember that I had to scream your name four times to get your attention off Dr. Rivera's house. You were distracted. You've been distracted for several months now. You've misplaced your reading glasses, the remote to the TV, your coffee cup, her diaper bag. And what about the laundry detergent I found in the fridge before we even moved?"

Denying I've been distracted would be stupid of me. I have misplaced items. I still don't remember putting laundry detergent in the fridge, but he said I did, so I guess I did. Could I have left my most prized possession on the dock? "Okay, I admit to misplacing items, but the baby? Steven, I would know if I left the baby on the dock or not."

Steven clears his throat. "That's not one hundred percent accurate. You left her in the car the day before we moved for ten minutes."

That was different. I'd been packing and had taken her with me to grab more boxes. It was a chaotic day.

"Were you rushing? Sometimes when you rush, you forget things. Important things."

"No…well…the clock was wrong." Whoever was in the house must have changed my clock setting. But why?

"The clock was wrong?" he asks slowly and heaves a frustrated breath. I hear a voice tell him his next patient is still waiting in Room B. "The one you set last night by your cell phone?"

"Yes." I don't offer my theory. He won't believe it. "Steven, I'm being serious. Someone broke into our house and played a record and then kidnapped Tara before putting her on the dock. I think I have to call the officers in on this."

"No!" His inhale is sharp. "No," he says more softly. "Gwen, we do not need anyone looking into us. Into you. Tell me you understand why. Surely you know why."

Unfortunately. We don't need to borrow trouble. I guess I'll have to protect our home and us myself. He's not giving me an ounce of help, including offering up himself.

"Yes," I snap. "I know why."

"You probably got the clock wrong and left the baby on the dock. As far as the record player, I don't know, but there has to be a more reasonable explanation than someone entering our house to play disturbing lullabies. Don't you think?"

Yes. He's right. None of it makes sense. And he doesn't even know about the little girl, the shadows, the way the house oozes with life, and not the evergreen kind. It's possible I did leave Tara out there myself. The fact she could have fallen into choppy waters isn't something I want to admit could have been my fault. I'm not a bad mother. I deserve children.

Don't I?

"I won't call the chief, Steven. I know we have everything to lose."

Me more than him.

Chapter Twelve

Black Capped Coffee is nearly empty when I step in just past 10:30 a.m. Two older men sit by the window, sipping black coffee and playing cards. Indie acoustic music drifts from the speakers, and the air is warm with the scent of roasted beans, vanilla, cinnamon and a hint of pumpkin spice.

Cady emerges from the back, wearing wide-legged jeans and a teal sweater that brings out the green flecks in her eyes. Her cheeks are pink from the heat of the kitchen, and she's smiling as she carries a tray piled high with freshly baked scones. "I was wondering if you were going to show," she says as I push the stroller to the counter. "Americano with honey?"

I nod. "And one of those cranberry orange scones."

"Just finished glazing them. My grandmother's recipe." She places the tray on the counter and makes my Americano with honey and heavy cream, then arranges a scone on parchment paper. After taking my money, she puts the fresh scones into the glass case and wipes her hands on the back of her jeans. "I'm going to make myself a coffee, and I'll be right over."

I wheel Tara to a quiet corner table, far enough from the

counter that it should stay peaceful even if the place gets busy. I take a bite of the scone—tart and sweet—and it's so good I could almost cry. If I made this a daily habit, I'd never shed the extra pounds, but right now, I don't care. I let myself savor it, just for this moment, trying to push away the fact that minutes ago I nearly lost Tara. That something—someone—was inside my home. Or maybe more than one someone.

My stomach twists at the thought, bile rising. But I take another bite anyway. I'm not wasting this scone. Cady arrives with her drink and a scone for herself.

"So. How are they?"

"If these were the way to take me out, I'd die happy." I sip my coffee as Cady peeks at the stroller. "She your first?"

No. "Yes."

"How old?"

"I've been blessed to have her for two months." I prefer to switch the subject from myself. I've never really liked too much attention, except for when I did, and that didn't go well.

"How about you? Kids?" We texted about the podcast and true crime but not a lot of personal banter.

"No children. I'd like one or two, but I haven't made a love connection. You'd think a coffee shop would be a great place to meet a man. I mean, he has to love coffee or it's a deal-breaker anyway, am I right?" She laughs, but distress and longing fill her blue eyes. She's young and has plenty of time for relationships, marriage and family.

"Strong women can intimidate some men. You own your business and are independent and smart."

"How do you know I'm smart?"

"I can tell these things." I grin. "You not only own this place but you use it for multipurpose events. You decorate well, which means you have a good eye for detail. You like cold cases, and your thoughts are keen. To name a few. And you always make my Americano perfectly."

Cady laughs, and it's soft and sweet like her. She's the only person in this town so far that doesn't set my teeth on edge. I'm comfortable around her and oddly feel maternal towards her. Something about her feels a little lost.

She reaches across the table and touches my forearm. "Speaking of mystery and cold cases, I talked to Chief early this morning when he came in for his cup of coffee. He hasn't heard from the medical examiner yet, but he says to pick a new crime to podcast because this one will go nowhere. I'm not so sure. I have to tell you something." Cady's eyes flash with wariness and grief.

"Okay, you can tell me anything."

"I don't talk about this. No one does, really, but I can't help wondering…if that femur bone is human…it might belong to someone I know."

My heart thumps hard against my chest. "Who?"

"My sister. She went missing when she was thirteen, walking home from school. Vanished. Over thirty years ago."

Was this what Teresa meant when she said no one went missing *recently*?

I frown, trying to do the math. Cady is way younger than her sister, and I met Marcia and Curt Tremell. They're mid-to-late sixties.

"I never knew her. She'd been missing four years before I came into the picture."

"Do you have any other details? Newspaper articles?" I sip my coffee as my brain moves at Mach speed.

Cady nods. "Not a lot because there just wasn't much to go on. When she went missing, it was local news. My parents don't talk about her. It's too hard on my mom. I get it. That's why she and Dad bought and renovated this place. To keep me close. Mom is overprotective to a fault, and I've always shown her grace—though I wanted to throttle her—because I can't imagine losing a child and never knowing what became of them."

My stomach roils at that. I can't even drink my coffee anymore.

"But what if..." Cady trails off, and I finish her question.

"What if your sister is buried in my woods?"

"I mean, it's possible, isn't it, if it's a human bone?"

"The national park brings lots of tourists, hikers, backpackers. Strangers to town. She could have been killed in the woods, taken from school to a more secluded area. Or it's someone else's remains. This Brad guy—he left in a hurry. He said he had to transfer to Japan. Maybe that's true, or maybe he had to run because of something he did."

Cady inhales and exhales, her eyes narrow. "I doubt it was him. But for the sake of brainstorming, if he was leaving because he murdered someone, then he would have had to dip a body in some kind of solvent to eat the flesh from the bones or it would have been, you know...gross. And I haven't heard or seen anything about a missing person since my sister vanished."

She makes a good point. "Maybe it wasn't a local girl. Maybe it was a hiker, backpacker, camper. And it's possible an animal ate the flesh from the bones and carried one away."

Cady's nose wrinkles, but she nods in agreement. "Well, we have possibilities."

"That we do. And I'm going to tell you something now." I hadn't brought up the woods in our texts. We've simply been getting to know each other, but now this changes everything.

She leans in.

"Last Saturday, I spotted multiple lights in the woods. At least three. Flashlights. Maybe it was teenagers. But I think those bones are human, and someone was searching for more, or covering what remains."

A low whistle escapes her. "That makes sense."

I want to do a little digging into Brad Langston. I don't think we'll land squarely on him. He's interesting, though, and not a stone to be left unturned. Why did he need a house that large? Teresa said he'd lived there eight years. That's enough time to let a body rot. And a reason to want the house—to own the land you buried a body on.

"Was Brad Langston a local?" I nibble on my scone, but I'm not all that hungry anymore.

"No. He lived in Oregon. Moved in around eight years ago. I know the Langston family, though, and I don't believe for one second any of them are involved in nefarious activities."

"People are good at hiding behind friendly masks, Cady."

"Not the Langstons."

"Good detectives cover all their bases."

She pinches a healthy portion of the scone and chews slowly. "What was being a detective like?"

Thinking of my career is bittersweet. "Rewarding." The pat answer. "Hard to handle at times. Especially cases involving child homicides. Those are always the most tragic." My most recent case comes to mind, as it always does. Teri Jo Tipton. Mother of three girls. Pregnant with her fourth. Drowned the ones not in utero in a kiddie pool in their backyard. How do women like her have babies like rabbits, and someone like me, who would be a loving, devoted mother, has miscarriage after miscarriage? I try not to think about her. About those lifeless little bodies all under the age of five, face down in the water. Of my partner, Kent Masters, holding me back, and my vow to make sure she received the punishment—the justice—she deserved.

But she didn't. Not exactly.

"I know. I hate reading about children being harmed or murdered. That's why I stick to making coffee and only talk about true crime involving adults. I'm not sure I could stomach seeing any of it." Cady finishes off her coffee.

My chest cracks into tiny splintered pieces. "No," I murmur. "No, it's not for the faint of heart, that's for sure." I pull out of the memory of Teri Jo Tipton, glance at Tara and then sigh. "Well, right now my main project is to work on the house. I hope it turns out as gorgeous as what you've done here. I love all the muted colors." So many variations of white, cream, brown and a hint of black.

"Thank you. I did a lot myself and picked out the color schemes to match the state bird."

"The black-capped chickadee? Like the name of your place."

"Yes. It's a beautiful little bird. My mom's a bird-watcher, so I've learned a few things."

I've seen the little birds. Pleasant and calming. Unlike the awful black birds that nest and circle my house as if they're drawn to the tenebrous energy there. I wish the place was inundated with the chickadees. I could use more beacons of peace and light.

I finish off my scone. "So your parents bought you this to keep you close? What would you do otherwise?"

"I don't know. I really like research. But I also like coffee. Kinda goes hand in hand. Need the caffeine to keep digging. I'm a part of several online groups around the country who try to solve cold cases. It's a whole web of average joes who have skills to help law enforcement. You can just about find anyone you want. Pretty neat."

"It is. Back in Baltimore, we used the same kind of citizens to aid us on cases at times."

"How did your parents feel about you going into law enforcement?" she asks.

"Oddly, okay. We're talking about parents who never let me out of their sight, even in the backyard. They kept a pretty tight rein, which led to some teenage rebellion. I bucked pretty hard at fifteen. Did some things I wasn't proud of." I regret it and wish I could go back and change things, but the past can't be changed. You can learn from it and grow, or you can sit in it and be bitter. I've done a little of both.

I don't like thinking of that year. Some secrets are best kept hidden. From Cady, who looks on with curiosity but isn't asking.

And Steven.

Some things I can't even share with him.

"So, tell me about this podcast you're planning to start." I need a subject change. The conversation is pressing too hard on old wounds, and I can feel the seams of my past beginning to give. If they split open, I'm not sure I'll be able to piece myself back together again. Not this time.

Cady's eyes brighten as she tells me about her love for unsolved crimes and the justice she would love to see brought to cases that end cold. "Like that bone?"

"If it's human, yes."

She's passionate as she shares several cases she's researched and her ideas on who might have been the culprit. She has a knack for this. "You should have been a detective."

Cady laughs. "My mother wouldn't have handled it like your parents. Too dangerous. She doesn't love the idea of the *Black Capped Coffee & Crime* podcast either."

"I love the name. It's perfect." I check my watch. We've been sitting here for an hour, and I still have to go by the hardware store. "Look, we may have a story here. But the only way to know is for me to go out there into the woods again myself. See what I see." I went out that night I saw flashlights, but I haven't had much time since dealing with house renovations. And then there's Steven hovering as if he's waiting for me to cross a line. I'm trying to abide by his wishes, which really aren't that unreasonable.

"Like freshly dug-up earth six feet long and deep." Cady gives me a knowing smile.

"Well, not six feet under or it never would have been uncovered. But a shallow grave, yes." I stand and remember the house across the harbor. "Hey, what do you know about Dr. Adrian Rivera?"

"He's great. He delivered most of the babies in this town."

Her mouth turns down. "But he has Alzheimer's now. Has to keep a live-in nurse."

"They the only two in the house?"

Cady nods. "As far as I know. His wife died. Why?"

I'm not quite ready to share the odd instances around the house, including the light mimics from Adrian's house. Cady needs to know me a little better first and trust I'm not a total whack job. "I'm not sure yet. I'll let you know what I find, if anything, in the woods." She sends me a scone to go and one for Steven. She's thoughtful that way.

"Hey," she says as I'm leaving. "We'll get to the bottom of this."

Oh, I'm in complete agreement.

I want to search those woods again just to be sure.

Chapter Thirteen

I lace up my boots in silence, the sound of the laces pulling tight far too loud in the stillness. The gun slides into my waistband with a cold finality. I take the shovel from the shed and head toward the woods. This wasn't how I pictured reconnecting with nature, but here we are.

At the tree line, I hesitate. The forest looms like it knows something I don't. But I'm going to find out. My skin prickles. My gut coils. It's the same feeling I get just before the panic hits, that breathless moment when the world feels like a thin veil and so wrong. I check my phone. The app with the video monitor shows Tara hasn't moved. I left the camera pointed at her. She's still right where I left her. It was haul her out here in a chest sling or leave her behind. I can see if anyone tries to steal her again.

And yet something within me hits an uncomfortable chord. No one took her. I might have left her, even if I don't want to believe it. I'm not fully convinced I didn't, and I'll take that to the grave.

No going back now, though. I enter the woods, the pine needles and leaves crunching underfoot. I'm not exactly sure where the flashlights were in relation to where I am now, but I'm not bad with directions and keep moving west, the trees pressing in on me. The rain that fell won't make this easy, but I've seen several burial sites in the woods in bad weather. I know what I'm looking for.

Checking my phone app again, I see that all is still well at home. My phone rings. Steven. Not answering isn't an option. I answer. "Hey."

"Hey. I had a minute and wanted to check in. How did the renovation shopping go and your coffee with a new friend? What was her name again?"

"Oh. Cady Tremell. It was great, and she made a cranberry orange scone to kill for. I brought one home for you. I haven't actually made it to the hardware store. I'm going after lunch instead." After I skulk through the woods looking for a burial site or a decomposed body.

"Good. You sound good." His voice is soft and filled with relief, or at least that's what it appears to be. Could be he's just checking in on me and making sure I'm minding my own business, keeping my head down and not attracting any more attention than necessary.

I force a smile into my voice. I'm not the only one who can mask emotion. "I am."

"No more freaking out over the record and the baby on the dock?" This tells me the truth. He's more concerned with me minding my business than if I'm actually good.

"No. Nothing to worry about, babe. You be home for dinner?"

"Yes, but I thought I'd run by the Blue Crab and pick up some cheddar biscuits and stuffed blue crabs. Reggie says they're wonderful."

Well, if Reggie Mansfield says it, then it must be. "Perfect." I didn't want to cook anyway. "Sounds yummy."

"See you around six thirty." Is that a warning to be home?

No. I'm paranoid. I've always been a little paranoid. I have trust issues thanks to past trauma, but I suppose I'm not alone. What human being who's lived any amount of time doesn't have personal trauma that translates into being leery of how every word or text comes through?

"See you then." After ending the call, I exhale a long sigh. I'm in this—whatever this is—alone. But I am in it. I resume my trek through the woods. The trees press in so tightly, they choke out the light. It's colder too without the sun to warm my skin. I spot something, and my pulse skips.

Fresh ground.

A grave has been unearthed.

Cold Harbor's police department looks exactly how you'd expect it to—unremarkable. A squat redbrick building, an American flag snapping in the breeze, and a two-engine fire station tacked onto the side like an afterthought. A few cruisers sit idle in the lot, but the place feels deserted. Maybe they shut down for lunch. Why not? In a town that prides itself on having no crime, what's the rush?

I ease the stroller forward and pull the sunshade down, shielding Tara from view. Though it's not her I worry about.

What if the bones buried out there belong to a child? The thought coils around my spine like ice. But child or not, the dead don't get a voice, not unless someone speaks for them. That's part of what drew me to law enforcement in the first place, giving voice to the silenced, the stolen, the forgotten.

The blood cries out from the ground—it always has. Since the beginning. Since Abel's blood screamed for justice in the dirt. Whoever was buried in my woods—disturbed, hidden, taken—they deserve the same. Justice. A name. A reckoning.

I have no choice but to come here and tell the chief what I've found. Someone was on my property—at least three someones. And they've dug up something.

I step into the station, and to my right, behind a pane of smudged glass, sits a middle-aged woman who looks like time moves a little slower for her. She's painting her nails a glossy cotton-candy pink that matches the too-bright lipstick stretched across her smile. The grin feels practiced, like it's been waiting all morning for someone to walk through the door. "Good afternoon. How can I help you?"

"I'd like to see the chief, please. About that bone Wilt Dinner found in the woods."

She waves me through. "Yeah, go on back. He's in his office eating a bite, but I'm sure he'll want to hear from you."

With zero security measures, she buzzes me back. Good thing I'm not here to detonate a bomb or shoot the place up. A woman with a baby never appears dangerous. But that's false security. I pause at the hall, unsure of which way to turn. She didn't exactly give me directions. An officer must notice my lost expression and asks if he can help me.

Grant Ellersby's door is open, and he's perched in a black leather chair behind his oversized desk eating a lobster po'boy and smearing steak fries in ketchup. My own stomach rumbles. He glances up and immediately motions me inside with one hand while wiping crumbs from his thick mustache with the other. I park Tara by the door, the back of the stroller facing us.

"Mrs. McDaniel. Good to see you. What can I do you for? I hope everything is okay. Most people don't pop in for good news, unfortunately." He points to the other untouched half of his sandwich. "You eaten? Want a bite?"

"Oh, no thank you, and I'm sorry to interrupt your lunch."

"Not at all. And anyway, Bev is going to let every woman through the door without hesitation. She's my own personal dating app. She's a receptionist, not a detective, for a reason." He points to my wedding ring and stroller, lifting his eyebrows and tossing me a knowing look.

I allow a laugh to escape my lips. He's charming on purpose.

As if I don't know all the tricks to lower a person's guard. "Well, I did hear you were the most eligible bachelor in Cold Harbor."

He laughs—a warm, easy sound—and his eyes are kind. But I know that won't last. Not once I deliver the news. I'll be the pebble in his shoe, the headache he didn't ask for. And honestly, I'm fine with that. What worries me more is how Steven will take it when I start shaking the branches he's worked so hard to keep still.

"I'm a bachelor. That's true. Eligible?" He toggles his head. "Debatable. How long you been married?"

Glancing at my ring, I say, "Eleven years. Not a newbie. Not exactly a veteran either."

He nods and holds up a fry. "You mind if I eat while we talk?"

"Not at all."

"Eleven years. I was married once. Four years in my early twenties. Came home one day and she'd cleaned me out and took our dog. I still miss her."

"Wife or the dog?"

He laughs for real this time. I can be witty too.

"The dog, of course."

"Of course. Dogs are loyal and stick around."

His jaw ticks. I've hit a nerve. I'm adept at reading body language, expressions. Was his wife unfaithful, or was he, or was it something else altogether? "That they are." He takes a bite of his sandwich and wipes his mouth, chewing and waiting on me to land the plane.

"Last Saturday I saw at least three lights in my woods—flashlights or cell phone lights. I went out to investigate, but they were gone. Today, I inspected the area in daylight. I suspect whoever was behind my house was out there in connection to the bone Wilt found. Digging up further remains or burying them. Not sure, but either way, they were covering up tracks, though not completely. Earth is still spongey." I hand over the phone with the photos queued up. "Unearthed ground."

He wipes his hands on his napkin, takes my phone and zooms in, studying each photo carefully. "You find any evidence? Bone fragments? Clothing, hair, nails or jewelry?"

"No."

"Can I tell you why you won't?" He hands me back my phone and opens a drawer. "Not that I owe you this, but here." He hands over a medical examiner's report.

I read the findings. Canine femur. Likely a coyote.

"Our town loves that they feel safe, that we keep them safe and people are good. I suppose many are, but I'm not living in Utopia here, Gwen. People can and will do bad things. Before starting a panic, I wanted to confirm the nature of the bone while keeping a confident calm. I can see why Wilt suspected a human—young or petite—but that belongs to an animal. Canine. No one needs to be concerned due to false information."

I hand him back the report. "He's adamant." And strange things have been happening in my house and on my property, lending to this theory of foul play. "What about the flashlights?"

"Gwen, you were on the force. People love stories. I have a number of theories. Could have been voyeurs wanting to believe Wilt and out for their own macabre search. Could be kids out there for fun—you do live in a house with some sketchy history, and kids love a good scary story, especially around this time of year. October is a big month in Cold Harbor. Could even be hikers from Acadia lost and off the beaten path—which has happened on several occasions."

He has logical explanations that can't be denied. Am I looking for something that isn't there because I feel lost, without identity, since leaving the force? If I left Tara on the dock, then it's possible I'm barking up the wrong tree, which will cause a lot of trouble in more than one way. "But the ground. Someone was digging. That's obvious."

Ellersby brushes aside his sandwich wrapper and rubs his clean-shaven chin. "Could've been an animal, following the scent of old bones—took what was left. Or maybe some kids or crazies poking around where Wilt said he found the bone. For all I know, one of the past owners buried a pet out there years ago, and something sniffed it up and dug it out."

He pauses, glancing at me. "I didn't see any human footprints. Did you? With all this rain, there should've been some sign—unless the digging happened before the storm hit and the rain washed it all away. Human or animal, either way, it doesn't match your theory about three people digging out there last week."

My stomach plummets as I realize I've been wrong. "No. I didn't actually see footprints around the unearthed mound of dirt. I did see prints nearby though." I show him those photos, but I know what he's about to say. I'd have said the same thing.

"Footprints prove your property was trespassed on, and I can't do much about that with only footprints. Look, I went out there myself after Wilt's dog found the bone and he brought it in. There's nothing out there. The fact there are no footprints around the mound of disturbed earth tells me they weren't at that specific location digging around."

My face flushes with lava temps, and my chest tightens. This is humiliating. "I'm very sorry." I return the report to him. "I don't know what else to say."

"I'd put cameras up or something. I need names, faces, if you want me to arrest someone for trespassing, but it's going to be common come October 1. Halloween's coming, and your house is haunted. Every teenager within twenty miles wants to come see all the ghosts in the windows." He grins, but a chill freezes my bones. He has no clue—or maybe he does.

He stands. "Aw—" he waves the spooky talk away "—it's just kids and urban legends. You have nothing to worry about."

If that were only true. I can't offer that weird things are happening in my house and not just around the windows. I need to look into my house and its apparent sketchy history. Cady's mom is the town historian and president of the historical society. If Cady doesn't have information, Marcia Tremell and the historical society will. Or, worst-case scenario, I go back to the White Pine Cone boutique and ask the girls working there. They'd spill.

"Again, I'm sorry for second-guessing and wasting your time."

Chief waves my apology off and shoves a fry in his mouth. "You got good instincts, Gwen. If my department had room, I'd talk to you about a job."

Is he messing with me? If he knows I'm a detective, then he has to know why I am not employed as one now, unless he's not done a thorough check on me. Just googling my name will show I was a cop in Baltimore. I've been a witness in court trials and mentioned in newspaper articles. If he's just googled me, that could work to my advantage. No point in asking how he knows. Don't need all that unearthed. I'd like to keep a few things buried myself.

"Thank you. Well, again, I'm sorry to have wasted your time."

"Not a waste. You been over to Michaud's yet? They'll treat you right. Give you a good deal on supplies for remodeling."

"Tad is knocking out some walls to open up the living space. He's there now. But thanks."

His eyebrows rise again. "You really are doing a full renovation. It's always been a beautiful home. Marcia's been trying to make it a landmark for ages. Doesn't quite meet the criteria."

I stand. "Well, I have no plans to do anything wild, so she can rest easy. Paint. New fixtures and lighting, gut the bathrooms and bring them up to date. That sort of thing."

He walks me down the hall making chitchat about weather

and the upcoming festival. When we enter the lobby, several officers are dragging out Halloween decor.

"Little early for all this, isn't?" I ask.

"Just getting it down to go through for now. Never too early for fright nights, though," Ellersby says.

Debatable, but if they never see the underbelly of humanity and real monsters, then this is their only hoorah for all things macabre. Me? I've seen the real deal.

As I push Tara down the chilly street, the clouds begin to gather again, growing ominous. Suddenly, a presence zips beside my ear, buzzing me, and I duck and shriek as a sickening thud hits the glass.

Black feathers whirl in the heavy air ripe with rain.

A massive black bird lies dead on the sidewalk, blood running from its beak. In the distance, a cacophony of crows wail as if singing a funeral dirge.

"You okay?" a man asks, startling me for the second time. My pulse is ticking double time, and I release a breath that's been trapped inside my lungs. "It's like it buzzed you on purpose."

Did it? I don't know much about crows except they hold grudges. They can identify and remember people, which I find unsettling. What kind of animal holds a grudge, besides humans? And what have I done to offend a crow other than move into the house?

I turn to the man, who is at least six feet. He's weathered like old leather, his thick gray hair brushed back from his head, and his wrinkled face looks like a lawn of gray scruff. "Wilt. Wilt Dinner," he says, offering his hand.

I offer him mine, but it's trembling.

"Gwen. Uh—Gwen McDaniel."

"Nice to meet you, Gwen McDaniel. Might want to hurry off soon. There'll be more to come. Crows gather for funerals. If they see you, they might blame you for this one's death.

They teach other crows how to harass those who have wronged them. Eerie birds, crows."

I glance up at the inky sky. Sure enough, the mourning wails grow louder as one after another black bird rests on the wires stringing from light pole to light pole.

"Is that true?"

"Mmm… Intelligent too. If you feed them, they'll bring you gifts."

I do not want gifts from a creepy crow. The number of birds has gone from ten or twelve to at least forty, and one flies to the sidewalk about ten feet from us.

"I know you found a bone on my property," I blurt, as each second passing gives me the willies.

"I did. I'm on my way to Ellersby's now."

"I already saw the report. It's canine."

Wilt laughs and tosses a curse. "Oh, I bet that's exactly what he said. You see the signature on that report?"

I look up from the dead bird into Wilt's icy blue eyes. "No. I didn't, actually."

"Get on home, Mrs. McDaniel. A storm's coming." He peers up at the sky, or maybe the birds, now so numerous it's frightening. Like part of the Halloween decorations flying in to take perch. Watch over the town, take names and number days.

I nod and hurry on down the cobblestones, then turn. "What kind of storm?"

"The kind that brings damage in its wake. No other kind."

Chapter Fourteen

Lily Ann

"Lily Ann." Daddy's home.

The door opened, and she heard Daddy's footsteps on the hardwood stairs that led to the basement. She spent most days in there. Daddy said it was for her safety. There are people who want to take her away from him, but he's the only one who can protect her from the bad guys.

Bad guys killed her real parents. That day when she went with him to the other side of the lake. They were shot and killed. But she's not sure if that's true. She didn't hear any gunshots. She knew what they sounded like too. Daddy and Grandpa used to take her shooting cans.

He entered the big room with brown carpet and painted a soft white. She had a little kitchen in the corner, a bathroom, and even a TV and video games. The corner opposite the stairs had bookshelves, and Daddy changed them out so she had a lot to read. He said she can visit anywhere in the whole world through books.

She just wanted to visit home. She wanted to see Gran and

her cousins and go to her school. Daddy homeschooled her. He was a good teacher. Always patient and rewarded her with her favorite ice cream. He was very nice to her. Didn't hurt her. But he also didn't let her call Gran or go outside.

Maybe today.

"Daddy," she said, but it was hard to call him that. He wasn't her real dad. "Can I go outside today? I bet it's a pretty day."

"It's cloudy, my little doll." He sat beside her on the couch and toyed with her braid. "Not today. How about we watch TV or play a game?" His smile told her he was in a good mood. Some days he wasn't in a good mood. Some days he frowned and wouldn't speak. He only watched her, and it made her tummy feel funny.

"What kind of game?" They had a lot of board games, but sometimes they played weird games where he asked her questions and she had to give him the answers he'd told her before. If she got them right, she was treated with ice cream. If she got them wrong, she had to write lines. She did not like writing lines, but he said the bad men would find her if she said the wrong answer.

"Let's play the question and answer game."

"We played that yesterday." She didn't like this game. It felt like lying.

His eyes stared right through her, and his cheek twitched. The impatient look. She'd learned to read his faces. Something inside her told her this was important.

"But okay, Daddy. If it makes you happy."

"I love that you want to make me happy, doll. All little girls should want to make their daddies happy. Now, what's your name?"

"Lily Ann."

He playfully tugged on her braid. "Good. How old are you?"

"Ten."

"Good. Good girl. Daddy is so proud of you." He leaned

down with his elbows on his knees and his chin rested in his hands. They were face to face, and he smelled of mint and coffee. "Where do you go to school?"

"Daddy teaches me. He's the best teacher, and he knows all things." That was the answer he wanted her to say. Yesterday, she had told him where she used to go to school, and that was the wrong answer. But she would get them all right today. And maybe he would let her go outside and play or call Gran.

"Yes." He closed his eyes, and a dreamy smile spread across his prickly face. Sometimes this late in the day, his chin whiskers were scratchy. "Where do you get your food?"

"From Daddy. Daddy takes care of me and makes sure I have food and clothes and fun things. No one else will give me these."

He tweaked her nose. "Excellent, doll. Who do you love more than anyone in the whole world?" He ran his thumb across her cheek.

Her eyes burned, and she wanted to cry, because she loved Mom and Dad most in the whole world. But they died. She loved Gran next. She bet she was sad without Grandpa or Dad. But she couldn't say Gran. "I love my daddy. I would do anything for my daddy. Anything in the whole world that would make him happy."

"Well done, doll. Well done. Strawberry ice cream with whipped cream?"

"Yes, Daddy." Her stomach didn't want ice cream. It was telling her bad things might happen. As bad as her parents dying. She'd eat it, though, because it would make Daddy happy. And that was her job. That's what Daddy was trying to help her understand. He was her world now, and she had to make him happy. Even if she didn't want to.

He kissed her head and went upstairs. When he returned, he had two bowls of ice cream. His was bigger. He handed hers to her and sat next to her. "You know, Lily Ann, when you get bigger, thirteen—when you become a woman—you won't be so sad anymore. We'll be happy. And I'll take even better care of you then. In a new way."

His words said one thing. Her stomach said he was lying, and she wouldn't be happy or taken care of. But she ate her ice cream and prayed God would see her and help her back to Gran.

Chapter Fifteen

Friday marks four weeks since we arrived Labor Day weekend and has brought a brief sliver of reprieve from the gloomy gray skies and scattered storms that ushered in October. A ray of light has peeped through the grayness, and I've been working in the flower beds, pulling weeds before storms roll in again.

The crows have lurked in the branches all day. I can't help but wonder if they're the same ones that watched one of theirs fly into the store window and if they've followed me home with some trumped up vendetta. As if it's my fault one of their own smacked into glass and killed itself.

Suicidal crows. Is that a thing?

I push away my intrusive thoughts and check my watch. It's almost five, and the sun is already making its way to bed; thunder rumbles in the distance, signaling more storms tonight.

Nothing but storms since we arrived.

Steven has been working late—an old habit I thought he'd break once we settled in. Doesn't appear to be the case. He's catching up on patient records, paperwork, unpacking. How much catching up does it take in a town the size of a cracker box? Okay, maybe a microwave oven.

I need to hurry and finish my last chore. I frown at the flowers I planted in the barrels—twice, to be exact. I can't seem to make them live. Or maybe they have no will to live, no desire to thrive in this house. The inside is coming along. Tad and his crew work fast, and now the main floor feels open and spacious. The paint has done just what I hoped—made everything light and airy—but it feels superficial. I still can't shake the eeriness of the home. I haven't had much time to dig into its history like I wanted to, thanks to the renovation. Steven keeps nudging me to start the attic, and I keep telling him our living space comes first. But the truth is, I don't want to go back up there after what happened last time. I haven't acclimated to the creaks and pops of the house. They're never the same.

Every night it's baby cries and unsettling noises. Every day it's like a blanket hovering over me, moving with me. Like the house's cold breath ribboning around my neck like a noose. And when it's not choking me, it's Steven or the bloated murder of crows surrounding my house like an enemy plotting to invade, pecking at windows as if hunting for weakened areas to enter.

I shove my spade into the potting soil and spread it around the new batch of flowers. Mums. Purple. Yellow. Rust. Pretty. I'm not a fan of Halloween. But I'm not sure if it's an evil holiday that curses kids behind closed doors and invites wickedness into the world or not. Seems to me, wicked already rules. I don't see how kids in cute costumes are harming anything. But to each their own.

For me, I've seen real evil. Faced monsters that go bump in the night. Professionally and personally. I don't want to celebrate darkness even if I'm not opposed to being scared for fun or eating delicious candy. It's just some days you get the good kind and other days you get razor blades along your tongue. I suppose that's true of life, metaphorically—and literally.

So I'm not going all out like the rest of the town.

I drink a swallow of water and glance at Tara sitting in a little bouncy chair beside me. "You like the flowers, baby girl? I know you do. Let's see if we can make this batch live. Mommy doesn't exactly have a green thumb." But the flowers were wilting when we arrived, so I guess Brad Langston wasn't exactly gardener material either. I strip off my gloves and carry Tara inside, where I hold her a few moments and then place her in the swing to wash my hands and make a glass of iced tea.

My phone dings—a reminder that I still need to shop for a dining room table. Now that we've opened up the space, Steven wants one big enough to seat twelve. He's all about dinner parties. Me? Not so much. I've never been drawn to polite small talk, especially when it veers into the medical world—something I know very little about unless it involves a suspect, a victim, or drugs. Not exactly sparkling conversation material.

I've had my nose to the grindstone for weeks, trying to stay focused since Steven's been nudging this dinner party idea along. He helps out some on Saturdays and Sunday afternoons.

These days, unless I'm talking to Tara—who can't talk back—I'm mostly talking to myself or to Cady. She did mention the historical society keeps records on the house, but she's been tied up at the coffee shop. I've done my own search when Steven isn't around, usually at night.

I've discovered that Thomas Barkley did shoot his wife in the kitchen, then his child—in the attic—on Halloween night in 1974, and that the fire in 1980 was set by the son of the Batterson family. He claimed his parents abused him for years, and he couldn't take it anymore. One night in December, he doused the floor around their bed on the main floor and lit them up.

They tried DJ Batterson as an adult and found him guilty. Two years after his sentencing, he was murdered in a gang-related stabbing in prison.

But these things that happened can't explain the weird phenomena I'm experiencing.

Wilt didn't seem to believe that the femur was an animal's,

but I'm sure Ellersby set him straight that day he visited the precinct, just like he'd done with me. And no one seems to be enthralled by it anymore. Except me. Even Cady seems to believe it's an animal and hasn't mentioned her sister who vanished, so I steer clear too.

Now we mostly chat about TV and coffee and all the usual true crime things. Maybe I'll invite her to the next dinner party. She can keep me company. Watch me play the role of the doting wife. Which I am—or I have been.

In the early years.

Steven and I met at the hospital after he'd treated an eight-year-old boy several times for broken bones, black eyes, lacerations. I was only called in after the final blow and ended up at the hospital.

"Hello, I'm Detective St. James with the Baltimore PD. I have the privilege of investigating Trevor Denny's homicide."

Steven said my eyes caught his attention first and then my sarcasm.

Turns out, Trevor Denny's father really did beat him to death at the dinner table—for not finishing his plate, which, heartbreakingly, was mostly made up of his own vomit after being forced to eat green beans he couldn't stand. That truth didn't come to light until later, after I broke the mother down in the interrogation room.

I liked Steven though. He'd tried to be proactive by calling social services on each occasion. But like most Child Protective Services, they were understaffed and Trevor fell through the cracks, until one crack robbed him of his life.

A week after my interview with Steven, he dropped by the PD to ask me, in person, to dinner. Steven had a brilliant mind and was a calming presence, and his charm and humor didn't hurt.

Steven was a good man. Now I think he's just a broken one.

Bitterness is an ugly weed with a root that wraps like choking vines, leaving no breathing room for grace and mercy to bloom. I see this in him, because I know it's in me too, and it's recognizable. A nasty bitter weed for every person who let me down, including myself. Myself maybe the most.

"Gwen! I'm home."

I rise from the kitchen chair as Steven enters the front door into our living room that is now freshly painted Bleeker Beige. I'm considering painting the earth-toned brick and hearth around the fireplace, but the flecks of brown look nice with the paint and give the room a cozy and peaceful feeling, and I could use some peace in my life.

"I'm in the kitchen. You're home early." I've been in here trying to figure out why I don't want to work in this room. It's not the little black-capped chickadees fluttering around the windowsills. They're adorable birds, and something about them soothes the itch in my chest. Maybe I should take up bird-watching. Become the bird lady.

"It's closing time. I'm not early." He breezes into the kitchen, lays his briefcase on the table and kisses my cheek. He's cheery. He used to look like that after diagnosing something challenging in a patient.

He studies the kitchen. He thinks I should paint it the same color as the living room. Once we change out the flooring and countertops, it'll be sunshiny. All that gorgeous light from the floor-to-ceiling windows.

I agree. I need the light. I've seen too much darkness. Too much darkness has seen me. Lives in me still.

Steven runs his thumb under one of my eyes, caressing the bruised half-moon. "You're not sleeping well."

Well, no. Of course I'm not. I haven't told him, but I'm still hearing baby cries at night and sometimes giggles as well as other noises that don't come naturally from an old house. Not from the attic, but like an echo I can't pinpoint. I lie awake with my gun in hand, skin cold and clammy, shivering in fear. Steven snores lightly each night, never waking.

"A lot on my mind with the reno."

Steven studies me, searching for the lies hiding in my eyes, and finally looks away and heads to the fridge to dig out leftovers. "You eaten?" he asks.

"I'm good, thanks." I haven't had an appetite, and a calorie deficit is my friend these days. "We'll be ready for the dinner party by early November. It can be a Thanksgiving-ish shindig. Show our gratefulness to the town and people." I'm so blowing smoke, and he'll know, but neither of us will care because at the end of the day, it's a clever idea.

"Oh, good. That will give us more time to redo the attic so they can see my new office."

A man's office is equivalent to a nine-year-old showing off his new bike he got for his birthday. He's going to indirectly force me up to that attic. I can't seem to change his mind. Which is odd because I usually have better ideas about spaces and lighting. Not so with the attic. Steven wants me up there ASAP. I inwardly cringe and try one more time…

"You know that room beside the bath upstairs has great lighting and gives a view of the harbor too. You sure you don't want to use that one?" *Please go with me, Steven.*

"The attic has an aerial view the second-floor bedroom doesn't. And it's quieter. I think I can take a few stairs to use the bathroom, Gwen. I'm set on it. Great idea."

He basically laid out his parameters and decided it was the only room that would work. It's like he'd already made up his mind after that solo walk-through—then dressed it up as if it had been my idea all along.

"But don't overdo it, Gwen. You need your rest."

"You can't have it both ways, Steven. Either I throw myself into a project or I don't. Nothing gets done when I'm resting." I don't mean to clip the words, but he's treating me as if

I'm fragile. And it reminds me so much that I am. An earthen vessel full of fissures so minute but enough that I'm slowly and almost invisibly leaking. And I hate this about myself. At least when I carried a shield, I felt strong and valuable and impenetrable. Nothing was leaking out, and nothing with shadowy tendrils could seep in. Gwen McDaniel caught bad guys. She made the world a safer place.

Now I'm just making a place pretty to pass time to indulge my husband. Real award-winning stuff.

He holds up his hands in surrender. "Put the gun down, Gwen. I'm just saying don't overdo it. It all looks great, and you're doing a fantastic job." He grabs a glass from the counter and then looks at me. "Chief came in today for a checkup. Mentioned you'd visited him about the woods a few weeks ago. Said you'd been out there investigating. Why didn't you mention it?"

"Because he confirmed the bone wasn't human. And I did find moved earth. He needed to see that, Steven."

He eyes me in the way an attorney would. "You didn't tell him anything else, did you?" He puts the leftovers in the microwave. "We talked about this."

No, he *told* me. But he was right. "Of course not. Once he showed me the medical report, I let it go. I'm putting all my efforts into the house, and you know this."

He sighs and leans on the island. I've never been a fan of islands. I'll likely rip this one out and send the new home trend people into cardiac arrest.

"You can see I'm over it," I point out. "Probably kids in the woods. You said it's prime for fooling around and having a few drinks, which doesn't seem to count as a crime." I shrug, and the microwave beeps. Steven removes his plate and sets it on the table.

"When are you going to start on the kitchen?" He cuts into his seafood lasagna.

"I'll have it done by the time you want to host a dinner party. I have a few other things to do." I don't want to stand in here and be interrogated.

After I put Tara to bed, lightning bursts into the bedroom, and thunder peals. I'm not going to sleep, and even if I wanted to, I'm angry. At Steven and the world and at myself for being afraid of shadows.

I blow out of the room, and Steven meets me at the landing. "What are you doing?" he asks as I carry my tool kit from the bedroom to the attic door.

I have to put my fears to bed before I can put myself there. "I'm working on your office. Isn't that what you want?"

He cocks his head. "Yes, if you want to. No, if you're mad about it. I can help you tomorrow since it's Saturday. Come to bed."

So I can prove how fragile I am. No. "Not tired. I'll be down later." I burst through the door and tromp halfway up the stairs before my arms prickle and the atmosphere turns icy. Well, I can't back out now. I've acted like a toddler throwing a tantrum for no reason. Might as well go all in now. I'll take fear by the horns and wrangle it to its death.

I don my N95 mask and knee pads and hold a flat pry bar. Beside me are pliers, a utility knife and a floor scraper. This nasty old carpet is coming up tonight. I'll pull it up and move furniture as I go.

The rain beats against the roof and lightning casts ghoulish shadows along the walls, but I drop and get to work, taking out my frustration and stubbornness on this nasty, dust-filled, filthy carpet.

I start at the far corner, removing the carpet from the tack strips. I'll have to cut away large pieces of carpet and roll them up to cart them to the rented dumpster too. As I pull and cut, I don't lose steam. I'm in here. I'm doing this, though my nerves hum and any moment I expect the record player to begin and lights from across the harbor to switch on as if to let me know I'm being watched by more than birds.

All I have is the lamplight.

Sweat breaks out along my back and neck and my muscles scream in agony as I rip and pull. Rip and pull. Rip and pull. Wind howls and smashes against the window, rattling it, but it's still freezing in here, like a cold breath along my neck. Instinct tells me to run. Stubbornness demands I stay.

This is my house. I'm not going to fear it. Whatever "it" is.

I stand and rub my back and see the light tick on in the attic across the harbor. I walk to the window and stare out, see the silhouette in between pulled curtains. My light stays on, and so does his. I don't have time to play this chilling game tonight, and I get back to the work at hand.

I finally pull enough to see that there is no padding underneath the carpet. I pause and run the back of my gloved hand over my brow, pushing away strands of hair stuck to my face. Who wouldn't put down padding? That's what makes carpet soft and comfortable.

The hardwood underneath is filthy and looks scratched, but until I can clear more, I can't be sure if it's salvageable. I grab an old white sheet that had covered one of the tables in the corner and use it to sweep the dust and dirt away.

Yep. Scratches.

Wait… Is that…?

I can't see well with the poor lighting.

Thunder breaks the silence like a trigger pulled too fast, the windows trembling in its wake. I flinch, heart slamming against my ribs until it hurts. For a second, I forget how to breathe. My fingers, trembling, hover just above the floor, where more scratches peek through the dust. They're not random. Not claw marks. No.

They're letters.

I lean in, a cold knot tightening in my stomach. The wood

grain seems to shift beneath my hand, as if it's breathing. Another roll of thunder growls through the sky, longer this time, a warning I don't understand. Like Wilt's words… *"A storm's coming."*

A storm is here.

And there it is—etched deep, frantic, carved by a hand that didn't seem to be able to stop—I AM NOT CRAZY.

Again.

I AM NOT CRAZY.

The same sentence, gouged into the floorboards again and again until the words bleed into each other. My hands shake harder. The air feels too tight, too still. I press my palm to the wood, needing to feel it—prove it's real.

Lightning flashes.

For just a second, the room explodes with light. And in that flicker, I see something—someone—crouched in the corner.

But when I look, the corner is empty.

Only those words remain, screaming silently from the floor.

I AM NOT CRAZY.

Part II

The Unraveling

"Three may keep a secret, if two of them are dead."

—Benjamin Franklin

Chapter Sixteen

The thunder hits harder this time, shaking the windows like a warning. A chill slips beneath my skin and stays there. I stumble back from the floor, gasping, my eyes locked on the words carved into the wood.

I AM NOT CRAZY.

I AM NOT CRAZY.

I don't remember the scream. Just the burn in my throat, the pressure in my chest, and the air that won't come fast enough. This can't be real. Who would write this? When?

Am I seeing this like I saw the flashes, the blurs and the young child?

The wind howls outside, and rain slashes against the windows in sheets. The room flickers with lightning—white, then gone—like time itself is glitching around me.

"Gwen?" Steven calls from downstairs, his voice saturated with concern. "Gwen, are you okay?"

I can't answer. I try, but the words won't come. My legs are frozen. The walls close in on me. Another flash of lightning, another glimpse of those words—

I AM NOT CRAZY.

Then Steven's rushing up the stairs, his footsteps heavy, but they're no match for the weight in my chest. He reaches the top of the stairs, breathless, and looks at me first. Then his gaze drops to the floor.

His brow furrows, and his eyes narrow as he takes in the words. He steps closer, crouching down, his face unreadable.

"What is this?" he mutters, more to himself than to me.

I back away from the floor, trembling, and point at the scratches, almost accusing. "So you see it too. What is going on?"

He takes his time, running his hand over the grooves, feeling the depth, examining the markings. "Huh," he says, standing up. "It's—well, it's scratches in the floor. I can't explain it, but maybe it was some kind of prank."

I blink, my heart pounding. "What? A prank? You think this is some prank? Who plays these kinds of pranks?"

Steven looks at me with a calm, almost detached expression. "I don't know. It could be more than that, but before you go jumping to over-the-top conclusions, it doesn't mean anything sinister per se happened here."

My blood begins to boil. He's not even shaken. No fear. No anything. Just this cold, calm rationality. He's utterly clueless.

"You're not getting it!" I snap, my voice rising in frustration. "There's something wrong here! Don't you see it? This isn't the first odd thing I've experienced, Steven. I'm…" If I tell him I've been seeing things, it won't go well.

He sighs, his voice soothing but condescending. "Gwen, take a breath. You're just—stressed. It's the storm. We'll figure it out. Okay?"

A knot of anger tightens in my chest. I want to scream, but instead, I grit my teeth and swallow it down.

Did Gina Barkley write this? She might not have been chased here—that was a rumor. But she did die here. Maybe she spent a lot of time here. The scratching is fairly deep and probably took time. I start ripping up more of the carpet, not caring about gloves.

"Gwen, what are you doing? Come to bed. We'll talk about it in the morning when we've had more time to think and are clearheaded."

He reaches for me, and I shove him away. "No. No, I have to know. Help me with this," I demand, but he shakes his head.

"I'm not going to be a part of this manic behavior, and you need to come to bed." Before I can protest, he holds up his hands. "But if you want to rip up carpet all night, go ahead. It won't solve anything, prove anything or help with anything."

I stand with my mouth open. "Something bad happened here."

His hangdog expression does nothing for me. "Gwen, we already know something bad happened here. The Barkley family. The family who was burned alive in their sleep. But we have no clue if one of them did this or not."

"Maybe there's something under the rest of the carpet that will tell us."

He pinches the bridge of his nose. "Gwen, this is not a case for you to solve. You don't solve cases anymore. And you know why. Don't let this be that, honey. Please. I'm begging you. Finish in the morning and we'll figure it out, rationally."

"No." I can't. I just can't seem to let myself calm down or be rational. I can't seem to make myself do what he's asking. "Something is wrong with this house."

He kicks at a piece of loose carpet. "You talk like the house is a living thing."

Because I'm wondering exactly that. "I'm not going to bed."

"Well, I am." He turns and slowly goes back downstairs, leaving me alone with the ghosts of this house, their stories embedded in the walls—and the floors—clearly demanding to be told. To be known.

Maybe to be solved.

Who lived in this house? Who resides here still?

I begin pulling, cutting and rolling. My body is on fire, but I press on until I've pulled all the carpet up.

The entire floor is covered with the same words. I AM NOT CRAZY.

Someone spent a lot of time up here, carving. I can't tell what they used, and it doesn't matter. What does matter is that it's here. Who—or what—would drive a person to do this? Was it a reminder that they weren't actually crazy? Did someone make them believe they were? Tell them they were?

I understand the need to carve the truth into something that can't be erased. Something that is absolute. An anchor to hold me to reality. Words to repeat and assure and remind.

I don't want to write I AM NOT CRAZY.

I want to write the opposite.

Chapter Seventeen

Steven is at work when he's not supposed to be working Saturdays but helping me. Says it shows he's willing to go the extra mile. I think he's avoiding the carvings in the attic.

I spent most of last night sitting in the attic pondering who wrote those words. And all today, it's plagued me. I could barely choke down breakfast or lunch.

Someone felt crazy or was led to believe they were.

The Barkley family was dysfunctional, and Thomas Barkley murdered his wife, Gina, and daughter, Lizzie, on Halloween. DJ Batterson set his parents on fire, though there wasn't much evidence they had actually abused him.

Cady's sister went missing over thirty years ago.

A femur bone was found on my property. A few nights later, people with flashlights snooped in my woods, where I found an unearthed grave—or what appeared to be. While I saw no footprints, that doesn't mean someone didn't cover those tracks. But I'll never know since so much rain has fallen since then.

I'm seeing things. Hearing things.

Are these events connected?

I check on Tara in the swing. "You're my only constant, little bit," I whisper as a car pulls into the drive.

It's nearly two o'clock, and I recognize Teresa's car. I texted her first thing this morning about the house but didn't hear back until a couple of hours ago. She has had back-to-back showings, Saturday being her busiest workday, but said she would stop in around two or two thirty.

She wears a cheery smile as she climbs the porch steps, and I open the door before she knocks.

"Come in. I have to show you something."

Her expression is a mixture of confusion and curiosity, and her perfume instantly saturates the atmosphere. It's so strong I wonder if she was using it to cover the stench of some sin she's committed.

"I hope there's nothing seriously wrong. It's out of my hands now anyway since you signed the papers." She's firm on this as if I don't know that I'm officially saddled to this horrible place.

"I'm not holding you liable, Teresa. Upstairs. In the attic." I start up the stairs. "I found something."

"Yes, you said that in your text." She follows, but she's slowed her step as if the second floor expects her to. As if she too can feel what I can in this house. A sinister energy. But if she does, her face doesn't show it.

The front door shuts, and Steven's footsteps clomp on the stairs until he meets us on the second floor. Guess he's not working all day today after all.

"Teresa, hello. I guess Gwen told you about the floor in the attic?"

"No. I'm about to see it." She frowns and holds his eye as if they're having a private conversation, and I wonder how two people who barely know each other can do that. That's reserved for longtime friendships, lovers, sisters and brothers. But they absolutely are speaking without words, and on his silent acknowledgment, she faces me again and nods for me to take her to the attic.

"I pulled up the carpet last night and found this." I point to the repeated carvings, which can now be clearly seen after I ran a broom over the floor to clear the dust and dirt.

I AM NOT CRAZY.

I AM NOT CRAZY.

I AM NOT CRAZY.

Teresa's eyes widen. It's there. She sees it, and it's as shocking to her as it is to me. I'm not blowing things out of proportion or believing it's a prank. Pranks bring laughter. This is not that. Maybe Teresa will back me up and prove to Steven and myself that my feelings are valid.

"I have no words."

I have enough for us both. "I need some information. You said Brad Langston lived here and moved abruptly?"

She frowns. "I wouldn't say abruptly. His job transferred him to Tokyo, and he spent most of his time traveling rather than living here. I seriously doubt he did this and carpeted over before he moved. The carpet wasn't new." She tosses Steven a wary look, and he returns it with a sympathetic close-lipped smile that I do not like.

She's right about the carpet not being new. It was an ugly avocado green, but not worn. After being installed—without the padding, which tips me off that it wasn't professionally done—no one seemed to walk on it much. Which makes sense. Most attics were used for storage space until the late '90s and early 2000s when it became trendy to turn them into bonus rooms thanks to HGTV.

"Who lived here before—in the '70s or even before that—besides the Barkleys and Battersons? Do you know?" The house was built in 1896. An expansion was made in the early '80s according to the house information on Zillow. But specifics were not in the property details. Names were not given.

Teresa clears her throat and rubs her fingers along the strap of her cross-body purse. "Before? I'm not sure. Before Brad, his great-grandparents lived here. Maybe fifteen or twenty years. This house is only my second sale, remember?"

"I do." I try not to look at Steven, but I can feel his gaze drilling into me. "No rumors of someone mentally ill living in the house?" This town is full of stories and rumors, so surely something has been passed down.

"Well, yeah, but nothing concrete," she says warily, and she backs up as if I'm the crazy one here. I didn't write this. I'm not hallucinating it. Is that what she thinks? That I'm a madwoman? Is that the look she's giving Steven and his reciprocating expression? They agree I'm unhinged? I can't deny that I've done things in the past that would come across as impulsive—manic, even—at times. But this is not about me right now. This is about the author of these words.

"Care to share anyway?" I ask.

She eyes Steven again as if asking for permission, and I move myself between them.

"Well, a woman named Rebekah Howler lived here with her husband, who was the mayor. The house was designed by the same architect who built the Bangor Mental Health Institute. The story goes that on one Halloween, she threw herself out the attic window. Kids like to come and see her ghost."

"I thought they came for Lizzie Barkley."

Teresa smiles apologetically. "They come for both. It kind of goes with the holiday, a twofer, I guess."

Great. Just what I need to add to my life. Teenagers trespassing in hopes of seeing ghosts, plural. "Fine," I say, annoyed. "What else can you tell me about Rebekah Howler?"

"She'd been a mental patient at the facility. There are lots of stories about this house since it's the second oldest house in Cold Harbor. A lot of ghosts." Teresa seems to notice my apprehension and forces a smile. "I can't be of much more help. I know who might, though. Deena."

The blueberry who brought me a goodie basket? "Deena Richardson? The Welcome Wagon lady?"

Teresa laughs. "Yes. Except Deena wasn't always the Welcome Wagon. She was a real estate agent. Retired five years ago. I took her spot. But she was actively working until then. She'd know who lived here, or you can look up property records at city hall. I mean, it's a room with a table and filing cabinets. Nothing online, but it might benefit you."

Right. I know this. I'm just not thinking clearly. If I don't sleep soon, I'll really be in a state. "Well, thank you for coming by."

"It's super creepy, Gwen. Who would write that?" She shakes her head.

"I don't know," I murmur.

After she clambers down the stairs faster than she came up them, I spin on Steven. "Do you know about the mental hospital?"

Steven massages the nape of his neck. "It's a rather well-known facility and has had several names over the years, but yes. Teresa's guess makes the most sense to me. Whoever wrote this may have been committed for carving the words—maybe this Howler woman—or the story is Boogedy Boo to scare kids. My guess is someone who lived here was committed at some point, and if he or she was etching this into the floor, then that is most likely where they belonged. Talk to Deena. But I don't think this is an unsolved crime. An unsettling mystery but not a crime, Gwen. You don't solve crimes anymore."

I'm sick to death of hearing him say that.

He kisses my cheek. "I just came home to grab the lunch I forgot and to see you a minute. But I need to get back. I'll try to be home by six, help you with dinner."

Dinner? He's thinking about dinner? Am I the only one who finds this to be more than a mystery? More than bizarre?

Am I the only one seeing…children who don't exist and hearing babies and noises in the night?

I need a break from that house after Teresa and Steven leave. Fresh air and seeing Cady will do me some good, and it's only 2:45. A coffee pick-me-up might help too. I ignore Steven's office building, where it seems he'd rather be on a Saturday. But every time I come downtown, it's worse. The whole town looks like it's been swallowed by Halloween. Paper skeletons sway in shop windows, some missing limbs. A scarecrow leans crookedly outside the florist, its stitched mouth sagging open like it's trying to scream. Even the lampposts have plastic cobwebs clinging to them, twitching with every breath of wind.

I push Tara through the damp park where I thought I saw a man preying on children, and my stomach tightens. There's a hay bale display by the fountain—meant to be festive, I'm sure—but one of the stuffed figures slumped against the bench has red paint splashed down its front. Or maybe it's not paint. The eyes are just black buttons, but they seem to follow me as I pass. Along with the dreadful crows. Not only do they surround my home but they're everywhere downtown. On wires, rooftops, trees. Growing like a massive, wicked army—tearing the sky to shreds, black wings cutting the air to ribbons, each ragged cry drilling straight into my skull. It's more than noise—it's a sickness, a rot that festers beneath my skin, crawling in slow, sticky lines across my nerves.

Their collective shadows ripple across the ground like oil swallowing the light in quick, greedy gulps. They see me, I know they do, those inky eyes glinting sharp as blades, watching with a patience that feels like hunger.

I just want them to go away. To lift with the pregnant storm clouds and rumbles of thunder.

Down at the harbor, the restaurants are lit up, cozy and glowing like always, but there's something about the jack-o'-lanterns lining the boardwalk that makes me uneasy. Too many of them. All carved with the same wide, jagged smile. Their flickering candles twitch in the wind like whispered threats.

This used to be my favorite time of year.

Now every cheerful pumpkin, every plastic bat, every child-sized ghost hanging from a porch hook feels like it's trying too hard. Like the town is hiding something—something old and decaying beneath the surface. Something no one wants to look at directly.

As I cross the street to Black Capped Coffee, I notice three black-capped chickadees fluttering on the bench in front of the large picture window. The same three outside my own windowsill?

They're whistling, and it sounds like they're calling out, "Phoe-bee, Phoe-bee, Phoe-bee." As I reach for the door handle, one flies up and sits right on it and peers up at me, its little black head cocked as if it asked me a question and is awaiting the answer.

"Sorry," I whisper. "I'm not Phoebe. I'm just Gwen."

"Black-capped chickadees are quite lovely birds," a man says. "Friendly too."

I turn and am greeted by a man in his mid to late sixties, tall and broad-shouldered, with a shock of ebony hair just beginning to surrender to gray at the temples. A few silver streaks run through the longer strands on top, pushed back in a way that suggests he still cares how he looks, even if time has had its say.

His eyes catch the fading light—icy blue beneath thick, bushy eyebrows that give him a permanent expression of scrutiny. He must've been a heartbreaker once. You can still see the shape of it in the line of his jaw, the tilt of his mouth. That kind of thing doesn't vanish—it just settles in deeper. There's a faint scent of pipe tobacco on his breath, sweet and cloying. Familiar. It hits me in a way I wasn't prepared for—like a ghost passing close.

"I didn't know that."

"Oh, yes. They also have exceptional memories. They use episodic memory to find numerous food caches they've left. The part of their brain that supports spatial memory—the hippocampus—expands in the fall in order to bank memories, and then it shrinks back to its normal size in spring. These little birds are special—they're survivors."

I've learned more about birds in the past month than in my whole life, and now I'm more convinced I should take up the hobby. I gaze at the little bird again, a survivor—and the word tagged onto this fragile, petite being brings burning tears to the backs of my eyes.

"I had no idea." I continue to watch the bird as he—or she—watches me. I can't tell the sex.

"Memories are important to them for their survival. Winter is a harsh season. Cold and barren. Hard to muddle through. Scientists often study chickadees to see how memory works."

"There you are, Dr. Rivera. You can't keep getting away from me like that. I'm going to have to buy a child's backpack with a leash on it. Neither of us wants that," a redhead teases. The little chickadees fly away upon her approach, leaving a dull ache in my chest. I wasn't ready to stop gazing upon the beauty of the three birds.

Their beauty is delicate, almost sacred—the kind you miss if you're not paying attention. Most people don't. They're too taken with the bold and the bright, the things that shout.

Like the crows.

They pierce—bleak, suspicious eyes, impossible to ignore.

But chickadees…

Chickadees are quiet.

They're for the ones who know how to look.

"I was just telling Cady about the chickadees."

She gives me a knowing look mixed with an apology as if he's putting me out.

Then his name strikes me as the thought of the birds dissipates. Dr. Rivera.

"Adrian Rivera?" I ask.

"Well of course I am, Cady." He smiles like I'm the one confused, and I remember this man has early-onset Alzheimer's. But he is the doctor who lives across the harbor. The house with the light in the attic window.

"This isn't Cady." The redhead extends a hand. "Kristin White. I'm Adrian's full-time nurse."

"Gwen McDaniel. We moved into the house across the harbor."

"Oh! Wonderful," Kristin says, and Dr. Rivera's eyes narrow. "I should have come already and brought goodies, but it's hard to get away." She side-eyes the doctor.

"I want my coffee, Kristin. Spit spot. It's after three o'clock." He throws open the door and enters.

"He's obsessed with *Mary Poppins*. I don't know why. Alzheimer's."

"I heard. Small town."

Her smile and blue eyes are bright against milky-white skin and flaming hair. "But coffee from here, he never forgets. And when he has a hankering, then we show up. It's usually around this same time." She tucks a stray hair behind her ear. "Nice meeting you."

"Same." I think about the light in the attic over there, the on-and-off game. "Oh, Kristin. Does he ever go up in the attic at his house?"

She frowns at my strange question. I can't blame her. "No. Why?"

Someone was in the top window of the house across the harbor. He escapes her in town. Chances are he's escaped her in his own home too, especially late at night. "I saw a light in the window a few weeks ago and thought it might be him."

She cocks her head. "That isn't possible. Adrian never goes into the attic because his wife killed herself up there over thirty years ago. Hung herself in the middle of the night. Tragic."

Ice spiders up my spine, quiet but insistent, like my body knows something my mind hasn't caught up to yet. "I'm sorry to hear that."

Dr. Rivera returns and pushes open the door, a scowl along his brow. "Cady, when are you due?"

Kristin face-palms herself. "Great. All we need are rumors that Cady Tremell is pregnant. And it's offensive. Adrian, this is Gwen McDaniel, and she has a baby already. She's not pregnant, and neither is Cady. Come on." She laughs and rushes inside, and I follow.

Cady pats her belly. "Just say I'm fat if you think I'm fat, Doc." She looks at me. "He's convinced I'm having a baby. Nice. I need a man for all that, Doc."

Kristin snorts, and they start talking about the pitiful dating pool in Cold Harbor. But my mind goes back to the window. If the doctor never goes upstairs, then who was up there? And why did Mrs. Rivera kill herself?

Chapter Eighteen

Cady wipes her brow and pulls a face that lets me know it's a busy, stressful day. She slides into a chair after her last customer leaves with his order. She sighs, then smiles at the stroller.

"She sleeping?"

I nod.

"I am exhausted. Everyone wants a late afternoon pick-me-up. I get it. Me too, but I'm wiped out, and Adrian thinks I'm pregnant. Nice."

I snort. Cady is trim and her tummy flat. No one is going to believe she's pregnant.

"I love owning and working at a café, but man, people are mean when they jones for caffeine." She grins, and I raise my eyebrows over the steaming cup of coffee.

"I think the real question is, how many cups have you had today?" She's a mile a minute with that mouth.

"More than you want to know." She waves a hand at me, brushing off her idle babbling. "What are you up to this afternoon?"

The bone may not have panned out as human, but where

one book ends, there's always a new book to pick up. "I think we might have us a podcast after all."

"I was going to tell you the same thing. Wilt was in here thirty minutes ago, and guess what he told me?"

I really hate when people ask you to guess something you would never know. "How about we cut to the chase and you just tell me?"

She nods. "He said he's still not buying the story about the bone being canine and told Chief as much. Told Chief he's just covering up crime so the mayor doesn't give him the boot and replace him with Lowell White, who has made it known he'd be a better chief of police than Grant. He also happens to be the mayor's golfing buddy, and it's known that Grant and the mayor have butted heads in the past."

Wilt is dead set on proving Chief wrong? Why? No one else is even talking about the bone anymore. Old news. No news. "Chief and Wilt got a beef?"

"A beef?" She gives me a look that says strap in for the gossip train. "Wilt's wife cheated on him with Chief a year after they married. My mom told me that. She says it's not gossip, it's talking history."

A laugh tumbles out, and I choke on my Americano. I never thought of gossip like that, telling someone's history. But in a way, I suppose it is. "Did they stay together?"

"No. Well, they did for a few years and had a daughter, but sometimes even if you forgive, you can't forget, and Wilt couldn't forget." She shrugs.

I think people remember what suits them—and twist the rest to fit whatever story they need to believe. Sometimes it's to erase what they've done, sometimes to justify it. We all have our own way of evicting the truth we can't live with and redecorating that space with the version we wish had happened instead.

"I saw the medical examiner's report, Cady. Looks like Wilt's trying to take a swing at the Chief's reputation—make it seem like Cold Harbor isn't as safe as he claims."

"I want to show you something." I unlock my phone and tap the photos icon. "I was pulling up some old carpet in the attic—and found this underneath."

I hand it to her. At first, Cady simply frowns, squinting at the screen. But then her expression shifts. Her mouth parts slightly, then drops open as the image registers. Her eyes widen—huge, round, unblinking. Like Frisbees.

She sees it now. "What is this?"

"I don't know, but it's nothing good. No one writes 'I AM NOT CRAZY' all over a floor—"

"Unless they are." Cady continues to stare at the phone.

"Or someone wants them to believe they are."

"Who do you think wrote it? When?" Cady hands me back the phone and picks at her apron string.

"I don't know. It could have been there for decades or just a few years."

"Maybe that's why it's carpeted. Whoever saw it thought, 'Yeah, that's icky,' and covered it up to forget, then just stored junk up there."

That was possible. "But here's the thing. Looking back after I found it, I didn't notice bloodstains on the floor. If Gina and Lizzie Barkley were killed in the attic, there would have been a mess."

Cady wrinkles her nose. "Maybe they cleaned up her mess, then carpeted it or replaced the previous carpet. Covering all the past. The murder and the madness." She shrugs.

"Could be. A crime may not have taken place. But it's bizarre and freaky, and I want to know who was upstairs in that attic. I want to know who wrote that. So I think we should work it like a cold case. Find out who lived in that house. Who were they? What happened there? And why did they write that?" It might not lead to a murder, but what if it does? My gut won't let this go. This isn't an animal bone in my woods. This is someone's pain and suffering and maybe torment in my upstairs attic.

Cady nods enthusiastically. "My mom might be able to help us."

"Good. I'm going to talk to Deena Richardson as soon as I can. See if she'll remember who owned the house before she retired." Do I want Deena to know what I'm doing? Might work best if she didn't. "Let's keep the writing in the attic between us. For now. All anyone needs to know is that I'm interested in the house's history, especially since Halloween is approaching and kids love to visit my house in the chilling hope of seeing dead Lizzie Barkley. And this Rebekah Howler character. What do you know about her?"

"Rebekah Howler is a ghost story about a woman who was married to the mayor of the town. That part is true. She was pushed out of the window by him and fell to her death. That part is a rumor. She was pregnant at the time, but he didn't know it. Also rumor. They say that if you approach the house before midnight on Halloween, you can hear her scream and her baby wail. But it's just a made-up story."

Except I am hearing baby cries.

"Do you know when she lived in the house? Can we find out information on her and her husband?"

Cady frowns. "I'm sure we can. I don't know the exact dates, but the house was built for him and her to raise a family. My mom is the history buff, not me and she hates scary stories, movies and books. Anything I know, I heard from friends at school. But we can find out dates. Maybe it was Rebekah who wrote the words—the stories about her mental illness are true."

Her version differs slightly from Teresa's story. But all campfire stories morph over the years, usually becoming scarier, more gruesome and more sinister.

"There has to be something." I pull out my phone and google the mayor of Cold Harbor and Rebekah Howler. A few articles pop up. "When in doubt, Google. It says here that he had the house built for them in 1896. Charles Howler." I stare at a photo of my home when it was fresh and new and a little smaller. "I'd still like to know more about them." I don't see anything on the mental institution in connection to Rebekah. "What do you know about the mental health facility in Bangor?"

"You think whoever wrote that could have been a patient?" she asks.

"Possibly. Teresa said Rebekah Howler had been a patient there. If it was in the late 1800s, early 1900s, the perception of mental health vastly differed from today. Back then it was kept a locked-up secret. Now people are far more open about mental health. It's not shameful or something to be hidden. In fact, she may not be the only one with mental health issues who lived in that house or resided in a facility."

The bell over the door jingles, and four middle-aged women step inside, laughing and chatting like they've known each other forever. There's an ease to them that tugs at something in me. I miss having that—miss the idea of it. But the truth is, I never really had friends. Not in the way that lasts. Trust has always come hard for me.

Sometimes it doesn't even take.

It's a wonder Steven and I ever fell in love. Vulnerability has never been easy. My job demanded a poker face, every hour of every day. Steven believes I've been honest. That I've told him everything.

What he doesn't know will protect him.

Cady hops up.

"We'll talk more later," I say.

"Keep me posted."

The women wave and smile at the stroller as I push Tara out into the cold air.

I'm on to something just like I knew I was on to something

with her. Teri Jo Tipton. Child killer. No business with that newborn.

And that reminds me I could call my old partner, Kent Masters, to help look into that femur bone or access a database I can't as a civilian to look into missing persons for the past thirty years. If that bone is human, it belongs to someone. But that would be all kinds of wrong. With our past and how he was responsible for my firing.

For my own good, he said.

No, he was nothing short of irate at my rejection.

He betrayed me.

And I betrayed Steven.

Chapter Nineteen

I make a bottle for Tara and settle into the rocking chair in the living room. It belonged to my grandmother—old, squeaky and a little uncomfortable—but it connects me to her, to a family I no longer have. Not counting Steven, who probably won't be home to help with dinner like he said earlier.

I've lit a fire, though it's not really cold enough. Still, it soothes me—the crackling logs, the squeak, squeak, squeak of the chair rocking over old joists. I'm trying to figure out how my life spun so vastly out of control. Why I made some of the choices I did. I wish I knew.

I wish I could go back and do it all over again. There are so many things I'd do differently. Holding Tara against me, feeling her tiny chest rise and fall, soothes something in me. She's my only solace these days. The only thing keeping me sane. Without her, I'd fall into tiny pieces—fragments so light they could be scattered by the wind.

If I could go back, I wouldn't have taken those prescription pads. I wouldn't have forged his name. I wouldn't have ruined him. We would still be in Baltimore. But I wouldn't be a cop.

Losing the baby before Tara—the second-trimester miscarriage. I delivered a beautiful baby girl, stillborn. That last hope…severed.

The days that followed were a blur of silence. The house felt too quiet. Too clean. I went back to work too soon, pretending I was okay, pretending I could still be who I was before.

A week in, Kent and I got the call—Teri Jo Tipton.

She met us at the door with swollen eyes and a swollen belly. Crocodile tears, mascara streaking down her face. She said all the right things.

I stood there, staring at her…and broke. Snapped.

But those prescriptions to dull it all…it's not the worst thing I've ever done to Steven.

Only he doesn't know that.

He stuck by my side and left his practice quietly to spare me. Well, he was asked to leave. If I confide my deepest secret, he won't stay. We're on eggshells as it is.

And it's not like he hasn't done things to hurt me.

We've been cut in two. I don't feel like we're one, not even when we're together intimately. But then, I've always felt a disconnect. A loss. This gaping hole within me that I can't fill.

I hum a lullaby to Tara. One I must have heard from my mother. Time robs us of memory. Robs us of the good moments. We think we'll remember them.

We don't.

But I remember every baby lost. Every tear cried. Every hope dashed.

I hold Tara closer, breathe in her powdery scent and kiss her velvety cheek. "I'll keep you safe, baby girl."

Looking around the house, I inhale the smell of fresh paint and wonder about the lives of those who lived here. A black pall hovers and sucks at the air, making it hard to breathe.

How do I tell Steven I want to leave? How do I explain that

a presence lingers and its shadowy ribbons slither around my soul? No amount of paint and new fixtures will change that.

A thump under the stairs raises the hairs on the back of my neck.

Thump.

Thump.

Thump.

Like maybe the sound of a tennis ball being thrown against the wall over and over. I set the bottle on the hearth and put Tara snugly in her swing, then inch toward the door.

I wrench it open and switch on the light.

Nothing. No one.

But it feels like the temperature has dropped again and I'm cold, chilled to the bone. Swallowing is hard. Still, I step deeper into the closet, stooping as the ceiling slopes down in the back. The walls seem to close in, narrowing, and I reach out, pressing a hand against one to stay upright. Everything's spinning now. The floor tilts. I sink, not like I'm falling, but like I'm being pushed until the back wall gives way and opens up.

I tumble into a blackness so thick my eyes can't adjust, and a startled yelp escapes my throat. My phone is still in my pocket, thank God. Hands shaking, I fumble to unlock it, the flashlight flickering on with a cold white beam. I'm in a room tucked behind the closet. The air is suffocating and musty, like it hasn't been breathed in years. I cough, choking on dust and the taste of mildew, and swat at cobwebs clinging to my face like fingers.

Something crunches beneath my foot.

I freeze.

Not dust. Not old wood.

Bugs.

A scattering of legs and shells and brittle bodies, all cracking under my sneakers like dry leaves. I lift my foot and see them—some crushed, some still twitching.

They're everywhere. Along the floorboards, clinging to the damp corners, skittering away from the flashlight's glare.

I don't mind chasing killers. But a room full of bugs?

Hard pass.

Still, I breathe through my nose and take another step. The air is dense, the kind that sticks to your skin. The flashlight beam wavers slightly as my hand trembles. The room isn't big. Maybe four by eight, barely enough to lie down in.

In the far corner sits a child's lawn chair, the kind with bright plastic webbing—except this one's been swallowed by grime. Filth clings to the slats, thick and sticky like old syrup. A lump of something dried and unrecognizable is stuck to the seat.

Beside it, on the floor, is a jump rope. Orange plastic. Purple handles.

I know that jump rope.

Just like the one the little girl was holding.

The girl that wasn't really there—or was she?

God, what is happening? Am I being visited by a little girl ghost? I don't believe in ghosts. But people believe in things all the time that aren't true.

And what was the thumping?

I see nothing that could make the noise...other than the jump rope maybe slapping against the wall, but that's impossible, and yet it's the same kind of noise.

Beside the jump rope, a green plastic pail sits, and inside, children's books. I kneel down and open the first one. It's a Ramona Quimby book, worn at the edges. Written inside, in faded pencil. *Lily Ann.*

Who is Lily Ann? Did she live here? Was she locked in this musty, dank room?

Did she...die in this room? Did she write the words up in the attic? Is that why I keep seeing her? What about the baby cries? Are they hers, or did a family once live here—one that might've looked like a picture-perfect family, living in a lovely place on the water, but was murky, filled with something sinister inside?

And then I see it.

Around the baseboards—claw marks. Deep scratches. A pattern of them, jagged and desperate.

My heart jumps into my throat. Quickly, I snap a few photos on my cell phone, trying to steady my hand. My flashlight scans the rest of the room. A spider scurries along the wall, its legs moving too quickly, too precisely.

I squat, trying to center myself, think logically. Maybe this wasn't a room of punishment but remains from a childhood hideout. A clubhouse, some secret place where kids used to play.

Maybe the marks are from an animal. Just like the bones in the woods that weren't human—just an animal.

As I'm rationalizing, something catches my ear. I hear it again.

Beautiful dreamer, queen of my song…

I pause.

My breath catches in my throat. The song. That horrible song. The record player. I kept it, didn't I? But I threw the record in the dumpster.

The cold air vibrates around me.

I hurry out of the secret room, back into the closet. Tara is in her swing, safe—for now. I don't want to leave her if someone's in the house, but I can't take her with me for the very same reason.

Truth? I don't think someone's in this house.

I think some*thing* is in this house. And I don't know if it's a danger to my baby or not. But could something have carried her off to the dock? No. I mean… I don't know. Maybe I left her out there myself. I just don't want to believe it. Yet again, belief doesn't make something true.

Leaving her here feels like the safer option.

The music is grating now, gnawing at the edges of my sanity. I bustle upstairs, duck into my bedroom, and grab my gun from under the pillow. Then I move to the attic door.

Like a horrible round of déjà vu, I climb the stairs, one by one, and the music grows louder.

List while I woo thee with soft melody;

Gone are the cares of life's busy throng…

No one is up here. I cut the record, letting the needle scrape across the vinyl. With a snap, I break the record in half, letting it clatter to the floor. I can't afford to let myself believe something supernatural is happening. But if a human is in this house, they must be getting in through secret passages. Like the hidden room under the stairs.

I rush to the bookcases and begin to push and pull, hoping to find some hidden compartment. But nothing gives. No indication of a panel or door. No crawl space.

Breathless, I peek out the attic window. And that's when I see the smoke—before I even smell it.

My shed.

It's on fire.

Chapter Twenty

Lily Ann

Smoke poured over the stove and choked her, and the fire alarm squealed. She'd burned the bacon, and Daddy would be angry. She was supposed to be making him happy. She waved a towel in the air like Mom used to when she was alive and set off the alarm. Dad—her real dad—would have laughed and opened the back door and windows to air out the house. She raced to the windows, but she couldn't open them. They'd been nailed shut. The door locked from the outside, and tears filled her eyes. After returning to the kitchen, she flapped the towel until the alarm stopped, but Daddy came upstairs with that scowl on his face she didn't like.

She tried to keep the good days going. Good days meant they went outside. Good days meant vitamin D. Who knew you could get vitamins from the sun?

Mom always gave her gummy vitamins. But she preferred the sun. She missed the parks and camping. Daddy said they could go camping again when she turned thirteen.

She'd be a woman at thirteen, and things would be different. She'd make him happy in new ways, but she still wasn't sure what he meant. For her last birthday, he bought a big cake with candles, and it was fun. He grilled hamburgers and fried tater tots—her favorite—and he bought her a jump rope and a few books. She liked to read, and he did too. Often at night they'd sit in the living room reading. He liked spy books and detective novels. He liked to build too. He made the kitchen table and chairs, and he was working on a rocking chair for her.

A wedding present.

Guess it'd take a while, then. She was too young to get married.

Daddy homeschooled her. She was very good at history and English. And she'd learned all the right answers to the questions he'd asked. She never got them wrong.

"Lily Ann, what did you do?"

"I was making you breakfast—to make you happy—but I burned the bacon." A tear slipped over her cheek, and her tummy hurt. He didn't like it when she cried. When she cried, she went to the Punishment Room. It wasn't that bad a place though. Just lonely if she was left in there very long.

She wiped her tears and apologized again.

But instead of becoming angry or scolding her, Daddy dropped to his knees, eye level with her, and smiled. "Oh, doll. I appreciate that. That you would want to make me breakfast. That makes me happy. It's okay. Look." He pointed to a metal dome above the stove. "That's a hood fan. It sucks up smells and even smoke. When you're cooking, you turn it on. See?" He switched the little black button to On, and the fan hummed to life. "You'll remember that next time, won't you?"

She nodded, thankful he wasn't mad. He'd taught her something new too. She hugged him around the waist. "Thank you. You're the best daddy and teacher, and you provide me with good food. I am very sorry I burned some of it." She answered his questions without him asking. He liked that a lot, and she'd been learning that it was true. She did eat because he fed her. She had a warm bed because he provided it. She had access to books, games, a jump rope and TV all because he gave them to her. He never hurt her either.

Even if sometimes he scared her. There was a darkness in his eyes at times. So black the whites of his eyes were nearly gone, and a coldness rolled off him in waves. It gave her goose bumps and made her feel like she needed to do number two. She did not like that look. Or the other look that made her feel icky. She didn't like it when he stroked her hair or rubbed her back under her shirt. But she never told him not to. She was too afraid.

Late at night, she pretended her parents didn't die on that camping trip while she was trying to find the best fishing spot. She pretended she was home with them and riding her bike and playing with friends in the cove. She went to real school, and the windows weren't nailed shut, and the doors were locked only at night. And there was no Punishment Room. No bucket for a toilet.

Those short moments before she drifted to sleep, she was happy, but it wasn't real happy because that life wasn't real. It was make-believe. She smiled up at Daddy. He didn't have to know she was pretending. All that mattered to him was that she made *him* happy.

Chapter Twenty-One

I call 911, already running downstairs to the main level. The shed—the one I meant to turn into a she-shed—is an inferno. Flames roar, and smoke rolls in thick, sooty waves.

I call Steven. "Something's wrong. The shed's on fire. You can't work late tonight. Come home now." I end the call. Did I do this? Forget something? Start it somehow?

No. I haven't touched the shed in days. But my mind—it won't stop circling, glitching.

Why now? Why fire?

To destroy something? Lure me out? Trap me in?

I return to the living room. Tara's still in her swing. Unbothered. Safe.

But everything inside me is screaming.

Sirens signal the fire truck is near, and then it's pulling up fast. Lights flashing against the dusky backdrop. Brakes screaming. Firefighters jump out, dragging the hose toward the shed. Water blasts. Steam billows. I follow to the back of the yard, watching them in horror.

Chief Ellersby strides over, flanked by an officer I recognize—one of the ones standing outside the station when I brought Chief my findings—or lack of them—from the woods. I straighten instinctively, but my hands are still shaking. My heart won't slow down.

Ellersby squints at the flames, then at me. "You all right?"

No. Not even close. But I nod. "It started fast."

He looks past me, toward the house. "Anyone inside?"

"My baby."

The officer stiffens. "Is she safe?"

"She's fine. For now."

I don't mean for it to sound so grim. But I don't know what's coming next. And I'm starting to wonder if any of this—the fire, the hidden room, the record playing—is part of something bigger. Or if it's just me, unraveling one thread at a time.

Ellersby raises his eyebrows. "Doesn't look like you're having a good evening, Gwen."

He doesn't know the half of it. I can't tell him a fourth.

I promised Steven. And he made good points—valid, terrifying points. We don't need the chief of police digging into our lives. Not in a town this small. Not when everyone's watching everyone.

"No," I admit. "I'm not. Why would someone set my shed on fire?"

Why would someone need a hidden room? Why carve words into the floorboards? Why play a record when I'm the only one home?

Chief Ellersby arches an eyebrow. "Did you see someone?"

"No. I was in the attic."

Trying to solve another mystery.

He raises his hands, already grinning under that bushy mustache. "I'm not saying it wasn't arson, but—"

"Don't," I cut in. "Before you start saying 'no crime.' How often does a work shed just catch fire on its own?"

He shrugs. "Faulty wiring. It's old. Could be accidental.

But Fire Chief Becker will do a full investigation. If it's intentional, we'll know."

The fire dies fast under the firefighters' assault. What's left of the shed is a charred skeleton, sagging and reeking.

I can already feel the smoke soaking into my skin, my clothes, my hair. I'm going to need another shower. Maybe three.

"Gwen!"

I turn, and Steven sprints toward me, still in his white coat. He pulls me into his arms without hesitation, holds me like he hasn't in months—tight, desperate, real.

I don't know if it's the fire or the fear or the way my heart is finally starting to crack, but I nearly cry into his shoulder.

"Are you okay?" he asks.

"I'm fine. They caught it before it went into the woods." That would have been a nightmare.

"They'll do the inspection to determine if it's arson," Chief Ellersby says, turning to Steven.

"Thanks. Might've been faulty wiring," Steven replies smoothly. "I noticed it wasn't up to code during the walk-through when we bought the place."

He side-eyes me.

No, I didn't go to the walk-through. I haven't even been inside that shed but twice. I just thought it might make a nice she-shed. Or maybe a greenhouse. Chickens, sourdough starters, jars of jam lined up like a Pinterest shrine. My own eggs. My own garden.

But that's not me. It never will be. I'll just keep envying the women who make it look effortless online.

"I don't think it's faulty wiring, Steven."

Chief folds his arms. "We can't really say what it was or wasn't at the moment." He glances back at the shed. "If you need anything, let us know. We should know more in a few days. But...*why* do you think someone set it on fire? Why not an accident?"

Steven's glare tells me to tread carefully.

How do I explain the record that played itself? The secret room behind the stairs that even Steven doesn't know about yet? Finding Tara on the dock when I was sure I brought her inside with me?

And what if—I can barely stand the thought—but what if I did leave her out there?

I swallow everything I want to say. "It could've been an accident. I guess the cop in me just...sees suspicion everywhere."

Chief chuckles. "Your words, not mine. I got that on record, right?"

Steven laughs. The other officers do too. I smile because I'm supposed to, but inside I'm crumbling.

Once the scene clears and the fire chief confirms they'll investigate, I'm alone with Steven again. The tension hangs heavy between us.

"What's going on, Gwen?" His voice is low, serious. "You need to talk to me. And you need to be honest. Are you...feeling anxious? Depressed?"

"I'm not slipping," I snap. "And I'm tired of every feeling being labeled as some kind of disorder. Yes, I have anxiety. Sometimes I'm depressed. That doesn't mean I'm hallucinating."

But maybe it does.

Do I show him the hidden room? Or will he take my concerns about it as proof that I'm unraveling?

He's never really understood.

I walk to the living room and lift Tara from her swing. Her tiny body melts into mine, and something in me unknots.

She anchors me.

Have I ever mattered like this to Steven? Or have I just been the shadow at the edge of his perfect life? I curl onto the couch with Tara nestled in the crook of my arm.

"This where you plan to be the rest of the day?" Steven asks.

My stomach tightens. "What exactly does that mean?"

"It means what it means." He throws his hands up, then rakes one through his hair. "Why is everything subtext with you?"

He's already turning away. "I'm going back to the office. Don't wait up."

Then under his breath, just loud enough… "Not that you would anyway."

My eyes sting, but I don't cry. "What about helping me with dinner?"

He slowly turns. "Do you really think you're going to focus on anything else or anyone else tonight, Gwen?"

Honestly? No. I'm a distracted mess. I want Steven home, but he's right. I won't pay any attention to him.

"I'll see you later then," I mumble.

"That's what I thought." He hangs his head and walks away.

This isn't living. This isn't what I signed up for.

When I married Steven, I imagined white picket fences, joyful chaos, romantic nights. Arguments didn't exist in that fantasy. Neither did grief. Or isolation.

But I was swept off my feet once before.

Not by Steven.

By someone who fed me stories of adventure and forever. Who made me believe I was worth something.

I gave up everything for that man.

In the end, he spit me out. Hook, line and sinker—left embedded in my cheek like the foolish fish I'd been.

That was the day I stopped believing in happy endings.

Since then, the glass has only ever been half empty. Every drop of hope wrung out by reality. Now, holding Tara, I realize I'm drowning in the same ache again—unloved. Unwanted.

And I'm scared that this time, I won't resurface.

Chapter Twenty-Two

Tara swings rhythmically in her seat, a little bead of milk resting in the corner of her mouth. I watch her, lulled by the back-and-forth motion—just like when I was a kid, waiting for Misty and Jada to swing the jump rope so I could run in without missing a beat.

Life feels a lot like that lately. Like I keep missing the rhythm. The rope swings heavy and smacks me in the head, and my feet tangle underneath me. Only now, it's not skinned knees I'm dealing with—it's a heart that can't find the pace.

Steven rolled in around ten last night and was up at his normal time today, mentioning finding a church. I rolled over, pulled the covers over my head and slept until after 10:00 a.m.

I finally pull myself together enough to dab the milk from Tara's lip, then slip back onto the couch with a cup of peppermint tea and my laptop.

The house is still chaos in most rooms. Boxes line the walls. I haven't sanded the attic floor or cleared out the rest of the rolled-up carpet. I'm a disaster. I can't think straight.

So I continue where I began—research. Maybe there's something in this house's history that explains the hidden room, the writing, the creeping sense that something's not right.

Nothing new springs from the online search.

I sigh, push off the couch, and head to the kitchen. Deena Richardson's business card she left with the welcome basket is in a catch-all bowl on the counter.

I call the number. "Hello. You've reached Deena Richardson..." Her voicemail greeting continues until the beep, and I decide to leave a message.

"Hi, Mrs. Richardson. This is Gwen McDaniel. I heard that you were the real estate agent who sold this house to Brad Langston and only recently retired. I'm trying to find a list of previous owners going all the way back to the Howlers." That's further than I need, but I don't want to give away too much. Steven asked for me to butt out, so discretion is now required. I give her the number so she can reach me and end the voicemail. I'm not one to answer calls from numbers I don't know, so I give her about ten minutes and still no response.

I text her the same information.

Nothing.

Maybe at her age, she's fighting technology. She strikes me as the type who posts "Facebook has no right to my photos" as her status and genuinely thinks it means something.

It's not quite four o'clock yet. I pack up Tara and leave for city hall and Black Capped Coffee to trade information with Cady. I need to get out of this house. The fact Steven is downplaying the writing on the attic floor is irksome to say the least. I haven't told him about the closet. Admittedly nothing is wrong with a secret hiding space, and it just contained some toys and books—and bugs. But the gnawing in my gut says that, coupled with the writing upstairs and the weird things happening and what I'm seeing, the secret room is nothing short of sinister. And I'm done sitting on my hands.

"Come on, baby. We have work to do."

I'm in the downtown square by 4:15. It's quiet. The shops glow with jack-o'-lanterns though the sun hasn't dipped behind the trees yet.

It's all meant to be fun, festive. But it doesn't feel that way to me.

It feels like a warning.

A scarecrow slumps on a wooden bench outside the coffee shop, its burlap face stitched into a crude smile. The crows aren't afraid of it and rest on and beside it; black beady eyes follow me, accusatory as I walk by. Their constant lurking is driving me mad.

Children's laughter echoes faintly from a nearby alley, but when I glance that way, no one is there. Just fog oozing from a sewer grate. It's going to rain again, and I'm over that too.

This is a communal place, which means constant bake sales, fish fries and clam bakes. Smiling faces. Shared hot dishes. That undercurrent of closeness that's both comforting and claustrophobic.

But this close to Halloween, the town feels like it's wearing a mask. Like it's pretending to be something it's not.

I bypass the coffee shop and head for city hall. It's close to closing, but the woman at the metal desk grins, and we make polite chitchat. Then I ask for the property records, ready to pay whatever I need to in order to find out who owned the house as far back as I can. The rest will have to be discovered through town history.

"Give me a minute, hon." Greta, who loves her job and can't believe the amount of storms they've had—it's unusual for them—finally returns from the filing cabinets with a scowl. "I'm sorry, but there are no property records for the Darkwater Road home. Not that it's odd. I mean, in a town this size, things are easily misplaced or not filed, and we don't really do the whole online update thing. Is there anything else I can help you with, Mrs. McDaniel? You know, I saw your husband last

Friday for a weird mole on my ankle. He put me right at ease. Not cancerous. He's handsome."

Does this woman take breaths? I'm overwhelmed at the mile-a-minute information dump and the fact that all the property records are misplaced. Coincidence?

Doubtful.

"No. No, I appreciate it." I don't bother to remark about Steven's good looks or her benign mole and instead book it to the Black Capped Coffee. Cady waves when I enter. "Hey, I got news. Hold up. You want your usual?" she asks, and I nod and find a little table near the window. I park Tara's stroller and keep the top over it for privacy.

Cady interrupts my thoughts as she brings me my Americano. "You've had a crazy twenty-four hours."

"Speaking of crazy. You're going to think I am. But I need to tell someone, and I feel like with our shared feelings of my house, you might believe me."

Cady leans in, and she's all ready for me to spill the tea.

"I think we can add on to the very bad things we already know happened in that house. And they may have stuck."

Cady twirls her blond ponytail end and cocks her head. "Like? And stuck how?"

"Listen, I'm not a believer in souls lingering in houses, but I'm teetering on becoming one. I've been toying with an idea that I really don't want to believe but… I think maybe Lizzie Barkley or some other little girl is still calling my house home."

She sputters on her coffee, wide-eyed, like the words just punched the breath out of her. "You think your house is haunted?"

"No." That's silly. And yet… "No. definitely not. But… perhaps?"

"Are you sure or are you trying to convince yourself?" Cady reaches across the table and squeezes my hand. "What's been going on? You have my word I won't call you out as a loon or spread it around town. You're a levelheaded former detective. Lay it on me."

And I do. From day one I tell Cady everything that has happened that she doesn't already know.

By the time I'm done, she hasn't moved—coffee cup full, hands clenched tight around it. "Whoa. And you think this little girl you're seeing is trying to tell you something?"

"I don't know. I'm coming up with every cockamamie idea to understand what's happening, because it can't be that I'm cracking up."

Cady snorts. "You're not. Your husband and even Teresa saw the writing on the floor. That was real."

"I called Deena for information and texted her too, but…" As if the stars have aligned or divine providence has granted me this favor, Deena Richardson is standing in front of the Tabby Cat, a bookstore, talking with a woman I don't recognize. "Hold up."

"No problem. I'll keep the baby company."

But I take Tara and her stroller with me. I rush out the door and jog across the cobbled street to Deena, and for a brief second, she looks terrified to see me.

"Hi, Deena. Did you get my voicemail and text?" I'm interrupting and couldn't care less. The other woman smiles tightly and excuses herself, leaving me and Deena all alone. Gotcha girlie.

"I'm afraid not. I've been so busy today. I'm on the Halloween Hoopla committee. Busy, busy."

"I wanted to find out who owned my property dating back to the building of the home. City hall has lost all the property records, and I do mean all of them. Since you were a real estate agent until a few years ago and lived here your whole life, I thought you'd know."

Something streaks through her eyes but is gone as quickly, and she clears her throat. "Are you having problems?"

Interesting question. "Define *problems*, Deena."

"I mean structural or water damage. Things like that." She glances at her phone and then back at me. "I mean, the home passed inspection, so there shouldn't be issues, but sometimes things slip through the cracks. The house is old."

"But it's had some updates and had been built on to over the years. Do you know who built on to it or anything like that?"

She blinks rapidly. "I really don't. It's out in the middle of nowhere and nestled in all those woods. Owners who have lived there clearly wanted privacy." She glances to the café window, where Cady sits watching us intently. "I didn't mean anything. I just… I heard you thought the bone they found was human and went to the chief about it. Now you want the property records. Seems you might be doing an investigation. Maybe to help Cady with a true crime podcast?"

"Would that be an issue?" Would a podcast about crime wreck their town motto and help kick Ellersby out of the chief's chair?

She looks back at me. "Her mother really doesn't want her doing that."

"Cady Tremell is an adult. I think she's long past having to obey her mother, don't you?"

"I just think you might be borrowing trouble."

I'm ten seconds away from really stirring up trouble. Why can't she just tell me who owned the house back before Brad Langston and his great-grandparents? "So you won't tell me? Someone in this town will."

Her eyes narrow, and then she's quickly back to being cordial. "Sorry I can't help you. Marcia is my best friend, and she doesn't want Cady doing true crime. You know her eldest daughter vanished. It's cruel what Cady is attempting, and I'll have no part in it. If someone else wants to feed into this podcast obsession, so be it. It won't be me, Mrs. McDaniel."

No, she's not sorry at all. She's hiding something, and all

she's done is pour gasoline on my fire, which reminds me of my shed gone up in flames. I stalk back into the shop. "Why wouldn't Deena tell me who lived in that house?"

"I don't know. Unless she thinks it's for a podcast. She and my mother have been best friends since elementary school. But before you saw her, I was going to tell you something else I heard this morning from one of my regulars who hunts with Wilt sometimes."

"What?"

"Wilt definitely thinks Chief had the medical report fudged because of the medical examiner who filled out the report."

My heart picks up pace. "Who was the medical examiner?"

"Jean Jackson. She dates Ellersby off and on, and they're on good terms. Like hookup good terms. Wilt is convinced Grant is covering up crimes so as not to give the mayor a reason to fire him and put Lowell White in charge. Crime on his watch means he might not get another watch."

Makes sense why he asked me if I saw the signature on the report. This changes things.

"Steven is working late tonight, yet again. Come by the house when you close. I want you to see what I've been talking about for yourself, but keep it quiet. The fewer people who know what we're up to, the better." I stand and jostle my purse on my shoulder.

"What are you going to do now?"

"See a man who might give me some answers."

Chapter Twenty-Three

OB-GYN Adrian Rivera lives across the harbor. I plug his address into my GPS and let it guide me through narrow, winding forest roads. The house comes into view just as the sun starts to dip, casting long, dusky forms over the drive. I pull up near the side, close to the edge of his property, where the trees seem to crowd in a little too tightly.

Kristin, the ginger, steps out onto the porch. She's dressed casually in jeans and a jade sweater that brings out her pale eyes. Her face is narrow, her features perfectly contoured. She's striking in her quiet way.

"Hi. What brings you here?" she asks as I roll down the window, then step out of the car, leaving Tara in her seat.

"I wanted to talk with Dr. Rivera. Just a little neighborly chat."

"You know his mind is fragile, right?" she says, her expression a mix of confusion and guarded concern. It's clear she's trying to puzzle out why a new neighbor would want to see someone whose memory is slipping away. But she wasn't concerned with me chatting with him at the coffee shop yesterday afternoon. Why is stopping by so concerning?

"I do. I just wanted to talk about birds," I say, forcing a casual smile. "He's a bird lover, and I need a hobby. After hearing him talk at the coffee shop about the black-capped chickadee, I thought he might know more. They fascinate me. Plus, if he has any bird books, I'd love to borrow one. I imagine he's got a whole collection." I shrug, a little too exaggerated, trying to seem harmless. "To be honest, I'm lonely. My husband works late most nights. I'm in a big, drafty house all by myself, and I could use something to get me outside."

The light is already starting to fade, and I want this done before nightfall.

Kristin tilts her head as though weighing my words, then nods. "I get that. I moved back after finishing nursing school in Portland. After leaving and returning, it's a culture shock—small towns. They have their own rhythm." Her lips soften, and her expression relaxes slightly. "Let me go get Adrian. He does better outside anyway. You'll likely see him on his dock from your windows. He could stand—or sit—out there for hours, lost in his thoughts."

She turns and disappears inside, and I let out a breath.

Sometimes my former job comes in handy. I've learned to improvise, to maneuver people in subtle ways to get what I need—whether that's a simple conversation or a door into someone's life. If birds are the key to getting Adrian talking, then fine. If it lets Kristin think I'm harmless and just looking for company, so be it.

But I didn't come here for birds.

I will do whatever it takes to acquire answers. If that means misdirection, then hasta la vista, moral compass.

Kristin returns with a handful of hardback books on birds, and Adrian follows with a smile. He's wearing black slacks and a gray sweater as if I've arrived at his practice and not his home. I'm a sweats kind of girl when I'm home.

"This is Gwen McDaniel, Adrian," Kristin says. "Your new

neighbor across the harbor. She's interested in learning about birds."

"Hi, Dr. Rivera. Do you remember us meeting at the coffee shop yesterday afternoon? You told me about the black-capped chickadees that had landed on the door. It was fascinating." My smile gains me one in return.

"The black-capped chickadee is a marvelous little bird. Friendly too. They also have exceptional memories. They use episodic memory to find numerous food caches they've left. The part of their brain that supports spatial memory—the hippocampus—expands in the fall in order to bank memories, and then it shrinks back to its normal size in spring. These little birds are special—they're survivors."

He's repeating what he told me previously, but I don't mind. We learn best through repetition. Even if what we are telling ourselves are lies.

"See, I need more of this. Could we chat about birds before the sun goes down?"

"Oh, yes, my dear." He holds out his arm for me to hook mine through, and I do. I won't go far—I can still see the car, see Tara in her seat. "I could talk about birds all day long."

Kristin chuckles. "I'll just be inside preparing dinner." She hands me the books, heavy hardbacks with cloth covers that smell like dust and sun. I leave them on the hood of my car for now. Who knows? Maybe I actually will take up bird-watching. It'd give me a reason to snoop through the woods with binoculars and a notepad—under the guise of harmless curiosity.

Adrian smells of pipe tobacco and Old Spice—warm, clinging scents that should be comforting. Familiar.

"How about we sit on my dock?" he asks.

It's in my line of sight. I nod. "Sounds good."

We walk the gentle slope toward the water, the grass uneven, wild. The air shifts as we near the rocky edge, the brine mingling with Adrian's scent. The sun is bleeding its way below the horizon now, painting the world in magenta, violet, robin's-egg blue and a fiery tangerine that seems too bright to be real. It's beautiful here. A different kind of quiet than at my house—less charged.

No wonder he sits out here often.

Two rocking chairs wait at the edge of the dock, facing the water. We sit. A canoe is tied beside us, and the small brass bell attached to the rope chimes softly in the breeze.

"How long have you lived in this house?" I ask. "And in Cold Harbor?"

Adrian inhales deeply, as though drawing the answer up from his bones. "Most of my life. Left for med school. Worked in Bangor a few years. Found out I'm just a small-town man. Small clinics. My wife needed more of my time."

"Oh? Why's that?"

"She's ill."

He says it in present tense. I wince just slightly.

"I'm sorry to hear that." It's public knowledge Mrs. Rivera hung herself in the attic. Because she was ill?

"Yeah. Did a little time in..." He hesitates. "Postpartum depression. Just starting to be taken seriously back then. I'd seen a few patients suffer. Ellen was the worst. She refused to care for Adrianna. Quite the strain. But she got better...until she didn't."

A fish plops in the water nearby, sending ripples out in ever-widening circles. One little movement. One disturbance. Affecting everything around it.

One bone found in the woods.

One sentence scratched into my attic floor.

One woman drowning in the depths of her own mind.

I understand depression. I know the murky gravity of it—the way it pulls at you, always just outside your vision. It blankets the joy, drowns the light. It doesn't shout. It whispers lies. Tells you you're alone. That you deserve it. And it's easier, sometimes, to stop fighting the current. Just close your eyes and drift. Let the quiet take you.

Except it's not quiet. Not really.

"Who was your neighbor across the harbor?" I ask, needing to redirect, needing to know. "They did a great job adding on."

Adrian's gaze drifts to the woods across the water. "They all die over there. Tragic."

My skin tightens. "Who all dies over there?"

"Always die." His voice is low now. "I saw him bury her myself. Dig the grave in those very woods."

He points. To my woods. To the stretch near where flashlights once swiveled under nightfall. Where soil was turned over like someone had been dug up.

"You saw who bury her?" I ask, too sharply.

"Doc, it's time to get ready for supper." Kristin's voice cuts through the gathering dark. She's walking toward us, brushing a copper strand of hair behind her ear.

"I'm having meatloaf," Adrian says. "It's my favorite. Next to lobster bisque. Do you like bisque?"

"I do, but—who buried the girl? In the woods? Who did you see?" My heart is a wild thing in my chest now.

"She died in a fire. Tragic." He stands as Kristin nears.

A fire? I thought a girl was buried.

This is what I get for trying to piece together the truth from a broken mind. But there's a pattern forming, however scattered the puzzle pieces.

Kristin tucks her hands into the sleeves of her sweater, her voice breezy, her smile stretched a little too tight. "You are definitely having meatloaf. With buttered noodles." She turns to me. "How was the bird talk?"

The sun is down. The dock is drenched in darkness. My skin is cold.

"We're going bird-watching tomorrow," Adrian says.

And I don't correct him. Because another day with him might give me what I need.

"Oh, Adrian, that sounds so fun." Kristin waits for him to

enter the house, then turns to me. "You know that's not possible, right? He won't remember tomorrow. Not in any reliable way."

"Would it be so bad to take him if we didn't go far? Or even leave the yard?"

Kristin's tone bristles. "He'll want to go into the woods. And when his mind is made up, no matter what state it's in, it's hard to change. He can get hostile. Physically combative when confused. It's best not to put him in that position, or into the woods where he could become lost."

"I understand." I do. But I hate it. "Can I visit?"

She softens again. "Absolutely. As long as it doesn't upset him. It's a day-by-day deal."

"Thanks. For the books too." I pick them up from the hood and slide them into the back seat beside Tara. I brush a hand across her soft blond curls and kiss her forehead.

I notice Adrian has returned and is standing by the door quietly, watching. How long has he been there listening?

Kristin waves.

Adrian waves too. "Have a nice night. And I'm sorry about your dock catching fire. I'm glad it didn't spread to the house. That could've been a nightmare."

My dock? It wasn't the dock—it was the shed.

He pulls an uh-oh face and waves as he disappears inside.

As I drive away, my mind races. Is he confusing events? Has it happened before?

I'll inspect the dock. I'll check the wood. See if it's newer than it should be.

Because something inside me is screaming now, louder than the lies depression whispers.

Something in me knows.

What's happening now…

Has happened before.

And my gut has yet to be wrong.

Chapter Twenty-Four

Cady lets out a low whistle as she stands in the attic, staring at the words carved into the floor.

I AM NOT CRAZY

I AM NOT CRAZY

I AM NOT CRAZY

"Anyone who has to say they aren't crazy this many times, might actually be," she says, squatting down and running her fingers along the jagged lettering. "This must've taken a while."

"Yeah. It's rough—probably done with a screwdriver or something similar. I'm no expert, but I once worked a case where someone carved hearts into victims' legs. No finesse there either."

Cady snorts. "I can't imagine the kinds of crimes you've seen."

I think of Teri Jo Tipton. The way she drowned her children. How she said her ex-boyfriend who still had a key must have come in while she slept and drowned them. I stayed on her like flies on a garbage can. During my on-shift hours and off-shift. I was determined to see her pay for what she did.

I still am, although with this new nightmare, I haven't had

much time to look at her social media account—she only has the one. But I would search it every single night, pulling up any information I could find. Talk to neighbors, old friends, day care and social workers who had been called out but never taken the children away from her.

Steven said the one thing he asked me was to stop thinking about her—Teri Jo.

She doesn't haunt my dreams like she used to—I have new terrors taking up space while I sleep—but I know she did it. Even if I couldn't pin it on her. She's out there. Living. And with a new boyfriend. I saw him too. A lowlife drug dealer.

There she was, two days after giving birth, a cigarette hanging from her mouth, the ashes dangled over the baby girl. And that two-bit dealer boyfriend with a rap sheet was on her doorstep with a bag moving in.

It was only a matter of time before that beautiful baby ended up dead too.

"The worst part is, they get three meals a day, TV time, education. And their victims sleep in the dirt. Their families never get peace. It makes me sick."

"You ever think about doing a podcast on those cases? If this one doesn't work out?"

I shrug. "I don't know what I'm going to do, Cady. I don't feel like I have purpose anymore." All that was taken away, and while I want to blame Kent for going to the captain, and Teri Jo for being a bad mom who killed her kids…no one made me self-medicate the pain of losing my own babies. That's what kills me the most. I did it to myself, and the fallout spilled onto innocent lives.

Cady nods thoughtfully. "You have purpose, Gwen. Do you not want to go back on the force? Shoot, you should steal Ellersby's job out from under him."

I half laugh. I wouldn't dislike being chief of police. But maybe not in this town. "I don't like golf."

Cady laughs. "Yeah, the mayor likes his game."

"Besides, I can't go back to law enforcement." I hang my head in complete shame.

"Why?"

I might as well tell her. She's the only friend I have, and I trust her. Feel a closeness with her that makes no sense since it's only been weeks that I've lived in Cold Harbor. I tell her about my miscarriages and how after delivering a baby girl stillborn, the pain was more than I could bear. They'd given me some pain pills for a previous back injury. "I took them. I kept on taking them. And it cost me my job." I don't go into the fact I stole Steven's prescription pads and forged his name.

That shame is too much to admit.

But he had to step down from his job when it came to light. That or they'd press charges against me.

So here we are. Kent ratted me out about coming to work on pain pills. Teri Jo filed a harassment charge and restraining order. And Steven settled for Nowhere, Maine.

"I'm so sorry, Gwen. Everyone makes mistakes. Some more costly than others, but you won't find judgment here. You'll find grace." She squeezes my hand, which has become her habit. "You get a do-over. Let's figure out this cold case, bring justice where it's due, if we can. And while we do that, you'll figure out what you want to do next. You have time, and Tara will be grown before you know it."

"You're right. Let's quit drowning in my sorrows and see if there's a crime that's gone unpunished."

Cady nods resolutely. "Okay, here's what we know. Brad Langston lived in your house for eight years. His great-grandparents before him. I saw Lana Bernard today. She's been around as long as Methuselah, and she said they moved out in the late '90s—the grandparents." She looks away as if she's holding back information.

"Is that all you know?"

Her top teeth slide across her bottom lip. "Mmm...yeah."

She's lying, but I don't call her out. I am disappointed. Why would she hide something from me? Or maybe I'm just used to people lying to me. "I know the Barkley family died in 1974. And the articles I read said they'd lived here almost ten years, so they must have moved in around '65. Other than the Battersons after them and the Howlers in 1896, we're stuck. After Rebekah was pushed or jumped—did Charles stay in the home? And for how long? Who lived here in the early 1900s? And who moved in after the Batterson home fire in 1980?"

"I'm not sure."

"I asked Deena. Got nothing. Radio silence. Makes me wonder if the chief's told people not to talk."

Cady frowns, then pulls out her phone. I hear it ring before a woman picks up.

"Hey, Mom. Who lived in the house on Darkwater Road before the Langstons?... No, I'm not doing a podcast on the house. What do you mean you can't remember? It's your job to remember." A pause, and then Cady sighs. "Can't someone just be curious about their house's history? You're the historical society president, for crying out loud."

Another pause. "Who? You think someone named Wagner? A first name? Come on, Mom. Think. Okay. Was that so difficult? See you later." She ends the call and lays her phone on the table. "The Wagners. Roger Wagner. Which means late 1980, maybe 1981. I'm not sure if the house sat vacant some years or not. She didn't say. Her mind is fuzzy in her old age without documents to refer to, so she says." But it's clear Cady doesn't believe it. Marcia Tremell doesn't want to remember. Seems like neither did Deena, and Cady did hold back something from me earlier. But now isn't the time to press. I need her resources, and calling her out might shut her up.

"My mom hates anything true crime. Thinks it turns tragedy into entertainment. And to be fair, I get it. My sister vanished, but this isn't about entertainment. I could bring closure to my family. If it turns out that femur was human. I like Wilt, but he has a lot of resentment toward Chief."

She looks away. Her expression shifts—softens. "She blames herself," Cady says quietly. "It was a safe town. Kids biked around, walked home alone. No reason to worry. And yet that mistake meant me never being able to go anywhere alone. Mom picked me up every day, hovered. It drove me crazy—but I understand now. I can't imagine losing a child and not knowing what happened."

My chest tightens. I think of my own parents. Hovering, then holding secretive discussions about me. My teen years were a battlefield. Maybe Cady's were too.

"How old would she be today?"

"Thirty-five."

I nod, mind already spinning. "You know, I visited Dr. Rivera earlier. He said he saw the man who lived in this house bury a woman in the woods."

Cady's eyes widen. "What?"

"He pointed toward my woods—same spot I found disturbed soil. He said it clear as day. People in that house always die." Of course he said my dock caught fire too, so…

"We need to find out more about the Wagners and how long they lived in the house, and the gap between the Howlers and the Barkleys. Wagners shouldn't be hard if it was in the '80s."

Cady crosses her arms, thinking. "We could always take a shot and look through the historical society documents. May not be anything there, but someone might know something. To be honest, I think my mom knows. She's just digging in her heels."

"And what if Adrian's not confused? Alzheimer's patients often remember the distant past better than the recent. What if he did see something? What if someone was buried here?"

"And Ellersby is concealing it to keep from getting the axe? Think the bone could be Candy's after all?"

"If it's an old bone from decades past, revealing the truth wouldn't affect Ellersby's job. But if it's more current, then maybe. Neither option explains the writing on the attic floor. I want to know who was upstairs etching it hour by hour, day by day. It could be the very same person buried in the woods."

"An adolescent, like a girl?"

"Could be. Or even a malnourished petite woman. Even a young boy, but my gut says female. This looks a little too feminine. But messy. The fact Adrian said female too makes me lean on a girl or woman."

"Candy?" She swallows hard. "She was only thirteen. Small. Adolescent."

"I won't rule it out. Not yet."

Cady bites her lip. "Then we fill in the gaps."

I nod. "And maybe we pay a visit to Jean Jackson too. See if the ME's report on that bone holds up. Shake her up a little."

Cady suddenly inhales as if new resolve has filled her sail. "Then we're gonna need a wicked good cup of coffee. I know just the place."

I glance once more at the carved words in the floorboards—jagged and desperate.

I AM NOT CRAZY

The room feels colder now. Heavier. Like we've disturbed something that doesn't want to be remembered.

As we turn to leave the attic, I pause on the threshold as a slow unease curls in the base of my neck and spreads downward.

What if the author of the writing isn't just trying to be heard? What if she's trying to come back?

Chapter Twenty-Five

A baby's cry rips me from a fuzzy nightmare I was already trapped in. I sit bolt upright, gulping air like I'm drowning in it. Sweat clings to me, my thin T-shirt glued to my skin like a second layer I can't peel off.

Steven jolts beside me, groggy. "Gwen, you okay?"

No.

The cries echo—thin, distant, like a pen of lambs bleating before a slaughter. My lungs lock up, refuse to cooperate. Since I showed Cady the attic three days ago, the baby cries have intensified, and my fuzzy nightmares have increased. I can't remember them, but I know with each one, I'm more terrified.

"Hey," he whispers, rubbing circles into my damp back. "Breathe."

"I'm trying," I snap, voice jagged. "I'm having a…a panic attack."

He rolls out of bed, shoves his glasses on. In the bathroom, water runs. When he returns, he's holding a pill and a glass of water. "Take half a Xanax. It'll help you sleep."

But I don't want sleep. When I sleep, I dream. And the

dreams are full of flames and screams and things with too many teeth. He breaks the pill, the powder dusting his palm.

I hesitate.

"Gwen," he says, voice low. "You're not sleeping. You have half-moons under your eyes. Talk to me. I barely see you—"

"You work late every night." I don't mean for it to sound like an accusation, but it is. "So soon. Already."

His jaw ticks. "I'm trying to settle in. Meet people. Reggie's helping me ease into the community. People don't trust big-city doctors off the bat. I'm doing the best I can."

I know. I do. But knowing doesn't make me feel any less alone. He's pouring himself into work, and I'm supposed to pour myself into this house. But this house is draining me dry.

"I'm sorry," I say. "I heard a baby cry, Steven."

"We've been over this."

I clench my fists so tight the crescent moons of my nails press into my palms. "I know what I heard. There's something wrong with this place. I know I picked it. I know I insisted. But something evil happened here. I feel it in the floors, in the walls, in the silence."

He draws back slightly, shoulders tight. I'm scaring him. Good. Maybe he'll finally listen.

"I found something," I say. "And I didn't show you."

"What?"

"A room. Behind the closet under the stairs. A kid's room. Hidden."

He frowns, already rationalizing. "Could've been a playroom. A hideout. Something fun."

Always logic. Always an answer with clean edges. But I don't think this place is interested in clean edges. This house is a wound that keeps reopening.

"You're probably right," I say, hollow.

That satisfies him. My heart's still pounding like I'm prey

in the brush and something with teeth is sniffing me out. My hands won't stop trembling.

"Do you still want this?" He holds out the pill.

"No."

He nods, takes it back to the bathroom, locks it in the box I don't know the code to. That's the point.

When he returns, he pulls me close. But his arms aren't safe anymore. They're a cage. When he starts snoring, I slip out from under him and pad over to the bassinet. Tara rests, small and perfect. Untouched by all this.

Downstairs, the kitchen feels off. I can't shake the image of that child fading into the island—like she was never there to begin with. Still, I need something warm, something to hold on to. I start the kettle and drop a tea bag into a chipped mug.

Outside, the shed is a blackened skeleton. How long before they say it was faulty wiring? Before someone buries the truth beneath red tape and small-town favors?

I need proof. But what if I find it? Will anyone believe me? Or will I end up scribbled into the margins of town lore as the local crazy?

The kettle clicks off.

And that's when I see it.

Movement.

A figure standing under the pine near the dock. Moonlight outlines it, distorts it. It's holding something jagged—like a saw or a blade. It's not moving. Just watching.

I snatch a knife from the block and throw open the sunroom door.

But the figure is gone. Like it never existed. Like it stepped out of a nightmare and dissolved into the shadows.

I'm barefoot. Shivering. Out here in a sweat-soaked T-shirt like a final girl in a slasher film who should've known better.

Back inside, I slam the door and lock it, heart thundering.

My phone lights up.

A text from Cady. It's nearly 3:00 a.m.

Deena Richardson is dead.

Chapter Twenty-Six

Deena is dead.

It might sound more ominous than it is—but if it was just something like a heart attack, why alert me at this hour?

I ignore the steaming cup of tea beside me and immediately call Cady. She answers on the first ring.

"I was hoping you'd be awake," she says quickly, a breathless edge to her voice. "But if not, I didn't want to call and wake the baby."

"You don't need to worry about that." My throat tightens. "What's going on?"

"A couple found her in the woods. On a hiking trail. She apparently tripped and hit her head on a rock—died instantly. Mom called me at one this morning and told me. Ronald, Deena's husband, reported her missing. They sent out a search party but came up empty. Then some teenagers out canoodling stumbled across her."

"That'll be the last time they do that—in the woods."

Cady snorts softly, but half-heartedly. "I just… I can't believe it."

"It is tragic. I'm so sorry. I know she was your mom's best friend."

"No, I mean—yeah, it is tragic. But what I was saying is I literally can't believe it. Deena Richardson's idea of a hike was waddling from her recliner to the pantry for a sleeve of crackers. I'm not trying to be cruel, I'm just being honest. She hated the outdoors—unless it was her outdoor kitchen, and even then, she barely used it."

She has a point. The day Deena brought me that welcome basket, she was practically wheezing from the slope in the yard. A hike through the woods? At night? It doesn't fit.

"But that's not all," Cady says, voice intensifying.

"What are you, an infomercial for criminal acts?"

She laughs again—shorter this time, almost forced. "Deena came into the coffee shop last night. Dressed in a pantsuit and flats. Sun's down by six. By the time she got home, changed clothes and went out? It would've been pitch-black. Nobody heads into the woods after nightfall unless they're up to something shady…or steamy."

I glance toward the windows, toward the hulking black trees beyond the yard. A cold thread winds its way down my back.

"So, what do you think really happened to Deena?"

"I don't know. Nothing good. And with a bone found in the woods…this can't be a coincidence. If Jean Jackson fudged the results on the femur, it makes me wonder if she's the ME for Deena too."

"Not to mention Deena refused to talk to me about this house. What if she wanted to and someone silenced her?" A cold flush spreads through my veins.

"The writing on the floor? Do you think it happened in the '70s because of the avocado-green color of the shag you ripped up?"

"Not necessarily." I grip the phone tighter. "Someone could

have laid it much later. People keep old things. I'm not sold on Brad Langston anymore. Not ruling him out either."

"You know where I stand on the Langstons. I told you they were good people."

"Good people can do bad things, Cady. I think whoever etched that writing into the attic floor did it a long time ago. Doesn't mean it was immediately carpeted over. Maybe it's been up there for decades for anyone to see and nobody cared." But she cared. Who could live with that kind of mystery and not ask questions, seek answers?

Millions. People buried their heads in the sand and turned blind eyes every single day. Shutting out torment, pain and evil like they didn't exist. Maybe whoever found it first put the lock on the door, sealed the attic and never went up again. Out of sight. Out of mind. Someone else's tragic past. Not their business or concern.

Cady slurps something on the other end—coffee or maybe something stronger. It derails my train of thought for a moment.

"I do," she says. "I care. And you do."

"We're on to something," I murmur. "Don't you think?"

"I think we're standing knee-deep in something sinister with no solid ground. We don't have proof a body was buried in your woods. Adrian saw something, but what or when is uncertain. We don't know Deena was murdered. And we can't prove the chief asked Jean to fake the report. What we do have? Weird carvings. A secret room. And a trail of coincidences."

"Okay." I exhale. "Let's both try to get a little sleep. I'm going to look into the Wagners today. Probably going to buff living room floors too."

"Ooh, adulting. When I get off work, I'll text you. I'd love to dig through this mess with you. I'll do some quiet digging on Deena too. Mom's grief might make her more open to talking."

I feel a flicker of warmth. Cady gets me. Doesn't judge.

Of course, she doesn't know everything about me either.

"I'd actually love that," I say. "So, are you going to gather all your facts before starting the podcast—or are you going to *Only Murders in the Building* it?"

"Please, that show ran off pure speculation." She slurps again. "And it was TV. They couldn't get sued. Fictionally, I guess." A sigh. "Gah, I'm going to be dragging all day. Wonder where I can get a good, strong coffee to keep me vertical."

I laugh softly. "Hmm. No clue."

She chuckles. "Text you later."

After the call, I dump the now-cold tea in the sink and stare into the blackness outside. The trees sway like mourners. The moonlight's thin and watery, stretching across the backyard and the glassy surface of the harbor.

Someone was out there. By the pines. I'm almost sure of it.

There's no point going back to bed. Not now.

It's time to see what I can uncover about the Wagners.

If I still had anyone in Baltimore who trusted me, I'd have a proper background check run. But I burned those bridges.

Well. Most of them.

I could call Kent. I could. Even if he betrayed me.

But I won't. Sometimes reaching out turns into reaching in. And reaching in? That's where the danger really starts.

What I'm doing now? It's already a kind of reaching in.

And it may have cost Deena Richardson her life.

The real question is—

Will it cost me mine?

Chapter Twenty-Seven

As the sun rises over the dense forest in shades of blush and lavender, I'm already on my fourth cup of coffee with nothing to show for it. I've dug through every Roger Wagner I can find on Facebook—dozens of them—but without a photo, I'm just guessing. I narrowed it down to men who might be in their mid-fifties to mid-seventies. Only three live in Maine. I've looked up news articles and checked archives, but Roger Wagner and his family didn't seem to be at all newsworthy.

I've also searched every report of missing girls around Acadia National Park in the last fifty years, starting at age thirteen—Candy Tremell's age when she vanished. Only a few cases came up. I may need to go back further. I have no idea how long ago that bone was buried in the woods—or if it was human. But Candy Tremell went missing about thirty years ago. For all I know, hundreds of bodies are buried out there.

What I really need is access to the NCIC—National Crime Information Center—Missing Persons File. But civilians aren't allowed access.

Kent Masters could do it. I'm not that desperate yet.

Steven is up. His footsteps cause creaks above me. I make another pot of coffee so his will be fresh. I'm trying. He just doesn't see it. And I suppose he's trying too. No, he is. In his way.

He clomps down the stairs in his sweats and a long-sleeved T-shirt, heading straight for the coffee like clockwork. In an hour, he'll lace up and run six miles before getting ready for work.

"How long have you been up?" He heads for the coffeepot. It hasn't beeped but he'll pour what he can. He's predictable.

"Couple hours." Or three. "Dining room table comes today, and some new fixtures. Going to install them." In between my search for missing girls and Roger Wagner. Might even take a trip to the historical society.

"I know this house has revealed some oddities—like the attic floor—but overall, don't you think it's peaceful? I see so much potential." He hands me my anxiety pill since I've beaten him out of bed this morning.

I want to quote *The Sixth Sense.* "I see dead people." But that will go over like a lead balloon, and I'm not sure I'm seeing dead people at all. My brain is glitching, and it's more concerning each day. I'd check the anxiety meds to see if Steven's prescribed new ones, but they're locked up, and only Steven has the key and code. He leaves a pill by the coffeepot each morning. Just one. He's not taking any chances on me relapsing.

"I do love the fresh air." When it's not smoke-laden. Fire chief called yesterday, and the shed had faulty wiring. I'm not buying that. Someone set my shed on fire. Can't argue with the fire department though. Steven wouldn't buy that.

Or maybe it did go up in flames on its own. I'm second-guessing everything I see and think.

He sips his coffee, studying me, trying to reach inside my mind and heart, but he won't be able to. I don't allow full access to those places, and he'd have a breakdown if he knew my new thoughts, saw what I've been seeing.

"Town's hosting a spooky movie marathon on the outdoor

screens this weekend. Bonfire and cider. I think it's the classic *Wolf Man*, *Dracula* and *Frankenstein*. You game?"

I have enough monsters circling my life right now. "Maybe."

He puts his coffee on the table. "Gwen, I've hesitated bringing this up, but at some point, that attic floor needs to be buffed or have new wood laid. I can rent a buffer and handle it this weekend."

Steven is right. I can't leave the attic covered in the writing of someone who tipped over the edge of sanity. But buffing it out or ripping it up feels a lot like letting it go, pretending someone wasn't terrified—due to reality or a mental break or someone causing their madness. Too many people have fallen victim in this house—to this house? An innate sense of justice compels me to search out the truth, bring it to light. Expose the darkness.

It's nearly impossible to explain. I don't have the words to describe the drive, the frenzied need to find truth, declare it, make it known. Something deep within me says that if I bring the darkness of this house to light, I'll be free. I just have no clue what I'll be free from. My own darkness? The shameful secrets that lurk inside me too?

"I'm not sure the writing can be buffed out. We can try. If you want to rent a buffer, go for it. I just haven't had time." Haven't *made* time, but we can't leave the written jagged pain on the wood forever. At some point, it needs to be smoothed out, with fresh flooring laid. But it won't erase the memory; that's imprinted in the house forever.

I think of the chickadees—how they shed old memories like feathers, making space for new ones. Maybe that's why they seem so weightless. There's freedom in the way they flit from branch to branch, trust in their eyes, joy in the beat of their tiny wings.

Not like the crows.

The oppressive birds hold on.

Remember every slight, every wound. Their eyes are charged

with distrust, thick with old grudges. They carry their past like a second skeleton—always there, just beneath the surface. And I wonder which I'm becoming. The one who forgives and flies, or the one who circles back, again and again, unable to let go, growing larger and darker and casting looming shadows over every inch of light.

Steven quietly drinks his coffee, then speaks, startling me from my thoughts. "Do you remember that year we carved a pumpkin and I ended up having to give you three stitches?" He laughs.

I haven't thought of that in ages. Funny how the good times get buried under everything else—the hard moments, the ones that linger longer than they should. It only takes a small nudge to bring the good ones back, though. And when they surface, they shine. They pull a laugh out of me I didn't know was waiting.

God knows I could use more of those.

"I do." We'd been married about a year, still full of bright hopes and dreams of a perfect little family. Steven had bought two pumpkins and big bags of candy—the good kind—to hand out to trick-or-treaters. Turned out I wasn't much of a carver. "I still have a scar," I tell him. "It's faint, but it's there if you really look."

I suppose that's true of all scars, inside and out. If you peer closely enough, there's always evidence—of pain, of trauma, of dreams lost somewhere along the way.

I wonder…if we scrub away the strange, unsettling things written in the attic, will the house still carry its scars too? Will they fade, or just settle deeper into the walls where only those who know where to look can see them?

Steven takes my hand and stares at my scarred finger, then gently kisses it. "I love you scars and all, Gwen. I always have."

I want to believe it's possible.

But it's hard when I carry the weight of everything I've done.

I wish I could set those memories down somewhere and walk away. Just let them go, clear the space they take up inside me.

Maybe then I could give him everything.

All of me. Even the parts I've kept hidden, the ones I've never trusted anyone with.

Not because he doesn't deserve them—he does.

But because I'm afraid of what he'll see when I finally let him in.

"I love you too." And I mean it. I love Steven. But that doesn't erase the ways I've hurt him—or the ways he's hurt me. Maybe we'll find our way back to each other. I hope we do.

But I don't have a road map for healing. It's a rough road, full of sharp turns and unmarked paths. You need someone who knows the terrain, someone you trust to lead.

And trust…well, that's where I come up short.

So instead, I change the subject.

Fear keeps me quiet. It wraps itself around my thoughts, making them too heavy to speak aloud. I want to give them to him—share the load—but I can't.

"I'd like to see about a sitter for Tara. I can take her shopping, but I'd rather not. I could move faster without her." I hesitate, waiting for Steven to bristle. He eyes me for longer than I'd like, but then he acquiesces.

"If you'll feel better and it makes your day smoother, then call Teresa. If she can't, one of my receptionists at the office is off today. I could call her. Lynn. Remember? You met her."

The perky and pretty brunette. Mid-twenties. "Yeah." I text Teresa to ask if she would be interested in sitting this afternoon if she doesn't have many listings. I don't see how she could. It's not a big town, and the entire company she works for is three people. Her, the owner and the admin assistant.

She doesn't respond right away, but it's early.

Finally, she does and says she's free from noon to five. "Teresa can come. I'll tell her to let the delivery guys in to put the table in the dining room."

Steven nods, but his jaw is tight. He doesn't like me getting babysitters, and he's always the one who chooses who may watch Tara. He's careful. Cautious. I understand why. Still, I wish he'd be more into the baby. But I can't force him to love her like I do, to need her like I do. She makes me feel useful, and Steven still has his career.

I don't think he's ever actually wanted children. His own father walked out on him and his mother after an affair with an eighteen-year-old he knocked up. He started a new life, and Steven was no longer a part of it. He didn't marry the girl, but he left them for her until she miscarried. Then he left her too.

But he never did go back home to Steven and his mother. The damage had been done. Steven hasn't spoken to his father since the day he walked out, though he tried a few times and was met with rejection.

At sixteen he had to take care of the family, be the man, and he has never forgiven his father for crushing them, abandoning his marital vows and his responsibility as a father. Steven says children aren't that important and we can be happy without them. I think he's afraid of hurting one. Disappointing them. He knows that pain. He's never admitted this to me, but he's also never told me no to having a child. It's not like I had to trick him to get pregnant.

It's because of this deep-seated belief Steven has about marriage that he even stays with me, I'm convinced.

And it's why there are some things about me he can *never* know. Because I don't want him to leave me.

Chapter Twenty-Eight

Cady is holding her purse and waiting on me when I arrive. "Where's little bit?" She hugs me tight. Her eyes are red-rimmed. Deena Richardson had been a second mother to her.

"Tara? She's with Teresa. I think this calls for no little bits." But I love that she's already given her a nickname, and something hovers at the edge of my memory. I pause, trying to make it come, but it's blurry.

That's not your name.

My chest tightens, and my insides flush like I've been on prednisone.

"You okay?" Cady asks.

"Yeah. Just…something's off. Since the day we moved in, I've felt like I'm standing just a little outside myself. Like the house doesn't quite want me there. Now Deena's dead, and it's suspicious at best. I'm so sorry, Cady."

She hugs me again. "Me too. It's awful. Ron is a mess. The kids too." She blows a heavy breath. "But no one seems to think it's odd, so maybe she did take walks in the woods regularly."

I let it go. She's hunting for a solid reason in her grief, and I give her that.

"More noises?" she says abruptly as if thinking of my horror show is easier than dwelling on her own pain. And I give her that too.

"Yes. They wake me most nights—but it has to be my imagination." Right? "Otherwise Steven would wake up too."

But he doesn't. He sleeps right through it.

Because nothing's happening.

Not to him. Only to me.

There's a shadow—drifting, curling through the air like it belongs there.

Some days, I can almost ignore it.

Other days, it wraps around me like a second skin.

Cady hugs me yet again, and I melt into it—because I can't remember the last time a friend hugged me. The last time I had a real friend. I hug her back and smile.

"You're my favorite person in this town, Cady. I'm glad I met you."

She grins. "I am pretty awesome. Or that's what my employees say—all two of them."

We leave the coffee shop and head toward the furniture store near Michaud's Hardware. Everything in Cold Harbor is within walking distance, and the air smells like the sea, pastries, soy candles and coffee. I want to love this town. I really do. But I don't. Not yet. Maybe not ever.

As we step inside the store, the scents of furniture polish and fresh wood greet us. A salesperson approaches almost immediately. Her name tag reads Barbara. She's probably in her fifties, maybe early sixties, and her smile is as bright as the noonday sun.

"Hi, Cady."

Cady waves. "Hi, Barb."

"I was so sorry to hear about Deena. I texted your mother to give her my condolences."

"Thank you. It's...hard to process."

Barb pats her shoulder and turns to me.

"Gwen McDaniel. Me and my husband just moved here."

"Oh, I know. We all know. So happy to have you. How can I help you?"

"I'm looking for an end table and an ottoman. But I don't know exactly what I want. I'm hoping it will jump out and tell me." I smile, but the wattage doesn't begin to match Barbara's.

"Well, sometimes it simply needs to sing. You walk on through, and if it does, you call me on over."

I nod, then pause. "Barb, have you lived here your whole life?"

"Oh, yes. Grew up right here in Cold Harbor and took over the family business. Once Cold Harbor's in you, it doesn't let go."

She's grinning, a twinkle in her eye, but to me, it feels… ominous. Like Cold Harbor has claws—and they're already in me, sinking deep, drawing blood with their death grip.

Cady has her own business too—gifted from her parents—but the truth still stands. Cold Harbor clings to her, the same way it clings to Barb. And the Michauds.

No one leaves.

No one wants to.

Except me.

Now that I'm actually here. "Did you know any of the former owners of my house on Darkwater Road? Before the Langstons?"

Barb's mouth forms a perfect O.

"Roger Wagner?" I prompt.

"Why on earth would you want to know about him? He's been gone for some time."

Finally someone actually knows something. "Just wanting to get a feel for the history of the house. History interests me." I shrug.

Barb's lips pinch, but she keeps her inner monologue to herself. "Roger was a nice man. Architect, I believe. He and his wife, Ann, and daughter…um…what was her name? I think she was in kindergarten when they moved here. Anyway the house sat vacant for about two years after DJ Batterson lit his parents on fire and went to prison. That boy was a right menace. But Roger, being an architect, didn't see a problem with fixing the place up and making some additions like the sunroom, and I think he built that shed, if I remember right."

"Do you know much about his wife? His little girl?"

"His wife, Ann, died when the girl…" She snapped her fingers. "Lily Ann. That was her name. When she was about fourteen or so? But she ran away when she was fifteen I think. Rumors were she was troubled. Probably due to losing her mom."

"And Ann Wagner. How did she die? Was she sick?" Mentally ill?

Barb opens her mouth, then closes it again, like she's weighing her words.

"Well, I think she had a stroke, and at such a young age. She was a homebody, and they were private people—like most who've lived in your house."

I'm not exactly an open book myself.

"Poor Lily Ann. No girl should be without a mom in a perfect world," Barbara says.

No, they shouldn't—unless their mom was someone like Teri Jo Tipton. Then distance was a gift. A necessity.

"I don't know if Roger ever found his daughter or not. Never talked about it that I know of. But he moved."

"Do you know when?"

"Oh…" Barb taps a nail against her front teeth, thinking. "It was '96, maybe, or '97. It's been a long time."

"Of course." But we have names now. We have years. Yes, there were still gaps, but we might be closer to finding the girl upstairs.

"What is this for again?"

I shrug. "I love that the house is practically a historical landmark. I'm thinking about documenting the history—maybe making a book."

It's a stretch. But if this were an interrogation room, it'd pass. Fair game.

Barb tilts her head toward Cady. "Ask your mother. She'd know more about the house's past if there's something to know. And I suppose all homes have histories—and mysteries."

She snickers at her rhyme. I toss out a customer-service laugh in return.

"But your house does have an interesting history," she adds. "Lot of tragedy and terror. Starting with Mayor Howler and his wife, Rebekah."

"People say it's just a story about her jumping or being pushed."

"Well, we'll never know that truth of how she went out that window, but he was the mayor, she was his wife, and he had a mistress."

That was new information. Rumor or true?

"All that is true and can be read in the library. Poor Rebekah suffered from depression, but back then they called it melancholy."

"Do you know the story, the truth?"

She leans in a little, eyes glinting. "Mayor Charles Howler locked his wife, Rebekah, in the attic after bringing his mistress to live in the house. That is lore but feels true."

Except there is a lock on the outside of the attic door, and it could be as old as the house. I can't be sure.

"It drove Rebekah mad—but the mistress lost her mind first. One Halloween, she crept upstairs and pushed Rebekah to her death. They say you can still hear her shrieking at midnight." She laughs again, delighted with herself. "You won't find that in any article. Some versions of the story say he pushed her.

Some say she jumped. But they were real people, and after Rebekah died in the early 1900s, Charles and his mistress lived in that house until they died. I don't remember exactly when."

A thin thread of unease winds through me, tugging at something quiet and buried.

What if she's still here—Rebekah? Wandering the halls. Her and that pigtailed little girl who might be Lizzie Barkley.

Could that really be possible?

Maybe.

More likely?

I'm coming undone.

"I've been out to the house on Halloween. Never heard a scream, but we sure scared ourselves silly."

Barb laughs. "We did too. Never did see any ghosts."

Cady looks at me. "But there is some truth to that story after all."

Someone in that house didn't think they were crazy or needed to write it to believe they weren't. Could it have been the Barkley woman? Rebekah Howler? Ann Wagner? Or could it have been one of the men who seemed to act irrationally? It could even have been the Batterson boy. I'd been assuming it was a woman.

It could have been a man.

How much more history will I find on this place? And as Barb said, do I want to know it?

Chapter Twenty-Nine

Cady and I walk along the riverfront, the cold wind tugging at our hair, forcing us to huddle against it, but it feels good. The bite of it reminds me I'm alive—and maybe on to something here.

"What do you think? Just scary stories, or a sinister past to the house that's leaked down through generations of owners?" I ask.

"I think either would make for a great podcast. Not to profit off anyone's misfortune, but people are always intrigued by the histories of old homes—what's happened in them, what's been left behind. But if you're saying the house is cursed, I don't buy it. I don't believe in luck, good or bad."

I sip my cider—fresh from the stand between the White Pine Cone and Tandy's Candies. If Halloween downtown wasn't already unmistakable, it really isn't now. Life-sized skeletons hang from lampposts, their bones rattling in the wind. Wrought-iron gates draped with fake bats flicker with dim orange lights. Every corner seems to hold something that grins, something that watches.

"Neither do I. But why do some houses carry such grim histories while others don't? Can a house draw in certain kinds of people? I was drawn to it." I can't believe I'm admitting this.

As we turn in to the town square, huge jack-o'-lanterns sit on the steps of the old courthouse, their carved faces glowing with flickering candlelight, casting long shadows across the cobblestones. Above us, the skeletal branches of the trees look like reaching hands, their twisted shapes silhouetted against the dimming sky.

Cady slurps her cider, then sighs. "I don't know. What do you mean you were drawn to it?"

"Can I share something? Off the record?"

With a laugh, Cady reminds me that she's not a reporter, and I'm not a cop. But to go ahead.

"I found this house two years ago, just browsing Maine real estate, houses, looking through Zillow at neighboring properties and Google satellite images. I kind of just fixated on it. Sat with it. Imagined how I'd renovate it, how it would feel to live in this small town. Quiet. Serene. I pictured Steven and me hiking through the woods, raising kids with no devices in their faces. Outdoors, all the time. I saved it, went back to it over and over. And then, one day, out of nowhere, it was on the market. My heart just—jumped in my throat. I called Steven, told him I'd found a house."

"You moved because of the house?" Cady's disbelief is obvious.

"No. We had to move." And I share about the depression from earlier miscarriages and then I decide to unload the rest that I held back earlier. And I tell her about Teri Jo Tipton and Steven's prescription pads, but I still hold back part of my past. I can't bring myself to share all my sins. "That's why I had to leave the job. We had to move. We were done there."

"Gwen, I'm so sorry. I can't imagine how hard this has been on you. Why Maine? Were you also drawn to Maine?"

"No. Well, yes. When I was a little girl, we vacationed in

Acadia National Park. When I hit my late thirties and my final parent passed, I realized that my childhood memories grew dimmer each day. My last strong memory was camping in the woods. Fishing in the lakes. After that…time robbed me of vivid memories with Mom and Dad. At least from childhood. I started thinking about that time here and I looked up Maine, looked at small towns around Acadia National Park. Cold Harbor popped up. Idyllic. Perfect."

An utter lie.

"Nothing has been perfect. Quite the opposite of what I'd built up in my head."

We walk a few moments in silence, sipping drinks.

Finally, Cady speaks. "Sometimes, we see something, and we fixate on it—dreaming about all the possibilities it holds. We think it's going to change us, make us new, give us hope. We build it up so high in our minds, it becomes like… I don't know…a kind of sanctuary. A place of worship. But then, when we finally get there, when we bow to it, it's nothing like we imagined. We're disillusioned. Maybe the trouble you were having in your marriage faded when you poured yourself into the house—when you dreamed about it, dreamed about being here. But now that you are…you're still left with the same discord. The same pain, the same empty promises. And now… you have regrets."

I ponder on Cady's profound words, especially for someone so young.

Is that what I did? Saw a house in a place near where I vacationed, a place of anticipated joy, and let it draw me away from the reality I was facing in Baltimore? When opportunity knocked, I didn't even consider other options but walked right into darkness. Mistaking it for light. My reality didn't change for the better, but added new frustrations and fear.

I can't deny I'm afraid of the house.

Which sounds like a three-year-old afraid to turn off a nightlight. But the light is what drives away darkness.

My home is a plague of it, so thick it's almost tangible, tasteable…unsettling.

"You're right, Cady. I did think our life could be picture-perfect here—because everything about this place looked perfect. But that's all it was. A photograph. A dream. We walked in with all our brokenness and just opened a new door. Painting the walls doesn't make it new. It only hides what's underneath. And that's the thing—it's all still there, just buried. Never really gone. That's exactly how these strange discoveries feel. Like they've been lingering the whole time, waiting to resurface."

As much as I may want to see justice for a potential victim or victims, I think I believe that solving the puzzle will quiet the house. Quiet me.

It strikes me how much I'm like this house—secrets tucked deep in the walls of my heart, brokenness and decay disguised as age, when really it's just neglect. A lack of care. Of maintenance. What once felt vibrant has faded, not with time, but with forgetting how to tend to it. My own turbulent history lurking within my veins, coming out in ways that scare me, hurt others.

I am this house.

And I have no idea why or how to fix me. I collapse on a bench as a flutter catches my eye. One of the little black-capped chickadees lies near a tree, its wing weakly flapping and its chirps faint.

My heart aches for the broken bird. I can't explain it, but I know these three birds I keep seeing are the same ones, and they've been a comforting presence when I acknowledge them. To think that one is on the precipice of dying sends a sharp ache into my chest. Gasping, I rush to the light pole and kneel, but there's nothing I can do to help him. Nothing to do but watch him fade away. It's like he stares up at me and there is no fear in his eyes. He's calm like he knows something I don't.

I glance up and see the other two birds. One is perched on the tip-top of the light post. The other hovers halfway down, as if studying the broken bird on the pavement.

Slowly, the fallen bird chirps once more. Then his wing flutters to a stop.

He's gone.

I can't explain why this strikes me with such force and grief, but tears spill from my eyes for this bird. It shouldn't be this way. This death feels so wrong. What did he do? Who did he harm? He brought nothing but joy and peace and friendship.

Yet he is gone. Like Deena Richardson. And I can't help but feel the pain of that too. What if I got her killed and it was no accident? Her family is grieving her either way. Cady too. Though she laughs and talks, the sadness and loss are in her eyes, haunting her. Deena was like a second mother to her.

"Gwen?" Cady lightly touches my shoulder. "Are you okay?"

"No. No, I'm not." I'm crying over a bird. I'm broken myself. "I don't think I've been okay in very long time."

Cady hugs me. It's tight, warm and everything I need. "Here's the rub, Gwen. Broken things can be mended. Healed. And made whole. I'm a person of faith. Even when things go sideways, I believe God can fix you when no one and nothing else can."

After I give her a quick squeeze back to signify I'm done hugging, she lets me go, and I stare at the bird one last time.

"We should be heading to the historical society," Cady gently says.

"I guess we should."

As I step back, the bird's wing flutters—slow at first, then stronger. His midnight eyes snap open and, just like that, he lifts off. As if he was never injured. Not dead, just resting. In an instant, he's in the air, wings slicing through the sky, chirping loud and clear. And somehow, everything that felt wrong a moment ago feels a little more right.

If he can rise again, maybe I can too.

Me.

My marriage.

This aching, splintered heart.

"Well, I didn't see that coming," Cady says through a laugh. "What a wonder to behold."

She's nailed it. A wonder. To be dead and then alive. Reanimated to take flight and be who you were meant to be.

Tucking her arm in mine, she pulls me close. "I never knew my sister, but I kind of feel like God gave me you. Can I say that after a month or so?" She grins, and I lay my head on hers.

"I feel the same way. I always wanted a sister."

My wings might not be quite as broken as I thought.

Chapter Thirty

The Cold Harbor Historical Society Center is a stunning 12,000-square-foot brick estate perched on a gentle hill overlooking the town and harbor beyond. Ivy curls up the corners of the building, and tall arched windows reflect the light like glass in a cathedral. Inside, polished wood floors stretch beneath high ceilings, and ornate crown molding lines the rooms with quiet elegance. Open Monday through Friday and Sunday afternoons, it offers museum tours that trace the layered, sometimes haunting, history of Cold Harbor. But it also doubles as an event space—and I can see why. The manicured gardens, wrought iron balconies and sweeping staircases feel like something out of a dream. I'd get married here in a heartbeat.

"It's a sight for a small town, but it is rich in history," Cady says as we stand inside, catching the whiff of the past and hints of berries. "I sound like my mother."

"Is your mom full-time?"

"She is. Gives her purpose and keeps her busy. She has rheumatoid arthritis and can't go up all three stories like she used to, but she never misses a day. She's a woman who loves the past, but hers is ripe with tragedy. I don't think I could spend all day dealing with what happened before—not knowing what happened to Candy."

I notice how Cady is only one letter shy of Candy, and something in my chest tightens.

She was the daughter born to replace the one who vanished. That's a heavy kind of inheritance—to grow up in the faded light of a ghost.

I wonder if she's ever felt it.

Or if she still does.

What did happen to Candy Tremell?

"Have you ever looked into Candy's disappearance prior to now?" With her love of true crime and solving mysteries, I'd find it surprising if she hasn't.

"Yes, but there isn't much to go on. No one saw anything. Not a lurker or anyone bothering her at school. No pervy teacher, and my parents can't talk about it. It's too painful. I did once ask Deena about my sister, and she started sobbing. She was her godmother." Her voice breaks talking of Deena. "The only thing she managed to say was that it changed my mom, robbed her of a piece of her soul. I would have liked to have known who she was before."

"I get that." I never met my babies I lost, but I know they were a piece of my soul, ripped away, changing me with each devastation. Marcia and I have that in common. She at least had thirteen years with Candy.

"But she never speculated as to what she thought might have happened?"

I study the framed black-and-white photographs that line the walls—sepia-toned portraits of stern-faced townsfolk and long-gone storefronts. Everything feels preserved in time, reverent and still, as though the walls themselves are holding their breath, listening, but not like the way the walls of my home seem to breathe.

"Not to me. Maybe to Deena. When I was younger, I imagine she didn't want to scare me. As I got older, I think she didn't want to let her mind wander to scary scenarios, so I stopped asking. No point contributing to pain, you know?"

"I definitely do." I don't need my mind to go there either. I've seen the aftermath of abductions, and it's chilling. Heartbreaking. Soul-crushing.

"Also, she's specifically asked me not to podcast it."

I pause as we stand in front of a table with the history of Cold Harbor's origin. "In that area. What do you mean?"

Cady leans on the table, though it explicitly says not to. "I'm adopted."

This is news to me. Surprising news. "Oh. I had no idea."

She shrugs. "I forget about it most of the time, to be honest. I've always been known as Cady Tremell, belonging to the Tremells. But I was adopted four years after Candy went missing. I uploaded my DNA and information to an ancestry website about three months ago, hoping to find my biological history—parents, family. So far it's been crickets."

Adopted. My stomach knots.

"And your mom doesn't want you to find them?"

Cady folds her arms over her chest. "No. She hasn't said that explicitly, but she's my mom, and Curt is my dad. Since I was born. I think it would feel like disrespect to her. Like I'm not grateful. So I did it quietly."

"What will you do if a match pops?"

Cady shrugs again. "Reach out. See if they want to meet me. I have no real expectation. I just would like to know."

She deserves to know. I take a more scrutinized look at Cady. Her jawline, the straight nose and thick lips, eye shape. Definitely doesn't look like Curt Tremell, but oddly, she could pass as Marcia's daughter. I've seen that before. Adopted babies looking like their adoptive parents.

"Maybe you'll find a match. For now, we have my house

to look into, the house that harbors dark secrets and lingering wickedness." I'm making light to mask the dread pooling in my gut. "Where do we even start?" I automatically whisper as we stare at a massive staircase.

"Archives. Historic homes are on the second floor. We might end up having a better shot at microfiche from the library. I'm hoping to catch Mom and just ask. She came into work to keep from thinking about Deena. The family is a mess. But they all seem to believe she died accidentally. No one, not even Ron, is hinting at foul play. So maybe…maybe it wasn't." She waves over a young woman who looks frazzled and in desperate need of a shampoo that helps with frizz.

"Cady, good to see you. What's up? I was so sorry to hear about Deena. I took a hot dish to Ron's earlier today. You holding up?"

"Hi, Elle. Thank you. And yes. Best we can. Funeral arrangements are being made. This is my friend Gwen. We're interested in the history of the house on Darkwater Road. Would you by chance know anything about its past?"

Elle shakes my hand, and even the vigor in it feels frantic. "You trying to confirm which stories about Rebekah Howler are true as All Hallows Eve approaches?"

"We're trying to determine if Rebekah Howler had melancholy and if she died by suicide or was pushed, yes," Cady says.

"She was real and fell to her death from the attic. It is true that Charles had a mistress—Annabeth Lemont. Rebekah did have depression. She did several stints in the asylum, and he took Annabeth into his arms and into the home while Rebekah was in the insane asylum from 1897 to 1898. Her story is filled with heartbreak and tragedy. She was quite younger than Charles and hoped to give him a son—a legacy—but she lost all her babies. Five in all, if it's true she was pregnant when she jumped, if she did. That could be rumor along with who pushed her, Charles or Annabeth. Either way, her losses—I believe—led to her being locked away, depression. It's said Charles kept Rebekah in the attic and away from people because of her strange behavior."

"What kind of strange behavior?" I ask.

"An old diary states she often sang lullabies wherever she went—in public or private. She once took a child from the general store. Her mother had gone inside to shop. They of course brought her back safely."

My stomach knots again.

Elle continues, her purple retro frames sliding down the long slope of her nose. "Honestly, I think a lot of her bizarre behavior was simply depression over the loss of her children. Annabeth became pregnant, and that sent Rebekah into a spiral. Charles was going to return her to the asylum on a Monday, but she fell to her death that Halloween night, which had been on a Saturday. More rumors circled that Annabeth pushed her, or Charles, because neither wanted to spend the money on an institute. But there was no proof or trial. So we'll never know for sure. Charles did admit to locking her in the attic for her own good, to keep her—and others—safe after she brought the toddler home from the general store."

"What do you think happened?" Cady asks.

Elle cocks her head. "I think she was a lonely, miserable, depressed woman, and she ended her own life rather than going back to an asylum that was known for being understaffed and overcrowded. The methods back then, too, were outrageous. Abuse, even. She saw no other way out but to end it, and if she was locked in the attic, jumping from the window was her only escape."

Cady and I exchange glances. We're both thinking about the lost babies and the cries I'm hearing. "Any other foreboding stories about the house, even rumors? Do you know who lived in the house after Charles?"

Elle nods. "Oh, yes." She pulls up a website on her iPad. "We have most of the history digitalized, especially your house since it's as old as it is." She taps on the screen and swipes a few times. "He lived there for fifty years. Annabeth passed on too. Their child also died. Polio. In 1947, a young family moved in. The Randalls. Darwin, Jenny and... Louise, Betty and Dianna."

"Any tragedies? Deaths?"

"No tragedies. Jenny died of cancer, the kids grew up, and I believe Darwin went into an assisted living center and died there. The kids sold the house to the Barkleys in '65. And that was a tragedy.

"Poor little Lizzie was only ten when it happened, when Thomas suspected Gina was having an affair. She wasn't. He was paranoid and suspicious. Controlling. And a drunk. He'd beat her up before, and she swore she had never cheated on him. She confided to a neighbor—who's dead now but who said the house told Thomas that Gina was unfaithful. I never knew why he had to go and kill Lizzie too. They found her in the attic. She played up there a lot, according to the woman who had known Gina. The neighbor tried to get her to leave him, but in that day and age, it rarely happened."

"Anything else?" At this point, I wouldn't be surprised if Thomas authored the attic carvings. It was possible the real estate agent at the time covered the flooring to cover up not only the words but the death of little Lizzie. Not like they had great aftermath recovery teams then. But I still think Rebekah could be a contender for the writing.

At least for now.

"Sorry. I wish I knew more."

"No, you've been a huge help."

"What exactly are you looking for?"

"Just trying to conjure a visual." Because I may have been seeing Lizzie Barkley and hearing Rebekah Howler's babies' cries.

"Funny how we deal with brutal death, isn't it? We turn it into spooky stories to warn children or teach them a valuable lesson. I guess that's easier than believing tragedy has no meaning, no purpose. I suppose it doesn't, unless we allow it to bring a purpose and meaning. Shame to let it go to waste and not use it for something good, or a warning to steer clear of something dangerous."

What good can come from the loss of my babies? From my substance abuse and the end of my career? From moving here to this horrible home that feels like a creature enveloping me more than a home shielding me? What good can come from my painful past? The secret I carry with me. One that no one knows. Anyone who did is now dead.

"Oh, hey, Marcia!" Elle waves at Marcia Tremell—a tall, willowy woman with a patrician nose and lips drawn tight like a seam. Wire-rimmed glasses perch precariously at the end of her nose, and her thinning hair is twisted into a clip, the roots silver-gray against a fading ashy blond. She looks like someone who once lit incense and marched in protests but now keeps her wildness folded away like an old scarf.

Deena did say that Candy's death changed Marcia. I wonder if Deena's death will change her further and in what way.

"Cady, what are you doing here, sweetheart?" She ambles over, and I notice the slight limp in her gait and the knotted knuckles from her arthritis. "Gwen. Good to see you as well. Are you here for a tour?"

"No. I would love to have one though. This is an amazing place. I'm enchanted. And I'd like to say how sorry I am about Deena."

Marcia's eyes fill with moisture. "Thank you. It doesn't seem real, so I'm just working until it does. We've worked hard to preserve history and make this place inviting for locals and tourists. So what brings you here, then?"

"We're looking into the history of Gwen's house. Elle just gave us a whole lesson." Cady hugs her mother lightly, being kind to her aching joints. No matter how closed off Marcia became after her daughter's death, she's done a great job with Cady.

Elle pushes her glasses back onto her nose. "I told them about the Howlers and on down through the Barkleys."

"Oh. Well, that does make for a fun project leading up to Halloween." Marcia chuckles and touches my shoulder. "Expect a slew of teenagers to gather outside your house to see little Lizzie Barkley and Rebekah Howler. They won't vandalize anything, but you'll hear their squeals. Kids." She waves off the notion.

Everyone thinks trespassing in the name of Halloween is good fun. I prefer not to have a brood of children and teenagers stomping around my house at midnight—any night.

"What about when Roger Wagner lived in the house? His wife died and then his daughter ran away, and he moved a few years later, right? Does anyone know what happened to Lily Ann?" Could she be the girl upstairs? The bones in the woods?

Marcia says nothing.

"Anything nefarious there?" I ask.

"I thought you were looking into the history of the home. Not nefarious deeds." Marcia narrows her gaze at Cady. "What exactly are you doing?"

I jump in to clear the heat from Cady. "I'm curious about the people who lived in the house before me. Property records can't be found. I checked." Who wouldn't want someone to know about the previous owners?

"I already told Cady it was the late '90s. And as far as I know, no one found Lily Ann. Tragic." She says it lightly, like it's just another piece of town trivia, but her smile doesn't reach her eyes, and something flickers behind her expression—too quick to pin down, but it feels like deflection.

"I have some cucumber sandwiches left in the fridge if you two are hungry," she adds, glancing at her watch like she's suddenly remembered an appointment. "Might even find a couple of cupcakes one of the volunteers brought. Strawberry."

It's generous, sure—but it also feels like a gentle nudge toward the door. Like we've stepped too close to something she'd rather keep tucked away.

"Sounds good. Thanks, Mom."

Marcia kisses Cady's cheek, then pats it with a tenderness that seems both practiced and genuine. She might have been overprotective, even rigid, but the love she has for her daughter radiates in that small, familiar gesture. It stirs something in me—a pang so sudden and taut it almost knocks the breath from my lungs.

I miss my own mother. Overbearing, yes. Impossible at times. She shattered my heart during those raw teenage years, ripped it out and crushed it underfoot until there was nothing left but a bruised, bleeding mess. But she was still my mother.

Now I'll never get to hear her voice again. Or my father's. Maybe we wouldn't speak even if they were alive. Maybe the silence between us would still stretch miles wide. But I like to believe I could've forgiven her—for what she did, what they both did to me.

Adulthood has brought perspective, but not peace. If anything, it makes the ache heavier. More permanent. I try not to dwell on it. If I do, I fear I'll unravel completely.

"It's so nice to see you again, Gwen. I had a lovely time meeting you at the Mansfields'."

"Same. Again, I'm sorry about Deena. I know you two have been best friends since school. It's such a terrible tragedy. I had no idea she even hiked." We're all throwing the words *tragedy* and *tragic* around like they are simple answers to a complicated problem.

Marcia's face betrays the slightest slip, and she tucks her bottom lip between her teeth to hold the tremble. "Thank you for your condolences. Her funeral arrangements are being made now. Life will be so strange without her."

Cady hugs her mother, and then we part ways and go upstairs, but after thirty minutes we've found nothing new about my house. Deena won't leave my mind. I still have a few hours before Teresa needs to leave. "I want to talk to Wilt about Jean Jackson and Ellersby in general and... How would you feel about stopping by Mr. Richardson's house? Pay our respects."

"Pay our respects or snoop?"

"Both."

"Okay, but Deena was like a second mom to me, Gwen, and I don't want to cause Ron any grief." She holds my gaze like steel.

"I'll be tactful, read the room and not bring him any extra grief. Fair?"

"Yeah. That's fair."

And if I don't like what I hear or catch a whiff of cover-up, I can always return without her.

Chapter Thirty-One

Ron Richardson sits at the kitchen table with a hangdog expression that tugs at my heartstrings. I know that grief—its silence, its strange, clumsy echo. He's the opposite of Deena. Lanky where she was lemon-drop round. Weathered to her fresh, dewy skin. Thick gray hair sticks up like he hasn't run a brush through it in days. A cup of coffee sits in front of him, a thin plume of steam curling up like smoke from an inky pit.

Cady reaches across the table and takes his hand. "I'm so sorry, Uncle Ron. Is there anything I can do?"

The house is quiet, mostly empty except for his son and daughter in the next room and a few scattered family members. Covered dishes line the counters like offerings wrapped in foil, and stacked paper plates. Jugs of iced tea and lemonade crowd a cart beside a tray of desserts.

"No, honey."

I clear my throat. "I am so sorry for your loss. Deena was the first person I met when I moved in. She brought me a welcome basket—vibrant and bouncy as ever."

I'm stretching the truth. She was a bit much. A little too in my face. But still.

"She loved welcoming new folks to town. A real people person," he says and sniffs, then sips his black brew.

Cady and I lock eyes. She nods, but there's caution swimming in her watery gaze. I have to remind myself—she loved these people. They aren't suspects to her. They're family. Friends.

"Ron," I say gently, "did she often go out hiking at night? Or was this more of a new hobby…a one-time thing gone wrong?"

He looks up, and his gray eyes latch on to mine, stormy and unblinking, like turmoil circling a drain. "She liked to walk sometimes," he says, voice tight and trembling. "Not exactly a crime." His hand curls into a fist on the table, knuckles going white.

The defensiveness prickles. My voice stays even. "I didn't mean to suggest it was. Sometimes the fresh air helps us think, helps us…cope. Was Deena coping? Was something bothering her?"

He pushes back from the table, inhaling sharply. "Why would anything be bothering her?" His voice rises. "Why are you asking me questions like you're still a cop? Last I heard, you were fired from the Baltimore PD." He lurches to his feet. "Leave my home. My wife is dead. Cady, don't bring her back here again." Then he stomps through the kitchen and disappears upstairs.

I sit there, the sting sinking in. Ron Richardson knows I was fired. But how?

I turn slowly to face Cady. She's staring at me, unmoving.

"That could've been just…grief blowing a gasket," I say softly. "Happens. Or something else. That level of defensiveness wasn't necessary, Cady. I never accused him of anything."

"No, you didn't," she murmurs. "I've never seen him like that. But…like you said. He just lost his wife. We should go."

We slip out the kitchen door and walk to the car. Once inside, she turns to me.

"I promise I didn't tell anyone about what you told me," she says. "That you were fired or why."

As far as I know, there's nothing online or in the news about me being fired. It was fairly discreet. Not for my benefit but to save face in the department. I could lie and get away with it. But what's the point? Lies do nothing but dig graves with the tongue. Little fleshy shovels.

"I believe you." Once I'm inside the car, she backs out of the drive.

"We need a murder board or something so we can connect dots."

I laugh. "You went into the wrong business, Cady Bug."

She grins. "Cady Bug. I like it. But I'm being serious."

"I know." I count off the truths like cards in a hand. "We know a bone was found on my property. Jean Jackson possibly lied on her report—if what Wilt Dinner said is true. I want to talk more to Wilt myself, but I'm one person and stretched thin." Steven's watching me like those wicked crows that keep gathering and brooding in the branches and wires, and when he's not around, I'm working on the house or doing online research.

If I was still on the force, this would be a moot point.

"We know my home has a dark past with several tragedies. Dr. Rivera said he saw *him*—whoever *him* is—burying a girl. That tells me we're not going all the way back to the Barkleys or the Howlers. This isn't ancient history. This is *now*."

I pause, watching the landscape slip by the window. "Someone or something is in my house, doing things. Someone carved I AM NOT CRAZY into my attic floor. Someone set my shed on fire—no matter what the report said. Deena is dead, and that whole situation doesn't sit right. Ellersby has people in his pocket, and he wants to stay in the mayor's good graces. Keep the motto alive. Calm Waters, Safe Shores, Strong Community. Who was it you said wanted the job and golfed with the mayor? Because there's a saying," I add quietly. "The enemy of my enemy is my friend."

"Lowell White," Cady says. She flips on her blinker and takes a left, veering away from downtown and the coffee shop. "Lowell's a good guy. Used to run a section of state troopers."

I glance over at her, heart ticking a little faster. This feels familiar. Not like snooping. Not like aimless suspicion. This feels like the job. Like working a case—chasing leads, bouncing theories, reading people. I've missed this.

Ten minutes later, we pull up to a home that looks like it belongs to a huntsman from an Appalachian folktale. A big cabin with tall windows, tucked among woods and not far from the water. The view's gorgeous, though not quite as lovely as my place. If only it wasn't a freak show over there.

The front door swings open before we even get out of the car. Wilt Dinner stands on the porch, arms crossed, jaw like stone. Khaki pants and a hunter-green sweater fit snug around his still-solid frame. He's in good shape for someone in his mid-sixties; the only real giveaway is a bit of recession at his hairline.

"Cady," he grunts in that gravel-and-smoke voice. Then he eyes me. "Mrs. McDaniel. Not witnessing more crow deaths, are you?"

"No. Not of late. They're all eerily alive." I step forward. "We came to ask a few questions about the bone you found on my property."

"Figured you would at some point. It's now known you were once a detective for the Baltimore PD." He steps back to let us in. "I just made coffee, if you're interested. And Cady—when are you *not*?"

He chuckles and motions us inside. The house is lived-in but not dirty. Smells like fresh coffee and old cigarette smoke.

"Real funny, Wilt," Cady mutters, smirking. "We want to know if that bone was your way of beefing with Ellersby—or if it's actually human."

He smirks and pours us each a cup of coffee, steam curling from matching brown pottery mugs. "I like direct," he says and hands me the coffee. It's hot and bitter and exactly what I need.

"Beefing with Ellersby," he continues, "would be setting Gwen up to meet the mayor and giving her golf lessons. The bone? It was a femur. Petite. Probably a young woman or girl." He leans against the counter, eyes hard. "Ellersby's nervous. He's appointed, but Mayor Jones isn't a fan of people disagreeing with him. Ellersby's done that on a few occasions, so I think he roped Jean into fudging that report. Who knows what he promised her. Not much we can do about it."

"Make a big enough stink," Cady says, sipping her coffee black like she was born for this, "and he might be forced to bring in a second examiner. Could change the narrative."

"No one wants to believe it," Wilt mutters, pouring the rest of the coffee into a dented thermos. "Because if it's true, it means something *bad* happened. Real bad. But it could also belong to a tourist. Someone got lost, died of exposure. Doesn't have to be sinister." He shrugs, then fixes me with a level look. "But it was human. I'd bet my house and every last cent on it."

He sips quietly, then shakes his head. "What do *you* think, Detective?"

I keep my expression steady. "I think you're on to something," I say slowly. "I've been researching the house I live in. A lot of wicked things happened there. That bone might connect to something inside the walls of that house."

Wilt watches me over the rim of his thermos, running his tongue along straight off-white teeth. "That house has a history, no doubt. But I can't say I ever heard of someone being murdered and buried in the woods. The murders that did happen? People *knew* about them."

"But can we ever really know what happens inside a house?" I ask. "People hide their worst parts behind closed doors. Domestic violence. Addiction. Sexual abuse. The kinds of things no one talks about until it's too late. How often do we hear neighbors say, *'I had no idea'*—then they find twenty bodies in the yard or stuffed in a crawlspace? Dennis Rader was a deacon in his church, for crying out loud. Homes hold secrets. Sometimes they rot the place from the inside out."

Wilt's eyes dim, like a curtain falling. "My wife had an affair. Right under my nose. In this house." His voice is quiet now. "Should've burned it to the ground, but I held on. Couldn't afford to leave. And things got better. Eventually. Before it went south again and she left."

An affair with Ellersby, but he doesn't offer up that morsel.

He sets the thermos down. "Suppose anyone could've pulled a hiker in from the woods. Brought them into the house. But not a family member. Not someone known. We'd have heard. Town's too small. People love to talk."

A hiker from the woods.

The phrase sticks to me like a too-heavy meal. Dense. Uncomfortable. Refusing to be digested.

I need access to a better database on missing persons. Tourists. Campers. Hikers.

What about Candy Tremell? She went missing. No one, not even Marcia, thinks that bone could belong to her? If my daughter went missing and I heard the slightest rumor of a human bone discovered nearby, I would be on it like gnats on a summer watermelon.

"The bone is human. End of story." Wilt looks at Cady. "Your mom went to him, you know. She was there the day I went in to see the report. I suspect she wanted to know the truth about Candy." He side-eyes me.

So they do think it could be her; they're just quiet about it.

"She knows about Candy's disappearance at thirteen," Cady says softly. "Mom never mentioned going to see the chief. But it makes sense. I wondered myself. It's such a delicate subject to broach." She wipes at her misty eyes.

"I've got a friend in Portland," Wilt says. "We were in the army together—he's a detective now. I could ask him to look into her cold case. No one here's going to help you. Grant'll shut it down fast."

"I have friends in armchair detective groups," Cady says. "I'll start there. If they can't help us track down what might have happened to Candy, they can check into other girls missing under the same circumstances in neighboring towns. If there are any cases. It's worth looking into."

I nod. We've got our own little squad now—me, Wilt and Cady. A motley crew if there ever was one. No one else thinks this is weird? Just us? Maybe. But maybe it doesn't matter. People turn blind eyes all the time. It's easier not to see than to unsee.

I should've seen it myself when I turned sixteen and fell into a deep trap.

The signs were there. Obvious if you looked. But I kept quiet. Held it inside like a locked box with no key. I wonder if my mother saw. If she looked away on purpose. If pretending was easier—until it wasn't. Until the evidence bled out, touching everything. Tearing lives apart. Including mine.

And still…all she did was make it go away. Neat. Clean. Hidden again.

Out of sight. Out of mind.

But there are things you *can't* unsee. Can't forget. Memories that brand themselves in your brain like fire on skin. You carry them around, even in sleep. They wake you up. A haze at the edge of a dream. You know it was *there.* It seeps in during quiet moments and anchors itself in every decision you make for the rest of your life.

Rebekah's depression.

Mr. Barkley's abuse and paranoia.

Candy's disappearance.

And my own worst secret.

My greatest regret.

I hold it like a feral cat—afraid to let go, but bleeding from the grip. Its claws sink deeper every day, shredding me bit by bit. The blood runs in a quiet stream I can't stop.

"Gwen?" Cady's voice breaks through the fog.

"Right. Yeah. Thanks for the coffee, Wilt."

He walks us out, and we climb back into her car. The woods press in on either side, tall and listening.

"This is going to be hard on your mom," I say. "You told her you wouldn't do a podcast about Candy, but what if she's the missing bone?" What if she's the etcher in the attic?

"I know." Cady exhales, pulling out of the drive. "It's why I haven't said much. But digging into people won't hurt anyone. Only podcasting it might, and we have to take that chance. I think it's worth the pain if we find the truth. Maybe even justice. What if we discover who took her—and they're still alive?"

She pauses, turning onto the road. "Don't you think it's worth it? Even if it means hurting someone to get there? Is that ever okay—if the end is truth and justice?"

I glance out the window, the trees flashing past in streaks of green and gray. "I don't know that harming anyone is ever good. But we'll try to keep it quiet. Try to protect people where we can. If there's justice at the end of it...maybe that softens the pain."

But nothing *eases* it.

Our ride back to Black Capped Coffee is quiet. Heavy with unspoken thoughts. Both of us wrapped in our own spiraling what-ifs.

If a missing girl or girls connect with that bone, then I know it's going to help me solve the mystery in my attic. I also know there *will* be consequences.

There always are.

Chapter Thirty-Two

"Dolly Bear, Dolly Bear, turn around…

Dolly Bear, Dolly Bear, touch the ground…

Dolly Bear, Dolly Bear, turn off the light…

Dolly Bear, Dolly Bear, say good-night!"

Giggling.

Fits of laughter.

"Shhh… Don't tell."

My eyes fly open.

A shadowy blur flickers across the room, pausing at the door.

My skin is ice. I shiver. Steven isn't on his side of the bed.

So cold.

In the distance, a music box plays. The kind with the tiny ballerina who pirouettes until the song winds down and dies.

I sit bolt upright, but my limbs resist. Stiff. Joints aching. My lungs are drawn tight, like a noose around a neck, suspended from a beam. Each breath burns. My throat scratches with every inhale of freezing air.

The shadow moves again—

In the hallway.

Thump.

Thump.

Thump.

I swallow hard.

Thump. Thump. Thump.

My feet hit the floor. Hardwood. Freezing. "Steven?" I whisper, though I already know—it isn't Steven out there.

I grab my phone. My gun. I turn on the flashlight and inch toward the door. Every muscle in my body screaming not to go.

Don't go. Run. Hide.

You don't want to see.

But I move anyway, past the threshold. At the end of the hallway—it's there.

Rocking.

Back and forth.

Back and forth.

Then it glides down the stairs.

Thump thump thump thump.

Faster. Faster.

It stops by the front door.

A child's oversized bouncy ball.

I take one chilled step after another, glancing around the stifling, silent house—but the silence is unnatural. Screaming, somehow, under the surface. Like the walls are begging me not to go farther. Tendrils of fear snake from the corners, clawing toward me, eager to drag me under.

I kneel at the door. Reach out. Touch the ball—red, the kind you buy for a couple bucks at a big-box store. Or the floating buoys from the dock.

It's real.

I turn on the lamp on the side table. Warm, dim light fills the room.

The shadows flee. But the ball stays.

The closet under the stairs is cracked open.

My stomach drops.

I haven't touched that door. I've *thought* about nailing it shut. But part of me—some stubborn, curious, foolish part—wants to go in. Dust it for prints. Collect evidence.

I open the closet door and shine my light inside. It's empty. I close the door, unsettled, and head into the kitchen.

And slide to a stop.

There's a figure outside. On the dock. Pulling a canoe to shore.

Steven wasn't in bed.

Why would he be on the water at two in the morning on Monday?

I don't go outside. Instead, I slip into the sunroom and sit in the dark. The half-moon is just bright enough to cast the figure in faint silver as he walks toward the house. I know the gait. The rhythm.

It's Steven.

He eases open the back door and slips inside. Quiet. Careful.

I wait until he's almost to the kitchen. Then I flick on the lamp beside me.

He jumps, then pivots to see me sitting on the wicker couch. "You scared me to death, Gwen." He clutches his chest, cheeks flushed red. From the cold? Or embarrassment?

"If I scared you to death, you'd be dead," I say evenly. "Why are you out in a canoe in the middle of the night?"

His eyes shift. They land on the window.

"I—uh. I couldn't sleep. Thought a row on the water might help. Tire me out. And it did." He laughs—but not genuine. It's that *polite laugh*. The one he uses for strangers at church. Bad jokes at dinner parties.

"I'm a detective. Try again." What can I say? I'm a pusher. I'll push it to the edge of a cliff and then right on over the side and drown it in icy waters if that's what it takes. The fact he's even trying to get one over on me is annoying and raising red flags.

Was he out there meeting someone? Teresa? Miss Perky from the office?

He scowls, and his cheek pulses. "You know, Gwen, not everyone is a criminal you need to interrogate. And the fact you can't anymore rests squarely on your shoulders. So don't give me the third degree. Do you know how many times I wake up in the middle of the night and you're not in our bed? Most of them. But I don't accuse you of anything, do I? No. I let you do what you do in the night."

"I don't canoe in cold weather at 2:00 a.m. and then get defensive."

"No, you just snoop around, grasping at straws for a crime scene you can investigate since you were fired. You're going to ruin everything for us here, and it's like you don't even care. Like the mess you put us through in Baltimore never happened. We moved because we had to. We moved for a low-key life—which I hate. I can't grow, can't do anything truly worthwhile except treat colds and flu and arthritis. Nothing challenges me. But do you care about that? No. So don't talk to me like I'm the criminal, because we both know it's you." He seethes, and his muscles are tight like a lion about to pounce on unsuspecting prey.

And he has, in a way.

His teeth go straight to my jugular. All I have left to do now is bleed out.

My mouth opens to respond, but nothing comes. It's as silent as the screams within the walls. He blows through the kitchen and clomps up the stairs. "And stop messing with the thermostat. It's freezing cold in here."

I haven't touched the thermostat. Ignoring the pain and biting truth of Steven's words, I rush into the living room to collect the ball and show it to Steven.

But there's no ball by the front door anymore.

Blood whooshes in my ears. Am I seeing things? Hearing things?

No. No, a ball had rolled down my hall, down the stairs and bumped into the front door. It was red like the balls on the dock. I rush out to the dock, barefoot, and use my flashlight to see, but I didn't count them, so I can't be sure if one is missing.

With nothing to show Steven, how can I convince him that it was here and real? That I am seeing things. Hearing things.

But are they real? Good night, am I having a psychotic break?

Steven is in our bathroom, the shower running and the door locked. His phone is on the dresser. I pick it up and glance at the bathroom, the light spilling out from the crack under the door.

I touch his phone, and the screen lights up. I enter the passcode, but I'm denied.

He's changed it. Why? I try his birthdate, our wedding anniversary, my birthdate, and then the year he won the big award at Johns Hopkins, and it finally unlocks.

Steven longs for what was. Every time he has to enter the passcode, he's allowed to relive the best time of his life—not our wedding date. Not our first date.

The one time he won an award stating he was valued as a physician.

I open his texts. His most recent is with Teresa from last Saturday after the shed fire. My heart pounds, and anger races through my bloodstream. I knew it.

Teresa Lindon: I'm sorry you're going through that. What are you going to do about her?

Steven: I don't know. I can't just throw her out. That would cause a spiral and at the moment I don't trust Gwen. Can we keep all this between us?

Teresa Lindon: I'm a vault. ;)

Steven: ☺ Thanks

I hurry and click the button to turn off the screen.

I set his phone on the dresser and walk out of the room. I can't be near him right now.

This might finally be the proof. The thing that confirms what I've suspected for too long. Steven is a cheater. A hypocrite. Following in his father's footsteps—an affair with a child, practically—and hiding behind a mask of moral superiority while doing it.

But I won't confront him. Not yet.

Good investigators don't tip their hand.

They build a case.

An *impenetrable* one.

Chapter Thirty-Three

Later after Steven leaves for work, the tension between us thick as fog, I finally exhale. I settle into the rocker, Tara tucked against me. I place the bottle in her mouth, my hand stroking the silky tuft of her hair. Her skin is velvet. Her breath gentle and steady against my chest.

I sing a lullaby I can't remember anyone ever singing to me—not my mother, not my grandmother. But it hums through me like an echo. Familiar, yet not.

"Lullaby and good night, With roses bedight..."

The words rise like they're floating up through molasses. Thick. Sweet. Slow.

"With lilies bedecked, Is my baby's wee bed. Lay thee down, now, and rest..."

I don't know this song.

But I keep singing. I can't stop. My chest tightens, panic flooding my limbs.

"May thy slumber be blessed. Lay thee down, now, and rest..."

Tears blur my vision. I lay Tara in her swing, the corner of her mouth beading with milk. I pace the floor, still singing, still trapped in the pull of something old and unseen.

"May thy slumber be blessed."

I don't *want* to sing it. But I have to. My voice won't obey me.

The song is *in* me. *Through* me. I'm not alone in here. I don't even know who *I* am anymore.

Then—my phone rings.

It cuts through the fog like a siren.

Cady.

I answer, breathless. "Hey. What's going on?"

"My dad came by the shop this morning and basically read me the riot act. My mom's losing it. She's convinced I'm going to exploit Candy. She wants me to stop looking, says I'm poking where there's nothing to find. But I kinda already kicked the hornet's nest, Gwen."

Her voice is shrill, frantic. I grip the phone tighter.

"I was up half the night searching missing girls in a hundred-mile radius of Cold Harbor with that online group I'm a part of."

"And?" I ask. I swear I can *smell* cigarette smoke—acrid and intense, like something conjured from my old rebellion. I don't smoke. Haven't in years. But I used to. Back when anger was a lifestyle.

"Nothing similar to Candy's disappearance."

She exhales hard.

I'm no closer to knowing who might have carved those words into the attic. Whose bone might have been discovered in the woods.

What I can work on is Candy's missing persons case. And I think of what Steven said. I feel compelled to turn everything into a mystery I can solve. Solving puzzles, whether crimes or not, makes me feel a sliver of peace. Like when the house is clean and a candle burns while a roast simmers on the stove. All is right.

It's not obsession. It's thirst. For justice.

"So what are you saying? You want to scrap the investigation? The podcast?" Surely she doesn't. I see the same light in her eyes that fires mine up when talking about finding truth. Yes, we're truth seekers, and there can't be anything wrong with that.

She huffs. "No, quite the opposite. I want to know more about Candy's disappearance. But I also don't want to give up on finding who wrote the strange message in your attic. Or why weird stuff keeps happening inside the house now."

A sigh of relief escapes me. "I want those things too. Let's meet at the library later this afternoon and see what we can dig up." I have somewhere I need to be before then. And I think I'll call Teresa and see if she's available. I have a feeling she's a walking sign that says Open for Business.

"Sounds good. I'll meet you there with coffees. And if you don't feel safe in the house, maybe you should get a hotel on Halloween night."

Steven might be having an affair and angry at me, but he would never hurt me.

I wonder if Gina Barkley thought the same thing before Thomas Barkley fired a shotgun shell into her brain for an affair that she never had.

Am I Gina…or am I more Thomas Barkley?

I zip my puffer coat because I haven't warmed up since early this morning when I chased a bouncy ball down the stairs. Cady's meeting me in town in an hour, but I tromp over fallen leaves into the belly of the forest, heading toward where Deena Richardson allegedly fell. Cady says it happened at a place called Fell's Fall—a small waterfall tucked behind the Richardsons' house.

I park about half a mile away and hoof it through the woods near their place. No need to risk anyone spotting me and calling Ellersby. Branches hang low, raking against my coat as I crunch, crunch, crunch over the leaves.

Teresa could conveniently sit for me at the house. I didn't ask any probing questions—just let her get comfortable, unsuspecting. If she's sleeping with my husband, I'll know.

From what I can tell, the Richardson home sits about two miles back. Two miles in this gnarly forest isn't easy. How did Deena Richardson manage it at night? If she was out here, why? Or what if she wasn't? What if someone dumped her to make it look like she fell? Why pick way out here, though? Anyone who knows Deena—or even who doesn't—wouldn't believe she was hiking. Unless I'm wrong. Maybe she did walk outdoors now and then.

My thoughts spiral back and forth, and I can't seem to make sense of what happened to Deena.

In the distance, the water rushes, like the sound of nature applauding. I'm close. The ground shows ATV tracks, and there are scads of footprints surrounding the area. I search until I find it—the spot where Deena died. She fell on a cluster of rocks, hitting her head, and some of the blood still remains.

My jaw slackens, stunned into silence. They didn't even collect a large bloodstained rock? This must be where she hit her head, but as I kneel and picture it, something doesn't sit right. A few feet away is another rock, small enough to pick up but bigger than my face. It's stained too—less blood, no spatter. If she fell and hit her head, blood would have sprayed in small dots, but this is a large, solid stain, with a few drops scattered elsewhere. As if she'd been bashed in the head with the smaller rock, then bled out on the larger one.

I don't take Grant Ellersby for a Podunk idiot cop. But maybe he is. If a town prides itself on being crime-free, especially homicide, maybe he doesn't have much experience with bloodstains or crime scenes. For all I know, he calls it *blood splatter* instead of *blood spatter.* That would tell me everything.

"What were you out here doing, Deena? And if you weren't here of your own volition, where are the drag marks?" This larger rock—it looks like she bled out here. A corpse doesn't bleed. Wet blood in her hair would have leached onto the rock, but not like this.

I can feel my pulse picking up. I lean toward the grim truth. She was out here at night. With someone. Someone she trusted. Why not talk in the house?

Or what if she didn't die at night? What if everything is a lie—including the time of death? But that can't be right. Cady saw her right before sunset. Could Cady be confused?

Frustration churns in my stomach. My hands are tied. I can't take the evidence or run a real investigation. I have only my experience and gut. But I can't take my suspicions to the officers. Even if I did talk to Ellersby, he'd give me the runaround. His seat of authority means more than justice.

I rise and walk over to the falls, the water powerfully crashing down into the creek that runs into the harbor. Suddenly, I smell smoke. Acrid smoke. It wafts into my nostrils, and I spin, scanning for fire—but it's quiet. Just a few snaps of twigs, squirrels cutting through branches, and the crunch of leaves underfoot.

No fire. The smell vanishes as quickly as it came, replaced by the heavy scent of rain and wet earth.

I turn back to the rocks, squatting down again just as a loud crack of thunder booms nearby. But it's not thunder.

Gunshot.

The bullet strikes a tree, splintering bark about a foot away from me.

I dive behind another tree, my back pressed against it, chest heaving as I draw my own weapon and wait for the next shot. But none comes. Seconds stretch into minutes, and when I finally move to the next tree, nothing happens. Using them as cover, I sprint through the woods, tripping and almost face-planting until I burst into the clearing.

My car is half a mile from here. I take off like a greyhound, heart pounding, until I reach my car and slam the door behind me.

Who would shoot at me? Who knew I was out here besides Cady? Was I followed? Was whoever killed Deena already in these woods?

My pulse still races and I need a moment. I take fifteen minutes to calm myself. When my pulse slows, I press the button to start the car and head straight to the police department.

I can't keep this to myself. Steven will be mad, but I've been directly attacked. Shot at in the woods. Whoever's behind this thinks I know too much.

I park in front of the police department like I did last time and adjust the rearview mirror, fixing smudged eyeliner and running my fingers through my hair to smooth it down.

Ellersby might have run a check on me, but he hasn't said anything. He does know I lost my job at the PD. If I push him, if I press too hard, he'll make life difficult for Steven and me. He could destroy us here in Cold Harbor.

But someone shot at me. I weigh the options and decide to go in as a victim, not an undercover cop wannabe. I march inside, stopping at the glass. "Chief Ellersby?"

"He's not in," the officer behind the counter says with a no-nonsense tone. Guess the personal dating app normally behind the counter has the day off. "Can I help you?"

The front door opens again, and a cold blast of air hits me. I turn and see Ellersby standing in the doorway, in street clothes and hiking boots. He spots me, irritation flashing for a moment before he smooths his features into his usual charming smile. I can see why women would be tempted to have an affair with him. Not only is he strikingly good-looking for his early sixties, but he has clout in this town. Men aging like fine wine is unfair.

"What brings you in today, Mrs. McDaniel?"

"Gwen," I say, walking toward him. "Someone tried to shoot me in the woods about thirty minutes ago."

Now I've got his attention.

"Are you hurt? Do you need medical assistance? Does your husband know?" He lays a hand on my shoulder, inspecting me.

"No. They missed. I ran to my car and took some time to get my bearings, then drove straight here. Chief, I think you have a problem in town. I wish you'd have that bone analyzed again. Correctly."

He nods to the man behind the desk and directs me through the maze of cubicles to his office. He closes the door behind us and pauses. "Are you comfortable with the door closed?"

"Yes, of course." But these days, a man needs to ask. Or he's up to something.

Ellersby sits behind his desk, leans forward, fingers tented. "Let's start at the beginning. You were in the woods behind your house—"

"No," I cut him off. "I was behind Deena Richardson's house. I parked away from her place, then trekked through the woods to Fell's Falls. I saw the rocks."

He leans back, grinning that condescending grin. "Then you saw nothing. Deena's death was a tragic accident. Nothing more."

Do I argue? "Why would a woman known not to exercise hike those dense woods at night? And the crime scene, the spatter patterns…they're off."

He sighs, his voice softening. "Gwen, I appreciate your instincts, but you're not a detective anymore. This was an accident. Land behind the Richardsons belongs to Wilt Dinner, and he's made it known that anyone is welcome who will hunt responsibly. You were probably in the wrong place at the wrong time, and a hunter fired at a deer or a fox. You slipped by. Could've hit you."

Is that possible? I have to admit, it is.

"Why would someone want to kill you?"

He waits patiently for my answer, but I can't give him the whole truth. Not yet. "I think that bone could connect to a girl who might've been abducted—perhaps Candy Tremell—and Deena knew something. She was killed for it. Someone made it look like an accident. I'm getting too close."

Ellersby inhales, long and loud, then releases it through his mouth. "If that were true, I'd say you make a good case. But how would this person know you were on to them? How would they know you were going to the woods to be in their crosshairs? What if Deena's death was just a tragic accident? And the bone is just an animal's? What if nothing's as complicated as you think?"

I hate that he sounds right. But he doesn't know everything. He doesn't know the bizarre occurrences at our house.

"I'm sorry to have wasted your time," I say.

"Don't be." He stands when I do and walks me to the door. "Gwen, it's hard to not be able to do what you love. It's easy to see something where there's nothing when we're missing what we love to do. I understand that. On a different level, but I do."

I stop in the doorway, meeting his gaze for the first time since I walked in.

His eyes remind me of Kent's. I glance down and blink. No. I've been staring too long. I'm not seeing what I think I am. No, I am.

"Thank you for understanding," I say, stepping out into the hallway.

Ellersby's boots are caked with fresh mud.

Chapter Thirty-Four

I'm sitting across from Cady at a small table in the back room of the Cold Harbor library, nursing my Americano. After I saw Ellersby's boots, this conversation wasn't one that could be had in the vicinity of listening ears.

I've told her everything—the gunshot, my talk with Grant Ellersby. "He makes some good points, but Cady, he could have been in those woods. I sat in my car long enough for him to have made it back to the precinct before I did, even though he came in after me. What if he was the shooter? Maybe as a warning. Or maybe he simply missed."

Cady's face doesn't budge. She's not ready to take that leap. "Why would he kill you? If he's covering up crimes to help keep his position as chief of police—if that's even true—he'd want you alive, not dead. And, I agree, he makes some valid points."

"He could always say my death was an accident. A hunter they can't find. I don't know, Cady. But weird things are still occurring in my house." I tell her about the bouncy ball that disappeared, how I searched for secret passages that didn't exist, but it's all I can figure when the doors and windows were secured. Except they weren't, actually. Steven went out, and the door was unlocked. The same thing happened the day Tara was on the dock—it was unlocked then too. So maybe someone got in more easily than I thought, without a secret passage.

I take a deep breath, hesitant, then change the subject. "Hey, random question. Do you know this song?" I sing the lullaby I felt compelled to sing earlier. I'm never going to win a reality singing competition, but I can carry a tune.

"No." Cady pulls out her phone. "Sing it again. Or say it. Just slower," she adds, grinning. "Not that you're bad, just…slower."

I raise my eyebrows at her, wishing I could pull off a single raised one, but I'm not that skilled. "Sure." I sing it again.

Cady pauses, tapping the phone screen. "'Brahms's Lullaby.' And now that I see the lyrics, my grandma might have sung it to me. It's familiar. You never heard it before?"

Perhaps at some point. But enough to memorize the song? "I don't know. But I definitely know the song." Or…someone does. A chill crawls up my spine, but I push it away. I do not believe in ghosts. I do not. Not at all.

"You find anything new?" I ask, eager to shift away from this unsettling thought.

"Nothing that would connect to Candy's vanishing or seems similar, but I did find something interesting. A Monica Betts and Brynn Walters, both thirteen, went missing in Acadia National Park," Cady says, tapping her phone. "Four years apart—Brynn was the latest, in 1983. Both were on vacation with their parents. Same story. Turned their backs for a minute, let them wander a little. Gone. Monica's family was from Oregon, Brynn's from Portland, Maine. Neither girl was ever found. And both disappearances happened just forty-five minutes from here. There was a man questioned for Brynn's vanishing, David Diamond, but he wasn't charged. Insufficient evidence. Nothing on who might have taken Monica. It's probably a dead end."

"What year did Candy go missing?"

"1992." She sips her latte, and a little foam sticks to her upper lip.

"No pattern. And not close enough to Cold Harbor to determine hunting grounds. I hope they do find out what happened to those girls, but I agree. They and Candy likely aren't connected."

She sighs heavily; the purple half-moons under her eyes look bruised with exhaustion. "I also found two other missing girls—Caroline Brandon and Abby Raines—both nineteen. Caroline was with her boyfriend when she vanished. They suspected him, but there was no evidence. Abby was with friends, drunk. They think she wandered off—maybe fell into the river, maybe a wild animal attacked her. But they didn't rule out abduction."

"I guess it's possible one of them could be buried on my property, but the bone is from a petite person, more adolescent."

"Agreed. Look what I found before you got here. A yearbook with Lily Ann's sophomore photo. Took a picture." She opens her phone and shows it to me. Lily Ann Wagner had been pale blond with haunted blue eyes. Petite. Frail-looking. What if she is the girl in my attic and the bone in my woods? What if she didn't run away at all? Or tried and Roger stopped her—permanently.

I stand and start pacing, needing to move to think, trying to make sense of the house, the history, and the missing girls, including Lily Ann Wagner and Candy Tremell.

Cady drums her nails on the table, thoughtful. "Do you believe everything happens for a reason?"

"No," I say immediately. "But I believe *some* things do. I don't think children being abducted, abused and killed has a reason. That's not fate. That's some sicko with free will and a wicked heart making a choice to destroy."

"I agree," she says softly. "But I also think sometimes—sometimes—things *do* happen for a reason. And maybe you coming to this house at this time isn't random." She lays her hand gently over mine. "Maybe it's for a purpose."

Well, it's a pretty crummy purpose. "I don't know." I hesitate, my voice quieter. "What reason could there be for me moving to small-town Maine other than to run from what I did? To start over." I pull my hand back and refocus. "I want to find Lily Ann Wagner. How old would she be now?"

"Early fifties?"

"She's the better option and easier to track than Roger. She'll likely have social accounts and a digital footprint. If she's alive."

Cady's eyes widen. "I hope she is. She may have the only answers."

I don't want to go back home, but my time with Teresa is almost up, and I want to have a little talk with her. If she's sleeping with my husband, I want to know.

The question is, what will I do about it?

The thought of losing him gives me anxiety. For all the junk we've been through, put each other through, I love him. I want our marriage to work. But he's cheating on me. How do I come back from that? How would I ever trust him again? I've never fully trusted him or I would have told him the whole truth about my past. But when you know someone won't forgive you, why tell them? If I don't have to hurt him with the truth, why not keep it to myself? What harm is in that?

Or, I don't know. Maybe it is a wedge between us. Are we truly in a partnership if I'm not being fully open and honest? Is he?

"You hear me?" Cady asks, snapping me back into the present and away from thoughts that give me anxiety.

"No. Sorry. I zoned out. Hey, what can you tell me about Teresa Lindon?"

She gives a headshake as if trying to deal with my quick change of topic. "I don't know her super well. But she comes in for coffees a lot. Nice enough. Why? Is she involved?"

"I think she might be having an affair with my husband."

Cady's eyes bug out. "Shut your mouth. How do you know?"

"I saw a few texts and he's staying out late. And he was out on a canoe in the cold at 2:00 a.m. this morning, and instead of simply telling me where he was, he got defensive and tried to gaslight me."

"Like sexy texts?" She crinkles her nose, and I shake my head.

"I didn't have time to scroll and see much. But they're keeping secrets from me. That much I know. I think he might want a divorce." The thought tightens my gut.

"In just a little over a month? He's so into her that he'd divorce you?" Her skeptical tone is loud and clear, and the face she pulls solidifies she's not buying it. When put that way, I see her side.

"We aren't in a good place, Cady. We moved here for a fresh start, and me looking into murders isn't exactly filling him with excitement. She's young and pretty—"

"You are gorgeous, Gwen. Do you not know that about yourself?" Her frown has me wondering.

"No. I've put on some weight, and my eyelids are wrinkling. You know how I know? I can't use an eye pencil on them anymore. I have to buy one of those glide-ons, and they're expensive. Things aren't in the same place they used to be. Forty isn't my friend, and forty-one is pretty much sticking it to me. Who knows what forty-five and fifty will have to say."

She snorts. "Girl, you look fabulous. You really do. I would kill for that thick hair you can wear shorter and those high cheekbones and defined jawline. You have lips people would suffer for and lashes people have glued on. But you know what? I get it. We never see ourselves like others see us. We see all the flaws and imperfections. Your feelings are valid. Whether the facts are skewed or not." She squeezes my hand again. "I'm sorry you're having issues in your marriage, and if you ever want to talk about them, I'm here. I may not have great advice. If what you tell me makes me mad… I'll strike a match and burn him to the ground for you."

I laugh. "I'm a former homicide detective. I know how to make people disappear."

I know that pretty well, actually.

Chapter Thirty-Five

Lily Ann

The sauce simmered and bubbled on the stove. Meatballs were browning in the oven, and the water for noodles was in the pot and ready to boil. She'd add them to the water when he arrived and then put the bread in the oven.

She no longer called him Daddy.

Not since she turned thirteen six months ago.

She called him Husband now. The questions have changed somewhat. And so have her answers.

Husband would be home soon. He liked dinner on the table twenty minutes after he arrived. He needed a beer and time to unwind. Husband provided for her in every way and was very good to her. Sometimes they'd even take drives in the country and go to a drive-through for ice cream. He liked strawberry, and she liked chocolate with chocolate chips. That happened on Sundays. The only days she was allowed to go out. He thought it was safer for her to stay inside.

She didn't need friends. He was her best friend.

They watched TV sometimes. *The Dick Van Dyke Show,*

Leave It to Beaver, and lately they'd watched *The Brady Bunch*. Husband said to pay close attention to the wives. That's what a wife should be. Well made-up. Seeing to Husband's needs.

He'd purchased her makeup at the store. Husband liked red lipstick and pearls. She wore them every day and did her hair just right. She didn't particularly like the style, but Husband knew best. He kept her safe and cared for her. She didn't mind being Wife. It wasn't that much different than being Daughter—except a few things had changed, but she didn't think about them. He called them wifely duties, and the Bible said she had to. She knew God existed and always hoped He'd heard her prayers, but she didn't pray too much anymore.

Husband said he was the god of this house.

The door unlocked. He said if she went outside when he wasn't home, he'd know. She tried it once when she was eleven. She'd just wanted to sit on the porch. But he knew. When he came home, she'd been in trouble. Had to take her punishment. She learned her lesson and hadn't tried again.

Where would she go? She had no family.

"Hello, Lily Ann." He slipped out of his work boots. She wasn't sure what he did for a living. He said he was a jack-of-all-trades. He drove a white van without windows, and he always wore dirty black pants and a short-sleeved blue work shirt. He put his keys on the table by the door then looked around the house. Husband ran his finger along the mantel and smiled. "Spick-and-span. Very nice, Lily Ann. What smells so good?"

"I'm making spaghetti and meatballs, garlic toast, salad, and for dessert I made chocolate pudding with whipped cream and cherries on top." She'd become a good cook. He'd bought her some Betty Crocker cookbooks at a garage sale, and she'd been practicing. "Not even out of a box. I cooked it on the stove."

His grin was wide, and he nodded once, approving. Then he walked into the kitchen and put his arm around her shoulders.

"You've made me so happy. I'm going to take a shower and put on fresh clothes. Be ready in twenty minutes?"

"Yes, Husband. It will be ready. Would you like lemonade or tea?"

"Lemonade sounds refreshing. Thank you."

Husband didn't often thank her, so she knew he was especially pleased and in a good mood. That didn't make her happy, even though she smiled. When he was in a very good mood, she knew what happened later that night.

Her stomach clenched tight. But she kept on smiling and dumping noodles into the boiling water. Sometimes when he ate a big meal, he became tired and slept in front of the TV without waking until morning.

She only hoped that's what would happen tonight.

She reminded herself Husband was good to her. He provided for her. Cared for her. But it didn't make her feel any better about what would come later.

Shaking it off, she recited her times tables while she finished dinner.

Chapter Thirty-Six

After I leave the library, I head to the market. Bread, eggs, pasta. I toss them in the basket like muscle memory. Grab ground beef. Tomatoes. Basil. I don't even like meatballs. But Steven does. Tonight, I want him full and comfortable.

Especially if Teresa Lindon confirms what I'm starting to suspect.

Outside, the sky is the color of bruised metal. Wind curls off the water, rattling the cart as I load the groceries in my SUV. The highway home coils along the edge of the sea—gray waves on one side, endless woods on the other. The kind of road where no one would hear you scream.

Rain spits against the windshield. The car jolts—once, then again. A deep, unnatural thud. I grip the wheel. Ease off the gas. Turn down the radio.

Something is off-kilter.

A louder crunch, then a violent jerk sideways. The car spins. My scream rips out before I can stop it.

The world blurs.

Trees loom—too close, too fast.

I slam the brakes, wrench the wheel. The car lurches left and slams to a stop just shy of a tree trunk.

Silence.

My breath saws in and out. My seat belt burns across my collarbone. I'm shaking. Hard.

For a second, I don't move. Then thunder rolls—close enough to feel.

I open the door and stagger into the storm. Cold rain slaps my skin, soaking me instantly. My boots sink into wet leaves as I round the front of the car.

The tire's gone.

Not flat.

Gone.

The rim's chewed up, bolts exposed like missing teeth. I freeze.

Tires don't vanish. Not like this. Not unless someone…

The thought forms fully, a single hard truth.

Someone wanted me off the road.

I back away, scanning the ditch, the woods. Nothing but rain and shadows. I climb the embankment, slipping in mud, heart hammering. The road is empty as I squint through the downpour.

There—farther up the shoulder, like a sick joke.

The tire, lying on the side of the road.

I jog toward it, soaked to the bone.

No accident. This was *deliberate.* Someone tampered with my car knowing the wheel would come off at some point and likely kill me.

A flash of lightning cracks overhead. For a second, the world is white. I half expect to see someone standing in the woods, watching. But there's no one. Not that I can see.

I leave the tire behind and sprint back to the car, breath heaving. I slam the door, dripping wet, fingers shaking as I fumble for my phone and call Steven. Straight to voicemail. Figures.

I try Cady next as lights flood the rearview and a car slows, then pulls over.

I tense. One hand on the gun inside my purse.

The driver's door opens. A figure in a poncho steps out, hood low, and they walk toward me.

Rain blurs the glass. My fingers tighten on the weapon. Then the figure lifts his head.

Wilt Dinner.

Relief crashes through me like a wave. I roll the window down an inch. "Wilt?"

"What in mercy happened?" he shouts over the storm. "You all right?"

"No. I—I need a ride."

He waves me over. "Come on. Let's get you out of this. I'll call a tow truck for you."

I grab my purse and run. Inside his SUV, it's warm. Smells like pine and leather.

Wilt pulls off his hood, glancing at me. "Hydroplaned?"

I shake my head. "The tire came off. It didn't pop. It was gone."

He looks at me, slow. Cautious.

"Gone?"

"Someone loosened the lug nuts."

"Are you sure?"

I nod and stare out at the trees, dense and black beyond the window. He picks up his cell phone, relays information to Two Pines Garage, ends the call and stares at me.

"This was no accident," I say quietly. "Someone wants me dead."

Chapter Thirty-Seven

"Who would want you dead?" Wilt asks, voice low, measured, as he drives toward my house.

I stare out at the rain-slick road. "I don't know. But Ellersby's bucking me the hardest. Where there's smoke..."

"There's fire," Wilt finishes, sighing. "Just ask your shed."

Exactly.

I don't care what the fire chief says anymore. That fire didn't start itself. The storm outside thickens, and the windshield wipers screech against the glass in a syncopated rhythm, grating against my fraying nerves. I shiver in my soaked clothes, my seat creaking every time I move.

"Ellersby's a horse's behind," Wilt mutters. "But he's not a killer. Still, he warned me to stop looking where there's nothing. Said Jean didn't do him any favors."

"But you still think that bone was human." I'm watching him now. Carefully. Is he backpedaling?

"I do. And I think he's lying. But Gwen..." He glances at me. "A liar's one thing. A killer? That's a whole different game."

He turns up my road. My house looms at the top of the hill.

"I didn't say Ellersby was a killer," I snap. "But someone sure wants me quiet." I tell him about the woods behind the Richardson house. "That shot didn't come from a hunter, and it wasn't random. And now this with the tire—someone's getting braver. These aren't warnings anymore, Wilt. They're attempts."

His hands tighten on the wheel. "What do you want to do?"

"I don't know." I fill him in on the new information Cady and I have found. "I want to find Lily Ann Wagner," I say. "She's the only one who may know the truth about the woods behind my house." About the attic. About Roger Wagner.

Wilt shakes his head. "I didn't know Roger well. Never did the gossip rounds. Maybe ask Dr. Rivera…though his mind's gone now. It's sad. He delivered my first grandchild. Doesn't even remember my name anymore."

Should I tell him? At this point, what do I have to lose?

"I did visit Rivera," I say. "And he told me Roger buried a girl in the woods behind my house. Said he saw it happen. Well, I assume he meant Roger."

Wilt stares straight ahead. Doesn't flinch.

"I don't know if Lily Ann really left town," I go on. "What if she's still here—or was—and the killer dug her up after you found that bone? What if this whole thing is bigger than we think?"

He finally speaks. "A cover-up? By who? Ellersby? How would he even know?"

"I don't know," I whisper. "But what if Rivera *is* right, and no one ever listened?"

He pulls into my drive behind Teresa's car. My house, lit from within, glares at me like a watching eye. No longer a home. A warning.

"Looks like our new real estate agent's still here," Wilt says. "Selling already?"

"No. She's babysitting."

He chuckles. "My daughter just had her second. Babies are such a blessing—until they're not."

I don't want to discuss babies. "Thanks for the ride. And the tow."

"You can pick it up in the morning with a new tire." He dips his chin to say you're welcome. "If you're right, Gwen," he says, "you're in more danger than you think."

"I usually am."

I dash to the porch, soaked and shaking. I don't care about the groceries I left behind in my car. The fire crackles inside. Warmth beckons.

But the house feels *off.*

Too still.

I shut the door behind me and stop cold.

Where's Tara?

The coffee smell is strong. I peel off my wet jacket, shuck my boots and tread carefully down the hallway. The kitchen is cold. Not physically—but *emotionally.* I've always felt it here, like something's watching. Breathing on me.

I pause in the doorway.

Teresa is in the sunroom, curled up with a mug, legs tucked beneath her like she lives here.

But Tara isn't with her.

Then I hear laughter. *Male* laughter.

Steven.

I stiffen.

His car wasn't outside—he must've pulled into the garage.

Why didn't Teresa text me?

Why didn't he answer his phone?

I slip into the shadow of the hall and watch through the glass.

Steven enters the sunroom with a coffee, relaxed. Like this is just another evening.

Like my tire didn't fly off the car less than an hour ago.

"You sure you don't mind me sticking around?" Teresa's voice is syrupy sweet.

"You don't need to be out in this mess," Steven replies, checking his watch. Again.

"This storm has really put a damper on my showings," she says, sipping.

He nods, distracted. "Small town. Can business even be that busy?" Then, "What time did Gwen say she'd be back?"

"Four. I should tell her she can stay out later." She smiles over the rim of her mug. Waiting.

Waiting for what?

Approval? An invitation?

Steven raises his phone. "I'll call her."

My blood turns to ice.

Why now?

Why not *earlier*?

I stay in the hallway, soaked and invisible, watching my husband sit beside the woman who was supposed to be watching our daughter.

The woman who didn't even *notice* I was late.

And I can't shake the feeling this wasn't just a ride gone wrong. This was *engineered*. Piece by piece.

I walk to the threshold. "I'm home."

Steven jumps to attention and takes in my soaked status. "What happened?"

I focus on Teresa. "Where's the baby? She's not in her swing."

Teresa sets her coffee on the coaster and unfolds her legs. "The bassinet upstairs."

"Gwen, what happened to you? No one gets that soaked from coming inside."

I ignore him. "Why are you still here if Steven's home?"

Steven lets out a sigh. "I've been home ten minutes, and I told Teresa she didn't need to be driving in this mess."

"I was just going."

"It's terrible out, Teresa," Steven says, and he's right. But I couldn't care less. She needs to go. Now.

"I'll be fine." She flashes me a tight smile. "I hope everything's okay," she mutters and flees the sunroom.

"What is going on? She's doing you a massive favor, and you throw her out in the storm and all but shoot daggers with your eyes? What is wrong with you? And where have you been? Why are you soaked to the bone?" Steven's questions fire like bullets. If he can shift the focus off Teresa, he will. Well, I'm not that easy to divert, and he should know this by now.

"Are you having an affair with her?"

He blasts a bitter laugh and rakes a hand over his face. "This again? Really? I don't know what else to say, Gwen. No, I'm not having an affair. I've never had one. I'm not planning one. But if you want to talk about cheating, then let's talk."

My face floods with heat.

Because he's not wrong.

Not physically, no. I shut that down in the women's bathroom when Kent made it clear he wanted more than hallway banter. But emotionally? That line blurred months before that incident. I'd leaned on Kent when I should have turned to Steven. Called Kent when I was spiraling. Let him carry pieces of me my husband didn't even seem to notice had fallen.

But I don't say any of that. I grip the doorframe to hold myself upright.

"Then where were you at two in the morning?" I ask. "Why lie? Why stammer around when I asked?"

Steven takes off his glasses and pinches the bridge of his nose. "I'm exhausted, Gwen. I'm tired of being put on trial in my own home."

I flinch. He turns from me, his jaw flexing. "You want the truth? Fine. I was taking Dr. Rivera back to his place. He showed up in a canoe, muttering about dead babies and girls in the woods. He was soaked. Confused. Ranting. I didn't want you waking up and hearing that and…spiraling."

He looks at me like I'm the problem.

"I was protecting you, Gwen. Not sneaking around. You happy now?"

Before I can respond, he storms out of the sunroom and up the stairs. I stand frozen, steam rising from my skin and clothes, dripping onto the hardwood floor.

Do I call Kristin? Verify his alibi? The detective in me is already itching to dig. But the wife in me…she's tired. And terrified.

I peel myself from the threshold and trail upstairs. He's on the edge of the bed, elbows on knees, muttering something too low to catch. A prayer? A confession?

"I'm sorry," I say. Two words, but they mean more. Not just for the accusation. For everything. For the miles between us I helped create.

He lifts his head. His eyes are glassy. "You could verify what I'm saying," he says quietly. "You always do."

I manage a smile. He knows me too well.

He studies me a beat longer, then frowns. "Why are you drenched?"

Do I tell him someone wants me dead? That the tire flew off my car and I could've been killed?

No. Not yet. Not until I know whether he's trying to protect me…or cover his tracks.

"My back tire came off on the road," I say instead.

He's on his feet in an instant, hands gripping my shoulders. "Why didn't you call me?"

"I did. You didn't answer. Wilt Dinner drove by, gave me a ride and called a tow. I can pick the car up from Two Pines Garage tomorrow with a new tire."

Steven's eyes flicker—an emotion unreadable—before he masks it with concern. "Someone loosened the lug nuts?"

I nod. "You tell me. You're the one who maintains the car."

He holds my gaze for a long moment. Too long. "No. That shouldn't happen."

But he doesn't ask for details. Doesn't rush to suggest we inspect the car. Just wraps his arms around me.

"I'm glad you're okay. Go warm up. I'll make dinner."

That's it? No questions. No follow-up. Just fettuccini.

I stare after him, unease prickling. Then I glance at Tara in her bassinet and feel the pressure of this house pressing in.

I head to the shower and stop at the door.

"You don't find any of this suspicious?" I ask. "The baby vanishing, then reappearing. The fire. Now my car? All this after I started asking about that bone?"

Steven doesn't turn around. Just runs a hand through his hair.

"Sometimes bad things just happen," he says. "Not everything's a conspiracy. And we promised, remember?" he adds. "Not to poke at things that don't concern us. We don't look into people. They don't look into us."

"I'm not doing anything crazy," I say.

"That's all I ask." His smile is tight. Thin. "Fettuccini, ten minutes."

Then he walks away.

And for a moment, I stand there—dripping, shaking, cold to the bone—wondering if I ever really knew the man I married.

Or if he's just been very good at pretending.

Chapter Thirty-Eight

It's well past eleven. Steven is asleep upstairs—or at least, I think he is.

Nothing feels right except Tara, warm and heavy in my arms. I rock her, the bottle tilted toward her soft mouth as I hum without thinking. "Lullaby and good night..." The words catch in my throat the second I realize what song it is. The rocking chair groans beneath me, but the rest of the house is cloaked in unnatural quiet. Even the waves outside don't sound normal—less like crashing and more like clawing at the cliffside.

Steven had wanted this place too fast—so out of character for his patient, logical personality. The fire. The late nights. The text messages that stopped when I walked into the room. The untraceable steps in the hallway. Could it be him trying to mess with me?

He prescribed my anxiety meds.

The thought plants itself like a splinter under skin.

Or maybe I really am losing it—off my rocker, like they say. Divorce had never been on the table. But murder...well.

Doesn't the Hippocratic Oath cover that? Could he be trying to have me committed?

I kiss Tara's forehead, soft and cool against my lips. "You're the only peace I have," I whisper. Rain hisses against the windows, a sound I used to love. Now it whispers, *stay awake.*

An abrupt banging jerks my eyes open.

Not thunder. Not Tara.

Outside.

Breath catches somewhere in my throat. I lay Tara gently in her swing and tiptoe to the side window. There—just at the edge of my vision—a figure, unmoving.

My heart slams. The gun is upstairs, under my pillow. If I go for it, he might disappear. I need proof. I need to *see.*

I grab a heavy bookend from the shelf, gripping it like a vise, and slip barefoot through the kitchen. The door to the sunroom creaks open, and the night air licks at my skin. The rain hasn't stopped but it's thinner now.

The figure is still there. Crouched. A black raincoat, hood obscuring his face, one hand tapping gently—rhythmically—against the basement window. Not trying to break in. Not forcing. Just…tapping. Like he's waiting for something to open from the inside.

I raise the bookend, pulse pounding in my ears. I'm close enough now to smell wet earth and mildew.

He turns.

"Dr. Rivera?" The words leave my mouth in a rasp. "What are you doing here?"

He lifts a black doctor's bag. "I came to help."

He looks…disoriented. Pale. Water beads in his hair, his cheeks flushed from cold or confusion. I'm not sure which.

"How did you get here?"

"My canoe," he says, simply.

Steven told me it drifted off.

"Who are you here to help?" I press.

"She's in a bad way," he says. "She needs me."

"Who?"

His eyes widen. His hands begin to tremble. Then—without warning—he bolts.

"Doctor!" I chase him, rain slicking the back of my neck. "Wait!"

For an old man, he's fast. I catch up to him at the back of the house, where he stands frozen, staring up.

At the attic window.

The one where I flicked the lamp.

On and off.

On and off.

A signal.

"She sends me messages," he mutters, eyes glassy. He grabs my shoulders. His fingers dig deep, bruising, urgent.

"Do you know who *she* is?" I whisper.

His eyes dart back to the house. "The devil," he breathes. "He's always lived here. In a man or a woman. Doesn't matter. It's always been him."

Lightning bolts overhead. For a heartbeat, his face is lit in stark white—a mask of fear—but his gibberish makes no sense.

"You're not safe here," he hisses. "The house—this place—it *feeds* on wicked hearts."

"What's the devil's name?"

"Adrian!"

The shout comes from behind us. Kristin's voice, slicing through the storm.

Dr. Rivera releases me. My arms are numb where he held me.

"You scared me half to death, Doc." Kristin jogs toward us, clutching her chest. She throws me a sympathetic look. "I'm so sorry, Gwen. He's been slipping lately. Houdini-level escapes. He'd had the bird books out, so I took a gamble and figured he might have come to see you."

"Like last night?" I ask quietly.

She frowns. "I'm not sure about last night. But tonight, yeah. Definitely." She wraps an arm around him. "Come on, Doc. Let's get you warm. Tea sound good?"

"Oh, yes. I love tea."

Kristin leans in close as they start toward her car. "He's been wound tight lately," she whispers. "Blames Halloween. He says someone always dies over here this time of year. Urban legends, ghost stories...just superstition. But kids'll be in your yard that night. Just FYI."

Another crack of thunder. The air vibrates around me.

"Go inside before you catch your death," she adds. And then they're gone.

I turn back toward the attic.

The lamp I switched on—once.

Adrian's lamp flicked on—twice.

Repeat.

Was someone in that room...sending messages? Or was this the raving of a man slipping into madness?

Chapter Thirty-Nine

When I enter the kitchen the next morning, Steven is at the table with a cup of coffee and a bowl of oatmeal. I check the time—it's early. He hasn't gone on his run. Stuck with his routine.

"What are you doing?"

He puts his spoon down, and it clinks against the bowl. "We need to talk."

I walk to the counter, pour a cup of coffee and take my anxiety pill, the same—now familiar—thick cold hovering in the atmosphere when I come into this room. The kitchen is supposed to be the center of the home. Not this home. This one has a pulse of its own.

Once my coffee is in hand and I've had a sip, Steven motions for me to sit at the table. I acquiesce, taking a seat opposite him, and wait for him to begin his speech. He's rolled it around all night, if I had to guess. Steven's a processor and thinker. Me? I'm a shoot-from-the-hip kind of woman.

"This has to stop," he finally says. "I've given up a lot to be with you—and I know you've given up a measure of things to be with me. But this constant assuming I'm being unfaithful is taking its toll. On me. On you. On our marriage. You know how I feel about infidelity. How could you even accuse me? You embarrassed me and Teresa, and she's done nothing but be kind and accepting of us."

His eyes hold mine. Unwavering. And he's right on all accounts. I've never had proof of his infidelities.

"I didn't mean to embarrass anyone, but your story was flimsy and…" I stop short. I can't bring myself to admit I went through his phone. Although shouldn't married couples be able to do that? But why would you need to if you trust your partner?

"And what?" he asks, his tone quiet. Calm.

"You're working late, and the women in your office are so much younger than me, and…" My cheeks balloon with heat. It's humiliating to say out loud. "I've let myself go. Age is showing in a dozen places. I can't compete with a twentysomething." I can't even meet his gaze.

Steven sighs, low and pained. His chair scrapes across the floor as he moves closer to me. He tips my chin up, and for the briefest moment, I think he might kiss me. I think maybe, just maybe, there's still a version of us that survives this house, this fear. But instead, he says softly, "Is this what's going on? Projecting your insecurity about yourself onto me? You don't see yourself as beautiful anymore, so you think I don't either?"

I've never thought of myself as beautiful. Average, maybe. Pretty-ish when my hair and makeup are done. Never beautiful.

"I don't know." Maybe. Maybe that's exactly what I'm doing. "I wouldn't blame you."

Steven frames my face in his hands, and his smile unravels me. It's what I first noticed about him—that warm, unguarded smile and the gentle eyes behind it.

"Gwen, you are beautiful. I don't want to run off with some twentysomething. I just want you to trust me. We've been married almost eleven years. In all that time, you've never truly done that. And you can't even tell me why."

"I don't know why, Steven. I don't know why I do half the things I do. I've never understood it." What makes us the people we become? Why do some people trust too easily and others not at all? For all the sharpness I claim, I'm so dull in places that matter. "It's not because of my job, but I think it's why I was good at it. Everyone is a suspect to me."

"I shouldn't be, Gwen. I should be your safe space. You should trust me enough to confide. You…you confided in *him*." He drops his gaze. That wound still bleeds, even now.

"I didn't confide in him like you think I did."

The most hidden parts of me—they stayed hidden. From Steven. From Kent. From everyone. Some days, even from myself.

"He knew you were staking out Teri Jo's place. Knew you'd become…more than normally taken by her and her new baby."

"She didn't deserve her. She didn't deserve any of them." Just seeing her hold that sweet, precious bundle with a cigarette dangling from her lips, ash inches from falling onto soft, innocent cheeks—it made my skin crawl. Would make any normal woman's skin crawl.

"I know," he whispers. "I have always admired your tenacity. You go after what you want, what you think is right, and you don't back down. But that's gotten you into some serious messes. And this prodding about the house is going to backfire. Please let it go. For your sake. Mine. Our marriage. And what we're trying to protect here."

My lungs tighten. I hate to admit it, but he's right about one thing. This is wearing on us. But he doesn't know everything. Doesn't believe everything.

"Steven, something is wrong in this house. Someone tried to kill me."

"No one tried to kill you, Gwen."

Except someone *did*.

"If you maintain the car like you say, I shouldn't have lost a tire. And if you didn't loosen the lug nuts, then who did?"

He stands, jaw slack, eyes wide. "You think I loosened your lug nuts."

"No. I'm saying you have to believe me. And if you don't—if you really don't—then you must have a reason. And the only one I can come up with is that you did it yourself. And we both know you didn't." I *pray* he didn't.

He removes his glasses and pinches the bridge of his nose, exasperated—it's his telltale sign. "Freak things happen. Fire. Lug nuts. The strange writing in the attic. And maybe this house has had bad things happen inside. That doesn't mean it has anything to do with us. Please, leave it alone, or it's over for us."

Out the window, I catch a glimpse of the shed—blackened and skeletal. Hollow. Like us, maybe.

"What does that mean?" I ask, my voice barely above a whisper.

"You know what it means. For me. For us. Remodel the house. Make friends. Go to true crime bingo and Halloween parties. See someone for the issues you have."

He's begged me to see a therapist before. But I can't. I don't know why. The idea sends my chest into a tailspin.

"What about your issues?"

Steven's jaw tightens. "I *am* seeing someone. That's what I've been doing late at night. Seeing a therapist to make it through our marriage. But if you won't try, then how can I do it alone? I can't. So either get it together on your own and back off the phantom mystery—or see a therapist. Or this marriage is going to look a lot like our shed."

He walks out, leaving me utterly alone.

Like he doesn't care.

Or maybe like he's finally giving up.

I sit there, the coffee turning cold in my hands, the silence swallowing the room. The air is still colder here. Not drafty—*dead.*

Steven has been seeing a therapist.

I've driven my husband to a shrink.
And now the question begs attention.
Is solving this mystery worth losing my marriage?

Chapter Forty

"I'm sorry. I can't."

I hate to disappoint Cady. She's been the only real friend I've made since moving here. But I have to make my marriage work. We've been through too much—done too much for each other—to let it burn to ash.

And I love Steven.

My actions haven't always conveyed that, but it's true. Even when I don't like him, I still love him.

"My marriage is crumbling, and if I'm going to mend it, I can't be a part of this hunt anymore. I have to trust the chief and believe these things are coincidences. The writing on the attic floor could've been left by someone who lived here years ago—someone struggling. Depressed. Mentally ill. I don't know. But it's not proof of a crime or that whoever did it was held here against their will. The urban legends are just that. Kids trying to scare each other."

Cady stirs her wooden stick in her latte, eyes downcast, watching the swirl of foam and coffee like it might spell out something different if she stares long enough.

"And my sister?" she asks.

Candy Tremell. I've thought about her, and all the other girls. My heart bursts for them. I want justice. I want truth. But I can't chase it at the cost of my marriage. Looking for Candy means poking through the shadows inside my house—and I've promised myself I wouldn't.

"I'm so sorry, Cady. You have the savvy and the drive to keep going. You deserve to know what happened to her. So do your parents."

I roll a paper straw between my fingers, the soft crinkling oddly soothing me. My other hand rocks the stroller back and forth, a motion that brings more comfort to me than to the baby.

Cady's eyes brim with tears. "I understand, Gwen. I do. It's just—easier to fight the good fight when you're not alone. Just me against whatever's hiding here? It feels so small. You gave me courage. Strength."

That takes me aback. No one's ever told me something like that before. Me—washed-up, frayed-at-the-edges me—giving someone else courage?

I take her hand. Her delicate fingers cling to mine, and something unspoken passes between us. We are tethered. I think, strangely, I might die for this girl.

And for one fleeting second, I want to change my mind. Tell her I'll keep searching. That we'll do it together.

But I can't.

"You *are* strong on your own," I whisper. "And I'm not going away. I'm here. I'll help however I can—but from a distance. If you get stuck, I'll point you in the right direction. But my marriage has to come first."

I pause, then add, "That probably seems selfish when you think about Candy—"

"No. It's not." She wipes at the corner of her eye, then looks at me, steady. "But Gwen…the things you're hearing and seeing. You can't ignore them. Unless you think none of it's real?"

She's giving me an out. Letting me say it's all in my head.

And maybe it is.

"I don't know," I say honestly. "It's possible the baby cries aren't real. That happens to women who've had miscarriages. Phantom cries. And the ball—maybe I imagined it. Maybe I left Tara on the dock and just forgot. It's easier to believe someone moved her than to admit I could've done something so… careless."

That truth stings deeper than I expect. It makes me more like Teri Jo Tipton than I want to admit. What if I'm not a good mom? What if I never will be? What kind of mother leaves her baby somewhere unsafe?

"You've had a lot on your mind," Cady says gently. "And you're not sleeping. Don't be so hard on yourself. You rushed back to save her. And you did."

She glances at the stroller, top pulled down to shield Tara. "Can I hold her? I know she's asleep, but I'll be gentle. I love babies. I want a house full someday. Can't even get a date though. Small-town life. Once you've made your rounds, you're out of options." She laughs, but there's longing in it.

"Never wake a sleeping baby," I say with a smile. "Come by the house later. You can hold her to your heart's content."

I'm not letting her—or anyone—hold Tara in public. People don't need to gawk or get too familiar. Steven and I agreed. The fewer people know, the better.

Cady nods. "I can't tonight. Deena's visitation is this evening. Funeral's tomorrow."

"Later in the week, then."

"Deal." She stands just as a group of teenage girls bursts into the coffee shop, cackling and carefree, like the world hasn't touched them yet.

Must be nice.

"If you change your mind..." she starts.

"I'll let you know."

I push Tara out of the coffee shop and walk the path down by the water before heading to the rental car. I'll pick up my own later.

I can do this.

I can focus on remodeling the house. Ignore the whispering woods and the mystery tangled in the trees.

Deena's about to be laid to rest.

And I force myself to believe it was nothing more than a tragedy.

Chapter Forty-One

Almost two long weeks have passed since I recused myself from the mystery to focus on my marriage and the house.

Steven insisted we go to Deena's funeral. Said it's what good community members do—especially when one of them is the town's new primary care physician. "We're part of Cold Harbor now," he said. "It matters." How noble.

Steven likes being liked. He won't admit it, but he thrives under approval. Needs it like most people need sun. I used to be that way, too. Maybe I still am, beneath the rust. But lately, I find myself caring more about surviving the day than impressing the people in it.

The funeral was more like a celebration—Deena's life, her friends, her goodness. Everyone said she was the kind of woman who left flowers on your doorstep just because. Who laughed with her whole face. I sat in the second-to-last pew, hands folded, eyes roving. I studied faces instead of the eulogies. Watched for anyone who looked nervous.

But everyone did. It was a funeral. That's the trap—grief makes everyone look suspicious.

Afterward, the fellowship hall felt too full. Too loud. Laughter that didn't quite land right. I picked at desserts I didn't need but couldn't resist. Chocolate lasagna, someone called it. Worth it.

Back home, I rubbed my hand across the bridge of my nose—itchy again. My nerves always wake up when I have something delicate to do. Maybe that's all this ever was, frayed nerves and an overactive imagination. The sounds in the attic. The record player. The little girl with the jump rope. Gone now. Quiet, mostly, since I backed away from investigating.

But the dreams have stayed. Not quite nightmares. Not quite sleep. Always the house, the cries, the girl's giggling. Always something buried.

Still, the other things—the strange noises, the flickering lights, the smell of smoke—they stopped. Like a fever finally broke.

Two days ago, Steven brought home a sander, and I spent hours trying to grind the words out of the attic floor.

I AM NOT CRAZY

I AM NOT CRAZY

They'd dug deep into the wood, deeper than I realized. We had to pull up the planks completely. I took pictures before they were gone, for proof. Steven thinks not seeing the message will help me move on. And he's not wrong. I feel lighter. But that doesn't mean it wasn't there. I wonder if that's how others who lived here felt too? Covered up. Concealed.

On the Sunday after I agreed to back off, we went back to church—the one on the water. The Mansfields go there. I still have questions about God, but it felt good to sit in the silence, to listen. To be part of something bigger than myself.

After the service, we laughed over fried shrimp by the docks and took a long walk without saying much. It was the best day we've had in years. That night, we watched an old movie in black and white, popcorn in our laps, Tara curled against me.

For a moment, it felt like the last four years had been erased.

But they haven't been. And one peaceful day doesn't scrub the guilt off your bones. The past always finds a way through the cracks. You can only patch so much before the rot shows.

Still, that night, I let myself believe in peace.

Now I'm outside, potting mums again. I can't seem to keep them alive, but I try. Seems like I'm trying to keep *a lot* alive these days.

I pat the dirt down and step back. "What do you think, Tara? You like?"

She blinks, the soft pink romper lovely against her milky skin. I pluck one of the blooms and tuck it into the band of her head wrap.

"You're as pretty as a petal," I tell her. And for a minute, I believe it. That this could be normal.

The sadness still lingers. Always just under the surface, like water pressed behind glass. But today, I fight it.

I sweep the porch. I set out pumpkins and hay bales. The house is starting to look like fall—without leaning into the macabre. No skeletons, no tombstones. Autumn can be beautiful without being grotesque.

Inside, the house is warmer. Lighter. Gold fixtures instead of silver. Warm wood instead of peeling paint. My body aches from the work, but it's a good ache. Productive.

There are three bedrooms on the main floor. I keep them shut for now—unused. I tell myself they're just...waiting for when we're ready. For more. For something better.

The attic will be next. New floors are being installed this weekend. I want to make it bright and cheery—the opposite of what it is now—with hopes that will fix everything.

I shower and head to the kitchen. Steven's office party is tonight, and I've volunteered to carve pumpkins for the decorations. It's a costume party—no scrubs allowed.

I'm going as Glinda the Good Witch. An old prom dress

from a thrift store, an even older wig. I thought about going as a cadaver, since I'm pale enough these days. Steven wanted me to go as a naughty nurse. He was only half joking.

Costume parties are strange when you're grown. Everyone pretending, trying on other selves. Monsters. Witches. Maybe it's harmless fun. Or maybe it's something truer—a night to let the darkness out in a way that won't raise eyebrows.

Steven's being clever. His costume is a play on words. I taped mini cereal boxes to a blood-spattered lab coat. He's going as a *cereal* killer. He loves a cheap pun.

I'm elbow-deep in pumpkin guts when he walks in. The thought of taking such smooth, innocent pumpkins and stabbing them into something sinister feels all kinds of wrong, but I'm doing it anyway.

"I smell paint and pumpkin," Steven says, kissing the top of my head. Keys and coins drop into the ceramic bowl. "Mums look great. You've been busy."

"I bought templates," I say, gesturing with a spoon. "If I mess one up, I've got backups for the classic triangle face."

"Whatever you set your mind to, you do." He grabs a San Pellegrino from the fridge. Glass bottles only—always glass with him.

I bow dramatically. "Your costume's on the bed. Seven o'clock, right?"

"Right." He kisses my cheek. "I'm proud of you. You've made progress. It's been good this week. I'm happy. Are you?"

I look up from the half-gutted pumpkin. "I am. The house is finally becoming a home. It's going to turn around. I promise."

"We'll pick up your car on the way to the party. Drive separate?"

"Perfect. Teresa's coming at six thirty." I invited her myself. A small act of goodwill. Of trust. I'm trying.

"I'll be upstairs—in the attic. Deciding which walls to hang all of my stuff on."

Tad Michaud is coming Friday to install the new flooring. Soon, no one will know someone once carved their desperation into the bones of this house.

I press the template onto the pumpkin and start carving.

My hands are slick with pulp when my phone buzzes.

Cady.

We've been texting all week—mostly about harmless things. Avoiding deeper water.

I wipe my hands and answer. "Hey girl. What's up? I'm eviscerating a pumpkin."

Her voice is tight. Electric.

"I found Lily Ann Wagner."

Chapter Forty-Two

Steven holds my hand. "Are you sure you're okay? You've been quiet since the pumpkins. They're not that bad," he teases, squeezing my fingers.

"I'm fine." I'm not, of course. I'm wired and frayed and pretending to be whole. Cady apologized for dragging me back in, but she found Lily Ann Wagner—now Cartwright. Divorced. Two kids. Living in St. Augustine, Florida. Cady wants to fly down Friday. She doesn't want to go alone.

"I'm just tired," I say. "Every muscle in my body aches."

"You need a good soak in a hot tub. Sleep in Saturday. Hey, sleep all weekend." He winks, and I manage a small laugh. He looks ridiculous and harmless and utterly trustworthy. Which should be comforting.

It isn't.

He parks in the lot, already crammed with cars. Down by the water, the pavilion glows with orange and purple lights. Elvis's "Devil in Disguise" spills through the air. Tables are dressed in black and orange, loaded with caramel apples and popcorn balls and pumpkin-shaped cookies. The scent of roasted meat drifts up from somewhere closer to the marsh.

It all feels too nostalgic. Like a memory about to rot at the edges.

I'm wearing a giant hooped dress that makes me look like a sugarplum gone sour. I should've added fake blood and gone as Carrie. Instead, I look like a ghost of my nine-year-old self—the last time I trick-or-treated. Pink wand. Glittery wings. Back before everything cracked.

"Cady mentioned a beach trip," I say as Steven grabs two pumpkins from the trunk. "Sun. Sand. Maybe some fruity drinks."

"When?"

"Friday through Monday." I pull the hoop dress free of the door so it doesn't get slammed shut. "She needs a break from her café. I need one from…everything."

He hefts both pumpkins like a pro. "You need vitamin D. Can't say no to that."

"You sure?" I ask. I half expect him to protest. To insist we've come too far, worked too hard on rebuilding trust for me to chase ghosts again like he knows that's the true motive.

But he just shrugs. "Go and have fun. I got things here."

"You will?" I glance at him sideways. Alone time with Tara could be just what he needs. Or a chance to do something I don't want to imagine.

"I got this," he stresses again. "You grab the other two pumpkins."

I wrestle them up, crown slipping sideways on my head. An omen, maybe. Or a metaphor. A falling crown, a fractured fairy tale. Dorothy returned to Kansas. I have no idea what happened to Glinda.

"Has she booked flights?" he asks as we head down the hill.

"Not yet. I wanted to talk to you first."

He smiles. Easy. Too easy. "You sure?"

"Positive." I force a smile. "You're right. I need a bestie."

He leans in like he might kiss me, but Dr. Mansfield calls his name. He peels off toward the pavilion. I linger behind, watching the way he slips so easily into social charm. It should reassure me.

It doesn't.

Back at the car, I set the pumpkins on the hood and dig my purse from the passenger seat. I call Cady.

"I'm in," I say when she picks up. "But this is covert. Steven can never know."

"Understood," she says. "We surprise her. Lily Ann won't see it coming."

But if Steven finds out?

He won't. He can't.

"We say it's a girls' trip," I tell her. "If we hit a wall, we let it go. But if she knows something…"

"We blow it up," Cady finishes. "Like dynamite."

I end the call and spin—only to find Grant Ellersby leaning on the car beside me.

My breath catches.

He's five feet away. Too close. Dressed in a long black coat and cowboy hat, fake holster hanging low on his hips.

"How long have you been standing there?" I ask, keeping my voice light, my panic masked.

He twirls the fake revolver on his finger and smirks. "Long enough to know you carry more than pumpkins." He taps the side of his temple. "Secrets make poor costume accessories, Gwen."

I try to ignore his barb and point at his costume. "Doc Holliday?"

"I'm your huckleberry." His eyes—unreadable—travel the length of my ridiculous dress. "And what are you?"

"I'm Glinda the Good Witch," I say dryly.

He cocks his head and smirks. "Mmm. Look more like a queen about to be dethroned."

My stomach twists. He knows. Or suspects. And the way he looks at me—like a wolf that's scented blood—makes my skin itch. He's going to tell Steven what he overheard, and that will dethrone me in a big way.

He leans in and slowly adjusts my falling crown. "Right back on the throne. For now, anyway."

Subtext thickens between us like smoke. I stiffen.

His eyes flick over my shoulder. "Saw your husband when he dropped off the pumpkins, talking to someone by the bar. Woman in a mask. Pirate maybe. Red coat. Looked like they know each other."

My blood turns to sleet. "Steven? Probably someone from the office."

Grant nods slowly. "Just seemed…intense, that's all. Made me curious."

My mouth goes dry. I glance over my shoulder, but the pavilion's a blur of costumes. I don't see Steven.

"Curious about what?"

Grant gives me a half smile that doesn't reach his eyes. "What kind of man sends his wife away while he whispers to masked women in secluded corners?"

My muscles draw tight. I want to ask him what he knows. What he's implying. But instead, I pick up the pumpkins, crown tipping again, dress swirling, and head back down the hill. Toward Steven. Toward answers I'm not sure I want.

And I wonder if *he's* the one I should be afraid of or if Ellersby is messing with my mind because he knows he can. But how would he know what buttons to press unless someone told him?

Chapter Forty-Three

We landed at JAX a couple of hours ago, and after picking up a rental car, we grabbed a quick bite at a little crab shack—its dim lighting and salty tang oddly reminiscent of a seaside graveyard—before driving into St. Augustine to meet Lily Ann Cartwright (formerly Wagner). Steven saw me off at the terminal with a kiss and a small gift bag filled with sunscreen, lip balm and a book by one of my favorite authors. It was thoughtful, but every kind gesture felt like another weight adding to my hidden guilt.

Lying to my husband has never been my intention. I know it's wrong. Yet here I am, treading on dangerously thin ice in a town where secrets echo in every hallway, and I can't let justice go unpunished—if justice is even possible when a monster is still at large. Monsters, I've learned, come in many forms, clothed in both beauty and deceit, male and female alike. And tonight, the mirror tells me I might be one of them.

"What if she's not home when we arrive?" Cady asks, her voice a welcome interruption from the relentless pounding of my anxious thoughts.

"Then we stake her out," I reply, adjusting the air conditioner vent that barely fights the sultry, stifling heat. “Good old-fashioned surveillance. We circle the block, scope out her driveway, see if there’s a car parked—anything to let us know she’s around.”

“Good plan.” She bounces in her seat like a kid on the verge of unwrapping candy at a haunted fair. “I know this is all awful, tragic even, but I can’t help the excitement.”

I pat her knee but feel a shudder ripple through me. “Calm down, doll baby. It’ll be okay.” My words crack in the humid air as my heartbeat stutters—a prelude to the all-too-familiar chill that sweeps over me, stealing my breath. Not now. Not here.

“Gwen, are you sweating? Perimenopause or something?” Cady leans forward, concern replacing her earlier buoyancy as she studies my pale, trembling face.

I shake my head, pulling over to park. “Panic attack. Just need to breathe. Get them sometimes.”

“Right. Just breathe.” Cady begins an absurd interlude of hee hee hoo hoo.

“Cady,” I pant, “that’s Lamaze.” I begin my seven in through my nose and eight out through my mouth.

Her sheepish grin fades as she apologizes in a whisper. “Right. Namaste…in…”

I can’t help but snap, “Cady, shut up.” Rising from the car, I bend over and struggle to regain control. Every secret seeps into my veins, a reminder of what I’ve risked and what I still might lose. Slowly my breathing steadies, the perspiration easing like an underground fountain finally ebbing.

Sliding back into the car, I offer a tentative smile. “Sorry for telling you to shut up.”

“No problem.” Cady rubs my shoulder gently. “You good?”

“Yeah. I just…the lies are piling up, and I’m feeling them.”

Cady adjusts the air vents to blast cool comfort our way. “I’m sorry. I shouldn’t have called just to tempt you.”

“Not your fault. I’m a grown woman, fully capable of deciding what I want—and what I don't," I reply, shifting into Drive as we meander through a sleepy suburb of cookie-cutter homes and neat little carports. Passing by Lily Ann's street, I catch a glimpse of her home. A cheerful lemon-yellow house trimmed with white and a tidy lawn.

"She lives alone, a single mom. Unless she's got two vehicles, she's home," Cady deduces, squinting at her barely visible social accounts. It strikes me how private Lily Ann keeps her life; the only image we have is a younger version from some old yearbook.

"Now, listen," Cady continues, her tone dropping to a conspiratorial whisper as we circle the block. "This might get us nowhere. She might not know anything. She might not even talk—and if she does, she might not be the Lily Ann we expect."

I nod, the hairs on the back of my neck prickling with foreboding. As I park the car on the road, my pulse begins a slow, anxious rhythm. We step out into the warm glow of a late afternoon. I'm dressed in a flowing green maxi dress and sandals—disarming and approachable. Cady wears white slacks paired with a blue halter top that mirrors her bright eyes. I knock on the door, and after a moment, it opens just enough to reveal Lily Ann's wary gaze.

"Can I help you?" she asks, her voice tremulous.

"Are you Lily Ann Cartwright?" I ask, deliberately omitting her maiden name.

"Yes," she replies, looking older than her fifty-two years, half awakened and suddenly alert. She's dressed in worn black yoga pants and an oversized T-shirt sporting a sea turtle. Her hair, once golden, is now a tangled mix of gray pulled into a lazy topknot. In her vulnerability, I sense someone used to hiding in plain sight.

"I'm Gwen McDaniel, and this is Cady Tremell. We're from Cold Harbor." I study her expression, which shifts from confusion to something close to panic. "I moved into your old house last month."

Her eyes widen as if haunted by memories. "I'm sorry. I don't know what you could possibly want with me."

"May we come in?" I ask softly.

"I'll come out," she answers, her tone cautious, then shuts the door behind her and gestures for us to have a seat on the plastic lawn chairs lining the small concrete porch. The breeze is pleasant and gentle—and for a moment, I forget the sinister forces that brought us here.

"How did you find me?" she asks.

"Oh, it wasn't too hard," Cady says. "We want to talk about the house you grew up in."

Lily Ann's laugh is forced. "I see. Is this about the urban legends concerning Rebekah Howler and the Barkleys?" It's pretty clear she knows it's not.

"Did you have carpeting in the attic back then? I pulled up green shag and was wondering."

"You came all the way to Florida to ask me about carpeting?" She pulls a pack of cigarettes from her T-shirt pocket, lights one and inhales deeply, waiting for me to land the plane faster.

"In a way, yes. Please indulge me."

Lily Ann takes another drag. "My mom loved the attic. Spent a lot of time listening to records up there. Old-timey stuff that people before her had left, I guess. I wasn't allowed up there—it was her space. Why?"

"Was there anything written on the hardwood when you grew up there?"

She frowns. "Written? No, not that I know of. But again, I wasn't allowed upstairs. My mom wanted her space—needed it. My dad could be…controlling. What exactly is this about?"

I glance at Cady, and she nods. "When I ripped up the carpet, I found chilling writing carved into the wood—'I am not crazy'—and I want to know who wrote that."

Lily Ann's fingers tremble, and she takes a puff to calm herself. "I don't know. I can't imagine my mother doing that…" Her eyes look skyward, but her mind is back in Cold Harbor, in that blank but forlorn expression.

She's not much help, but it could have been her mother. She believes that. If so, why? "What can you tell me about your father? We can't seem to find him, as if he vanished too. Have you spoken to him recently?" I ask.

Lily Ann's eyes narrow. "As you probably already know, I ran out when I was fifteen. Hopped a bus with some cash I stole from him and came to Florida. Never looked back."

"That couldn't have been easy, to make your way at fifteen." I can't think about the things she might have had to do to survive.

"I got a job waitressing for cash. Little sunny-side-up diner. One of the servers took me in. But no, it wasn't easy. Life isn't easy."

"No, it's not. So…you haven't seen your dad since you were fifteen?"

She shrugs. "If you're trying to find out who wrote on the attic floor, I can't help you. I guess it's possible it was my mother. He made us feel crazy. Maybe we were. Maybe I am," she murmurs.

"How did your father make you feel crazy? You mentioned he was controlling?"

She lets out a loud, humorless laugh. "My father was a very bad man, Mrs. McDaniel. Though no one ever would have known."

"Bad *how*?"

She swallows hard and closes her eyes.

"For one, he liked young girls."

Chapter Forty-Four

Lily Ann's words lodge in my throat like a noose, pulling tighter until I can hardly swallow. Arriving at homicides is always depressing, but crimes against children unsettle me in ways I can't even put into words. I'm a tight ball of nerves, but I have no choice but to ask the next question.

If what she's saying is true, then it's possible that Roger Wagner abducted Candy Tremell at age thirteen.

"What do you mean by 'liked young girls'? How young?" I ask carefully. "And how do you know this?"

Lily Ann pulls the pack of cigarettes from her T-shirt pocket again and taps one loose. She leans forward, flicks the lighter resting on the plastic side table, and lights up. The acrid scent burns my nose, and I try not to cover my mouth or cough.

"Doesn't really matter how young, does it? Young is young," she mutters, exhaling smoke through her nostrils. "I don't want to talk about it." She stands and turns toward the door, shoulders squared, like she's ready to bolt.

She's not wrong, but if he has a certain type, the sicko might be responsible for some of the missing girls. One of them could be the author of the frantic writing.

"My sister went missing," Cady says, her voice quivering. "She was thirteen. Walking home from school. She was never seen again."

Lily Ann pauses mid-step, one hand gripping the doorframe.

"If your father liked young girls," Cady continues, "then it's possible he hurt my sister. I never even got the chance to know her. My parents…they've never been the same since she vanished. Please…please talk to us." Her voice drops to a whisper. "We need you."

Lily Ann turns slowly. "Your sister disappeared?"

Cady nods.

"Lily Ann," I say, my voice low. "The day I moved into your house, a bone was discovered behind your property. A femur." I swallow hard. "And now, more than ever, I'm starting to believe that bone belonged to Candy Tremell. Maybe your father did something to her."

She was local. The other girls who went missing weren't. He could have watched her, followed her. Roger Wagner might not have taken the others, but it's very possible he took Candy.

Her watery blue eyes shift between us. She takes a long drag, exhaling as she sinks back down onto the wicker couch.

"Thirteen. That's how old I was when my father started coming into my room at night." She flicks ash into the tray, not looking at either of us. "That's all I'm going to say about *that*."

My chest tightens. Her words cut deep.

"But I think my mother knew," she goes on. "She would go up into the attic for hours. Music cranked so loud the windows shook, especially at night. I think… I think she was trying to drown out what was happening. I don't really know."

She shrugs, a bitter little motion, and stubs the cigarette out hard.

"She died when I was fourteen, and then it was just him and

me and…no buffer anymore. I ran a year later. He'd never have thought I'd do such a thing. I'm sure it infuriated him." She lights another cigarette and exhales slowly.

I feel her pain like it's inside me, clawing at my ribs. I want to sob for the girl she was, locked in that house of horrors, bottled up for years like a scream in a sealed jar.

"I'm sorry that happened to you, Lily Ann," I say. "I would've left too. What you did was brave." I hesitate. "How did your mother die?"

"Heart attack, but she was young. Younger than they told anyone. Once she told me she was only thirteen years older than me. Either way, I found her in the basement. Dead on a Saturday afternoon. I always suspected stress did it, but who knows?"

I close my eyes and wait for the lump in my throat to ebb. "Can you tell me…did you ever see him with any other girls? Or was it just…was it just you?"

Not every abuser harms outside their own family. But if he did—if he took Candy—there could be a pattern.

Her fingers tremble as she presses the cigarette to her lips again. "I never saw him with anyone else."

"Were you allowed to have sleepovers with friends from school?"

Her nod is barely perceptible, but it's there. "I had friends over some, before thirteen. After that… I never invited anyone again. But not because I thought they'd get hurt. I was scared they'd find out about me. That he'd come into my room while they were there, and they'd see."

Without thinking, I reach over and grasp her clammy hand. "I'm so sorry." The words feel weak, useless. But they're all I have. If I tried to explain the way I feel her pain—how deeply it resonates—she wouldn't believe me.

She stares down at the floor for a long moment. "I did hear something once. Right before I decided to run away. The nightly visits…they'd started to taper off some by fifteen. I was grateful for that." Her voice cracks on the word *grateful.*

It turns my stomach. No one should ever have to be grateful for less abuse.

"What did you hear?" I ask gently.

"Kailey Bechtel's mom caught my dad peeping in her little sister's window. I overheard her talking about it at school. I was in the stall next to hers. Said he was a kiddie peeper and they went to the police department. Told Detective Ellersby. He said he'd handle it."

She clamps a hand over her mouth, and a ragged sob breaks through. "How awful is this," she says, "but part of me…part of me hoped he'd pick someone else even though I'd never wish it, never really want that to happen. Just that I wouldn't have to endure it anymore." Her eyes meet mine. "I know that makes me a terrible person, but—"

"No," Cady says firmly, handing her a tissue. "It doesn't. You were a child. You were scared. You were being abused by the person who was supposed to protect you. Anyone would have felt the same."

Lily Ann dabs her eyes, composing herself.

"Do you know where your dad is now?" I ask.

"No." Her answer is clipped. "And I don't want to. I never want to see him again. I assumed he was still in that house or dead. I'd prefer the latter."

"Did he ever talk about where he might go? Mention family? Parents? Siblings?" Maybe I could find him. Destroy him.

She inhales the cigarette deep. The end glows bright orange before dimming again.

"He never talked about his family. I never met anyone. No grandparents, no cousins. I asked my mom once, and she said she never met them either. They eloped, she said. Ran away together."

Or he'd abducted her too. If she was only thirteen years older than Lily Ann, she was a child.

Her eyes go distant, like she's putting together pieces of a puzzle too long ignored.

"Do you know how old he was or should be now?" I ask. I need an age to help me find him. He could be dead from old age.

"I think he was born in 1958 or '59, maybe. She would say they were just like Jerry Lee Lewis and Myra." Her eyes search mine. "I don't believe that for a second. I think she lived in a fantasy world to survive the nightmare that was her reality."

"Was your mom from the South or just a Jerry Lee Lewis fan?"

"Tennessee. Always had a little accent."

"And your father?"

She opens her mouth, pauses and shakes her head. "Honestly? I don't know. Never heard much of an accent from him. Didn't sound local either. I always assumed he was from Tennessee too. He has a degree from there, I think. Architecture." She exhales, smoke curling around her face. "Truth is, I never really knew my father. I don't think anyone did. But he was well-liked, respected. We went to church every Sunday, but that was clearly for show even though I actually liked being there. Only time I truly felt safe."

She leans forward, elbows on knees, voice low.

"But inside the house? It was like living in a vacuum of fear. A cloak of heaviness hung over everything, and it was always so darn cold."

"What about the secret room under the stairs? I found a pail with books, and your name was in them. Did he ever make you go in that room? Or was that a hiding place you felt safe?"

She frowns. "We never had a secret room under the stairs, or if we did, I didn't know about it. Wasn't forced in there."

Then it must have come after she left. He would have wanted

another girl. To replace her. He may have kept Candy Tremell in there. His own daughter from birth would have been easier to control, and so would Ann Wagner, especially if he had her from thirteen or earlier. But a new girl, one who wasn't under his thumb for decades, might be harder to control.

And he had to go to work. He'd need a place to hide her away. Keep her quiet. Submissive. Afraid. Dependent on only him.

"I used to think it was ghosts—Rebekah Howler or Lizzie Barkley—but the real monster wasn't in the past," Lily Ann continues. "He was made of flesh and blood. He prowled our halls and slipped into rooms at night." She closes her eyes, voice almost a whisper. "He preyed on innocence and fear."

I feel this deep in my bones. I've had my own personal bogeyman, too.

And I've never told a soul.

Chapter Forty-Five

The long drive up Darkwater Road hits different now. The trees lean a little heavier, the shadows stretch longer, and everything feels steeped in that damp, creeping kind of cold that never quite leaves your bones.

It's a sharp contrast to where we were yesterday—stretched out on a sunny Florida beach, sand clinging to our skin, books half read and drinks sweating in our hands. The sky was so bright it felt unreal, like we'd wandered into a dream. We mostly talked instead of read, letting the waves muffle the world. For a little while, we didn't speak of Cold Harbor at all. It was girl talk. It was easy. It was a lie.

But the lies never really leave, do they? They cling to the underside of every laugh, every easy moment. I don't like lying. I tell myself it's not who I am at the core.

But maybe that's a lie, too.

Maybe, deep down, we're all better at deceit than truth. Maybe honesty is the real performance—one that comes with effort, fear and guilt. The fear of being caught. The guilt of knowing you've hurt someone. The shame that you've done it at all.

"Hey," I say, glancing at Cady, "you up for talking to the Bechtel family? I don't see why we can't hit them up right now. Teresa has Tara while Steven works."

"I'm a savvy driver, and we're closed today. I'm down for anything." She does a smooth U-turn, flashing a grin.

"That's illegal."

But I no longer carry a shield.

"Sue me." She laughs, turning us down a side road.

We coast into an older neighborhood nestled in the pines. The homes are modest but well-kept—mature ranch styles with fresh paint, trimmed hedges and wide-open yards. I notice the absence of privacy fences. It feels…exposed.

Cady parks in front of a redbrick house from the fifties. A bay window juts out from the front like a soft smile, and inside it, a fat tabby cat naps in a slant of sunlight.

I miss Florida. I miss the sun. I miss pretending.

"Mr. Bechtel lives alone now since his wife passed. His name's Chris," Cady says, knocking. "But he might not remember. It's been a long time."

"Cady, you never forget a man peeping in your daughter's window."

The door creaks open, revealing a man in his late sixties, maybe early seventies. His smile widens when he sees Cady.

"Delivering coffee now, Ms. Tremell?"

She grins. "No, but it's not a bad idea. Mr. Bechtel, I'd like you to meet my good friend Gwen McDaniel. She used to be a homicide detective in Baltimore and now lives here with her husband—the new doctor."

"Oh, nice." He offers his hand. His grip is surprisingly firm. His hair is shock-white but thick, his eyebrows bushy and black—just like his eyes. But his gaze is kind, at least for now.

"How can I help you?" he asks. "If you're selling cookies or candy, I'm going to buy you out of house and home."

"Good to know," Cady says, glancing at me. My cue.

I step forward with a practiced smile. "Actually, we've been looking into some of the history behind my house on Darkwater Road. We were hoping to ask you about an incident involving Roger Wagner—something from years back."

The kindness drains from his face like warmth chased away by an oncoming storm. His eyes narrow.

"What kind of incident?"

His tone tells me everything. He remembers, and he hates the man. That alone lends weight to what Lily Ann told us.

"Your daughter Kailey said your late wife—" I soften my voice "—and I'm so sorry for your loss—saw Roger peeping in your youngest daughter's room. We wanted to confirm if that's true."

His gaze flicks to Cady. He sighs, then frowns.

"Is this for that podcast about the cursed house?" he asks. "Your mom helping you with this?"

"She's not," Cady says, calm but firm. "We're just curious about the people who lived there. Seems like the men were violent, and the women…broken."

Chris studies her for a long moment, then opens the door wider.

"Come on in. No point standing out here shivering in the wind when you could be warm."

We step into a house that feels untouched since his wife passed. It's clean but lived-in, a place suspended in time. He motions toward the kitchen, and we sit at a rickety old table scarred by decades of meals and memories. He takes the head of the table like he never left it.

"Roger always seemed like a stand-up guy," he begins. "Family man. Never found him at the bars, never chased skirts."

"So you didn't catch him on your property one night?" I ask.

"I didn't say that." He sighs.

"I'd noticed footprints outside the windows before," he continues. "At first, I thought Kailey was sneaking boys into her room again. She'd done it before—teenagers, you know. Boys aren't the only ones with raging hormones."

He waves a hand, brushing it off like dust.

"But one Friday night, Carlene stayed up late to watch a movie. A noise outside caught her attention. She went to catch Kailey in the act—but Kailey was fast asleep. That's when she saw someone at Olivia's window. Her room was across the hall, facing the backyard."

"How do you know it was Roger?" I ask.

Chris leans forward, elbows on the table.

"She woke me up. Told me someone was outside, watching. I grabbed my gun, went out the front, crept around back—and sure enough, there he was. A man in a black jogging suit, staring into the window like…well, let's just say he was enjoying the view."

I feel the air leave my lungs. "How old was Olivia?"

"Twelve. Almost thirteen." He scoffs and shakes his head. "I fired a warning shot into the air. He bolted. I chased him off. The next morning, when I was putting in new locks, I found his wallet in the dirt. Roger Wagner."

Cady and I share a glance.

"Did you confront him?" I ask.

"No. I called Chief—he was just a detective back then. We'd been friends for years. He came by, took the wallet, said he'd handle it. Said Roger wouldn't come around again. And he didn't."

"But he wasn't arrested?"

"Said all we had was trespassing. Voyeurism. He'd get a slap on the wrist, maybe. Told me he'd be more effective without me knowing details." Chris pauses. "Honestly, I hoped he roughed him up a little. And part of me wondered if Roger had gotten the wrong window. If he'd meant to look in Kailey's room. Still disgusting—but a child?"

His voice tightens. "Then a year or so later, Candy Tremell went missing. And I told Grant—I told him it could have been Roger Wagner. If he was the kind of man who watched little girls sleep…"

The dryer buzzes, abrupt and jarring. He excuses himself and disappears down the hall. A moment later, we hear the soft thud of him restarting the cycle.

When he returns, I ask, "What did Grant say when you suggested Roger took Candy?"

"He didn't think so. Said Roger had an alibi. Told me it was a false lead. Said he even searched the house himself, didn't find anything." Chris shakes his head. "But that girl could've been there and gone by then. You know how that is. Still… I trusted Grant. If he said it wasn't Roger, I believed him."

"What does Grant think happened to Candy?" Cady asks quietly.

"He said someone passing through saw her, took her. Crime of opportunity. Said he thought she was dead…but your parents never stopped looking. Not even after they adopted you." His expression softens. "You brought them joy, Cady. You gave them purpose again. We were all so happy for them."

I let the silence settle before asking, "Did anyone else around here have the same experience you did? With Roger?"

He splays his hands. "If they did, I never heard about it. And I didn't exactly go around telling people. Just told Grant."

And Grant said he took care of it. Took care of it how? Or did he turn a blind eye?

What mask is Grant Ellersby hiding behind? Is he a monster too?

Chapter Forty-Six

I sit in my car down the street from Marcia and Curt Tremell's house. After leaving the Bechtel home, Cady drove me back. Steven assured me he'd be home after lunch and swing by to pick up Tara from Teresa's, but he wasn't there. So here I am, parked in front of the Tremells' two-story brick home with its manicured lawn full of cutout black cats and scarecrows. Marcia's porch is covered in mums, scary jack-o'-lanterns and witches' brooms that probably smell like cinnamon.

The whole street is decked out for Halloween approaching at the end of the week, Saturday. Some yards are cute and kid-friendly; others are covered in fake tombstones and trash bags shaped like corpses rolled in black plastic. Vampires and Ghostface masks perch beside front doors, waiting to terrify children. I've never thought scaring children was funny, especially the little ones.

I'm not sure anyone's here—Marcia might be at the historical society. Curt's work truck isn't out front—it's too long for the garage—which brings me a wave of relief. I think I can crack

Marcia—but only if Cady's not here. There are things daughters shouldn't hear their mothers say.

And if I'm honest with myself, I don't want to face Steven. Things between us have been looking up, but I haven't decided if those texts he sent Teresa about "throwing her out" are nefarious—or something else entirely.

It's now or never. I walk up the drive and ring the doorbell.

After a few moments, Marcia Tremell opens the door, a dish towel slung over her shoulder. Her hair's pulled back, but a few wisps have come loose, her face flushed like someone who's just leaned over a hot oven. A wave of cinnamon and vanilla greets me, warm and familiar. Cookies. My stomach growls—I haven't had lunch. I never pass up a cookie, though I probably should.

"Gwen, hello." Her eyes flick over my shoulder, searching for Cady. "Come in. I thought my daughter might be with you. How was Florida?"

"Sunny and perfect." I keep it vague, not mentioning the real reason for our beach visit.

"Well, come in then. I made snickerdoodles. Fall Fest at the historical society—we like homemade treats."

Of course they do. It's the kind of town where everything looks perfect. But I'm starting to see the cracks. Feel them. Underneath all the charm, nefarious things are lurking. I just have to find proof before anyone will believe me.

"Thank you." I step into her kitchen—recently renovated, cozy and filled with ceramic Halloween decorations. A pumpkin cookie jar. A baker's rack lined with little black cats.

Then a real one saunters into the room like royalty, green eyes fixed on me. She sniffs the air and turns up her nose.

"That's Midnight. Not an original name, I know, but Curt found her at a worksite—starving, abandoned. How could I turn those green eyes away?" The cat winds around her legs, tail curling possessively.

"She's gorgeous. Did she inspire the collection?" I gesture toward the lineup of black cat knickknacks.

Paddywhack. Give a dog a bone.

The phrase slides across my mind, a fragment of some childhood rhyme. I don't know why it surfaces now, but it leaves me unsettled.

"Oh." She laughs, waving it off. "I've been collecting black cats since Candy was a preschooler. She loved them. Had a little stuffed one. It's on the mantel in the living room." Her smile falters, her gaze drifting for a moment. I've seen that look before—the distant, glazed-over expression of a parent remembering a child they can't touch anymore.

She pulls herself back. "Cady told me you know about our first daughter. Candy."

"Yes. And that's actually why I'm here, Marcia. I've heard some disturbing stories about Roger Wagner."

She stiffens, blinking fast. "What about him?"

"That he used to peep in windows. Young girls. Around twelve or thirteen—the same age Candy was when she disappeared. With the bone found in the woods…"

I let the thought trail off, let her mind fill in the rest. She already has.

She lifts her chin. "That bone was an animal. Grant wouldn't lie. He sent it off for testing, and a medical examiner gave him a report."

"A medical examiner he's quite friendly with."

Her mouth flattens. Her eyes don't leave mine.

"Come on, Marcia. You have to see it's possible. Grant's covering something up."

Marcia slides the pumpkin and black cat dish towel from her shoulder and twists it between her fingers. "Grant wouldn't lie, and certainly not about that. We all went to school together and have been friends for ages. He's a good man, and he would not cover up human remains. Why would he in the first place?"

I give her the *come on, you're smarter than that* look. "Ellersby isn't exactly in the mayor's good graces, from what I hear. I know he wants to keep his job. And if I've heard it once, I've heard it a million times. No crime happens here. It's a safe place. But Rebekah Howler wasn't safe. Lizzie Barkley and her mom weren't. The Batterson parents weren't either. That's just for starters." I refrain from bringing up my wild card—Lily Ann. For now.

She scoffs through a laugh as the oven beeps. She opens the door and grabs a pot holder before removing a batch of snickerdoodles. "That's absurd." She puts the hot pan on the stove and turns. "Is this about the podcast? Cady thinks you can get me to accept the fact she wants to exploit Candy? I won't change my mind. I can't stop her, though we've tried. But I don't have to participate or approve of it."

I sigh and forgo a cookie. I should have taken one before bringing up a sore subject. Now it would feel wrong. "I understand that. And it's not about the podcast but justice. Don't you want to know what happened to Candy? What if Roger Wagner harmed her? Don't you want to know? And what if we could find him? There's no statute of limitations on murder. He could go to prison for hurting her." Killing her. "I would see to it that he paid for his crimes."

Her eyes fill with tears. "I wish it was that easy. That cut-and-dried. You make it sound like we can just drive up at his new residence and take him away. You don't even know where he is. I've made peace—as much as I can—with the loss of my daughter. Now all I can do is focus and find joy in the daughter who is alive and here. All you'll give Cady—us—is false hope. And I won't stand by and be a part."

Her hesitation makes more sense to me now. She's been using the ill taste in her mouth over the podcast to cover up the fact she can't force herself to hope again. It would be easier for her to keep it all buried and locked away tight. Oh, how I get that. I've buried a lot myself.

But what if it isn't false hope? What if it can be real hope?

She pulls down a small plastic bag with fall leaves on it and places four cookies that were already cooled inside. Then she hands it to me. "Here."

Her gesture moves me, and I take the cookies. "I do know something about false hope, Marcia. About disappointment. I understand your need to bury it all. It's easier. Keeps you safer inside. But that's not true. It's always lurking underneath. Think about it. That's all I'm asking. If Cady does do a podcast, it would reach thousands or more, and these people might be able to help us find Roger Wagner. Find the truth."

"We don't even know it was him."

"We also don't know it wasn't. Think about pushing Grant or going over his head somehow."

I thank her again for the cookies and show myself out. As I step onto the porch, I hear her on the phone.

"She's been here. Cady is still going through with that podcast, and her first episode is going to be about Candy. I think that's pretty obvious now."

I pull the door almost closed but not quite as I listen.

"What else can we do?"

I'm still wondering who Marcia was talking to on the phone as I pull into my own driveway, my hands gripping the steering wheel a little too tightly. My heart's not quite right—something is off-kilter. Maybe it's the way Marcia's voice sounded, strained, like she was hiding something. Or maybe it's just me, overthinking.

After leaving the Tremells', I went by Teresa's and picked up Tara. She wasn't as friendly as she has been, and I can't blame her. But I chose her to keep Tara while Steven worked—a good faith thing and all that he's not sleeping with her and lying to me.

Now I release the car seat from the base, my eyes drifting to Tara's precious face, her small form so serene after a weekend away. I didn't realize how much I missed her until I saw her again. I carry her inside, my legs feeling like lead, my thoughts a tangled mess. The luggage can wait. I'm starving.

I text Steven that I have Tara and not to rush. I stare at the pantry, trying to distract myself from the uneasy feeling gnawing at my insides. Two cans of tuna stare back at me. I could make a tuna salad for lunch. Simple. Easy. He likes his with eggs, no pickle relish. I can eat it either way.

I place the car seat with Tara still in it on the kitchen table, the sound of shoes clicking against the hardwood floor drawing my attention. My body locks up, neck prickling. My purse, my gun, are on the table next to the car seat.

I turn, my pulse spiking as I go for my purse. But it's not an intruder.

It's Steven.

Not coming through the garage but the front door. Like a visitor and not someone who lives here. He stands there, blocking the hallway, his presence filling the room with something fierce and volatile. His neck is flushed, red and raw. The quiet rage in his eyes unsettles me—more than if he were shouting. It's a stillness that speaks volumes, a storm just waiting to burst.

My stomach tightens, but I force a smile, trying to steady myself. "Hey. You hungry? I was going to make tuna salad."

He steps forward slowly; the way his shoes scrape the floor makes me shiver. "No. How was your girls' trip?" His voice is too calm, too controlled. It feels like a trick question.

I try to hold on to the thin thread of normalcy even as I sense the heaviness in the air. "Fine. We soaked up the sun and drank fruity drinks. Gabbed, as girls often do." I force the smile wider and turn toward the pantry, trying to focus on the task. "Tuna salad sound good for lunch?" I ask again.

"All you do is lie to me." His voice is barely above a whisper. "You lied about the oxy. You lied about your job. Lies. Lies. Lies." The quiet fury in his voice wraps around me like a chokehold. "You lied about adhering to the restraining order against Teri Jo Tipton, and you still harassed her—"

The words hit me like a punch in the belly, and something inside me snaps. Anger floods my veins, black and hot, spreading through me faster than I can think. I spin around, my fists clenched, but I don't raise them. I can't.

"I never harassed Teri Jo Tipton," I say, my voice trembling with rage. "That woman murdered her children. Drowned them in a kiddie pool in her backyard. I was building a case. I was stacking evidence."

He shakes his head, a bitter laugh escaping his lips. His nostrils flare. "Yet you found nothing. Nothing at all." He steps closer, the distance between us shrinking, and I feel like I'm suffocating. "I told you to back off or you'd end up in hot water. But you never listen. You're a block of concrete when you think you're right. News flash, Gwen. You aren't always right."

I recoil. "Well, neither are you," I spit back, harsher than I intended. "I needed you to back me up. I needed you when I was going through one miscarriage after another. And what did you do? You pumped me full of antidepressants. Like I could fix myself with a pill."

He steps back, his hands shaking, and there's a flicker of guilt in his eyes. "You were depressed. I begged you to see someone. You refused."

"You couldn't separate being a doctor from being my husband. You couldn't see that I was dying inside. I wanted you. I needed you. But you couldn't be there for me. I was alone," I say, my voice breaking. The pain feels raw again, like the wounds never healed. "And you just kept going to work. Pretending everything was fine. We lost our children, one after another. And you wouldn't even hold Tara—the Tara before her." I point to the baby in the car seat.

His hands curl into fists at his sides, and his breath hisses out between his teeth. "Has it ever crossed your mind that holding her was too painful for me? Cradling her in my arms, lifeless, cold—was that what you wanted? Not everyone mourns the same way, Gwen. I don't sink into depression and drown in it like you do. But if I don't, then I must not love enough, right?"

For the first time, I see something in him I didn't before—pain, raw and jagged, just like mine.

"Why are we arguing?" I whisper, my voice cracking. "What is going on?"

"Don't act innocent. Why did you really go to Florida?" His eyes narrow, accusing.

My heart trips, thudding painfully in my chest. He knows. Grant Ellersby must have told him. My pulse races. What else has Grant said? What else does he know? I glance at Tara, the calm in her expression mocking the storm I feel rising inside me. For a second, I consider lying. But I can't. He's already suspicious.

Our marriage hinges on this one answer.

"You have to understand," I say, my voice steady but taut.

"I have to understand?" He laughs bitterly, a harsh, hollow sound. "Like I had to understand that your job came first? Like I had to understand why you needed the pills? You had to steal my prescription pads and falsify my signature to feed your addiction, Gwen. I lost everything because of you!"

He's right. Everything he worked for crumbled. My actions—my pain—tore everything apart.

"Like I have to understand why you keep parts of yourself hidden from me," he mutters, his voice barely a whisper, but the accusation is clear. "But you could stay up talking to Kent Masters for hours? How many times do I have to forgive you before I say enough? I warned you this would blow up in our faces, Gwen."

I press my hands to my eyes, trying to stem the tide of emotion rising in me. "What happened?"

"Grant Ellersby came by about thirty minutes ago." His voice cracks, and I see the rawness in his eyes. He ticks off everything, including my visit to Marcia Tremell. Was it him she was talking to?

Panic claws at my throat. "He knows everything. And he thinks you need to be in a mental facility. Maybe…maybe I do too."

My mouth goes dry. I feel like I'm losing my grip. The room tilts around me.

"I'm not crazy." The words hang in the air, heavy, suffocating. Same as what's etched in the attic flooring. They hit me like a blow. It's this house. This house is making us unravel.

"No?" His finger points sharply toward Tara. "This is normal? This is how a sane person behaves?"

My throat tightens, my heart beating so fast it feels like it might explode. "She's not a 'this.' She's my daughter. My only comfort. I need her."

"You need to need me!" His voice rises into a roar, and before I can react, he jerks Tara from her seat. Her tiny body is so fragile in his arms, her head lolling slightly.

"Steven, stop!" I reach for her, but he pulls her away, his hands trembling with rage.

"I'm here! I've always been here!" His voice shakes with fury. "You ignored me for her. I started working late back in Baltimore because you wouldn't talk to me, same reason I see a therapist now. But you talk to her!" His gaze locks onto Tara with a hatred that makes my blood run cold.

I step forward, desperate. "Give her to me, Steven. Please. You're going to hurt her."

His eyes turn as black as a storm cloud, fury mixed with something colder. "Hurt her? *I'm* hurting!"

And then, in an instant, he hurls her.

Her tiny body sails through the air, a sickening crack echoing through the room as she slams against the wall. The sound—like breaking glass—echoes in my mind as I watch her fall, limp, to the floor. My blood turns to ice.

Someone is wailing, but I don't know who.

No, I do. It's me.

Steven stands frozen, staring at her, his mouth open, his face a mask of disbelief.

I collapse to the floor, my scream shredding the silence. My whole body trembles, the world slipping out of focus.

Chapter Forty-Seven

Tara lies on the floor, her neck twisted at an odd angle, legs bent behind her back in a grotesque imitation of a broken doll… but…she *is* a doll. My hands shake as I kneel beside her, my sobs wracking my body. *I needed her.* I still do.

"I'm sorry, Gwen. I didn't mean to do that." Steven's voice is so detached, so matter-of-fact, as though he hasn't just thrown my only link to my stillborn baby into a wall.

"She's all I have." My voice cracks, the words barely a whisper, but they hang in the air, heavy and pleading.

He sighs, a low, irritated sound, and squats beside me. He doesn't touch me. "She's not even real, Gwen. I am flesh and blood. And you had me."

He might as well have slapped me, but I don't react. I can't. I can't feel anything anymore but the empty hollowness that's been growing inside me for months. Years.

He stands abruptly, keys jangling in his hand. His shadow looms over me as he walks toward the side door. My throat tightens, and my vision blurs with the salt of my tears. But I don't look away. I can't.

I reach for Tara, the reborn baby I'd had made piece by piece, based on the photos of Tara that Steven hesitated to let me use. But he didn't tell me I couldn't have a doll. Dolls help grieving mothers. I wasn't the only one in those groups, those social media circles where women cry over painted eyes and soft vinyl skin. It was a way to cope, they said. A way to hold on to something when everything was lost.

But Steven hadn't understood.

When I started making formula with baby powder and water, he balked. When I bought the stroller, the little beating heart mechanism that made the chest rise and fall as if it were alive—he grew silent, too silent.

And then I painted a nursery. Bought furniture. When he saw it, his face drained of color, but he didn't say anything. He didn't understand, but he allowed it. He indulged me. As long as it stayed in the house.

But that was before. Before I couldn't go anywhere without her. Before I couldn't breathe if she wasn't next to me. I feel her lifeless, silicone form against my chest, and my hands tremble as I place the little heart back into her chest, pressing it with desperate, shaking fingers until the soft, rhythmic beat fills the silence.

"This is unhealthy, Gwen." Steven's voice cuts through my fragile thoughts like a razor. I close my eyes, hoping it's a nightmare, but it's not. "Pretending you have a real newborn isn't going to heal you. I'm not going to say I understand because I don't, but I hurt, too, at losing Tara. She had my dimples. My nose. My chin."

I don't reply. I can't. I want to scream, but I swallow it. She *had* been blessed with his dimples, his nose. She was beautiful. But she's not here. She's gone, and all I have left is this plastic thing in my arms that feels like everything and nothing at once.

I remember what I said to him when I had her made. *"It's*

just for a little while," I whispered. *"I need time. Please. Let me be a mom, just for a while. Let me heal."*

I can hear him moving behind me now, his footsteps heavy on the floor as he gathers his things. His keys jingle again. I don't want him to leave. Not again. But he is.

"Where are you going?" I ask, my voice so small, so fragile, I can hardly recognize it.

He turns, his face grim. He has a suitcase in hand. When did he even pack it? How long has he been gone? I can't remember. Time has slipped through my fingers like sand.

"I can't anymore, Gwen." I grasp the finality in his voice, but my mind can't stop buzzing enough to fully register what he's saying. "This was the last straw. I've done everything for you. From begging them not to prosecute you to stepping down from my job to protect you. I've tried to keep you off Grant Ellersby's radar, but it's too late. He knows. He knows everything. How long do you think I can keep my job when everyone finds out my wife totes around a doll? Has a babysitter for her. How do you think I have felt explaining the situation to Teresa? Paying her? No wonder she didn't want to take our money. To watch a doll do nothing but swing? We might as well kiss this town goodbye—everything I warned you about. You just couldn't listen to me."

I know I made mistakes. I know that. Calling social services was wrong. But I *believed* it. I *felt* it in my bones. Teri Jo was capable of hurting her newborn. She was capable of anything. And I wanted to protect that child. No one would protect that baby. I had no choice but to keep vigil over her and had even considered taking her myself.

Teri Jo lied to my chief. She was never *afraid* of me. I didn't take the baby… I just wanted her to be safe, and that meant keeping my eyes on her every second I had available. And sometimes that meant during my working hours.

And now? No one keeping watch. It's only going to be a

matter of time before I hear that she's been drowned in a kiddie pool too.

"I didn't lie about Baby Tara," I say, my voice breaking. "It was real to me. She's been real to me."

He sighs, dragging a hand through his hair. He looks tired. So tired. "It was a mistake, Gwen. All of it. You've crossed too many lines."

"Grant...he's..." My mind spins. "He's after me." My chest tightens. I struggle to breathe.

"Too late, Gwen. Even if it was true, which it isn't." His voice is cold. Detached. "No matter what you say about bones in the woods or carvings in the floor or how many times you point the finger at the chief, you look mentally unstable. Like a madwoman raving and trying to hold on to a life she lost."

I shake my head. "I'm not mentally unstable, Steven." But here I am, holding a doll. Clutching it like a lifeline.

"You don't get it," he mutters, his voice trembling with frustration. "You have no ground to stand on. I look like a fool. I'm a *doctor*—and I'm letting my wife carry around a *doll*. You've made a mockery of everything. Of me. Of us."

This truth cuts deep, deeper than I care to admit. I want to push him away. I want to scream, to tell him that he doesn't understand—that he never will. But I can't. I'm too broken.

"And all the while," he continues, his words slow and heavy, "I've been trying to hold us together. But you—" He gestures around the room, the world closing in around me. "You don't even try. You refuse help. You refuse to see a therapist. You refuse everything that might fix this. You hold on to a *doll* and tell me it's real, and for side notes accuse me of affairs. This makes the fourth time. I can't keep doing this, Gwen. I can't. Watching you deteriorate is killing me."

My mind spins, dizziness threatening to swallow me whole. I close my eyes, clutching Tara tighter, feeling her cool, unyielding form against my chest. She's my daughter. *She's my daughter.*

Except she's not.

"I don't want you to leave," I whisper, my heart breaking at the thought of losing him. Of losing everything.

He looks at me, his face softening for a moment, before a single tear slides down his cheek. I don't know if he's crying for me, for us or for something else. But when he speaks again, it feels like a death sentence.

"You're not giving me a reason to stay," he says, his voice so broken, so defeated. "I love you, Gwen. God help me, I love you. But love isn't enough when it's *killing* me."

And with that, he walks out the door.

I hear the soft click as he closes it behind him. The sound reverberates through the house, and I feel it in the marrow of my bones. It's final. This is it.

I don't deserve his love. Not after everything I've done. I don't deserve his forgiveness. But he gave it to me, time and time again. And now it's gone.

I lay my head against the wall, the ache in my temples unbearable, my heart pounding so loudly I can't hear anything else. The emptiness grows. It's swallowing me whole.

And then it hits me. The only thing I do know in this moment is that I still don't feel alone in this house.

Part III

The Reckoning

"Everybody feels the evil, but no one has courage or energy enough to seek the cure."

—Alexis de Tocqueville

Chapter Forty-Eight

The sun has buried itself beneath the horizon, and duskiness has descended on the drafty house. I think I've been on the kitchen floor for hours. Crying until my eyes went from puffy to Rocky-Balboa-in-a-fight swollen.

I accused Steven of affairs, of betrayal, and found circumstantial evidence where I *wanted* to. Why do I do this? Why do I sabotage the only good thing in my life?

I knew something inside me was broken before I turned sixteen. What happened to me after that only deepened the cracks. My marriage's collapse is my fault. I own that. I carry it like a stone in my chest. And yet—I don't know how to fix it.

In my head, I do. Quit chasing ghosts. Quit seeing patterns that may not be there. If I've been wrong about Steven, maybe I'm wrong about Roger Wagner. Maybe I'm wrong about the bones, the house, the whispers.

Maybe I'm wrong about everything.

But not Teri Jo. She drowned her children. I know that. She got away with murder, but it haunts *me* day and night, and I can't do a single thing about it.

Maybe the ghosts I'm chasing are my own. Maybe I'm just haunted by myself—blurry, bone-chilling visions that surface in dreams and drag me awake in cold, choking terror.

Eventually I drag myself up from the floor and pick up Tara, placing her in the carrier on the table. My whole body aches, like I've been trudging through waist-deep sludge for days. I have just enough strength to make it to the living room. I light the fire, collapse on the couch and pull a throw blanket over me.

I'm exhausted in every way. Mind, body, spirit. I whisper a prayer—not for clarity, not for forgiveness that I don't deserve, just for God to *see* me. To lift this veil that's been draped over my soul for decades.

The fire staves off the cold but doesn't chase it away. As my eyes begin to close, I let sleep take me. In sleep, I don't have to think about my future. About the possibility that I don't have one.

Thud.

I jolt—but not fully. I'm groggy. Drenched in that heavy, velvet fog of sleep that won't let go. A child laughs, high and tinkling. It's followed by a bloodcurdling scream.

Then the slap of a plastic jump rope against concrete.

Slap.

Slap.

Slap.

Dolly Bear, Dolly Bear, touch the ground…

I bolt upright.

It's coming from the basement.

I know I shouldn't go down there, but I can't pretend I didn't hear it. The noise still echoes faintly—plastic on cement, far below.

I make my way to the kitchen, to the basement door, and pause. My hand hovers on the knob. I don't want to do this.

But I *have* to.

Only… I don't.

Because something is down there. Something that feeds on fear.

I back away and bump into the kitchen island, then slide down beside it to even out my breathing. When I toss my head back, I knock it hard against something beneath the Formica overhang. Maybe the size of a quarter.

I pull my phone from my pocket to use the flashlight for a better view and see three missed calls from Kent.

What could he possibly want now? After what I said to him before I was fired?

Ignoring them for now, I turn on my phone light and aim it at the underside of the counter. There, painted the same dull brown as the cabinets, is a button. Hidden in plain sight.

I press it.

A buzz echoes.

The island shifts with a low groan. The countertop slides open like the bed of an MRI machine, revealing concrete stairs descending into a void.

I didn't see any other stairs from the basement side. Just the main steps opposite the storage wall.

What is this?

My heart begins to hammer. I move toward the opening and slowly descend the twelve concrete stairs. The stench of mildew and rotten earth swallows me whole. I gag and bat away cobwebs thick as gauze. At the bottom, I find a light switch.

The fluorescent bulb flickers before humming to life. A twelve-by-twelve room. Concrete walls. Dust thick as wool.

A cot in the corner, long abandoned. An old brown rug. Two large paint buckets, one cracked. I cover my mouth.

Someone built this to *hide* someone. Not shelter. Not protect. Imprison.

It's not just secret. It's *sinister.*

Roger Wagner was an architect. He would have had the skills to design this kind of access.

Lily Ann said she was never kept in a hidden room. If she

didn't know about the tiny room under the stairs, then she probably didn't know about this. She'd been open about everything else.

The buckets. My mind doesn't want to go there, but it does. Someone had to use them. No plumbing. Just stone and silence and rot. He kept someone down here.

The room begins to tilt. Nausea hits me like a wave breaking against stone. I barely make it to one of the buckets before I retch.

I stumble back upstairs, shaking, and set the bucket outside, then return and rinse my mouth in the sink. My fingers tremble as I text Cady.

Come to the house ASAP. New news.

She responds instantly. On my way.

I hit the button again, and the countertop slides back into place. The island looks normal. Like nothing is buried beneath it. Like nothing ever happened.

Who else knows?

Teresa? Deena?

My phone buzzes.

Kent again.

Please call me. It's about Teri Jo Tipton.

My stomach drops.

I tap his name, and he picks up on the first ring.

"Hey," he says gently. "How are you?"

I pinch the bridge of my nose. "Acclimating." I don't tell him about Steven. He doesn't need to know that.

"Good. Good," he says. "I—well, it doesn't matter. I just wanted you to know...last night, Teri Jo's ex-boyfriend confessed. Cracked right after his rock-solid alibi fell apart."

I freeze. "What?"

"He and his 'other' girlfriend broke up. She came running with the news that he wasn't with her after all. She'd been lying because he asked her to lie. We brought him in, and he spilled. Said he'd been high and angry Teri Jo had kicked him out. Found out the youngest baby wasn't his. The oldest girl let him in while Teri Jo slept. He told her not to wake her mom. Said they could all go swim out back. Drowned her first. Then the three-year-old. Then the toddler."

I press my hand to my chest, trying to breathe.

"She didn't do it, Gwen. She's in rehab. She's working, taking parenting classes. She's clean."

I was wrong. All this time—I *was* wrong. I've been wrong about everything.

Steven was right.

I am chasing ghosts.

"Gwen. Gwen, I thought if you finally knew the truth, it might offer you some peace. The new baby is with Teri Jo's sister, who is a kindergarten teacher. Married with two kids of her own. She's safe while Teri Jo gets the help she needs. This…this makes you feel better, right?"

I slump into a kitchen chair, staring out into the hush of night. Moonlight slices across the tile, casting fractured shadows. Yes and no. I lost my career over nothing.

Although that's not really true, if I want to be brutally honest with myself. There would have been another Teri Jo sooner or later. I was already losing it before she ever came into the picture.

I rake a hand over my face. "I'm sorry, Kent. For what I said to you when you went to the captain with my problem. I should've thanked you."

"I know you. That you didn't actually believe I'd betray you for rejecting me. Rejecting…us." His words are laced with regret.

"I didn't. I was just angry at the world. At me. At Steven."

"I assume he's not having an affair, then?"

He isn't. Hadn't. My fears and paranoia were easy to project on him, on anyone. "No, but I've ruined it anyway." I don't go into any more details.

"I still..." Kent says softly. "Doesn't matter. I hope it works out for you, Gwen. All I've ever wanted was for you to be happy."

A pair of headlights flashes across the window. Cady's here.

"I know that too. Thank you. Look, it's crossing a line, but I need your help." I give Kent the bullet points regarding the missing girls, specifically Candy Tremell and what has happened tangibly since coming to Cold Harbor, which includes the secret rooms and what Lily Ann told us. "Can you help me? With everything. Roger Wagner. Grant Ellersby. And if there's any way you can get info on the bone from the woods..."

"I'm on it. But watch your back, Gwen. If you're right, you're in real danger."

I glance at the kitchen island, at the hollow space I now know lies beneath it.

I've been in danger all along. If I keep going...

That danger may lead to *dead*.

But stopping?

That might be worse.

Chapter Forty-Nine

"What is going on?" Cady asks, and I don't even know where to start.

"Steven left," I say. "I expect divorce papers within the week."

I manage to keep my voice steady, but my eyes are still swollen, and tears threaten to rise again. I hate crying in front of people. Hate the weakness of it.

"I'm so sorry, Gwen." She hugs me, and I let her, even though it pushes me closer to the edge.

"No," I say, pulling back just before I splinter. "This isn't your fault. I could've said no. I didn't. And there are things, Cady—things you don't know. But you should. And I'll tell you. But first… I need to show you something."

I move to the island and press the hidden button beneath the counter. A soft mechanical click, and the side panel shifts. The countertop slides open toward the door, revealing the concealed stairs to the basement.

Cady steps back like she's seen a ghost. "What the…?"

I don't answer. I just start down, and she follows. The fluorescent lights buzz to life with a flicker that makes my skin crawl.

"I know of one former resident capable of building something like this," I say.

"Roger Wagner," she breathes.

I nod. "Cady… I think he might've kept…"

"Candy," she says, barely audible.

"It's possible." I keep walking, even though the air is colder down here. "I've got a detective friend digging into Roger, seeing if there's any trace of him left. I also went to see your mom after we got back from Florida. I didn't tell her why, just asked about Roger. She gave me nothing. Still trusts Grant, too."

She stays quiet, her face pale in the humming light.

"I asked my detective friend to look into the bone," I add.

Cady collapses onto the nearest chair and grips her head. "I'm freaking out, Gwen. I can't stay down here."

"I know. Me too." I follow her back into the kitchen. Her gaze shifts toward the car seat in the corner. She frowns, then tilts her head, reaching down with deliberate slowness to touch the baby's cheek. Her fingers brush against the silicone skin, soft and impossibly lifelike.

She looks at me. Really looks.

"Gwen?" she says, standing, cradling the doll now. My heart skips. I think this might be the moment she leaves—calls someone, backs away, decides I've gone off the deep end.

I stay very still. "There's a story you need to hear. But it starts before Tara."

I gesture to the doll.

"When I was sixteen, I thought I fell in love," I begin. "With a friend of my father's. He was…twenty-five years older. I was angry all the time. Or sad. Or both. Sometimes I hurt myself just to feel in control again."

Cady doesn't interrupt. Her eyes shine.

"He said I was beautiful. That my parents didn't understand me. That I was a woman. He'd pick me up from school, take me out, buy me things. And I fell for it. I thought he saw me."

I look down at my hands.

"He was grooming me. And I didn't understand that until I was pregnant and he wanted me to abort it and left when I refused."

Cady's hand moves to her throat.

"I didn't want to get rid of her. I wanted her. I told my parents, hoping they'd help me. They said I could have the baby—but not keep her. I was too young. Too damaged. So I lied and told them I didn't know who the father was. But I did. I knew."

"How old would she be now?" Cady asks softly.

"Twenty-five. I named her Tara. I don't know what she's called now. It was a closed adoption. They gave her to a couple who couldn't have children. I never even saw them. They just...took her."

Cady wraps her arms around me again. This time I let the tears fall.

"I've been pregnant four times since," I say. "Four losses. The last one was second trimester. I thought maybe I deserved it somehow. That I was being punished, and to some degree I think maybe I still am, for my choices and lies and rebellion."

Cady shakes her head fiercely. "No, Gwen. You weren't. That's not how this works."

She turns to the kettle, fills it, starts it boiling. "We need tea. Or tequila. But tea's closer."

I almost laugh, and it feels strange, like I've cracked something open. She pulls down two mugs and reaches for the tea tin.

"She hasn't actually healed you, has she?" she asks after a beat, nodding at the doll.

I glance over at her—my Tara.

"No," I say quietly. "She comforted me for a while until she became so real, a habit to hold. I found this community online, people who lost babies. They had these custom-made dolls. Some looked just like the babies they'd lost. I sent in a photo. And when she arrived—it was like holding my daughter again. Just for a moment."

Cady doesn't flinch. She pours the water. Keeps listening.

"I know it's not normal. But it helped. For a little while, until it made things worse. I kept telling myself that nothing was wrong and it would only last a few days while I grieved, and a month turned into two months." Everything escalated until it was an avalanche out of control. I thought I was coping with the loss of the babies, the punishment for letting my parents give the one child I could carry away to strangers. But I lied to myself. Used the doll to live a fantasy instead of working through the pain in reality.

Cady slides a mug toward me and leans on the counter, her expression gentle but not pitying. "Bad things happen that we can't always explain—like losing babies. But it is not punishment for past sins. It isn't some kind of cosmic just desserts. You were sixteen. Under your parents' authority. They probably thought they were doing the right thing, even if maybe they weren't."

"I want to believe that."

"Then believe it, because it's true." She studies the baby. "This is why you kept the shield down and wouldn't let me hold her. But you told me to come by later."

"I was going to cancel on you. I love having you in my life. I thought if you knew I had her, you'd think I was mad and run for the hills." I swallow hard, holding back the flood of tears.

"I wouldn't have. I'm not judging your actions or your feelings, Gwen. You've gone through so much trauma in your life, carrying it around like an anchor around your neck. I won't tell you I think this is healthy, because deep down you know it's not. You know this isn't a coping mechanism that will bring you lasting peace."

"No. You're right."

She reaches out, then pulls back. "Can I hold her? Now?"

"Of course."

She glances at me for reassurance before picking Tara up from the car seat. "Wow. She is really lifelike. Her chest even rises and falls… Her eyes…" She tilts her head, watching the delicate blink.

I inhale deeply. It feels good—almost cleansing—to confess what I've been concealing for so long. But the one person I should be confessing to, I haven't. I've let him walk away, even if it's only fifteen minutes away. He's gone.

"Now," I say softly, "what were *you* going to tell me?"

She holds Tara a moment longer before gently placing her back in the carrier. "I went to my mom again—about Candy when I was working on her disappearance alone."

When I'd backed off to save my marriage and didn't.

"I told her about the possibility Roger could have harmed Candy. Before we knew what we do now, it was plausible. She shut it down as always, so I went behind her back, and I did something."

She pauses and I wait for her to continue.

"I found some of Candy's old things. There was a toothbrush wrapped in plastic and a lock of her hair—my mom kept them in the freezer, believe it or not. Back then, people saved anything with DNA. Just in case your kid ended up on a milk carton." She shrugs. "I guess she forgot about them or wanted to hang on to a piece of her."

"Smart," I say, feeling a chill slither up my arms.

"I used the raw DNA and requested a DNA kit. I had it expedited, then entered the information and uploaded it before we left for Florida. I thought maybe if she didn't die, she might be out there somewhere. That maybe she uploaded her own DNA, or she had kids and they uploaded it. Or maybe we could get the DNA from the bone—I knew you had contacts—and match it to the DNA from her hair and toothbrush. It's a long shot, slim. But I'm desperate."

"Of course you can hope," I whisper.

She touches Tara again. "If you'd like, I can purchase a DNA kit for you too. We could use it to maybe find your daughter. Would you want to try?"

I stir honey into my mug, feeling the steam warm my face. "To find my original Tara," I say, my voice barely audible.

She nods.

"Yeah. Maybe." I sip my tea. "I've thought about it. For years. But I always had reasons not to."

"What's different now?"

"Steven's leaving, and I am truly alone. He doesn't know about that part of my past. The man I was with…he was married."

Cady reaches across the table, her hand closing over mine. "You should tell him. He needs to know the root cause of your desperate moves to make things right, Gwen. That's all I'm saying. I won't push you. But I think we should one hundred percent find your daughter."

And for the first time in a long time, I nod *without* hesitation.

Chapter Fifty

I smell smoke. Acrid, thick.

My eyes snap open. I sit up in bed, but there's no fire.

A little girl stands at the foot of my bed.

I rub my eyes. I have to be dreaming. But when I look again, she's still there. Pale as moonlight, with dirt smudged around her mouth and one pigtail hanging loose, like it's been that way for years.

She begins jump-roping. Giggling.

"Let's pick a color," she chants, skipping over the rope again and again. "Let's pick a color, but please not red. Red is the color that makes you dead."

She stops. Looks straight through me.

My heart stutters. I clutch the tangled sheets around me.

"Find me," she whispers.

She turns toward the hallway.

Footsteps echo on the wooden floorboards—heavy. Steady.

"He's coming. Hide. Hide, Dolly."

Then she's gone. Nothing left but heavy silence wafting from the walls. I've gone days without experiencing this terror. But she's back. Now. Today.

Maybe I'm dreaming it. Now that Tara is out as a doll, I'm conjuring up every possible explanation that would make reasonable sense and not lead me down a ghostly road revealing Lizzie Barkley or even Candy Tremell calling from beyond the grave to enlist my help in solving the matter.

But here I am, a former detective. In this house.

Could Cady have been right? Is that why I'm here at this time? Is it my purpose to find justice for what I am sure Roger Wagner has done to his own daughter and potentially other young girls?

Maybe it's not the Darkwater Road home reaching out with sinister claws to drag me in and drive me mad. Maybe it's something lighter drawing me here for this. But the shadows are thick and blot out the light. It's hard to see, to feel the warmth. The fear of this living, breathing monster feels bigger than the light. Like the crows, bigger than the chickadees.

And yet they never stop visiting my windowsill in the morning light. Tapping at the window in a friendly request to beckon all three inside. To live and bring me joy, friendship and happiness.

All the while, the crows congregate and grow larger in number until the sky is a sea of black. It's so hard to see the little birds when a curtain of midnight hangs thick in the background.

I crawl out of bed and don my robe to make extra strong coffee and ponder on purpose. The eerie song from the attic takes on new meaning all of sudden.

Beautiful dreamer...wake unto me...

Am I living in a dream and not reality? It's easier. Who is Gwen St. James McDaniel?

I know who I've been. I can't say who I am now, but I have an inkling of a dream about who I would like to be.

As I wait for the coffee to brew, I check my phone and see

a text from Kent. A light catches my eye outside. A flashlight maybe. Then I hear something like rocks on glass. What on earth? I race back upstairs, grab my gun and return to the kitchen. No more lights.

But I hear something. Movement.

The coffeepot drips, drips, drips, and the room smells like bitter brew.

I sneak out the kitchen door and into the night; the wind bites and nips underneath my robe as I stick close to the side of the house, inching my way around back. Whispers catch my attention, followed by a girl's giggle, and that disturbing chant from the child at the foot of my bed echoes in my head.

"Let's pick a color, but please not red. Red is the color that makes you dead."

I fear what I'll bump into in the dark when I finally round the corner. The canoe bumps against the dock.

Thud.

Thud.

Thud.

My heart is in my throat, but I keep moving and peep out to see four teenagers. Three have beer cans in hand. One of them is pelting the attic window while the girls are repeating the same words and giggling.

"If you aren't serious about it, you won't see Lizzie Barkley in the window. Get serious," one of the boys hisses. The girls try to straighten up, but they're drunk or just stupid. Likely both.

"Okay, Riley. Chill," a girl scolds. She locks arms with the other girl, who is taller. "This is why I hate you being the DD. You're no fun."

"Bloody Lizzie Barkley, Bloody Lizzie Barkley. Please appear. Use the window as a mirror. Let us look into your face. If we scream, we'll take your place."

Oh, for crying out loud. It's almost 4:00 a.m. Are these kids for real? They're out here trying to conjure the very thing I want to go away. They don't know fear.

I listen to them say it four more times as the boys jest something is appearing in the attic window and the girls cling to them.

"I think I see her."

"I don't want to see her. I don't want to die!" the other girl says, speech slurred.

Is this what I'm going to endure all week until Halloween this Saturday? Well, if they want to be scared, I'll give them scared. Misery loves company.

On their last chant, I hold my cell phone under my chin and switch on the light. "Bralalalalalalala!" I scream in my deepest, most maniacal voice. They all squeal, including the designated driver, drop their beer cans and flee for the woods.

I laugh, and it feels good to laugh. That's what they get. I'm marching over to throw away the beer cans when I spot a light flicker on across the harbor at the doctor's house. The attic light.

On. Off. On. Off. On. Off. On… Off… On… Off… On… Off… On. Off. On. Off. On. Off.

I watch it repeat two more times before the light stays off permanently. I gather my robe tighter around my chest with one hand while I dump the half-drunk cans of beer onto the grass and carry them to the garbage can outside. The paint bucket that's inside still reeks of vomit. I hurry and close it, then go inside and lock the door.

Enough shenanigans for one night. I remember Kent's text and check it.

Nothing on Roger Wagner. Can't even find that he sold the house on Darkwater Road. He's a ghost.

I stomp my foot in frustration. I am over Halloween words and no answers but more questions. Deena isn't around to explain this. Teresa doesn't know enough, being so new to the occupation.

He moved in '96 or '97 according to a lady who works in the historical society.

Candy Tremell went missing four years earlier. Could he have kept her here in this house under everyone's noses?

Back in 1991, Jaycee Dugard was kidnapped at eleven. She was held for eighteen years down the road from her house.

Can you find me a Brad Langston from Cold Harbor? He moved to Japan, I think.

Maybe he can help me with the carpet in the attic or say if he'd seen the writing himself. More and more I'm believing that Candy Tremell is the girl upstairs.

Why is there no proof of sale from Wagner to the Langstons? Why would anyone cover that up and remove or destroy the property records?

Unless there never was a sale. My blood turns cold.

What if that bone in the woods was Candy Tremell's? But she wasn't the only one out there?

What if Roger Wagner's bones are out there somewhere too?

Chapter Fifty-One

Downtown is a nightmare dressed up in cobwebs and candy. I've been dreading this day. Each time I've come here, the decor has grown more over-the-top, but tonight, Halloween, it's grotesque. Every lamppost is wrapped in fake bloodied gauze, and jack-o'-lanterns with gaping maws line the sidewalks like warning signs. There's a giant inflatable clown on the courthouse steps with fangs bared and eyes that flash red. I swear it's watching me.

Children scream with joy—or something close enough to it—while adults sip cider out of skull mugs and pretend the world isn't falling apart under their feet and this town is safe and always has been. Everything's dialed up too high. Too much color. Too much sound. Too much malevolence, masked as tradition.

And I wonder, is this who we really are? Is this festival of gore and make-believe just a cover for what's been here all along?

People grin behind their painted faces, but I see it now. The corrosion. The way shadows cling to corners, to doorways, to people who stare just a beat too long. A man in a butcher's apron with fake blood down his front laughs with his friends. But his cleaver looks legit. The blood looks real.

I feel it deep in my bones—that something is very wrong about tonight. More wrong than it usually is, and it's not the drama at my house, running off kids in droves who came to catch a peek at bloody Lizzie Barkley with her head half blown off, or to see the ghost of Rebekah Howler plunge to her bloody end.

This darkness—it's not just around us. It's inside us. Inside me.

I've spent so long trying to hide mine, to bury it in denial and distractions.

If I'm going to even attempt to save my marriage, I have to come clean with my biggest secret and fear—the fear Steven won't just leave for the inn but for good. But how do I tell him I'm exactly like the young woman he blames for stealing away his father?

How do I keep him with the truth?

I haven't really had him with lies.

I'm unsure what to do, and I offer up a silent prayer for mercy and guidance, because guiding myself has landed me nowhere. Literally nowhere.

I move through the crowd like a ghost, ignored, unseen—except by a girl in a porcelain doll mask who stares without blinking.

I don't belong here. Or maybe this is exactly where I belong. Among the monsters. To fight them or remain one is the question.

For the past four days, since texting with Kent, it's been radio silence, which likely means he hasn't found anything concerning Roger Wagner or Brad Langston.

I'm convinced Roger took Candy.

I'm not convinced he's still alive.

Someone found out about Roger's evil deed. Ellersby knew he was a pedophile. Chris Bechtel. There could be others.

Including Adrian Rivera.

Not only were his rants in line at times, but he peered in my basement and attic window, convinced a girl needed help, and each day that passes, I'm more convinced a girl did need help. Maybe all the girls and women in this house needed help that never came.

His Alzheimer's might have fractured his memory, but he saw something here. Knew something. The lights from the other night—on, off, on, off. Was he trying to communicate with the person in my attic, the person from his past that seems to still haunt him too?

I walk past the White Pine Cone, and of course I bump right into Grant Ellersby. Out of uniform. Faded jeans, black T-shirt, green-and-black flannel, scuffed work boots. The casual look doesn't soften him.

My pulse spikes. He knows everything, and maybe he always has. The heat that floods my cheeks feels like a full-body hot flash.

"Grant," I say, refusing to call him Chief. I think he's a snake.

"Gwen." He smirks. "Saw your husband's car parked over at the inn the past few nights."

His mouth twitches. He's enjoying this—every bit of my undoing, my lack of credibility. It makes him look completely sane.

"Did you?"

"Mmm. Notice you're not carrying your baby today."

My jaw tightens. My hands clench. For a second, I consider decking him. He doesn't get to judge me. He hasn't lived my pain.

"Notice you're not in uniform. Looks more honest." I shoulder past him—hard—then look back. "You're covering up a crime. Obstructing justice. Maybe even accessory after the fact…or maybe *you* killed Roger Wagner. Wouldn't blame you. He was a perv. I'm going to find out, Grant. I'm coming for you."

He smiles like he doesn't have a care in the world. "I haven't done anything criminal, Gwen. Can't say the same for you. Who's going to listen to a woman who drags a baby doll around and calls it her daughter? You've made false accusations before. Didn't go so well. I promised your husband I'd be discreet about your…situation. But if you push, I might not keep that promise. How many more small towns do you think will welcome a husband with a wife who has 'problems'?"

He's got me by the throat, and he knows it.

"Roger Wagner took Candy Tremell. You know he did. I found secret rooms in that house."

His eyes grow wide at that, but he closes the distance between us and leans in, his breath sour with coffee. "I think he did. I agree with that. But unlike you, I need proof. You can't arrest someone on a hunch, Gwen. You can't just go throwing accusations and calling it justice. That's not how the law works. And secret rooms do not prove criminal activity."

"You took care of it, according to Chris Bechtel," I snap. "And then later Roger Wagner just…moved? Sold a house that was potentially never listed. Records missing. And the real estate agent dies in a tragic hiking accident? Deena Richardson didn't hike a day in her life."

"I can't explain that," he says. "Records got lost all the time before digital systems were put into place. Maybe he sold the house quietly. I don't know. And the Langstons are gone now."

"You're dodging."

"I'm telling you the truth. You're chasing ghosts. Other than Roger and Candy—I agree—you're seeing things that aren't there."

It's something. Not enough, but something.

And he's not wrong. I am seeing things that aren't there. But what if I'm also seeing things he's not—or doesn't want to see? "Did you ever search his house?"

"On a hunch? No. You need a warrant for that. Unlike you, I don't break into homes."

Low blow. I might've done that once—to Teri Jo Tipton. I thought I had cause. I thought she killed three of her children. Naturally I assumed the newborn was next. But Teri Jo hadn't killed anyone. The boyfriend had.

I *was* wrong.

He sees the silence in me and smirks. "Be careful out there. Kids get rowdy on Halloween. Your house is the bull's-eye. If it gets too crazy, call. Try not to shoot anyone."

He walks off like he's already won, and I stand there fuming, surrounded by the smell of strong coffee and old regret.

I hate that man.

Even if he might be right.

Inside Black Capped Coffee, Cady's nowhere in sight. A teenage boy with a head full of what looks like a home perm greets me at the counter. Please don't let that style be making a comeback.

"I'll take an Americano, heavy cream and honey. Is Cady in?"

"She went home sick about an hour ago."

Sick?

"Add a chamomile tea. I'll take them to go," I say. Might as well bring her something.

Five minutes later, drinks in hand, I slide into my car. Just as I press the ignition button, my phone rings—unknown number.

I answer. "Hello?"

"Hi. Uh, this is Brad Langston. I'm returning your call. Just so we're clear, I'm not liable for anything with that house."

"No, thank you for calling, Brad."

"I live in Japan, and it's been hard with the time difference, but I'm in Chicago this week. What's this about?"

"You bought the house from your great-grandparents?"

"Yeah," he says cautiously. "My great-aunt bought it for them as a gift. Said it was so they could be closer to her. I thought it was impractical at the time—I was just a teenager—but I didn't question it. After they passed, I asked to purchase it from her. She agreed, said it was important to keep it in the family. I'd tell you to ask her, but she recently passed away. I wasn't able to make her funeral."

Funeral?

"Deena Richardson?"

"Yeah. She was my great-aunt."

Chapter Fifty-Two

I watch the waves slam into the jagged rocks below as I wait for Cady to answer her door. I now know what she's been keeping from me, why she dodged the Langston conversation. She was protecting them because they are like family. But I told her I didn't think it was Brad.

No point holding it against her when I've not been the most honest person in the world. I texted to give her a heads-up I was stopping by, and she said that was fine. But now I'm not so sure.

The white-capped water crashes again and again, only to fall away—erased. It's a losing battle, and I wonder if I'm fighting the same one. Dredging up the past, clawing through secrets buried for decades—what if it doesn't help anyone? What if all it does is hurt the people I care about, destroy what little peace they've managed to build?

Cady opens the door in yoga pants and a thin white tank top with a bird sketched across the front. Her hair is pulled up tight like a ballerina's. She looks calm. Too calm.

"I brought you tea," I say, holding it out.

She doesn't look sick.

"Thank you. That was sweet."

"Are you sick?" I step inside her cottage-style home. It's bright and eclectic—just like her. "You look and sound fine."

"I'm sick and not fine," she says, shutting the door behind us. "But not in the way you think." She gestures toward the couch, where a multicolored quilt is draped over the back, frayed and faded. I relate to it more than I should.

"I need English, hon," I say as I sip my drink—honey, cream, and just enough caffeine to cut the fog in my brain.

She walks to the counter and pulls out a small stack of papers, handing them to me without a word.

GenomeConnect.

It looks like a CSV file. Clinical. Cold. But the words slap me. *Chromosome, genotype, match.* I flip to the next page and freeze.

A tree. A long genetic branch. Two raw DNA sequences, side by side.

"Is this…a match?" My stomach coils. "Is this a mother–daughter match?"

"Yeah," she whispers, her eyes red, glistening with new tears. Crumpled tissues litter the coffee table. "It's not yours, though. It's mine."

My body stiffens as if hit by lightning. Words fail. The room quiets around us, save for the soft sniffs from Cady.

She crumples on the couch. "I got the email this morning and opened the results in my office, then printed it all out. I thought it was a glitch. But it wasn't. We share over 3,400 centimorgans across multiple segments—that's mother–daughter level. The site flagged it as a *very close relationship*, but the detailed breakdown confirmed it."

"You aren't adopted, then," I squeak.

Cady shakes her head and covers her face with her hands.

She can't be when she's a match to Candy Tremell. And not any familial match.

A mother–daughter match.

Candy Tremell isn't Cady's sister.

She's her mother.

We sit in utter silence for what feels like eons, absorbing the information and what it means.

Finally, I ask, "And your dad? Did you find him?"

She shakes her head. "No. Which means his DNA has never been uploaded."

She dabs her eyes, voice hoarse. "Help me make sense of this."

I can't. I'm still reeling. "Have you talked to your mom?"

"No. As soon as I realized what it meant, I left the café. Told the staff I wasn't feeling well. Came straight home. Gwen…so much more is on the table now."

My mind spins. What have I missed? How off base have I been?

I take a deep, slow breath and release it. "Okay. A few things come to mind," I say slowly. "Candy could have run away, not vanished, and gotten pregnant at some point. Called your parents and they adopted you, but she wouldn't come home—though she would have been a minor, so they could have made her. But it's possible."

This would explain why she looks so much like Marcia.

But Grant Ellersby believes Roger Wagner took Candy. That could be true, or Ellersby is using Roger as some kind of a patsy to cover up what actually happened to Candy Tremell. Maybe the birth had complications and she passed, but they never wanted to admit she'd been pregnant—by Roger? someone else?—so they claimed she'd gone missing. That's why they don't want a podcast. Because it's not a cold case. It was solved thirty years ago. And if Cady looked into her birth, that would reveal the very result they tried to hide.

"But then where is she?" Cady asks.

No, that theory doesn't add up.

By the numbers, Candy would've been sixteen—figured from her age when she disappeared and when Cady was born.

"I'm not sure. Let's work it like a cold case and follow the lead that she was likely taken by Roger Wagner based on what Lily Ann and Chris Bechtel said, and what Grant Ellersby told me—that he believes Roger abducted her."

Cady lets out a strangled sob. "That makes me Roger Wagner's daughter. My father is a pedophile and a rapist!"

I set my drink down and wrap my arms around her, rocking her gently. I don't care what the test says—Cady Tremell is not some monster's legacy. "Listen to me," I whisper when her crying slides into quiet shudders. "We don't know if he's your father. But even if he is, that doesn't define you. You were raised with love. You are bright and kind and good. You're *not* him."

"What else could it be?" she murmurs in desperation.

I don't know. But if my math is right and Candy was taken at thirteen and Cady's nearly thirty-one, Candy would've been sixteen when she gave birth. That means he had her *here* for at least three years.

The basement. The room behind the stairs. The attic.

Candy Tremell is now my best guess for who wrote the words in my attic. I AM NOT CRAZY.

What kind of mind games did he play on her?

And what about Ann Wagner? Lily Ann? So many victims, hidden in plain sight. The age gap between Ann and Roger was huge. Thirteen seems to be his magic number.

The only person who might hold answers is Dr. Rivera. His mind is a maze, memory slipping like sand through fingers, but he knows something. Something terrible happened in this house. To Candy. Maybe to others.

Did the Tremells ever find out the truth? Did they get their own revenge? Is that what Ellersby's been covering up? But if they murdered Roger Wagner, then where is Candy Tremell?

"You need to talk to your mom," I say gently. "But don't expect her to tell you everything. Even if the DNA doesn't lie."

Cady is nothing if not curious. She *won't* let this go. And if I had to guess, Roger Wagner is buried somewhere in those woods. If Ellersby killed him for stealing and impregnating a child… I can't say I blame him.

But I don't know if I can turn a blind eye either.

It's not my job—or Grant's—to play God. To decide who lives and who dies. I've crossed lines before. And those lines always cost something.

I think about Teri Jo Tipton. About the times I wanted to play God in her life.

Now the question is, what do I do with this?

If I'm right…if the Tremells or, more likely, Grant Ellersby killed Roger to protect their daughter and bury a horror no one else could face…do I protect the only family Cady's ever known?

What will she want to do?

And where is Candy now?

I'm reminded of the call with Brad Langston—Deena Richardson's great-nephew. "I know the Langstons were Deena's parents and Brad was her nephew. He called me."

Cady's cheeks flush scarlet. "Are you mad I didn't tell you?"

"No, but I wish you would have." Her holding back information and being adamant they were good people now makes sense.

"I might not have known Brad well, but I did know Deena's parents, and there's no way they'd have done anything like this. I didn't want you to think I was being biased, so I let you run your own investigation, see for yourself he's clean—they were. I was afraid you'd keep me out of the loop if you knew how close I was to the family." She cringes. "I'm sorry. I felt guilty about it."

"You're actually right." I would have thought she was biased and potentially kept anything I found on him to myself. I grin. "But from here on out, let's not keep things from each other." As if I have the right to ask that. I'm still keeping the truth from Steven about my past.

"Pinky promise." She holds out her pinky. I can't help but snicker and curl mine around hers, and we shake. "I'm going to talk to Dr. Rivera," I say. "Maybe I can catch a few moments of clarity. Now that I know more, I can ask better questions."

I think about those lights. Quick bursts. Long pauses. Rhythmic and strange.

His cryptic speech.

He knows something, even if his mind won't allow him fluid memory. And I'm going to find out what it is.

Chapter Fifty-Three

I need to think. Really *think*. Let it all slow down, spool back. Make sense of the thousand jagged images slicing through my brain. So I climb into the canoe, lower myself into its creaking belly, and push off from the shore before nightfall arrives.

The water is black glass, shivering in the wind.

Paddling across the harbor will burn off some of the nervous energy ricocheting through my limbs like a pinball. Each pull of the paddle is punishment, therapy, propulsion. The wind resists me, biting at my skin, dragging the boat sideways. I grit my teeth and paddle harder. Let it hurt. Let it *all* hurt. My muscles are already fried from the remodeling and repainting—might as well rip them raw.

I left Cady still reeling, quiet only because she was exhausted. She was heading to her mother's house to chase answers before the streets flooded with plastic masks and synthetic screams once the sun fully set. Apparently my house is always the major stop on Halloween. I left a bowl of candy out in case I'm not back before they start arriving. The "haunted" house on the cliff.

But it's not haunted.

Is it?

Maybe the child I keep seeing is Candy Tremell, and she was small for thirteen. Or maybe it's Lizzie Barkley. Either way, she wants something. Help. Recognition. Justice. And the *HE* she's hiding from—maybe that was Roger Wagner.

But if Wagner was alive, Kent would've found a paper trail. A bank statement. An address. People don't just disappear. Not completely. Not unless they *want* to. Not unless someone *makes* them.

I keep paddling, muscles screaming. Theories knot tighter in my skull.

I keep digging, unraveling, twisting every thread in my mind like a forensic spider. Wagner panics, kills Candy. But not before she gives birth. Ellersby finds them. Sees the baby. Maybe Wagner confesses. Maybe Ellersby loses it. Buries Wagner in the woods. Takes the baby to the Tremells. They cook up a story. "Adopted." After four years of mourning their missing daughter, no one asks too many questions. But someone had to forge birth certificates, adoption papers. I think of Pat Dunham, family lawyer and Grant's golfing buddy. He could have done his old friend a solid.

Deena and Marcia—best friends. Convenient. And now Deena's dead. Walked into those woods like she *knew* the person waiting for her.

My arms burn with every stroke. My thoughts blur from possibility to madness.

Why kill Deena? She wasn't a threat. Not unless she was ready to talk. Confess. Maybe she was silenced due to all my questions. Maybe not by Ellersby at all. There's more than one secret rotting in Cold Harbor. More than one grave.

And my house? I bought it from Teresa, not Deena. The sale was rushed, last-minute, spontaneous. A fluke. I saw the listing while stalking places near our old vacation spot. Jumped on it. Signed within days. Before Deena even knew it was gone.

Maybe she didn't *want* it sold. Maybe she was trying to keep something buried.

Now she's buried instead.

The harbor narrows. Rivera's house peeks through the trees. The attic window is empty.

I tie off the rope, turn, glance back.

My house looms across the water like a corpse risen to its knees—white, tall, watching me.

And when I turn around, he's already there.

"Hello, Gwen." Dr. Rivera's voice is flat but alert, his eyes not the glazed mirrors I've come to expect. He's lucid. Aware.

"Doctor," I say, breath clouding. "I need to ask you some questions."

"About the birds?" He wraps his flannel tighter around his narrow frame.

"No," I say quietly. "About the basement across the harbor. About Candy Tremell. And her baby girl—Cady."

His eyes widen. He points a trembling finger toward my house. "That poor girl. All those poor girls. They all *die* over there."

A cold tremor dances across my skin. "What girls, Doctor?"

"She needed help. I helped." His voice cracks. "I did what I could. But she's dead. She's *dead*!"

Kristin appears, breezy, bright. "Adrian! I'm going to put bells on you like a kitten." She flashes me a sunny smile. "You canoed over?"

"I did."

"Goodness. Come in and warm up. Tea?"

"Please," I say, but my eyes stay locked on the old man. The cracks are showing. Something real is leaking through.

Inside, the sunroom smells like pumpkin bread. Shelves groan under bird books. The stove hums, casting everything in flickering orange. Rivera shrugs off his coat and sinks into the couch.

Kristin bustles into the kitchen. "Peppermint okay?"

"Perfect," I say. I feel like I'm floating inside someone else's memory.

Rivera thumbs through a book. "Birds are free," he murmurs. "They go where they want."

"Dr. Rivera," I say, crouching beside him. "Were you in the attic last night?"

He tilts his head. "Rebekah Howler. Poor woman jumped. Awful business. The Barkley women…dead too. They all die over there."

Of course. He's back in the fog. Or maybe not. Maybe the attic *is* haunted. History lingers. Pain haunts the air like spores. That house on Darkwater Road is no Halloween game. Not anymore.

Kristin returns with tea. "He's been more obsessed with your house than ever. No idea why. Half the time he's talking nonsense."

"I wanted to ask about Roger Wagner." I wrap my hands around the warm mug.

Kristin's expression stills. Rivera's hands clench into fists.

"That man is *vile.* I tended the baby, you know."

Cady. He *has* to mean Cady. But I can't trust the wiring in his brain. The lights flicker too often.

"You tended half the town, remember?" Kristin teases gently.

"I fought in the Civil War too."

"Oh, yeah?" I ask. "What side?"

"The North," he says proudly. "To free the people. Birds are free," he repeats. "But some are caged." He knocks on the wooden armrest.

Tap-tap-tap. Tap…tap…tap… Tap-tap-tap.

My blood turns to ice.

It's *Morse code.*

Someone signaled him. From *my* attic. And he tapped back.

Lily Ann wasn't allowed up there.

Was it her mother? Candy?

He's drifting again. Eyes glossy. Words tangling.

"I should go," I say. "Thank you for the tea."

Kristin walks me out. "Sometimes he mentions a doll. That's about it. He used to be brilliant, Gwen. If anything clicks again, I'll let you know."

"I'd appreciate that." I step into the canoe, stomach churning. I'm missing something. *Something huge.* I need Rivera to remember. To *clarify.*

My arms shake with the first pull into the water. My brain is sludge. My heart, sore and bruised. Steven hasn't called. I haven't either. Tara is home, in the carrier, and as much as I want to stay immersed in the fantasy that I'm a mom to a living, breathing baby, I can't. Seeing Steven sling her against that wall did something in me, dislodged the dream and woke me to the realization that the doll isn't making me better. It's just patching something fractured.

Each stroke through the water feels like a dream. Or a nightmare. My vision blurs. My head throbs. I'm so *tired.*

I reach the shore, my muscles screaming.

And then I see him.

Standing at the edge of the dock. Still. Silent.

Grant Ellersby.

Chapter Fifty-Four

My insides flush hot. Nausea crests in waves. My vision smears like oil on glass, and there's a bitter, anesthetic tang coating my tongue.

The tea.

How did Grant know I'd be at the dock? Why would Rivera's nurse—Kristin—drug me?

Am I being paranoid again?

No.

Something is *definitely* wrong with me.

And Kristin's a nurse—with access to all kinds of things.

"You're lookin' a little peaked, Gwen." Grant steps forward, flannel sleeves rolled up, his sidearm slung at his hip. "Let me help you."

I take his hand because I have no choice—I'm not sure I can make it from the canoe to the dock without collapsing. The dizziness swells, relentless.

"You out for a jaunt? Little cold for that, don't you think?"

Sweat breaks out across my forehead, beads along my temples, slicks my upper lip. "I… I'm not feeling well."

"I can see that." He points to a dock post. "Hold on to this while I tie off."

I grip it, weak with gratitude. Maybe I *am* sick. Maybe this isn't something sinister.

"Where've you been?" His voice sounds like it's coming from underwater.

"Oh… Dr. Rivera's. He has bird books." The words are slurred and sticky.

"Taking up bird-watching now?" He offers his arm, and I loop mine through it. "Come on. Let's get you to the house."

I lean into him. My legs feel like sacks of wet cement. "Yeah. I like birds. What…what are you doing here?"

He smiles, but there's nothing warm about it. "Truth is, I came to tell you a story. Let you choose the ending. Like those children's books I used to read. Turn to one page, the story ends one way. Choose another—different fate."

My brain struggles to keep up. "Okay."

"Over thirty years ago, Candy Tremell was walking home from school. Mr. Wagner offered her a ride. She always complained to her mom that her backpack was heavy. Figured she said yes pretty fast. He kept her in his house—*your* house—for four years. We looked. Marcia. Curt. Me—I was a detective back then. We all *knew* it was him. He was a known pervert. Peeking in windows. But we never found her…"

Because of the hidden rooms. The one behind the stairs. The one in the basement.

"You killed him."

"Would *you* let a man like that live? A man who stole a child and got her pregnant?"

No. No, men like that don't deserve to breathe.

"It's not our job to exact justice," I whisper. My tongue feels thick. My voice, alien. "I need a doctor. Call Steven. Something's wrong…"

We climb the hill—but he's *not* leading me toward the house.

"Where...are we going?"

My shirt sticks to my back, soaked in sweat. I can't fight him. I don't have the strength. I have to go where he leads.

I don't want to go.

A child's voice floats through my skull, faint but sharp.

Pick a different ending.

"You'll be fine," Grant says. "Kristin—my niece—she handled your tea. Called me when you started poking around the house again. Talking about Roger Wagner. You talk, Gwen, it gets back to me."

My heart pounds. Whatever Kristin gave me, it's still coursing through my veins. "You don't deserve a badge either," I croak.

He laughs. Not kindly. He yanks me toward the edge of the woods.

The sun is dipping low. Soon it'll be night, and kids will come out to play at being scared. If only they knew—real horror walks on two legs.

"I helped Marcia and Curt survive after their world was ripped apart. You think you're helping, but you've made everything worse. Cady knows now—about her mother. You tore that open."

I stumble. "What happened to Deena? You killed her?"

He scoffs. "You really think I'm the only man you should be afraid of?"

The words are slurred in my ears. My thoughts splinter, chased by memories I didn't know I had.

"Hi. Aren't you just the prettiest little dolly. Come on now. The park's on fire."

My pulse jumps. Smoke. I smell smoke. But there is no fire. Am I hallucinating? *Have I always been hallucinating?*

"Deena got scared when you started sniffing around. She thought telling *part* of the truth might shut you up. But here's the thing, Gwen. You can't rewrite history. Even if it's built on a lie, the story has to stick. Deena was a loose thread."

My legs collapse under me. He tosses me to the forest floor like I weigh nothing, then props me against a tree.

"What if I said I'd keep your secret?" I whisper.

Grant squats. Gently tilts my chin. "I *know* you will."

"What about Cady?" My tongue is dry. "Will you kill her too?"

He doesn't answer.

"Deena," I rasp. "Why did you—"

"You know, Gwen," he cuts in, voice rough, "if you distrusted *every* man like you distrust me, maybe Steven had reason to walk. How many times have you accused him of cheating?"

The fog in my head thickens, but something flickers behind it. A memory—faint as mist.

"You're crazy, Dolly. That's just crazy talk. I'm your daddy. I've always been your daddy."

I see the girl now. Candy. Trapped in the basement.

"If you're good, I'll move you to the attic. You can listen to records, play with the dollhouse."

The air shifts. Something ancient and decomposed coils in the dirt around me.

"Daddy, don't leave me down here. I'm not Dolly. I am not crazy..."

The words fall from my lips, and Grant stares like he's seen a ghost.

Because he *has*.

And I think maybe—I've seen one too.

Chapter Fifty-Five

Grant lifts my chin and tsks. "I wondered. You have her eyes, but I wasn't completely sure until now. It's been thirty years or so since I last saw you. Since I took you to the fire station. And you think *I'm* the bad guy, here? I gave you back to your parents, Winnie. Although you're going by Gwen now—Gwendolyn."

"What are you talking about?"

Grant makes no sense—and the sun has set, leaving us swathed in darkness that brings with it the whispers of ghosts fluttering through leaves. A round of laughter rides the wind, too.

Teenagers.

Making their way to my house.

Grant is running out of time—and so am I. He's going to use my gun to make it appear like I've killed myself. Everyone, including Steven, will believe it. He's set it up to be that way. The ball. The music. Moving Tara to the dock. Setting my shed on fire and loosening my lug nuts. I don't know how he did it all, but I know he did.

I don't have to understand his cryptic statements. But somewhere deep inside me, I know he's telling the truth about *something.*

"The night I found you, Gwen. You were only eleven years old. Huddled in a corner of the forest with an old screwdriver, bloody hands and splinters. You don't remember, do you?"

His hand covers mine. It's big. Warm. Familiar in the worst possible way.

"I got you, sweetie. You're safe now. I'm going to make sure you get home safe. See your mom and dad."

"He's my daddy. My parents died in a wildfire at a campground."

"No, he just made you think all of that was true. He's a bad, bad man. But he won't hurt anyone anymore."

"I'm not crazy?"

"No, honey. You're not."

"Can I take my ball and my jump rope?"

"You can take whatever you want."

As if something explodes inside my head, the fuzziness continues to clear.

The girl jumping rope. Giggling with a friend. Bouncing the ball. Asking for help.

She's not a ghost from the past, and yet she is.

She's…me.

Chapter Fifty-Six

"I was in this house," I whisper. He knew it and used it against me.

"Yes," Grant says softly. "And this is why it pains me to end you here, Gwen. I saved you once. I tried to save you again. Maybe it's better this way." His voice lowers, nearly a whisper. "All that trauma Roger Wagner inflicted—it broke you. And I'm sorry for that. Sorry you spent a year in his house of horrors. After I saw your bloody, splintered hands and then the writing in the attic, I knew you'd done it to stay in reality and not disappear into Roger Wagner's sick fantasy."

Me. I carved those words. Line by line.

"I imagine it was so terrifying that you locked that time up tight inside yourself. And I'm sorry I had to make you feel crazy... *again.* But more lives are on the line than you can imagine."

The laughter grows closer, and Grant swears under his breath, rage flashing across his face. He shoves my own gun against my lips, but I purse them tight, fighting against the pressure, using everything I have to keep him from pulling the trigger. My limbs are syrupy and slack, but I have to fight.

Protect myself. Live.

"I'll take her and run away. Protect her. He's not going to let you keep her, Lily Ann."

"Yes. He will. I'm his wife now, and he takes care of us. He provides for us. He loves us. She'll be fine. I'm tired. I need to rest."

She closes her eyes, and I take the baby wrapped in a plaid quilted throw and slip her into my arms, the screwdriver still in my hand. She's sleeping, and her face makes funny shapes. I'm not supposed to ever leave the house. But...he's going to hurt this baby. And she's all that matters right now. I have to be brave. Run. Through the woods. I don't think he locked the door behind him.

I'm scared. Breaking rules brings punishment. I don't like the creepy basement under the kitchen. But the lights across the harbor...

I know Morse code.

And the lights across the water know it too. I talk to him with the lamp sometimes when I'm in the attic with the screwdriver. Daddy didn't like it when I wrote in the floor, but he didn't make me stop.

The man across the lake. He can help me.

Adrenaline surges through my body, like it remembers what I've forgotten. I twist. Grab the gun. Slam my knee into Grant's groin. He folds just enough for me to wrest the weapon free.

I *have* to fight.

We grapple—bodies rolling through the leaves, the gun scraping against roots and bark. Then—footsteps. Voices.

The teenagers?

This could get them all killed.

I pray they don't find us.

Grant slams my head against the tree. My skull cracks and the world goes fuzzy again.

My vision blurs.

"*Stop!*" someone yells.

Has a teenager found us?

A gunshot erupts.

And my world fades to black.

★★★

When I open my eyes, I'm in a man's arms. I kick and flail, panic blooming in my chest—until a voice steadies me. Familiar. Soft. Safe.

"It's me, Gwen. It's Steven. You're safe."

We're at the edge of the woods. My head is pounding, but I remember.

The walls of the house and the fight to survive—again—has unlocked memories I never knew existed. I thought it was normal to not remember a chunk of my childhood, but I don't think that's true anymore.

Tears flood my eyes. I don't try to stop them. Steven kisses my forehead as the strobe of blue lights flickers ahead, washing the trees in pulses of light and shadow.

"What's going on?" I whisper. "What happened to Grant Ellersby?"

"He's dead," Steven says. "I shot him. Used your backup gun you keep in the safe."

Standing at the edge of the yard is Cady Tremell.

The baby I rescued thirty years ago—for her mother, Candy Tremell—who I knew as Lily Ann.

"Steven," I say quietly, "I wrote those words on the attic floor. It was me."

"It's okay," he says. "How's your head? I checked it quickly, but you might have a concussion."

I'm nauseous and my skull throbs, but for the first time in forever, I'm seeing everything more clearly than I ever have. Some pieces are still missing—but the fog has lifted.

Paramedics rush toward me, and a whirlwind of questions begins. Officers fan out into the woods while others approach me with notepads and flashlights. A cluster of teenagers stands nearby, cell phones aimed in our direction.

Great. I'll go viral before midnight.

I'm already part of this house's dark history.

I refuse a trip to the hospital. My husband is a doctor.

My husband. Steven left—and then he came back. He rescued me. He was willing to die for me.

He's standing beside me now, his hand warm in mine. When the ambulance pulls away and the officers finish their questions, Cady runs to me and wraps her arms tightly around my neck.

"You saved me," she whispers.

I've always felt a strange closeness to her—like she belonged to me somehow. And now I know why.

We share a past.

I was in the house when Candy—called Lily Ann—was pregnant. When she gave birth to Roger Wagner's child. *I took Cady and ran.* I remember the man who found me hiding in the woods taking her from me and giving her to another man—Dr. Rivera. He tended to her.

And a woman was with Ellersby and the man.

A woman I can't quite remember.

I cling to Cady with one arm as Steven holds me with the other. The puzzle isn't complete, but I'm alive. Steven is here. Maybe there's hope for us still.

"If that's all," Steven says gently but firmly, "I'd like to take my wife inside. She needs rest."

The yard buzzes with people in costumes—Disney princesses and horror villains mingling beneath the flashing lights.

None of them frightens me as much as Roger Wagner.

Inside, Steven tends to my wounds, washing dried blood from my hairline and asking me the standard questions. Is my vision blurry? Can I say my ABC's? I pass the test, barely. I'm more lucid, but my muscles are still weak.

Finally, I take his hand and look into those warm, steady brown eyes.

"How did you know where I was?" My voice breaks. "Why did you come looking? I thought… I thought you were done with me. That this latest sin put the final nail in the coffin. That I'd pushed you away for good."

The tears come hard now—hot, relentless. I don't deserve him. For so long, I saw him as the enemy. As someone working *against* me.

But I was wrong.

He's always been my ally. My protector. Even when I pushed him out—he never truly left.

Steven tucks my damp bangs behind my ears and cups my cheek.

"Cady called," he says. "She confronted her mom about the DNA results—about being Candy's daughter. Marcia broke. Told her everything. And that she'd told Grant you'd come by after your beach trip. Grant said he'd 'take care of it.'"

I look past Steven and realize—Cady is still in the room.

"I was afraid he'd do to you what he did to Deena," she says, her voice cracking. "And anyone else who got in his way."

She wipes at her eyes, sniffling. "I told Steven the truth."

I study her face. My throat tightens. "And what is the truth?"

Cady hesitates. Then shakes her head softly.

"I think you need to hear that from my mom."

Chapter Fifty-Seven

The small jail is tacked onto the backside of the police department—an old annex that smells faintly of bleach, coffee and time. It's dressed up in 1980s-style Halloween paper cutouts. Witches with warty green faces, grinning jack-o'-lanterns, wide-eyed ghosts and smug little black cats. Black-and-orange crepe paper streamers droop sadly across the bars of the holding cells, like party favors no one remembered to take down.

I guess it's the only way to spice up the job. And why shouldn't criminals get to celebrate Halloween? In some twisted way, it belongs to them—the ones who go bump in the night, who slip through shadows and haunt us long after they're gone.

But the ghosts that haunt me don't wear masks. Mine live in the deep vaults of memory, stitched into the hollows of my childhood. And now I understand why my parents watched me like a hawk and told me that childhood photos from years ten and eleven were damaged by water in the basement—they had no photos of me during that time.

I couldn't remember what happened to me that year, so they never spoke of it, hoping they could forget too. Now I do remember being called Winnie, but it's fuzzy. I mostly remember them calling me Gwen. Had I researched missing girls younger than thirteen, I would have stumbled upon my own case. Would I have realized it was me? I didn't recognize the ghost of myself, not even the blond pigtails.

I've worked enough abuse cases to know that trauma is a master escape artist. It slinks down into the subconscious, hiding in locked rooms with no doors, waiting to come out when you least expect it. When I glance back—really look at the jagged trail of my life—it all makes sense. The mistrust, the wild-eyed defiance, the crying out without knowing what I was crying for.

Even when I threw myself into a married man's arms at sixteen. He'd said all the right things. I had been there before—though I didn't know it at the time. I didn't know how broken I was, but he'd seen it. He'd preyed on me and all my fear and called it love. Messed with my head like Roger Wagner, whose face is now crystal clear.

First from memory. Then overlaid with the image of a young Jeff Bridges—kind blue eyes, a soft rasp of a voice. A wolf in the skin of a friend.

I shiver as I make my way toward the holding cell. It's just after 6:00 a.m., the morning after Halloween, and the world is still quiet. Marcia sits on the cot, her hair in wild disarray, a crumpled tissue clutched in one hand. Her face is worn down by decades of guilt and exhaustion.

I don't know why she's here exactly—accessory after the fact, maybe. But no jury on Earth is going to convict her.

Roger Wagner had a pattern. Thirteen-year-old girls. But I had only been ten. That's the part that doesn't fit. And maybe it never will. I don't think he touched me. I don't *remember* him touching me. But memory is tricky. Mine still hides things in the dark.

Steven and I talked last night, but I was in and out from the concussion. He dropped me at the door to park. I don't want to face anything else without him. Not the truth. Not the grief. Not the final locked box of secrets I've kept even from him.

Especially not Tara—but not the first Tara.

Because now I know why I named all my babies that name. Why my favorite doll shared it, too.

Candy Tremell had named *her* baby Tara. Cady. The first.

And the second…was mine.

The daughter I gave up for adoption. The child I never told Steven about. But I will. Today. And when I do, there will be no more secrets. He'll know everything. Then he can decide whether to stay and help pick up the pieces—or walk away.

Marcia lifts her head as I enter. Her voice is hoarse.

"Gwen. I'm so sorry for all of this."

"Me too." I swallow. "Did you know it was me? The little girl me?"

She shakes her head slowly. "Not until Grant told me. He thought you remembered everything—and that you'd come to extort us. That's why he was cold. Why he tried to twist your mind. That record—'Beautiful Dreamer'—was playing when I got to the Wagner house that night. Thursday. Roger bowled on Thursdays."

Of course. If he could make me look unstable, no one would believe a word I said.

"I didn't know about my past," I murmur. "It was repressed."

Marcia nods faintly. "The brain protects itself. Even when the heart breaks."

"You went to the house that night? You *called* Grant?"

Her eyes are red and swollen, her voice thin. "When Candy vanished, we both suspected Roger. Grant even went to the house, asked to search. Roger let him—once. He found nothing. But he kept going back until Roger filed harassment charges. He dropped them only when Grant agreed to stay away."

She draws in a trembling breath.

"I even broke in once. When Roger was at work. Found nothing. No trace of my daughter. Eventually I had to let myself believe she was dead. I told myself that lie for years, though deep down, I held on to hope."

"I'm sorry," I whisper, hollow with grief. "I can't imagine."

"I was talking to Adrian one day," she continues, "and he told me the attic lights would turn on and off. He would mimic it. I'd never been up there. But he swore it was a child. Who else would play like that?"

I remember. That lamp. The flickering Morse code.

"That Thursday night," Marcia says, "around eight thirty, I went back. Roger's car wasn't there. The back door was open. A record played upstairs—'Beautiful Dreamer.' I saw something I'd missed before. The kitchen island was open, and it led to the basement. Hidden. A soundproofed room."

Her hands begin to shake. Her voice trembles.

"I found Candy on the bed. Sixteen. Covered in blood. Glassy-eyed. Hysterical. She kept asking where Tara and Dolly were. I didn't know what she meant, but I could tell she'd given birth." A choked sob escapes her mouth.

She meant me.

I was called Dolly.

Dolly Bear... Dolly Bear...

We played jump rope together. She sang me...the lullaby. "Brahms's Lullaby"...

Hazy things. Fractured memories that began to surface living back in the house of horrors. I was drawn to the Darkwater Road house and had no idea why.

Steven enters then, with an officer at his side. He joins me, hand in mine, and together we face Marcia as she continues her march down memory lane.

"I only wanted to get her out. She was barely coherent. Then Roger came home. I wasn't expecting him. He looked like a monster. His eyes—black, Gwen. Like deep ocean water just before a storm."

She shudders.

"And I shot him. I pulled the trigger and watched him fall dead to the floor. I wasn't even sorry. And I'm still not."

It wasn't Grant Ellersby who killed Roger. All this time, I thought… "Then how did Candy die? If you shot Roger… who killed her?"

Marcia's face crumples. Her voice breaks into a ragged whisper.

"I did."

Chapter Fifty-Eight

"You did?" I'm stunned. My voice sounds far away, and Steven glances at me, a look of horror twisting his face. "How? Why?"

Marcia wipes her nose with the back of her hand. "When she saw me shoot him, she lost it. Came at me, screaming, attacking me. I killed Husband. He provided for her. He took care of her. He protected her. I tried to calm her down and reason with her—I was shocked—but she was hysterical."

"She was traumatized," Steven says gently. "She'd just given birth. She *was* a child. Candy likely had Stockholm syndrome. He'd conditioned her to believe those things."

Marcia nods slowly. "Yes. I know that now. Back then, I just wanted to help her, but she scratched and clawed and hit me over and over. I ran upstairs and she followed, repeating, 'How could you kill him? How could you kill Husband? He loved me. He takes care of us.'"

Us.

"Who was *us*? Me?"

"Yes. You. And I suppose…the baby—Cady." Her voice quivers. "She grabbed a knife and came at me. I tried to stop her. We struggled and… I killed her. In self-defense." Her shoulders collapse inward as the sobs take over, heaving.

The child she'd spent four years trying to save…she killed.

"I called Curt in a panic. He called Grant. We'd all been friends for years. It was an accident—I never wanted to hurt my daughter. I wanted to kill Roger."

She lifts her gaze. Her eyes shine, but there's a hard glint behind the tears. "But I'm not sorry about him."

Honestly, neither am I. I'd gotten it all wrong. I thought Grant killed Roger. I thought Roger killed Candy.

"What about Deena?" My voice is quieter now, but it cuts through the room. "Who killed Deena?"

Marcia sighs and removes her glasses. She rubs at the tearstains with the sleeve of her Halloween costume—a faded black cat, the ears sagging on her hood. "After Curt and Grant got to the house, we had to act. The attic had that writing, which we thought at first Candy had done."

I AM NOT CRAZY.

I wrote those words. Over and over. I wasn't Dolly. Roger Wagner was not my father, though he said he was and that I was crazy for thinking anything else. But I needed the reminder. I vaguely remember it, slamming the screwdriver into the wood and scraping over and over and over again.

Marcia continues. "Roger was dead—I killed him in cold blood. How were we supposed to sell a house with a dead man in it?" She presses the heels of her hands into her eyes. "Curt had some old carpet in his warehouse. Said we could toss it down fast. 'No buffing that out,' he said."

They couldn't. I know that firsthand.

"Curt called Ron and Deena first. Then, once they found you with splinters in your hands, the screwdriver and Cady, we had to call Adrian to check you both out. Later we enlisted Pat Dunham—an attorney. That night, the night it all went down, was a panicked frenzy, but we had the sense to know we'd need help with adoption papers and a birth certificate. When they arrived, we all made a plan. Grant and Ron took Roger's body to bury it. Deena, Curt and I stayed behind, trying to clean up all the blood—from Roger and Candy and from where she gave birth. It was all too much, and we didn't have time. The town talks. So Deena said she'd make it look like Roger approached her to sell the house, and her parents needed a place quickly since they weren't in good shape."

"She fudged the paperwork."

"Yes. I don't know exactly how, and I never wanted to. Deena's parents were feeble and never went upstairs, which gave us time to quickly cover the floor in carpet Curt had in storage. The property records weren't missing. They never existed, so Deena took all the ones before too to be safe."

"What was she planning to do when her own parents died? How would she know she could sell it to Brad or any other family member?"

"Once they died and Brad needed it, she knew he wasn't going to remodel because he traveled all the time. If he ever moved, she planned to burn it to rubble," Marcia says.

Burning it the night of Roger and Candy's murder would have drawn too much attention, raised too many questions, and they risked a wildfire in Acadia National Park if it got out of hand.

"But the house sold like lightning before Teresa had a chance to even put the sign out. She listed it, and hours later, you put in an offer. Right out from under Deena. She hoped you'd let Curt remodel. He would have ripped up the flooring without you knowing, and if there was any blood evidence left, he'd get rid of it. But you didn't."

"So she tried setting the shed on fire, hoping it would catch to the house and burn it all down."

Marcia nods. "She never wanted to hurt you or Steven—or the baby she believed was real."

"Go back to that night all those years ago. You said you called in Adrian."

"Yes. He told us he thought a child was in the house but too young to be Candy. He'd even come over a few times but found nothing. I assume Roger locked you and Candy in the basement during the day and let you out when he returned home at night after work."

The buckets in the basement. I remember using them now.

"Adrian did an examination on you and the baby. She was perfectly healthy, and he found no evidence of sexual abuse on you, Gwen. I imagine your family took you to doctors and therapists and found the same."

A blurry memory resurfaces of me sitting on a black couch while a woman talks to me. Talks to my parents. *"She won't speak about it. She's locking it away, and it's best she keeps coming. I'll help her."*

"No." My dad is talking. "If she can't remember, that's best for her. We don't want her to."

They argue about my health and what's best, but we leave.

I know now why the idea of seeing a therapist terrifies me.

Because I've been through something terrifying—and my mind locked it away, sealed it tight, thinking it was protecting me.

But it didn't.

"The anger as a teenager, the paranoia…the way I can't trust people—men, especially," I say quietly, not quite looking at Steven. "It all makes sense now."

He doesn't say anything, just sits there beside me, steady and still, giving me space to speak.

"It's the behavior of a child who was abused," I whisper. "A child who couldn't remember. Who didn't understand why she does the things she does now."

My throat tightens, but I push through. "I used to think there was something broken in me. Like I came out wrong. But now…now I think I just never had the chance to heal."

Steven reaches for my hand. He doesn't say it'll be okay. Doesn't offer to fix it. He just holds on.

And in that silence, something shifts. Not relief. Not yet.

But maybe the beginning of it.

I switch gears and go back to Adrian's findings. If I hadn't been sexually abused, why take me?

Lily Ann, Roger's biological daughter, escaped, though the abuse became less as she aged out of his particular desire. It's possible he collected me to groom me longer, to prime me for when Candy aged out. She was sixteen, and the real Lily Ann said he slowed his nightly rituals at around fifteen. He was evolving over the years. Getting more cunning, calculating.

Like most predators.

I'm physically sick and want to vomit. "How did you know who to give me back to?"

"A year earlier, we'd seen a report about a missing child in Acadia National Park. We recognized you. But we couldn't return you publicly—it would raise too many questions."

"What about other girls? We found a few missing. Not locals."

"No, he only had Candy and you."

So the other girls who went missing had their own horror stories, but Roger Wagner wasn't the monster in them.

"What did I say that night?"

Marcia paces the cell, her arms crossed tight. "Nothing. You wouldn't speak, except to say, 'Keep Tara safe.' You were wide-eyed. Dazed. In total shock. It broke my heart. The next morning, I cleaned you up, changed your bloody clothes—Cady's blood, maybe Candy's—and Grant took you to a fire station anonymously. From there, they returned you to your parents in Portland."

I frown. "I didn't live in Maine. We lived in Maryland. We were just vacationing."

"No. You were vacationing *from* Portland. Hiking. Your parents were setting up camp near a lake. You wandered down and disappeared. They told police they'd seen a park ranger—but no one matching that description worked for the park. They thought someone impersonated one and took you."

"What about Dr. Rivera? He said he saw a girl being buried, that he had to help her. Was that Candy?"

Marcia nods. "Yes. Grant said it was too risky to move her far. We buried her away from Roger. Quietly. But then her bone was found, and we moved her. She's close now. Near us. Where she always should've been."

"That's what I saw. The flashlights in the woods." I turn to Steven. "That was them."

"I'm sorry," he whispers. "I'm so sorry."

"The baby cries I kept hearing—they were real but from the past. Cady's cries. The night she was born." I squeeze his hand. He doesn't need to be sorry. He believes me now.

But it still doesn't answer everything. "Deena. Why did Grant kill her?"

Marcia closes her eyes and tips her chin toward the ceiling, as if hoping for mercy. "He didn't. I did."

Silence spreads like smoke.

"She wanted to tell the truth," Marcia says, her voice thin. "After all these years. You scared her with your questions. She was terrified. We went for a walk to talk it through—her kids were visiting, and Ron didn't want it brought up again, so we met by the falls. I begged her. Told her it would ruin us. That we had children. Families. If we just stuck to the plan, it'd be okay. It was an accident."

I would never have believed Marcia Tremell could kill her best friend or even make it out to those falls with her arthritis, but maybe that was the point. Maybe it was more premeditated than she's letting on. They could have talked in a car ride around the block if it was nothing more than meeting to discuss the circumstances.

But I'll let a jury decide that.

Her hands tremble. "I picked up a rock. I didn't mean to. I panicked. I was afraid."

She covers her face as if she can block out the guilt, the shame, the consequences of what she's done.

"If you killing Candy was self-defense, then why cover it up all these years? A jury would never have found you guilty for killing Roger Wagner." He had stolen her daughter, abused her, abducted me, and no one would have convicted her even if it had been in cold blood.

"I was afraid. Grant said it might not work out in my favor. I shot him in cold blood. And even if it was second-degree, I could get some time, or they'd give Cady to someone else. We could have lost her. She was all I had left of Candy. So we buried Roger. Said he moved because it was too hard to stay knowing Lily Ann was gone and Ann dead. Deena moved her parents in, and Pat handled the legal papers. That was that. It was over. But the guilt...no one prepares you for that. It drapes you like a hot, wet blanket, constantly smothering. Never feeling free even if what you did felt right. Shooting him *felt* right...until it woke me most nights. The agony of taking my own daughter's life... That night has plagued us all in many ways."

Marcia Tremell had lived in a black cocoon all these years. Grant Ellersby hadn't killed anyone. He'd just cleaned up his friends' messes. Shielded them. Justified it all because one child predator was gone. But I'll let the law and judge and jury decide his, Curt's and the attorney's fates too.

Steven wraps an arm around my shoulders as we leave the holding area. He pushes the heavy door open for me.

An officer steps in, escorting a woman in cuffs.

She turns, and I falter.

Kristin White stares back at me, no remorse in her eyes or posture for drugging me at Ellersby's request. She'll likely say he forced her; he didn't. Everyone has a choice. She's only sorry she got caught.

Chapter Fifty-Nine

Steven leads me to the car, but I pause. "Can we..." I hesitate, then glance toward the water. "Can we walk for a bit? I need the air."

"Of course." He shuts the car door gently and slides his arm around me as we follow the cobbled streets down to the path along the harbor. The breeze is biting and briny.

"I can't imagine it," he says softly. "Killing your own daughter and her abductor. Calling your husband and confessing. The kind of courage—and fear—that must have taken."

I nod. But I have a confession of my own. One just as painful. Fear has kept me quiet for years, but Steven deserves the truth.

And there are things I still need to do. I want Roger Wagner out of my woods—gone forever. And I want more answers about my own abduction. I want to find that therapist in Portland if she's still alive and ask her to pull my records. I want to take care of Cady since her entire world has crumbled, and help Adrian Rivera now that his nurse has been arrested. With his Alzheimer's, he won't see prison time as an accessory, and really, he wasn't.

I'll do all those things. For now, it's time for me to do what I should have over eleven years ago. To shed shame that doesn't belong to me and build back a solid bridge over the chasm I've made between me and my husband.

"Steven," I say, "I've been keeping secrets. But I don't want to anymore. Secrets destroy people from the inside out. They fester and twist everything. I know you came back for me, and I'll always love you for that—even if you leave for good."

He stops near a park bench beneath an old swing set. I turn to face him. He's quiet, searching my face.

"I don't want to leave, never did or I would have left Cold Harbor," he says. "I just needed to know where your heart was. If you really loved me. I'm sick of the secrets too. And knowing what I do now…it explains so much. But you hated the idea—"

"I'll see a therapist now," I blurt out. "I need one, and now that I know why I've been reluctant, terrified even, it actually gives me strength to go. To find help to heal and cope. In all the right ways."

He kisses me—soft, aching. Like the first time. But there's pain in it too. I've hurt him. I know I have. He may never look at me the same.

"We'll go together if you want. I'll never leave your side. I never really have."

I hold up my hand. "Wait. I need to tell you something. About when I was sixteen."

So I do.

I tell him about the married man who made me feel seen, special, wanted. How I clung to his attention because I was angry and broken and didn't know why. I tell him about my first child, Tara. About the adoption. About Cady uploading my raw DNA to an ancestry site—with hopes of one day finding her.

And I explain why I never told him. The fear. His hatred for his father after the affair with a younger girl. I might as well have been that girl—the homewrecker.

"You've carried that all this time?" His voice cracks. "Through the miscarriages..."

His hands cradle my face. His eyes shine. "I love you. I wish you'd let me carry that load with you. I could've helped. I don't blame you, Gwen. You were preyed on. You were hurting and didn't even know why."

"You don't hate me?" I ask, barely a whisper. "You're not leaving?"

"I'm not going anywhere." He grips me tighter. "I became a doctor to help people, but somewhere along the way it became about the prestige. The name. You woke me up. If you hadn't done what you did back in Baltimore, I'd still be lost in it. I forgot who I wanted to be."

He kisses me again.

"I love you. We can mend this. If we're honest. If we keep choosing each other."

"No more secrets," I say, voice firm now.

"No more secrets," he echoes.

Chapter Sixty

Eight Months Later

"You outdid yourself, Gwen," Dr. Rivera says, grabbing a peanut butter cookie from the tray on the island.

I'm still in the house on Darkwater Road. We sealed off the secret basement room and installed a new island. Turns out it's not islands I hate; it was that particular island.

After Halloween night, Steven called Teresa to put the house on the market. At first, I was on board. We were going to get out of Dodge and had asked Cady to come with us, wherever that might be.

The next morning, I noticed something.

The crows were gone. The hovering, beady-eyed beasts that cast shadows in my yard had suddenly vanished. But the little chickadees landed on my kitchen windowsill and sat singing for an hour, and I stood there watching, crying. It was like an anthem of hope in those little birdsongs.

I also noticed the house didn't feel so frightening. The walls no longer closed in like they had the past month and a half. I realized that while the insidious past still lived within the walls, it couldn't reach out to harm me anymore. Because I was free from its prison. Free to sing like the chickadees. It was like they were coaxing me to find a new song.

A song of deliverance.

One that was just my own. No one else could sing that song—except the three chickadees who seemed to always abide near me as if they'd been here all those decades ago too, singing, knowing one day I would be free to sing too, to dance, to find joy.

Horrible acts have happened in this home, not just to me and Candy Tremell but to Rebekah Howler, Gina and Lizzie Barkley. The Batterson parents. Lily Ann Wagner. And who knows how many more? Every house holds secrets.

Until someone is brave enough to set them free.

I wasn't just held in bondage in this house. I saved a child here. A child who is now my best friend. I protected her. I picked her up and ran with her to keep her safe.

I loved her. I loved Candy Tremell too, though I knew her as Lily Ann.

What had been meant for evil in this home had now been used for good. And I think that's what makes those people who smile easy, who laugh with gusto and give generously, the way they are—because no one makes it through life unscathed. Darkness bumps into us all.

It's what we do with the darkness that matters. Those who live under its shadow adopt its attributes, but those who look to the light and let that sweet light transform them lift the weight of oppression…they use that for good things.

My marriage was almost destroyed, but oddly, it was healed. Here in this house.

I told Steven I didn't want to leave. I wanted to make some changes. Cut off the dark parts. Seal them all up. I'll never revisit them.

And Steven agreed. Cady too.

I found my old therapist. She's retired and lives in Portland. My parents had been beside themselves but didn't want me to remember, so they left. She feared that without proper help, my life would take a downward turn. She was spot-on.

Now I see Tammy Wineberg at Hope for Healing counseling services. Steven and I have been seeing her almost a year, and I've recovered most of my memories from that time I spent in captivity. I've learned new coping skills, and our marriage grows stronger every day.

I still don't believe everything happens for a reason. But I do believe that the worst things in life don't have to be wasted. I'm not wasting what happened to me. I'm using it in my own way now. A better way.

"What are you in deep thought about?" Adrian asks me as he snatches another cookie.

Adrian Rivera actually does not have Alzheimer's. And he was never charged for anything. He wanted to tell what happened that night and voiced it to Grant Ellersby over two years ago, along with the fact he was having health problems and reflecting on the past. It, and the guilt over his wife's suicide, had been giving him nightmares. He'd come home after Candy and Roger died with blood on his hands. Unable to carry the pressure, he'd unloaded it onto his wife. She'd wanted to go to the state police, but he wouldn't let her.

Things changed between them. That secret didn't bring them closer. It divided them. Like secrets do. A few months later, she'd hung herself in their attic, unable to live with knowing that her own husband had been involved in a covered-up murder.

And Adrian lived with that. Ellersby told him no one could ever know. If he spoke out, he'd end up next to Roger Wagner.

Around the same time, Adrian had also told his Nurse Practitioner, Kristin White, that the IBS meds he was on, which are known to mimic early-onset dementia, had caused confusion and hallucinations.

Grant hatched a plan that led to Kristin's pharmacist friend putting wrong pills in Adrian's new pill bottle and Kristin moving in as his full-time caregiver. Both of them are doing time. Now, Adrian visits us a couple times a week. He and Steven have grown close—Adrian becoming the father figure Steven always needed. And Wilt has become part of our little family as well. He's running late as he always is. He's been helping Cady with her podcast and teaching Steven how to track deer. Steven's taken up all kinds of new hobbies. Except birdwatching. That's a me and Adrian thing. But sometimes his daughter, Adrianne, comes in from California and goes along too. She almost died when she was twelve in a fire, and now Adrian's stories of fires make more sense.

"What time is it?" Adrian asks, and my nerves jolt. I glance at the clock—the clock Ellersby had slipped in to mess with. I don't leave doors unlocked anymore. And as it turns out, there is a secret passage from the attic to a tunnel out of the basement from the bootleg years. That's been sealed up too. I don't want to think about the tunnels in this house or my life. Not today.

Today is the Fourth of July, and we're celebrating freedom—of all kinds.

"She'll be here any minute." I mess with my hair and glance at the sunroom, tables decked in red, white and blue. Charcuterie, berries, lemonade, iced tea. I can't wait for Laken Creed to arrive—with eight-week-old baby Nora.

My daughter.

My granddaughter.

I may never have children of my own, and I am at peace with that now, but I've been given the gift of a grandbaby. Cady's work on ancestry sites led me to Laken. We've been in touch for six months now. Steven and I flew to Alabama twice, even made it for Nora's birth. As a single mom, Laken accepted our offer to live with us while she gets on her feet. Maybe she'll stay. Her life turned out to be pretty good up until about three years ago when her adoptive parents died in a boating accident.

"Car's here!" Steven calls, and we rush to the door. Cady waves. Steven and Adrian grab bags while Laken steps inside, Nora in her carrier.

A real, breathing baby. I can hardly stand how beautiful she is.

Laken looks like a younger version of me, though she has her father's dimpled chin.

"I think she's gained weight since our last FaceTime," I say.

"Don't I know it." Laken laughs. "Who needs a gym when you're hauling a baby around? I love the house. It's beautiful."

Beautiful.

That word used to feel out of place here. But now…it fits. Beauty for ashes. I can't erase the past, but I can rebuild. I've stripped this house down—started with having Tad rip out the attic floor and replace it. And I've been doing the same with myself. Gutting the broken parts. Rebuilding with faith and hope for a better future. Maybe the kids will stop telling ghost stories about this house.

Maybe the chanting at the windows will finally fade.

Maybe, one day, this place will be known not for what was taken—but for what was given back.

I hug Laken, and she places Nora in my arms. Her eyes blink open, and her tiny mouth forms a perfect O.

I smile.

For a moment, almost everything feels right. Is right, here.

But monsters still lurk even if they don't haunt this house any longer.

"I still can't believe you're not chief of police," Laken says.

Cady catches my eye and winks. She visits her parents once a week. Curt was sentenced to five years, but he'll likely be out in three. Marcia was given twenty-five with a chance at parole at ten years. The court was lenient.

"I don't want to be chief. Lowell will do just fine." I've been helping Cady with her *Black Capped Coffee & Crime* podcast too. Our first story—*our* story—has over twenty million downloads. Cady has even opened up a little merch shop in the café.

I have a purpose. I know this. But it's not sitting behind the top desk at the Cold Harbor Police Department.

Steven scoops Nora from my arms and raises his eyebrows. "Hey, let Pop have a turn." He and Adrian steal her away, beaming.

I hug Laken again. "Let me show you your room. You can settle in, get some rest, then join us for food. We might even take the kayaks out later."

As we leave Laken's room, Cady closes the door behind us. "That information you asked for is in my car. We can go over it later—after family time."

I glance back at Laken's door, then head downstairs to find my husband rocking our granddaughter while Adrian shares stories from his doctor days.

But our story isn't over.

Stories only have chapters.

Some end with pretty bows. Others with cliffhangers.

Like the fact that, despite months of searching—even with Curt Tremell's help—we never found Roger Wagner's grave.

His bones are still buried somewhere in my woods. Too deep for dogs. Too long gone for aging minds to remember the spot.

Am I at peace with that?

No.

I'm going to find him.

Chapter Sixty-One

Lily Ann

Husband brought me flowers and take-out for my fifteenth birthday. We ate it on the back patio and watched the sun set. Today is my sixteenth birthday, and he says he's coming home with something very special for us both. I've been anticipating it all day. A puppy? I've been telling him how much I'd love a little puppy. I don't even care what kind. My days get lonely, but I have more freedom than ever, and the nights of having to make him happy upstairs are growing fewer and farther between. That feels like a little gift.

He told me not to cook today, but to dress my best, so I'm wearing a flowery sundress to end the summer though it stays hot long into September here. It looks too little-girlish for me, but he likes bows, ribbons, lace and white socks with lace trim and Mary Jane shoes. My hair is in a French braid; his favorite is pigtails. I'm too old for them though.

It's almost five o'clock, and his white van pulls into the drive and then into the garage. My stomach lurches with nerves, as it does every day, but today there's some excitement. I'm getting a birthday cake and ice cream and maybe a puppy.

But when the door from the garage to the kitchen opens, I see he's not bringing me a puppy.

My mouth falls open as he walks in, carrying a little girl on his hip. She clings to his neck, blue eyes wide, her blond pigtails hanging limp.

"Lily Ann, meet your new playmate. Dolly. Dolly is going to be staying with us. And you will be her mommy. We'll teach her how to make me happy just like I taught you how."

My stomach sours. I'm getting too old to make him happy, but soon this new Dolly will. Will he keep me or make me leave? While I don't want to stay, I have nowhere else to go. And he provides for me and takes care of me.

"Okay. Thank you," I say. He won't like it if I don't appreciate the gift of this little girl.

"Hi, Dolly. I'm Lily Ann."

Her cheeks are streaked with dirt, white lines cutting through where the tears ran.

I remember crying, too, when he became my daddy.

Even more when he became Husband.

"Can I clean her up, Husband?"

"Of course. Take her upstairs. I bought her a dress, and I brought pizza!"

I love pizza. "Oh, good! Thank you." But inside, my stomach churns, and I want to puke. "Come on, Dolly."

"My name isn't Dolly."

"No," Husband says. "That's crazy. Your name is Dolly. It's always been Dolly. You silly."

I take her hand and lead her upstairs and to the bathroom at the end of the hall.

"My name really isn't Dolly."

I sigh and wet a washcloth with warm water. "I know. But you have to go along with it. How old are you?"

"Ten. He says for now I'm his little doll, but in a few years, I'll be his Lily Ann. How can we both be his Lily Ann?" While I don't know for sure, I have a fair idea and shudder.

"He said my mom and dad died. He's my daddy now. But now he says he's always been my daddy. I'm confused." She starts to cry again, and I try to calm her. Tears anger him, and I'll be the one to take the punishment. But I understand her grief. My parents died, too, and as I've aged, I wonder if he killed them to take me away.

"It'll be okay. I'll take care of you." I wash away the dirt along her cheeks and nose. She's quite cute, and I think of what's coming. I have to protect her. I will protect her. Whatever it takes.

No matter the cost.

I'll wear the pigtails. The little girl dresses. Anything to keep him from going into her room. I try praying again. It may not help, but it can't hurt.

I bring Dolly downstairs as Husband has asked. She does look like a doll.

The pizza box is open on the table, and birthday plates and cups are laid out with a big bottle of grape soda. My favorite. "Come and sit down. Let's eat. Dolly, you sit by me."

She comes to the table and sits beside him, and he piles two pieces of pizza on her plate and pours her a cup. I don't like the way his eyes roam over her. I fix Husband and myself plates and drinks and sit at the other end of the table.

A knock startles us all.

No one ever comes out here. No visitors. No guests. A long drive leads up to our house, which is surrounded by evergreens. Husband says that our safety and privacy are of utmost importance.

His eyes darken, and he holds up a finger to his lips. "Sit right here and say nothing. Do you understand?" His voice is rough and cold.

"Yes, Husband." I take his spot at the table and cradle Dolly into my lap, hoping and praying she doesn't scream or cry. Maybe… I can risk us getting out. If I can see who might be here. They could help us. Free us. We'd figure out where to go and what to do.

"You stay here in the kitchen and be quiet as a mouse, and I'll give you a cookie," I whisper.

She nods and crouches in the corner of the kitchen as I tiptoe around the corner, where I see Husband at the front door—but he can't see me.

Husband opens it with a fake smile.

A woman with pretty blond hair in a short ponytail stands on our porch, and she's not smiling. In fact, she looks furious like Husband when I used to answer the questions wrong. I don't think Husband notices her serious face.

"Can I help you?" he asks. He's always pleasant.

Until he isn't.

"You don't recognize me?" she asks and takes a step closer to Husband, and I feel this sensation in my chest. Admiration. She's not afraid of Husband, not like I am.

She's strong and brave. I can tell. I know in this instant I want to be exactly like her someday.

"I'm sorry? You must have the wrong house."

"I don't think so, *Daddy*." She spits out the word *Daddy* like it tastes bad in her mouth. "It's me… Dolly."

Dolly? I'm confused. Dolly is in the kitchen.

Husband's face turns white like he's seen a spooky ghost. He starts to slam the door shut, but the woman puts her foot in it and shoves a gun in his face, presses it right into his nose, smashing it flat. Deep down, I hope she pulls the trigger.

Noise sounds outside. From the living room window, I see police officers running. They're everywhere like when I stepped in an ant bed.

"Curt Tremell told us where you were buried, but he was wrong—though he thought he'd simply forgotten the right location. But then I got to thinking, Roger. I'm going to call you Roger now, though you deserve so many other names."

"I don't know who you are. You're crazy."

She laughs, but she doesn't sound happy. "You tried to make me think I was. No, Roger, you don't forget where you bury bodies. So that got me to thinking…maybe Curt was right. Maybe when Marcia shot you, you didn't actually die. You clawed your way out of that grave to haunt other little girls."

She leans in; her eyes are cold and yet warm.

"See, I'm tenacious like that, Roger. A dog with bone. Can't let it go. Sometimes it lands me in trouble. And other times, well, other times I travel to Arkansas and I find you, you wicked, soulless monster. Your days of being the bump in the night are over. How many other girls have you stolen and broken in all these years? Maybe we'll know. Maybe not. Either way, it's the real end of the line for you."

"I have no idea what you're talking about." But he does. His voice shakes, and his hands tremble.

She holds out a paper and shoves it in his chest. "This is a search warrant for the Pulaski County sheriff's office to search your home. Will we find a new Dolly or a Lily Ann?"

That's me. That's us.

I motion for Dolly to come to me, and we step out from behind the corner as police officers make their way inside the house.

The woman sees me. Her hardened features soften, and tears well up in her eyes. She's like a superhero, dressed in all black.

"What are your names?" she asks as she approaches us, Dolly hiding, clinging to my legs like a cat. "I'm Gwen."

"Lily Ann," I say, and one of those tears spills down her cheeks.

"No, baby, what's your real name? Can you remember?"

Yes. Though I haven't said it in a very long time. "Maizy Dyer."

She looks at an officer and nods. "It's her." Then she looks at Dolly. "What's your name?"

Dolly looks at me, and I give her the okay while the officers shove Husband—Roger—against a wall and wrench his right arm behind his back. He cries out.

He's got a scar there between his shoulder and his chest. He said a bullet knocked him unconscious and the enemy took him for dead and left him to die during a war he fought in. The bullet is still there, reminding him he's a hero, but I don't think he's a hero.

Deep inside my heart, I know what he is.

Wicked.

"What's your name, sweetie?" Gwen asks Dolly again.

"Abby Kate Wilkerson. I'm ten."

She cocks her head, runs her hands through Dolly's pigtails and whispers, "Just like mine."

Like hers? When she was his Dolly? I'm so confused, but I'm too afraid and happy to ask her questions. "She came today. But I came when I was ten. Today's my birthday, actually. I'm sixteen."

Six years I've been with the Daddy-Husband-Monster.

"My parents died in a park fire when we were camping," I say. "What will happen to us now? Will I go to an orphanage?"

"Mine too," Abby Kate says. "Can I go to the orphanage with her?"

Gwen wraps us in a big hug and holds on so tight it almost hurts, but it feels really good too. Her voice cracks when she speaks. "No, sweet girls. Your parents are alive."

Alive? She must be mistaken, but I hope. I dare to hope that my prayers have been answered after all this time.

She leads us outside onto the porch, where officers hover and cars with blue lights now flash. We didn't see them before. They might have been hidden.

Another woman with long blond hair and an older man with black glasses approach, and he kisses Gwen on the forehead.

"I'm so proud of you, babe," he says.

"You did it, Gwen," the woman says. "You found that dirtbag just like you said you would." She wears a necklace that reads Cady.

I look up then and blink. No. I'm imagining it. I have to be.

But I'm not.

I see my real mom and dad. Older. Grayer. Thinner. Some wrinkles, but they have never looked better in my whole life. They really weren't dead. Not ever.

He lied.

When they spot me, my mother falls to the ground in a gut-wrenching sob, and Dad helps her up, but he's crying too. I've never seen my father cry. I look to Gwen.

She grins and nods that's it's okay for me to go.

But I hug her first. She rescued me. Found me when I never thought I'd be found. "Thank you. I think maybe God sent you and answered my prayers."

She hugs me back. "I think you're right. You will be okay in time, Maizy. I promise. Now go."

I begin walking toward my parents.

I hear Gwen behind me. "The Wilkersons reported their little girl missing today. Call and let them know Abby Kate has been found. And she's safe. And thanks for letting me be the knock at the door. I needed that."

"You earned it, Gwen," an officer says. "You're the best private investigator I've ever met."

And then I'm running into my parents' arms.

★★★★★

Acknowledgments

The Girl Upstairs started out with my longtime desire to write a "murder house book." When my mom came to visit, I told her I wanted to write one, and she started throwing out ideas—which were just terrible (don't worry, I already told her this, so it's not a surprise to her), but she did help me spark better ideas. From there, I knew I had something. Then the following week, my sister called me. Mom had mentioned that I was trying to write a murder house story and told her what we'd (and I use we'd lightly) landed on. She called to give me the big twist idea. It was brilliant! But to make it work, I had to plug a lot of holes, which took me a couple of months working through it, which is why I didn't dedicate the book to her. I did all the work. Thank you, Celeste, for that twist, and, being a therapist, helping me understand repressed memories due to trauma. Any stretch is my fault—or Mom's. Let's blame her like old times!

From there, Susan L. Tuttle, my fabulous craft partner, helped me brainstorm and read my early draft. Your ideas were gold.

Thank you to Laura Ott for helping me work out of a plot hole.

Thank you, Kristine Delano, my sweet friend, for answering endless questions about Maine! You were too kind to answer them all; any mess ups are all mine.

Then my rock star editor, Shana Asaro, who used her expertise on it, helping me make it stronger, as she always does. Thank you for your eagle eye and insight. One day, I'll nail a timeline, but maybe don't hold your breath.

Special thanks always goes out to my amazing agent, Rachel Kent, for always championing my books (even if it scares her a little to read them) and being a wonderful friend. I'm so grateful to you.

To my husband, who travels and takes photos of my books in every store he goes in, you are amazing. Smile more in the photos next time maybe. People might realize you do it of your own volition that way.

To the team at Harlequin, for their incredible work and support, thank you from the bottom of my heart.

To my launch team, you are gold, and I appreciate all your support and help. Thank you for helping me name the road, and to Kailey Bechtel for going with Darkwater. I hope you enjoyed seeing your name in print!

And to my readers. Mercy, I love you all so much. I thank God for you every day. You are why I write.